THE LUMINARIES

SUSAN DENNARD

 Daphne Press

First published in the UK in 2022 by Daphne Press
www.daphnepress.com

A CIP catalogue record for this book is available from the British Library.

Paperback edition ISBN: 978-1-83784-000-7
eBook edition ISBN: 978-1-83784-001-4
Waterstones exclusive edition ISBN: 978-1-83784-006-9

Printed and bound by CPI Group (UK) Ltd, Croydon CR0 4YY.

1

For the LumiNerds,
who brought this world to life even when
they were trapped in a garage

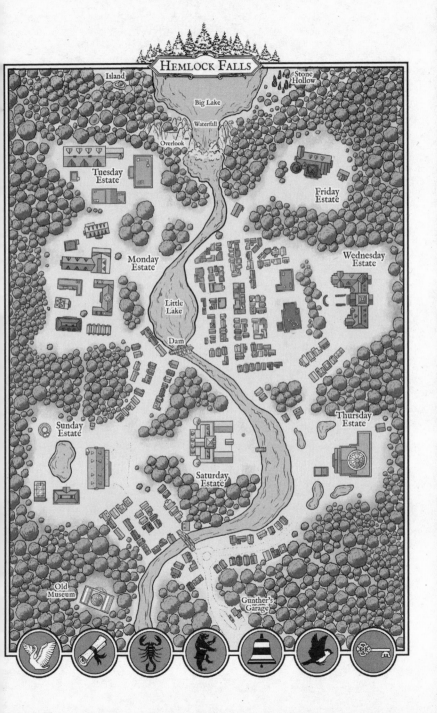

THE NIGHTMARE

The forest comes for the boy on his thirteenth birthday. He is not the first to catch the forest's notice. He will, however, be one of the last. Others have received bits of woven twine from a banshee or a shiny snail from a melusine, but he finds a wolf's jawbone on his pillow when he opens his eyes at dawn.

He was having the nightmare again. The one where his father has a face and his mother is still alive. It always begins a happy dream, until the shadows arrive. First they claim his father. Then they claim him too while his mother weeps and screams and begs the forest to change its mind.

But the forest never changes its mind. Not in the dream and not in real life either. Which is why, when the forest calls for the boy, he enters. And when the forest is done with him, he leaves. No longer a boy. No longer entirely human, but rather a ticking time bomb waiting for the forest to one day spark his fuse.

CHAPTER

1

They say that spring never comes to the forest by Hemlock Falls.

It isn't true, of course. Spring comes right after winter like it's supposed to. What *is* true is how different the spring is in Hemlock Falls from the rest of the world. It's quiet and lethal. Lonely and inevitable. It sneaks up on you, shaded by winter grey that doesn't like to let go.

Even now, a month into the season, frost still clings to the north side of trees. And though the sun might rise momentarily, it won't reach this dirt road. It won't reach Winnie Wednesday as she muscles a clunky four-wheeler with no assisted steering toward the Wednesday clan meeting point.

Mist exhales from the forest like smoke from a censer. The four-wheeler lights flash and reflect, making shapes where Winnie knows there are none. It's only the maple and fir saplings of last year's spring, skeletal in the predawn darkness.

Her front teeth click together as she drives. Today is her sixteenth birthday. And today, everything is going to change.

When her headlights beam over six black SUVs, Winnie rumbles the four-wheeler to a hemlock—the tree, not the poisonous plant, although those grow here too and no one knows for which the town is named.

She flips off the lights, pulls up the hood of her sweatshirt, and waits. Fog coils around her, an octopus embrace. She imagines what tonight's trial will be like. How it will feel to hunt a nightmare instead of just read about it.

Her mum won't talk to her about hunting—at least not anymore. Not since the *incident*. But Winnie has read the Nightmare Compendium a thousand times. A thousand thousand times. She has sketched every creature in the forest, every nightmare the American Luminaries must face. And she has pretended to face them herself, stabbing a droll in the fleshy part at the base of its neck or a manticore where the cephalothorax and abdomen meet. She has jumped and rolled and jumped and rolled so many times her body does it without thinking.

She'll be ready.

She has to be ready.

Minutes tick past. A wolf howls. A real one, she thinks, although she can't be too sure. The Compendium does describe a few nightmares that look like wolves or sound like wolves or briefly become wolves entirely.

Winnie shoves her glasses up her nose and keeps waiting. And waiting. Her stomach grumbles; she wishes she'd eaten breakfast. She also wishes she'd slept more, although she ought to be used to the insomnia after three weeks of it. Ever since her birthday month began and the reality of what she has been planning these past four years settled in, sleep has been elusive.

The wolf howls again, though it's farther away this time. It sounds lonely, lost. Winnie hates that she understands the feeling.

She hasn't told anyone she's going to attempt the first hunter trial tonight. If they find out, they won't let her. Aunt Rachel will lose her mind; Mum will lose her mind; the Council will lose their collective minds; and they'll find a way to intervene. But what they don't know, they can't stop.

Plus, nowhere in the rules does it say an outcast can't enter. Nons are forbidden, sure, but there's definitely no mention of outcasts.

All Winnie has to do is show up with the other hunter applicants tonight, and the Thursdays in charge of the trial will let her in.

They *have* to. Winnie really doesn't know what she'll do if they don't.

Eventually, she can't hear the wolf anymore, and eventually, the sky begins to lighten. The night is over. The forest's slumber is complete.

Wednesday hunters emerge from the trees on silent feet. A few hunters from other clans mingle within the ranks, replacements for anyone who's hurt or sick or just has a kid in the Hemlock Falls drama troupe. Ever since a Saturday hunter died two months ago and a Tuesday hunter died three weeks ago, the Council has beefed up hunter numbers each night.

All around the world, the Luminaries live near fourteen sleeping spirits. Each night, when the spirits dream, their nightmares come to life. And each night, the Luminary hunters guard the world against those nightmares, one clan for every day of the week. Last night belonged to the Wednesdays—Winnie's clan.

Or it *was* Winnie's clan until the incident, when her family was sentenced to be outcasts.

There are forty-eight hunters right now, several of whom are second cousins or cousins of cousins. They've definitely forgotten it's Winnie's birthday and wouldn't have cared even if they'd remembered. Dressed in matching black Kevlar and matching frowns, some are now bloodied, some have broken bows, a few limp.

Only Aunt Rachel speaks to Winnie, leaving the rest of the hunters to approach with a map in hand. SUV headlights beam over her like a stage light. She is gruff and perfunctory in her movements, as is Winnie's mum. But where Mum's hair is fully grey, Rachel's is still glossy and black.

They have the same hooked nose, though. So does Winnie.

"Here." Rachel holds out a map, a bad copy of a copy of a copy. "The nightmare bodies are marked, and we've got two nons this time too. Though fair warning: this one near the high school is just a halfer."

Halfer. Half a human corpse. Not common, but not uncommon in the forest either. Rachel hands the map off to Winnie, already glancing toward the SUVs and forgetting her niece is standing there.

This is how it usually goes. Aunt Rachel says a handful of words and then, like every other Wednesday and every other Luminary, she goes back to pretending Winnie doesn't exist. She even walks away before Winnie has fully grasped the map, leaving Winnie to swipe it from the air as it falls.

Once Rachel joins the other hunters, they all cram into their SUVs. Electric engines hum to life. A slurp of tires on fresh mud marks their exit.

Winnie doesn't watch them go. She has been doing corpse duty for three years now and even if today is her birthday, even if her stomach is as knotted as a harpy's braid, the familiarity of routine soothes her.

Corpse duty might be a job no one else likes—cleaning up the nightmare bodies left behind in the forest each morning, as well as any human bodies—but Winnie has always enjoyed it. Her brother calls her morbid; she calls him boring.

Sure, it's a grim job, but someone has to do it. Otherwise, the corpses that don't magically vanish at dawn will reawaken as revenants, and that's *always* nasty. Besides, corpse duty is the only time Winnie gets to flex her knowledge of the Nightmare Compendium, and each new body is a riddle to be solved.

She studies the map, her front teeth clicking. There's the halfer, not far from the Friday estate. And then a second human is marked about a mile away from the first, by the lake. Two is a lot for one night. There's been a definite uptick lately.

Click, click, click. Click, click, click.

"Winnie?" comes a voice, and Marcus, Aunt Rachel's son, steps out from under the hemlock. An eighth grader who has only just started corpse duty, he is nice to Winnie when no one else is around. But get him outside of the forest, and he—like everyone else in the Luminaries—delights in calling her *witch spawn.*

Winnie dreams often of punching out his front teeth. They're just the *perfect* size for smashing and would add some much-needed colour to his olive-pale skin.

Behind him are two other teenagers: the pretty Wednesday twins, Black girls with rich umber skin and dark tourmaline eyes. The dimples in their cheeks are the envy of everyone in town.

Their family moved to Hemlock Falls the year before, transplants from the world outside because their parents are networkers—that special variety of Luminary who live in the non world, working to ensure no one ever learns of the Luminaries or the forest.

Like most people in the Wednesday clan of the American Luminaries, the twins have no blood connection to Winnie or Marcus, and as sophomores like Winnie, they're easily the most popular girls at school. Which of course means that Marcus has it bad for them. Like, real bad. He doesn't seem to understand that they're only nice to him because they're nice to everyone. Including Winnie, no matter how much she frowns.

She *wants* to be nice back—she really does. But if she lowers her guard for even one minute, there's a risk someone might slip in. *Witch spawn, witch spawn.*

"Happy birthday!" they sing in unison.

"We got you a present." Emma offers a box with perfectly wrapped edges and a perfectly curled bow.

"Uh, thanks." Winnie takes the box; it's heavy. "I'll open it later."

A flash of disappointment crosses their faces. Their smile dimples smooth away, and Bretta, who currently wears corkscrew curls (while Emma has long braids), says, "Oh, but we want to see your reaction."

Winnie tenses at those words. Fear spikes up her arms, as if the box is made of banshee tears. They've pranked her. It's probably dog poop inside, and when she opens the box, they'll snap a video with their phones to show everyone at school.

Except no. Winnie shakes her head. The twins aren't like that. Besides, contrary to the rest of Hemlock Falls, they have always been genuinely nice to Winnie. The Luminary rules are pretty clear on how to treat outcasts: *ignore them.* Yet the twins never have.

Winnie pushes her glasses up her nose, inhales a steeling breath, and finally tears into the wrapping paper. It rips loudly across the silent dawn, and in less than a second the name *Falls' Finest* peers up at her in the same swirly gold lettering as the shop windows wear downtown.

She gulps, hating that she's suddenly excited. Hating that the twins have probably gotten her something expensive, judging by the box's heft, and that she's probably going to like it. She almost prefers the dog poop.

But she can't stop now. Emma and Bretta are bouncing with excitement.

She pries off the box's lid and discovers a leather jacket. The sort of item that Winnie will never be able to afford unless it's *very* used. And the sort of style that will look good no matter its age, no matter the decade.

She gulps a second time. It's the perfect shade of cinnamon brown to complement her auburn hair.

"Because you're always cold on corpse duty," Emma explains. "This will keep you warm!"

Though she doesn't say it and definitely doesn't mean

it maliciously, the subtextual reality is inescapable: *You're always cold and will continue to be cold because while we will stop doing corpse duty soon, you, Winnie Wednesday, will keep doing it forever.*

"Try it on!" Bretta urges, dimples returning. "We'll exchange it if it doesn't fit."

Winnie obeys, and of course the jacket fits perfectly. Even over her green hoodie that says SAVE THE WHALES. She bends her elbows. The new leather squeaks. She tries the zip. It slides up and down like a scalpel through vampira viscera.

She should refuse this. Yes, she should refuse this. Thank the twins politely, but say it's too nice a gift for her to ever accept.

Winnie doesn't refuse it. She feels too badass, like a photo her mum has of Gran Winona, bow in hand, nightmare viscera splattered across her body, and a wide, vicious grin bright as the sun rising behind her.

Winnie summons a similar smile, one with actual teeth, and says: "Thanks. This is really . . . well, nice of you. Thanks."

Emma beams, Bretta claps, and not for the first time Winnie wishes they were the stereotypical mean girls they're supposed to be. She knows where she stands with the rest of the town—with brats like Marcus. With the twins, though, who are *almost* her friends, but not quite . . .

That uncertain "between" makes her gut twist uncomfortably.

She clears her throat, unzipping the jacket. Then zipping it again. And again and again, because for some reason her fingers won't stop. It just moves so easily.

"When's your birthday?" Marcus asks the twins with an eagerness that suggests there might be awkward flowers in their future.

"Next week," Emma replies—at the exact same moment as Bretta. They laugh, a bubbly sound that erupts whenever they speak in unison.

Winnie's fingers freeze on the zip. Next week doesn't give her much time to find them a gift in return.

"We're hoping to have a party," Emma continues. "You'll both be invited." Marcus looks like he might swoon with joy. Winnie just feels faintly nauseated. Outcasts aren't exactly welcome at the various Luminary parties.

So she changes the subject. As the oldest of their group, Winnie is in charge of corpse duty. "We've, uh," she begins. *Zip, zip, zip.* "We've got a halfer near the Friday estate. Let's start there?"

"Aye, aye, Captain." Bretta pops a little salute. Then she, Emma, and Marcus pile into the flatbed. Winnie cranks the engine. Exhaust puffs, melting into the fog.

Dawn has arrived, pearly grey above the trees. Winnie flips on the headlights for good measure. Forest shadows scatter. The winter grey does not.

CHAPTER
2

Winnie's plan is a simple one: pass the three hunter trials, restore her family's status in the Luminaries, and become a nightmare hunter like she has always been destined to be.

Her mum was a hunter.

Gran Winona was a hunter.

Great-Gran Maria was a hunter.

And if not for the *incident,* Winnie would be fully trained and welcomed to the first trial tonight with open arms. But as she knows in all-too-intimate detail, it turns out that having your dad be a spy for the Dianas, the Luminaries' ancient enemy, doesn't go over well—even if you, your mum, and your brother had no idea what was going on.

You should have known, the Council said four years ago. *A true Luminary would have known. A true Wednesday would have known.* Then they laid down a punishment of ten years as outcasts for Winnie, Mum, and Darian.

And that had been that. Dad was gone, having fled as a spy, and the old life as respected Luminaries was finished. Ten years as outcasts. The end.

Winnie hadn't thought it could possibly get any worse . . . until she realised that her sixteenth birthday would arrive during her ten-year sentence—the *hunter trials* would arrive, and she would miss her one shot at taking them.

Which meant that if Winnie wanted to do this—and oh god, she wanted it then and she wants it now—then she couldn't let her sixteenth birthday slip by. She was going to have to attempt the first trial. She *is* going to have to attempt it.

It's her only chance to make everything right again and her only chance to go after the thing Dad tried to take away.

She just prays this new leather jacket will bring her luck.

CHAPTER
3

Winnie parks the four-wheeler on a trail thirty feet from the halfer. The headlights beam through mist, turning the forest to a pixelated haze. In under a minute, Winnie has found the human remains. Three years of corpse duty, and she knows where nightmares usually deposit their prey. This particular clearing, surrounded by blue spruce and maples, is a regular feeding ground for vampira.

At the sight of the halfer's exposed spine above the shredded remains of a waistline, Marcus gags. And at the sight of the exposed anklebones where the feet used to be, he turns and flees for the trees.

Which amuses Winnie. "Welcome to the forest," she calls after him, and Bretta gratifies her with a giggle. Emma, however, takes pity on Marcus, and moments later her dulcet tones drift over a rebellious throat and the spray of vomit on pine needles.

Winnie and Bretta don't wait for them. They pull on disposable gloves that are as blue as the cornflowers just appearing in Winnie's front garden, and Bretta withdraws a body bag from the teal backpack she always carries. A bag of crisps rustles. Probably salt and vinegar, knowing her. Or maybe it's Emma's preferred sour cream and onion.

"Nothing on him," Bretta says after checking for ID. Her gloves are already brown with blood. The guy's jeans are even worse. "Should we search for the other half of his body?"

"Nah." Winnie unfolds the body bag, which is really just an enormous ziplock. It's even transparent like a ziplock too, with comparably poor seal quality that requires careful, patient unzipping. Nothing like Winnie's new jacket.

Whenever a non is allowed into the Luminaries' world, they're always horrified that corpse duty goes to the thirteen-, fourteen-, and fifteen-year-olds. *The children!* they say. *Their impressionable minds!* To which Luminaries snort and reply, *Exactly.*

Death is a part of life in Hemlock Falls. It's a part of life beside the forest. You lose your family, you lose your friends, you lose yourself. The sooner "the children" learn what the forest can do to them, the safer and happier they'll be.

Winnie learned that the hard way.

"This is a vampira kill," she tells Bretta, draping the bag beside the corpse. "You can tell from what's left behind. See how all the parts with organs are missing? The torso and head have the most nutrients, and vampira hordes need those to survive. They like pieces with high-iron content."

"Oh." Bretta frowns at the body while Winnie hangs her leather jacket on a black walnut branch. Then, with a grunt, they grab the body, lift it, deposit it. Plastic squishes. Congealed blood squirts like toothpaste. The girls each grab a corner of the ziplocking mechanism and start sealing.

"Why are the feet missing too, then?" Bretta asks.

"Well, the story goes that vampira like feet because they don't have any. But then again, melusine and harpies don't have feet either." Winnie shrugs. She once asked Professor Anders about that, back when she was still allowed at the Luminary school, but he'd only glared at her and said in his Swedish accent, *If it's not in the Compendium, it's not important.*

So Winnie had checked the Nightmare Compendium—

and not the short field guide that hunters use, but the full, massive tome as big as her torso that resides in the Monday library. She hadn't found an answer, though.

"So why do *you* think they take the feet?" Bretta asks.

And Winnie flushes.

It's a weird heat. Part delight that Bretta would ask about her theories. Part shame, because she knows what will happen when she shares them. Even if Bretta won't laugh, she'll probably tell someone else who will tell someone else, and soon enough the Luminaries will TP Winnie's house again. Or spray-paint her mum's ancient Volvo, on which the last smear of red still hasn't fully faded. Then Winnie will hate her dad even more than she already does, and she'll hate her mum for ever loving her dad . . .

And yeah, she just doesn't want to go there. Not on her birthday.

So she shrugs and mumbles, "Dunno."

Footsteps clomp through underbrush. She twists, expecting Emma to reappear with Marcus on her arm. Instead, a boy with flaxen hair that blends into ashen skin emerges from between two saplings.

"Ugh." Winnie scowls at him. "Jay."

He draws up short at the sight of her. For once, he doesn't look stoned so much as tired, like he was out all night with a beer in one hand and a joint in the other. His broad shoulders hunch inside buffalo flannel, his hands are stuffed into faded jean pockets, and his black motorcycle boots are streaked with red soil.

He is a burst of colour in this forest made of grey, and Winnie suddenly wishes she still had on her leather jacket. Something about Jay requires armor.

Beside her, Bretta has gone very still. Like a ghost-deer spotting a human.

"Why are you here?" Winnie asks, but Jay ignores her, scrubbing a hand over his already mussed hair and taking in the scene before him. Not the people, not the body, but the forest. Its leaves and moss and mud. The subtle markings left behind by monsters in the night.

Winnie can't help but wonder what he sees. He passed the three hunter trials over a year ago.

"I was getting ready for school," Jay says eventually. His voice, like everything else about him, is threadbare and tired. "I saw tracks and wanted to make sure nothing had escaped the boundaries." The Friday clan estate, where Jay lives, is one of only two estates that directly abut the forest—the other being the martial Tuesday clan's. "Vampira?" he asks.

"*Yes,*" Bretta rushes to say. "We know from the missing torso."

Winnie side-eyes her. While she supposes she ought to be annoyed that Bretta has just claimed knowledge Winnie gave her, she's more startled by the breathlessness in Bretta's voice. And the intensity of her smile.

Not that Jay notices, and when he speaks again, it's directed at Winnie. "Any ID?"

"No," Bretta answers.

"Huh." Jay shoves his fists deeper into his pockets, spine stooping as if the forest canopy is too low. And though Winnie hates to admit it, there is something strangely small about the clearing now that he's in it.

"I can ask if my aunt saw anything," he offers. "She might have had her cameras set up—"

"Don't," Winnie interrupts at the same time Bretta sighs, "Yes, please." Winnie glares at her. Then at Jay. "I don't need your help, Jay. I know exactly what happened here. *Vampira.*" She points at the body. "*Horde.*"

His pewter eyes thin at this declaration, but he doesn't contradict her.

Notably, he doesn't confirm her assessment either, and Winnie finds her ire rising. She used to know everything Jay was thinking. Now she can't tell a thing. "I don't need your help," she repeats. "I can handle corpse duty on my own."

"I know," he says, and Winnie hates that he actually sounds like he does. "I was just trying to help, Win." He turns to go. At the tree line, though, he pauses long enough to call back, "Happy birthday," before the forest swallows him whole.

"See you at school!" Bretta shrieks into the pines, but no answer returns.

She deflates; Winnie's front teeth start clicking. She's glad Jay is gone and annoyed he remembered her birthday. Most of all, though, she's annoyed that in the five seconds he was here, he managed to poke a hole in her vampira theory. He said he had followed tracks to the body, but vampira don't leave tracks. Their stilt-like legs end in needle-sharp points that barely graze the ground.

She scans the forest floor, eyes squinting behind her glasses. What did Jay see that she missed? Did a sylphid do this? Or maybe a kelpie? She supposes she could chase after him and ask. She supposes she *should* chase after him and ask. After all, it would be the responsible thing to do as corpse-duty leader—and what a future hunter would do too.

But she isn't going to. Not in a million years.

"He never notices me," Bretta says mournfully. Then almost as an afterthought, she adds, "Or anyone else, really."

"Huh?" Winnie shoves her glasses up her nose and blinks at the other girl.

"Jay Friday," Bretta explains. "Me and Emma might as well be invisible whenever he's around. He's, like, *so* in his own head." The way she says this makes it sound like an appealing trait. "We go to every one of his shows at Joe Squared, you know, but he always leaves right after performing."

Winnie doesn't know. She avoids the local coffee shop like a nightmare avoids running water. She *has* heard that Jay's band plays there on Saturday nights, though. And she *has* noticed that half of Hemlock Falls seems to be in love with him.

It makes no sense, really, since Jay seems to have absolutely no interest in—or even awareness of—anyone in town.

Then again, maybe that's part of the appeal.

Against her better judgment, Winnie takes pity on Bretta. "He doesn't perform for attention, so I'm not surprised he leaves after the show. If you want to talk to him, try going to Gunther's after school."

"The non petrol station? Outside Hemlock Falls?"

Winnie nods. "He's there pretty much every day working on his motorcycle." Or his aunt's motorcycle, but Winnie doesn't see the point in specifying.

Bretta's eyes widen, her dimples crease inward, and Winnie can practically see her connecting thoughts one by one. *Gunther's petrol station leads to motorcycle leads to Jay leads to time with Jay leads to getting noticed . . .*

She claps her bloodied cornflower hands. "Oh, thank you, Winnie! I . . . *we* will definitely do that today. But how do you know so much about him? Are you two friends or something?"

"No." Winnie tugs off her gloves. They *thwack!* like gunshots across the forest. "Jay is not my friend."

CHAPTER

4

He used to be, though.

That's why Winnie knows about him. That's why Winnie hates him. Because the truth about Jay Friday is that he and Winnie *used* to be friends, along with Erica Thursday. They were an inseparable trio. A triad. A triangle. Anything with "tri" in it, they had declared themselves to be at some point or another over their seven years of friendship.

Wednesday, Thursday, Friday. A perfect arrangement of clans that made the initials *WTF,* which never failed to make them laugh.

Jay was a year older when they all met, but their respective parents (or in Jay's case, his aunt) were all buddies, so a carpool had been born. Every afternoon, they had ridden together to the sprawling Sunday estate, where all the Luminary classrooms and training halls are housed. After enough time spent debating Pokémon, then debating nightmares, and finally debating which professors were the scariest, they forged a bond that they truly believed could never be broken.

But that's the thing about the forest: it can break just about anything.

And it did. When Winnie's family became toxic because of her dad, Jay and Erica ditched her like everyone else in Hemlock Falls. *Hard.* Jay fell in with a bad crowd; Erica fell in with the most popular.

Just like that, the inseparable trio, triad, triangle was split in two: A right angle on one side, still welcome in the world of the Luminaries. A lost hypotenuse on the other, cast adrift, floating and alone.

CHAPTER

5

As the eldest on corpse duty and the driver of the four-wheeler, Winnie delivers the bodies to the Monday estate after everyone else has gone home to prep for school. There's a trail through the forest that will spit her out onto the Monday lands. It's covered in tire tracks from the Tuesday clan the day before. Winnie always tries to drive in their grooves when she sees them. As if by following what they do, she'll be like them.

Everyone loves the Tuesdays.

This part of corpse duty—the drive to deliver bodies—is Winnie's favorite part of the day: the time when she's all alone and can sketch out new nightmares in her mind.

Today, they retrieved an intact earth sylphid. Winnie has never seen one before; she hadn't realised quite how . . . *human* they are. Like miniature people with bark for skin and stone for teeth and horns. She'll need to redraw it in her Compendium. She can already see how she'll do it too, small hatch marks for the texture on their faces, a thicker pen to capture the full blackness of their eyes.

The other two nightmare bodies they retrieved are manticore hatchlings, which look like dog-sized scorpions. Winnie picks them up basically every other week, and they're easy to draw. All carapace and legs. Simple, clean lines.

Maybe it's because Winnie's attention is so focused inward, her gaze so locked on Tuesday tire marks, or maybe it's simply because the forest has a plan, but when Winnie reaches a familiar hill with a familiar red stake in the ground, she notices something out of place beyond.

Two feet.

Or rather, what's left of two feet. These are bloodied, pale, and missing toes.

She hits the brakes. The four-wheeler stops, mud splattering over the red stake that marks the farthest spot that nightmares might appear. Each night, when the mist rises, the nightmares form. Most stay within the heart of the forest, near the sleeping spirit, but some try to walk outside. Some leave in search of humans for their nightly meal.

Which is why the Tuesdays have sensors to detect when a nightmare crosses into the wider world. In *theory*. But clearly a nightmare crossed the boundary and left feet here—which Winnie definitely needs to tell someone about. She also needs to get those feet.

She hops off the four-wheeler and grabs an old grocery bag from under the seat. It presumably held someone's snacks, but for months now it has served as nothing more than a crinkly annoyance she's been too lazy to remove. Now it will serve as a crude body bag. Or . . . foot bag.

With her hand in the bag, she picks up the two corpse remains like she used to pick up Erica's dog's poop. Crinkle, crinkle. One foot. Two. They're surprisingly heavy, and there's hair on the bridges surrounded by deep, bloodied gashes, almost like they got caught in a lawn mower.

A wave of nausea hits Winnie. She hastily closes the bag. She'd mocked Marcus only an hour ago, and now she's on the verge of puking herself. It doesn't bode well for tonight's trial.

You're hungry, she tells herself. *And sleep-deprived.* Even Mum and Gran Winona must have felt woozy from time to time, and they were both Lead Hunters for the Wednesday clan.

Winnie shoves a stick into the spot where the feet were. Red clay crunches up. The stick breaks at the tip, but it's a good enough marker. Mario at the Monday lab will be able to find it.

After depositing the feet beside the nightmares and nons in the four-wheeler's flatbed, she sets off once more. This time, she doesn't pay attention to the Tuesday tread. She just drives. Fast. Until at last she reaches the edge of the Monday estate.

Cold blusters against her without the forest to protect. The grounds are quiet, the grass crispy with frost. Two crows take flight as Winnie thunders by.

It's like a university campus. Or at least what Winnie imagines a university campus might look like, based on what she's seen on TV. Ahead is the main building, with its brownstone and crawling ivy that's more like rattly spaghetti without its green coat. Then surrounding the original estate are all the annexes, seven in total: three laboratories, two libraries (historical and scientific), a hospital, and an office building for all the Mondays working to expand Luminary knowledge.

Intellect at the fore. Knowledge is the path. That's their motto, and not for the first time, as Winnie passes the two library buildings, she kind of wishes she had been born a Monday. It wouldn't have changed what had happened with her dad, but at least then she, her mum, and her brother wouldn't be *quite* so hated. The Mondays are always polite to her; the Wednesdays never are.

After all, the Wednesday motto is *The cause above all else. Loyalty through and through.* What could be more disloyal than living with a Diana? Those witches who steal magic from the sleeping spirits around the world? Who want to *wake up* the spirits and unleash nightmares on humankind?

As far as the Wednesdays are concerned, ten years as outcasts isn't severe enough for Winnie's, Mum's, and Darian's crimes. And frustrating as it is, Winnie can't even blame them for that. The Dianas are bad. Her dad is bad. End of story.

Used to be, back in the early days of the American Luminaries when the spirit here had only just awoken, the Dianas fought to gain a foothold in the forest. They would bury their sources all around—the crystals, metal spheres, wooden talismans, animal bones—hoping to absorb magic from the spirit into them. Then they would use their devices to craft spells.

It seemed like sources were everywhere in those days, tucked under roots or into stone crannies, draining the forest bit by bit. Often it was the kids on corpse duty who found them—and often the sources were booby-trapped.

Winnie's own great-grandfather lost his thumb that way.

In the end, though, the Luminaries of Hemlock Falls had been stronger than the Dianas. The witches hadn't been able to claim the spirit's magic, and so they'd gone back into hiding around the globe while the old siren installed downtown to warn of Dianas had stopped its frequent howling.

They're still out there, though. The Dianas. They still want to take control of the spirits and overrun the world. They still sneak in sources and steal magic whenever, wherever they can. Winnie's dad is living proof of that, and her family is living proof of what can happen when vigilance slips.

Winnie drives past the main Monday estate, and though she waves at two people in lab coats, they ignore her. Once she reaches the hospital, she circles behind to the morgue entrance. The lead nightmare researcher, Mario, meets her.

He nods at Winnie, his always-in-the-lab pale skin alight in the morning sun. A pink bubble pops from his lips. "Ugh," Winnie groans. "I thought we'd agreed no gum while I'm around."

"And I thought we'd agreed you would be on time." He taps his watch. "A guy's gotta fill his life somehow." He blows another bubble. *Pop!*

Winnie cracks a smile. She likes Mario. He never acts like she shouldn't be here, never rolls his eyes at her or ignores her wave. Maybe it's because his nephew Andrew and Winnie's brother Darian are boyfriends, or maybe it's because he was tight with Winnie's dad before the *incident,* but either way, she appreciates having an ally—even if she's never allowed to follow him into the morgue or exam rooms.

And even if he is like a walking piece of bubble wrap, always pop-pop-popping to the great annoyance of literally *everyone.* Even his mother, when she visits from the Italian branch of the Luminaries, scolds him.

"I found something." Winnie cuts the engine, hops to the pavement, and holds up the grocery bag. Blood is visible through the plastic.

Mario squints. "Are those . . . feet?"

"*Yes.*" She hurries toward him, waving with her free hand toward the flatbed. "And I found them outside the boundary. I'm pretty sure they belong to the halfer. No," she amends once she reaches him, "I'm positive they do. You know what this means, right?"

He sighs, and his face scrunches with a grimace that can only be described as *long-suffering.* "I certainly have a theory, but I suspect you have a different one. One that's highly improbable."

That's rich coming from Mario, who is somewhat infamous for his own off-the-wall ideas. "A werewolf did it," Winnie declares.

Mario blows another bubble. *Pop!*

"I'm serious." Winnie thrusts the feet at him. The plastic rustles. "What else can leave the boundary unnoticed, Mario? It's either a changeling or a werewolf, and changelings don't mutilate bodies."

WERE-CREATURES

Human by day and monster by night, these rare day-walkers blend in easily and are unrecognizable from other humans in their daytime form. The most common animal form is werewolf, but there are records of were-lions from the Kenyan spirit and were-leopards from the Pakistani spirit.

They can rip apart a body (nightmare, human, or animal) when the full frenzy of their nightmare mutation takes hold, but such frenzies occur rarely. Typically, they kill only to feed or defend. While they do hunt other nightmares, they prefer to hunt humans.

There is no cure for the nightmare mutation, and to be bitten by a were-creature is to become infected by the mutation. Incubation time varies by victim species, age, size, and type of were-creature. Some records exist of humans able to resist the mutation, though these are rare and unstudied.

Were-creatures, when in their animal form, are almost unkillable. However, like the non legends, they are hurt by silver—and, in some rare cases, by gold.

"They're also extremely rare. We haven't had one in seventeen years. And it was . . ." He shakes his head. "It was bad, remember?"

Winnie doesn't remember, since she hadn't been born yet. But she certainly knows the stories about how a non-turned-werewolf killed six people in as many days, and the entirety of Hemlock Falls was on lockdown until the Tuesdays finally shot him. Ever since then, that siren downtown that had been built to warn of Diana attacks has also been used for any daywalkers on the loose.

Winnie chews her lip. She doesn't want to make light of what happened seventeen years ago . . . but she also thinks she's on to something. "Just imagine it, Mario. This werewolf is in the middle of eating when the night ends. He still has the feet in his mouth as his body begins to change back into human form—"

"Now the werewolf is a he?"

"—and he just . . ." She mimics walking with her fingers. "Marches right out of the forest. Then he drops the feet and enters our world."

Mario does not look moved by this theory. If anything, he looks mildly agitated. Like he has somewhere to be and Winnie's tall tales are keeping him from it. He does, at least, accept the bag from her grasp. "Interesting story, as per usual, Winnie. But imagine this instead: It was the same vampira horde the hunters have been tracking for the past three nights. The hunters finally killed the horde— presumably mid-meal—and the feet got flung over the boundary." He shuffles toward a rolling table nearby. The stainless steel gleams in the rising sun.

"That was my first thought too." Winnie follows him, and when he grabs the table, she grabs the other end. They roll it to the four-wheeler. "But the marks on these feet aren't consistent with vampira. Just open the bag and you'll see!"

Mario doesn't answer, but Winnie can see he's mulling her words. He always chews louder and blows more bubbles when his scientist mind is whirring. *Pop-pop-pop!*

Winnie helps him load the first non body onto the table's lowest shelf. It's an older woman, her eyes turned to stone in what was clearly an unfortunate basilisk encounter. Then they load the manticores onto the middle shelf. Next, the sylphid (which Mario excitedly "oohs" over), and lastly, the halfer onto the top shelf.

"Definitely vampira," Mario says after a cursory examination. "But I do like your theory, Winnie. It's very . . ." He pauses as he does every week when Winnie offers her latest out-there idea.

"Inspired," she finishes for him. She can't keep the disappointment out of her voice. She really thought she'd gotten it right this time. A werewolf would have explained Jay's weird assessment of the clearing, and she had even heard all that howling at dawn.

Mario gives her an apologetic grin. "We make quite the pair, don't we? But I *do* like how your mind works."

Winnie shoves at her glasses. Her thumb smushes a fingerprint onto the left lens. "Did Aunt Rachel tell you they took down a vampira horde?"

"No," he admits. "The Wednesdays haven't turned in their kill coordinates yet, but I will bet you a week's supply of coffee that it *wasn't* a werewolf."

This is also what Mario does every week: he bets a week's worth of coffee that her hypothesis is wrong. And of course, whenever he's the one with the kooky theories, Winnie wagers the same.

Winnie studies the halfer again. Sunlight glares on the plastic. The grocery bag with the feet now rests below the shredded ankles. Yes, it does look like a vampira horde did this . . . but then why were they eating the feet? According to the Compendium, the vampira don't eat feet. They just remove them.

Winnie sets her jaw. There's more to this than what she's seeing. Even Jay noticed that.

"Okay." She shoots her gaze to Mario. He's writing on a clipboard that swings from the table's edge. "A week's supply of coffee."

He pauses his scribbling. "Huh?"

"A week's supply," she repeats, and she thrusts out a hand. Then she remembers she hasn't washed it yet and hastily withdraws. "I accept your wager. Shall we say coffee from Joe Squared?"

"You're that confident?" Mario squints at the bag of feet. *Pop-pop-pop!* Neither of them has ever actually gone through with a wager before. "You're even willing to pay for the expensive stuff? All right." He shrugs. "It's your funeral. If that turns out to be a werewolf kill, I'll buy you a week's supply of coffee from Joe Squared—or if you prefer, I'll make it a meal for you and a friend at the Revenant's Daughter."

You and a friend. As if Winnie has any of those. "I'll take the coffee," she replies.

He doffs an invisible hat. "And I'll email you when I hear from the Wednesdays."

"Excellent." She doffs a hat right back, then hops once more onto the four-wheeler. Spring wind bites against her. The smudge on her glasses distorts the day. Downtown, the bells in the Council building toll eight o'clock, meaning she has an hour until school begins.

School always starts late in Hemlock Falls, to accommodate corpse duty or last night's hunters.

"*Get ready to lose, Mario!*" Winnie hollers as she drives away. Mario's popping bubbles chase after her.

29

CHAPTER

6

T he Revenant's Daughter is part bar, part diner, all grease. Winnie doesn't normally stop by the restaurant before school, but her mum made her pinkie-swear the night before. "It's your birthday. I want to see you on your birthday morning." So now Winnie is here.

She parks the four-wheeler beside the dumpster out back, in the alley between Falls' Finest, Joe Squared, and the Wednesday-owned grocers that price-gouges everything because it's the only one around, so they can do that.

The smell of hot oil melts over Winnie. Both disgusting and mouthwatering. Nothing at the Revenant's Daughter is particularly good or gourmet, but it's battered and fried so deeply, you don't really notice. Plus, ketchup. The restaurant goes through a lot of ketchup.

Winnie clicks her front teeth in triple time as she marches toward the heavy back door propped open with a rock. Greasy heat billows into the morning. She wishes she had time for some breakfast.

"What's wrong?" Francesca Wednesday asks the instant Winnie steps into the steamy kitchen. Her mum is in the middle of sliding two plates of hash browns onto a tray that's already overloaded with eggs and toast and coffee.

Archie Friday, meanwhile, cooks more of those hash browns and doesn't look up from the griddle. He's a man of few words and mostly grunts.

"You look like something is wrong." Mum frowns, the lines between her eyebrows slicing deep. The yellow undertones of her skin look almost sickly in the kitchen's light. "Did corpse duty not go well?"

Winnie gulps. She's not a very good liar. Even the simplest of white lies is impossible for her to conjure. For example, she has never successfully convinced her brother Darian that she really *did* like the mustache he had last year. And when it comes to the big stuff . . . Well, she has only managed to hide her plans for the hunter trials by avoiding her mum.

Fortunately, as she stretches her brain for an answer, she zips up . . . and zips down the leather jacket. Mum's dark eyes laser onto it. "Where did you get *that*?" She strides over to Winnie, her tray balanced on one shoulder, and scrutinises the leather with a hunter's trained eye. "Did you steal it?"

Winnie laughs. A feeble sound that only makes her mum look that much more suspicious.

"*No*, Mum. Emma and Bretta Wednesday gave it to me."

"Oh." Mum blinks. "Wow." Her cheeks flush. She glances toward the back of the kitchen, to where a yellow gift bag waits beside the industrial coffee machines. "Well, you're, uh . . . you're going to be disappointed by my gift, then. But go ahead." She dips her head toward it. "Open it, and I'll be right back."

Mum shoves into the dining room, handling the tray with a lot more grace than she had four years ago, when the Luminaries first cast her out and she had to pick up two jobs to pay the bills. Winnie had never appreciated how comfortably they'd lived with Mum's hunter salary—until it was gone.

While the swinging door pauses at the height of its opening, the already buzzing drone of voices hyped up on cholesterol and caffeine crashes over Winnie. She catches a glimpse of the nearest booth, which houses Imran and Xavier Saturday (seniors, popular, not related), Marisol Sunday (junior, popular), Casey Tuesday (sophomore, popular), and Erica Thursday.

Erica's eyes, almost russet against her warm, amber skin, catch on Winnie's. Then they lurch away as quickly as Winnie's do. The door swings shut. Archie barks, "Order up!" And Winnie makes a beeline for the coffee machines. Her heart is thundering. Her teeth are clicking.

That is another reason why she doesn't come to the Daughter in the mornings. It's where the popular kids eat breakfast before school.

It's where *Erica* eats breakfast before school. They haven't spoken in four years, and though Erica doesn't call Winnie *witch spawn* or *Diana scat,* she also doesn't interfere when everyone else does. She just watches, expression inscrutable on her cold, perfectly made-up face. She'd just been getting into eyeliner and contouring when she and Winnie had still been friends. Now she is never without it, and her clothes are always designer, always new.

Erica's dad, who hails from the Mexican Luminaries originally, is always one of the best dressed in Hemlock Falls, so it's no surprise Erica is too. And though Erica's dad still uses the last name Jueves, Erica was born in the American Luminaries. As such, she has the last name Thursday like her mum—who also happens to be head of the Thursday clan.

Everyone expects Erica to follow in Marcia's perfectly placed three-inch heels. The way Erica looks and speaks and moves these days, she's already most of the way there.

Winnie reaches the yellow gift bag and recognises the unicorn tissue paper from last year's birthday. *New pens,* she thinks, since that's what Mum always gives her. Except when she dives in, she finds a fancy plaid glasses case instead.

Excitement wells inside her. She'd been saying she wanted new glasses, but she hadn't realised Mum had been listening.

Winnie pops open the case, and while the glasses winking up at her aren't smudged like her current pair, they *are* kind of scuffed around the edges. And they're also at least three years out of style, the frames thick when the style is thin.

Winnie swallows.

"I got the wrong kind, didn't I?"

Winnie jolts. She hadn't sensed her Mum approaching. Even still, Fran moves with the stealth of a Lead Hunter.

"Are they knockoffs? *Crap.*" Mum swipes the case from Winnie's grasp. "I really thought they looked fancy."

"They're not knockoffs." Winnie grabs for the case.

Mum easily scoots out of the way. She is scowling at the glasses. "I knew I should have waited until after your birthday, when I could make the trip to Chicago, but I was just so pleased to find these cheap. Dammit, Fran."

"*No.*" Winnie grabs her mum's biceps. Then she squeezes. "They're great, Mum. Exactly what I wanted. See?" She grabs the case and hastily changes pairs. No more smudge over the left eye, only crisp clarity as Archie shouts in their direction, "Order up!"

Winnie smiles, and Mum flushes all the way to the edge of her greying roots. Winnie hates how desperate it makes her look. Mum wants to believe Winnie, and Winnie wants Mum to believe too. Like, never in her life has she more fiercely wished she were good at this whole lying business.

But alas, Winnie just isn't convincing enough, and Mum sighs. It is a sound of such dejection and self-loathing that Winnie is struck, for the eight millionth time, by how much she hates her dad. He did this to Francesca Wednesday. He broke her heart—broke all their hearts—and made the toughest hunter in the Wednesday clan into . . .

Into this.

Not that Mum is broken. Anything *but*. She is Winnie's hero and always will be. But before Dad betrayed them, Mum never had any doubts. She was Lead Hunter for the

Wednesday clan, and she lived by the Wednesday motto. She hammered loyalty into her kids; she hammered loyalty into Winnie.

Then Mum caught Dad in the middle of a spying spell that would have fed Luminary secrets directly to the Dianas. She'd tried to turn him in. He'd knocked her out. And the rest is shitty history.

"How do I look?" Winnie offers her goofiest smile for Mum, tongue out and teeth bared, and to her relief, Mum grins back.

"*Order up!*" Archie barks, louder now.

"You look fantastic, Win." Mum pulls Winnie in for an awkward hug (they've never been one for touching) and kisses her hair. "Happy birthday to my most favorite daughter in all the universe—"

"*Order.*"

"—I hope it's a good day, and don't forget: we need to practice your driving—"

"*Up.*"

"Hellions and banshees, Archie, *I freaking heard you!*" Mum scowls, looking much more like the hard-ass Lead Hunter Winnie grew up with. A pat on the head for Winnie, then she's already stalking away to grab more breakfast.

And to serve all the Luminaries who will no longer let her in.

CHAPTER
7

It isn't that most Luminaries are cruel to Winnie or her family directly. After the spray-painting incident of freshman year had yielded actual punishment from the Council, most of the local Luminaries shifted to ignoring Winnie, Darian, and their mum.

At least to their faces. Behind their backs, however, they do love a good snicker. Or a good whisper. Or even the occasional *Oops, I spilled my chai latte all over you. So sorry!*

And when Winnie says "behind their backs," she means it literally. In homeroom, she is forced to sit in the second row because of Ms. Morgan's inane seat assignments that arrange everyone by grade, which means that today she gets to hear Dante Lunedì whisper-sing "Happy Birthday" at her with slightly modified lyrics and a nice accent.

He and his family might have moved here only two years ago from the Italian branch of the Luminaries, but outcasts like Winnie are despised in all fourteen branches around the world. So even though newcomers regularly join the American Luminaries, they all know exactly how they're supposed to treat Winnie, Darian, and Mum.

"Happy birthday to you," Dante sings, *"happy birthday to you, happy birthday, witch traitor, happy birthday to you."*

Well, at least someone remembered her birthday. Winnie supposes that must count for something, right?

She doesn't turn around, because she never turns around. She just drags her No. 2 pencil over a corner of maths homework. Here are the sylphid's horns. Its teeth. Its bark-textured skin. Winnie isn't in homeroom at all, but back in the forest while the hemlocks and spruce trees breathe. While humidity beads on her skin and the cold sharpens her senses.

"Happy birthday to you, happy birthday to you, happy birthday, Diana spawn, happy birthday to you." Then he adds a spoken "Don't take my finger bones as a source, *sí*?"

Most of the classroom is laughing now. Quiet, subtle laughs that are just soft enough they can be silenced in a heartbeat. The only person not laughing is Fatima Wednesday, whose mum is head of the Wednesday clan and therefore a councilor. She whisper-hisses "Stop" at Dante, as well as "No Diana would want your gross fingers."

As much as Winnie wants to give Fatima a grateful glance, she dares not turn around. She's afraid if she does, it will somehow confirm that no Diana would want his gross fingers. Then people will question how Winnie knows such a thing, and it won't matter that she doesn't. That even to this day, she has no idea what her dad's source was made of or where he may have buried it in the forest.

Twelve more hours, Winnie tells herself. In twelve more hours, she'll be starting the first trial. She presses her pencil into the paper and sketches out a long sylphid finger, almost rootlike in its gnarly shape. *Twelve more hours, twelve more hours.*

Right as Dante is going in for a third round of song, this time with Peter Sunday on harmony, Ms. Morgan arrives. She isn't a Luminary, but a rare non folded into the Hemlock Falls mix because she has been dating Mason Thursday for a bazillion years. With alabaster skin and round, glowing cheeks that she expertly streaks with shimmery highlighter, she has the look of a hippie art teacher. Her long mousy-brown hair is always pulled into a single braid, her clothes always billowy and free.

Aunt Rachel was actually the one who vetted Leona Morgan to ensure she had no shady past or Diana connections before she was allowed into Hemlock Falls. That was when Rachel had worked in the bureaucratic Wednesday offices before taking over as Lead Hunter.

Winnie has always wondered who vetted Dad; she has always wondered if Dad had been a Diana before he came and the Wednesdays just missed the signs . . . or if he joined the witches after moving here.

The entire room goes quiet at Ms. Morgan's arrival, and she flings out a knowing glance from behind her thin, metal-framed glasses. The exact sort of glasses that Winnie was hoping to get.

"Good morning." Ms. Morgan waves a loosed-sleeved arm at the room. "Is everyone finished being a childish asshole yet? Because if so, I'd like to take attendance."

Dante chokes. The rest of the room goes silent—and Winnie wishes very much that she could curl under her desk and die. Having Ms. Morgan defend her is even worse than enduring the childish assholes.

Twelve more hours. Twelve more hours.

Ms. Morgan bares a brittle smile before spouting off names. Everyone is there except Jay Friday, which isn't surprising because he's never there. And if Winnie hadn't already seen him that morning, she would have assumed he was out getting high.

Actually, she supposes he could still be doing that. He'll probably shamble in during second or third period, eyes bloodshot and hair extra mussed. His signature buffalo flannel will stink of stale cigarettes, even though she knows he doesn't smoke—just the older jerks he hangs out with do at the abandoned Luminaries museum on the south side—and he'll coast through the rest of the day without taking notes or paying much attention to anything.

Against her better judgment, Winnie wishes Jay *were* here instead of out getting high. Like Fatima, he doesn't laugh with the other assholes. But unlike Fatima, something about his not-laughing often gets the rest of the class to shut up. It's weird because he's not popular. He's a Friday. As the smallest, least powerful clan, Fridays are automatically off-limits for popular.

But Jay also became the first hunter in his grade, and rumor has it he might make Lead Hunter before he's even eighteen. In other words, people low-key fear or are high-key enamored with Jay, and as far as Winnie is concerned, that's way better than being actually popular.

"Hey," Fatima says, pausing at Winnie's desk on the way toward the door after homeroom ends. She wears a silky cobalt hijab that brings out the blue in her eyes. "Sorry about Dante."

"Don't be." Winnie musters up a smile.

Fatima smiles back, wide and open, revealing braces on her bottom teeth. "Well, happy birthday." She wanders into the hallway. Winnie stays put.

It's only once everyone else has left that she finally stuffs her maths homework, now adorned with a sylphid's torso, into her backpack and heads for the door. Unfortunately, she doesn't quite make it before Ms. Morgan hurries into her path. She grabs Winnie's sleeve; her pointer finger has a plaster on it.

Please don't mention the application, please don't mention the application.

Ms. Morgan, of course, mentions the application: "Have you given any thought to that summer program at Heritage, Winnie?"

Winnie's organs wince. Her face winces too. Three weeks ago, Ms. Morgan had approached her about this summer art program for high schoolers at Heritage University four hours away. *I know one of the professors who teaches it, Winnie, and I think you would just love it there. Here, take this application and give it a read. I can really see you flourishing at a place like Heritage after you graduate. So many subjects to explore, so many new people!*

All Winnie had heard in Ms. Morgan's speech, though, was: *You should really give up on being a Luminary again and find a solid backup plan. When you graduate, there won't be a place for you here.*

"The applications are due soon," Ms. Morgan continues, oblivious to Winnie's misery, "and I can email it directly to my friend Philip. He'll approve you, I'm sure of it. You have too much talent for him not to."

"Um."

"And if money is a concern, there's a financial aid option. It was on the second page of the application. Or . . ." Ms. Morgan's hazel eyes narrow. "Maybe it was the third page?"

Winnie doesn't know. She took the application, stuffed it at the bottom of her locker, and hasn't looked at it since. Drawing is something she enjoys doing, but only if she's drawing *nightmares.* Only if she's drawing *for the Luminaries.*

She shakes off Ms. Morgan's hand and murmurs, "I'll get on it, Ms. Morgan. Thank you." Then she beats a hasty retreat from the classroom, head ducked low into the sudden onslaught of traffic.

Bodies clot the arteries of Hemlock Falls High, hiding its nondescript walls built forty years ago and its floors carpeted only slightly sooner. There are no mascots at HFHS, no sports teams, no gym facilities, and no guidance counselors. All but three of the teachers are Sundays, and so, when the half day ends, they leave along with 99 percent of the students, who go to the sprawling Sunday grounds. *There,* you can find sports teams, several gyms, even more guidance counselors, and nary a sagging locker in sight.

Winnie misses it so badly sometimes that her chest hurts. She should be accustomed to the ache by now, yet somehow she isn't. And today, as all the students stream around her—some of them discussing tonight's trial because they'll be there and *welcomed*—a new sensation hammers atop the usual tightness. It's like she's been drugged with a phoenix feather and now her heart is going to explode.

Happy birthday, witch traitor, happy birthday to you!

She has tried, for four years, to approximate what they do at the Sunday estate. Jogging, sprinting, an obstacle course that is really just the inside of her house when no one is home. But there's only so much she can mimic on her own. She hasn't trained with actual gear in four years—she hasn't held a bow or thrown a flash grenade in *four years*. Hell, she couldn't even ID that halfer correctly this morning, so really, what chance does she have against the forest tonight?

Winnie drags her feet. Her heart is hammering harder now. The world is spinning too, and when she reaches her locker, she rests her forehead against the neon-yellow slats. Twelve hours seems impossibly far away. And also terrifyingly soon.

What if she fails? She has tried—with great success—to avoid even considering that possibility, but *what if she fails*? What if she can't find a nightmare, she can't track it, and she can't kill it? You can only attempt the hunter trials once. There are no do-overs. If she fails, then she will be back here tomorrow, still an outcast. Still pretending she doesn't hear everyone whispering about her as they pass.

Don't take my finger bones as a source, sì?

What if art school *is* her only option? Ms. Morgan will have had the right of it, and Winnie will be *right back here,* digging an application out of her locker. Then she'll spend the rest of her life drawing . . . Drawing what? She doesn't even know. She just knows it won't be nightmares.

The smell of bergamot and lime drifts into Winnie's nostrils. Then a familiar voice asks, "You okay?"

Winnie pries her face off the metal and finds Jay beside her. He leans against the next locker, no books in hand or backpack in sight. There is, however, a crease on his forehead that suggests he might have just awoken from a nap.

His grey eyes reach Winnie's then quickly skate away.

"Werewolf," Winnie says. She turns toward him and mirrors his pose, one shoulder against the locker. "That's what you thought it was this morning, isn't it? You didn't think vampira horde, you thought it was a werewolf."

"Hmmm," he replies, staring over the top of her head. "And why do you say that?"

"Because I found the halfer's feet outside the boundary. There were teeth marks on them. *And,*" Winnie adds, "you said you'd followed tracks. Were they wolf tracks?"

He doesn't answer. Instead he shifts his attention to the thinning traffic. "And I presume you told someone?"

"Of course." She fiddles with her jacket zip. "I told Mario."

"Anyone else?"

"Well, no." *Zip, zip, zip, zip.* "Should I have?" She doesn't add that she avoids the Council if she can. The last time she went to them about what she was *certain* was a melusine kill, they dismissed her with laughs that were a lot harder to stomach than Mario's.

Melusine don't kill, Dryden Saturday had said. And then Erica's mum, Marcia, had added, *Don't blame yourself, Winnie. It's not your fault that you're so out of practice.* Except the way she'd said it had made it sound like it was definitely Winnie's fault and she should definitely blame herself.

"Mario will pass along the info if I'm right," Winnie adds. "He's waiting to see the Wednesday kill coordinates before he confirms."

"Interesting," Jay murmurs, though nothing in his tone sounds interested. He looks like he is about to fall asleep standing, and Winnie abruptly realises that Jay isn't waiting for her to answer him so much as telling her, *This is not my problem, speak to someone else.* "Well," he says with a pat on her shoulder, "keep up the good work." He pushes off the locker as if to leave.

But Winnie grabs his flannel sleeve. "Why didn't you say something?"

"About?" His eyebrows lift. The red mark from his nap stretches long.

"About the halfer. You could have just told me it was a werewolf kill."

"Except," he counters, prying her fingers off him with a gentle but firm grip, "we both know you wouldn't have listened. Now, if you'll excuse me, I'm going to be late for Spanish."

"Like you care about being late."

He doesn't disagree, just flips a hand in the air and strides away. And as much as Winnie dislikes him, she does appreciate that he stopped to check on her. Somewhere inside all that lean haggardness, a heart still resides.

CHAPTER
8

It is raining as Winnie waits in front of HFHS for Darian to arrive. Because it is her birthday, he insisted on picking her up, and because she would always rather have a ride than take the local bus, she accepted.

As one of only sixteen students who don't attend the Sunday estate in the afternoons—and as the *only* student who didn't willingly give up Sunday training because she wants to move out of town one day—she waits alone in front of the school. The other students are already gone or huddled together, their own special clique who can't wait to leave Hemlock Falls and the world of the Luminaries behind. They would have taken an application from Ms. Morgan and filled it out right away.

Meanwhile, for Winnie, there has never been a single day when she felt she wanted to leave. For a few years after Dad's departure, Darian had decided *he* would. Unlike Winnie, he'd never wanted to be a hunter. His dream was bureaucratic: to one day lead the Wednesday clan and be on the local Luminary Council. But thanks to Dad, that dream had been obliterated.

An outcast—even if it's only temporary—can never join the Council. Ever. Unlike the rules for hunter trials, that conveniently never mention outcasts, the rules for Luminary councilors are very, painfully clear.

So off Darian had gone into the wider world, hoping he could find a place for himself outside. But after one semester at Heritage University, he'd come right back. Because at the end of the day, even if he's stuck being a coffee boy for the Council, it's better to be *here* in the world he knows. The Luminary cause will always define him. He will always be loyalty through and through.

Culture runs thicker than blood. It was something Dad used to say about the clans, and though Winnie hates admitting it, he wasn't wrong.

Winnie is also loyalty through and through. Hemlock Falls is all she has ever known. Fighting nightmares is all she has ever wanted to do. So while it's great that those *other* people want to leave town—while it's even kind of nice that Ms. Morgan sees so much potential in Winnie's art—here is where Winnie is meant to be.

When at last Darian arrives in Andrew's old white Ford Ranger, a drizzle thickens the air. Winnie's hair is soaked through. Her jeans too, and her hoodie because she'd panicked over her new jacket and shoved it into her backpack. Is leather waterproof? Is *that* leather waterproof? She decided to take it off just in case.

Darian stops in front of Winnie, brakes squeaking. "Are those the new glasses Mum got you?" he asks the instant Winnie swings open the passenger door. His skin is sallow—almost anemic—in a way that can only mean it has been an especially tough day working for Dryden Saturday.

"Yes." Winnie sighs and slumps inside. Her backpack lands on her feet with a thud.

"You should just wear your old pair."

"I can't." Winnie sighs a second time and yanks off the glasses. Water droplets coat the new lenses. "It would hurt Mum's feelings. Are they really that bad?"

Darian doesn't answer. Just pushes his own glasses up his own hooked nose. Unlike Winnie, he inherited the Wednesday Mediterranean hair: so brown, so glossy, so thick.

"Check the glove box," Darian says as he pulls onto the main street that cuts through Hemlock Falls. The pavement was empty thanks to the rain, and the truck's slashing windshield wipers are the only sound.

Everything is grey.

Winnie obeys, a smile perking her lips, and she quickly opens the glove box. Because Darian is the living embodiment of a colour-coded spreadsheet, and because he will organise anything that anyone will ever let him near, each item is in its proper sleeve, each emergency supply (matches, snacks, and even a glass-hammer in case the truck ever ends up underwater) in its proper cubbyhole.

He would have done so well as a Thursday. (Family motto: *Always prepared. Never without a plan.*)

Nestled within the orderly lines of the glove compartment is a tiny, grey velvet box. Too small to be pens or markers or a new sketchpad. *Curiouser and curiouser.* Winnie slides it out and opens it, holding it to the hazy afternoon light.

A locket winks up at her, a crescent moon and stars stamped into the matte gold. It's the symbol for the Luminaries, and when she clicks open the thumbnail-sized circle, she finds a picture of Darian on one side and herself on the other. Old photos, from when she was eight and he was thirteen.

She tries to grin. She really *wants* to grin, but instead, she grimaces. Then bursts into tears. Not normal tears either, but the gross, hiccuping kind, and the next thing she knows, Darian has pulled into a parallel parking spot in front of Odell Wednesday's bakery.

"Oh my god, what's wrong? Winnie, what is it?" He reaches for her across the seat, but Winnie *really* doesn't like to be touched when she's crying.

"I'm"—*hiccup*—"doing"—*hiccup*—"the trial tonight."

Darian doesn't seem to understand. He frowns at Winnie and slides off his glasses. "You're what?"

"*I'm doing the first trial tonight!*" She practically wails the words this time. Then she too yanks off her glasses, and buries her face in her hands.

This is embarrassing. She is not a crier. And yet for some reason, she cannot seem to stop. Even as she senses that Darian has gone extremely still beside her. Still as a vampira stalking its prey. Still as a brother who has no idea what to say in the face of a hysterical little sister.

After several minutes of Winnie's gulping tears and the clacking windshield wipers, Winnie finally gets herself under control. She wipes her eyes and snuffles onto a tissue Darian is now offering.

Then, as if he's afraid he might scare her, he says very softly, "You're doing the trial tonight. Is that even allowed?"

"Yeth." Winnie blows her nose. Then she explains how she checked the Rulebook and even copied the relevant pages. Any Luminary can take the trials during the month of their sixteenth birthday, but they only get one chance. To fail marks the end of their hunter career before it can even begin.

Darian swallows. His fingers—his middle finger bearing a ring on it that matches one Andrew wears—start tapping the steering wheel. "You need to tell Mum."

"She'll just stop me."

"Which maybe isn't a bad thing." He sighs and shifts toward her, drawing one knee onto the seat with him. "Win, people *die* taking the hunter trials. And those are people who've been training for years. You've seen what nightmares can do to a person."

Winnie blows her nose again, then stares at the gross tissue now clutched in her hand. "Darian, you know this is all I've ever wanted." Her voice is very small. "This is my only shot at it. If I can't do it now, then I can't ever."

His lips compress, the skin around them turning pale, and Winnie knows he's thinking about his own lost dream. She would feel guilty about that if she weren't so desperate to convince him.

"Plus," she forges on, "if I could become a hunter, it might help *all* of us. You, me, Mum. We might actually be welcomed into the Luminaries again. No more waiting six years for this stupid punishment to end."

Darian's lips compress even more, and he notably says nothing—because there's nothing he can say. Being a hunter carries clout in Hemlock Falls. *Big* clout. Enough to count for something with the Council.

And with the Wednesdays too.

He pushes his glasses back on. "What were you gonna tell Mum you were doing?"

"I was just going to sneak out."

He glares. "And then show back up all busted and muddy at three A.M.? No way. The forest is dangerous for a Luminary untrained, remember? It's like the first thing we learn, Winnie."

"And I'm not totally untrained." Winnie sets her jaw. "I've been practicing on my own."

Darian's glare turns suspicious. "How long have you been planning this?"

She fidgets with the tissue. "A while." *Since we first got kicked out.* "The first trial is the easiest, Darian. All I have to do is kill a single nightmare. And when I do that, then I can move on to the second trial this weekend—"

"'When'?" he repeats. "More like 'if.'"

Winnie shreds off a corner of the tissue and ignores him. "*When* I pass, I'll move on to the second trial and survive a night in the forest. Then I'll move on to the final trial, whatever it might be." She pins him with a stare. "Maybe you're right. Maybe it's *if*, not when, but I have to at least try, Darian. Think about what it might do for our family! Having a hunter again—proving our loyalty to the clan. *Proving* that just because Dad turned out to be a Diana doesn't mean we haven't always been Luminaries to the core."

Darian chews his lip. Winnie can see that her arguments are starting to wear him down.

"Does getting Dryden Saturday's coffee make you happy? Does having him scream at you that he wanted *two* creams make you happy?"

"Of course not." He is glowering at the rain on the windshield now.

"Well, an art program at Heritage doesn't make *me* happy! Darian, they call me 'witch traitor' and 'Diana spawn' at school. Like, every day."

"Who?" He rounds toward her. "Who does that?"

"*Everyone.* They even did it today." For some reason, she has started crying again. "We're living the punishment for Dad's crimes, and I can't do it anymore. We don't deserve this. We *deserve* our old lives back. We *deserve* to dream again. So please, help me, Darian. Please help me take the trial."

For several long minutes, the only sound is his careful breathing. He watches Winnie, a line in his shoulders that screams of angry brother just itching to go on the rampage. Right when Winnie isn't sure she can handle the silence a moment longer, though, he says, "Okay, Win." His shoulders sink. "I'll help you."

"Really?" The question is a squeak.

"Yeah, though god help me, this is a mistake." He returns his feet to the pedals and shifts the truck into drive. "The trial starts at nine, right? That only gives us the afternoon to get you ready."

"Thank you," she tries, but he cuts her off with a wave. He clearly hates that he's agreeing, but he also realises that he—like her—is too unhappy to keep living this way for another six years.

The truck's blinker ticks; Darian rumbles them back into traffic; and Winnie stares, with clicking teeth, at the misty brown river that pythons through town, fed by a distant waterfall and a lake filled with nightmares.

CHAPTER

9

Darian's flat is a lofted, industrial affair over the Très Jolie. Other than the Revenant's Daughter, the Très Jolie is the only restaurant around. Unless, of course, you want to drive an hour to the nearest non city. Unlike the Revenant's Daughter, though, it serves "fancy" food, meaning Winnie and her family only ever used to visit on special occasions and now never visit at all.

The flat always smells like fresh baguette, and Winnie is always hungry when she walks into it. Which, bless Andrew's soul, is why he always abandons his desk to make her a snack in the open kitchen when she comes over.

Today's snack, waiting on the island / dining table / bar, is a cake, which he clearly made himself. "It will taste better than it looks." Andrew's puppy-dog eyes dart to drooping candles shaped like the numbers 1 and 6. His sharp cheekbones, a dark, warm shade of brown, flicker in the dying light of the candles. His parents both hail from the Kenyan Luminaries, but since Andrew was born here, he uses Monday as his last name.

He's in training to become a medical assistant, and in the brief gaps between studying, he attempts to replicate what he sees on *The Great British Bake Off*. This particular cake has chocolate frosting and blue swirls that will probably taste better than they look.

"Thanks, Andrew." Winnie attempts a smile, but it feels forced—and he clearly senses that, because he glances between her and Darian. "What's wrong?"

"Nothing," Winnie starts.

But Darian, who *literally* just swore he wouldn't tell Andrew, says, "Winnie is entering the trial tonight. Please convince her not to." Then, at Winnie's sputtering glare, he adds, "Sorry. We don't keep secrets from each other." He stalks to Andrew, rolls onto his toes to give him a peck on the cheek, and then continues stalking into the bedroom under the loft.

Andrew just gapes at Winnie, and she in turn blows out the candles with furious force. *Please let me pass the trial,* she wishes. *Please, please, please, forest spirit, let me pass the trial.*

Andrew leans over the island. He is the opposite of Darian's prim sweater vests and perfectly ironed button-ups. He is rumpled T-shirts with sports logos and sweatpants.

"You can't enter the trials, Winnie," he says.

"I can." She yanks out the number 1 candle and licks off the frosting. "Nowhere in the big, full Official Rulebook does it say I can't."

"When did you look at the Official Rulebook . . . Oh." He scowls. "*That's* why you wanted to go to the library? I feel so used. Abused. And confused." He yanks the cake away from her. "How long have you been planning this?"

"A . . . long time."

"And have you, ya know, trained any?"

"Yes," she says at the same moment Darian shouts from the bedroom, "Not properly, she hasn't." Then the man himself reappears, holding what looks to be old hunter practice gear. "Which means not only is she going to fail miserably, but she also might die. Here. Try this on." He dumps a heap of black, padded clothing onto the counter.

Winnie blinks, briefly forgetting how he just declared she would fail and probably die. "Where did you get this stuff?" She pulls it to her: Kevlar vest, Kevlar thigh shields, and two poison-mist traps.

"They're Andrew's," Darian says while holding the vest toward her body, and Andrew winces. He has a very expressive wince that covers a wide range of emotions. This particular one says, *I am embarrassed.*

"I wanted to be a hunter," Andrew explains. "Or I thought I did, until I met Darian and realised maybe there were other things to live for than just the forest and the Luminaries."

"Psshhh." Darian rolls his eyes—though Winnie doesn't miss the blush creeping up his neck. "He just means his dad finally said it was okay for him to go into medical training instead."

"That too." Andrew grins and shoves the cake back Winnie's way. She swipes off the other candle (before he can change his mind) and sucks at the frosting. Her stomach gurgles.

"It's not actual hunting gear. It's just meant for training." Darian opens the vest in a *rriiiippp!* of Velcro. "But at least you won't be going into the woods without any protection." He drapes the pieces around her and she sets down the candle. Vest first, thigh shields next.

"It's . . ." She swallows. "It's too big."

Darian pauses his Velcro closure. "You don't have to do this, Win."

"I do."

"If you fail—"

"I *won't* fail." She doesn't want to have this conversation again. She doesn't want to see how much he doesn't believe in her.

And above all, she doesn't want to see how much hope is still hiding behind his eyes. He wants her to succeed as much as she does. He wants to be welcomed by the Council; he wants their family to be respected again; he wants to make enough money that Andrew isn't paying most of the rent.

When Dad disappeared, Darian had been hurt more than any of them. Darian and Dad didn't just have similar facial features; they walked and talked and organised alike. Where Winnie was all hard edges like Mum, Darian was soft and gentle like Dad.

And where Winnie and Dad had shared games together—scavenger hunts and secret codes—Darian had shared the deep stuff with Dad. The books and music, the late-night philosophy debates and disagreements over local politics. Most special of all, though, Darian had shared Dad's love of plants and growing wild things.

There is not a single piece of greenery in his flat now.

There is, however, a framed drawing that Winnie made of Darian and Andrew holding hands and smiling. It's not the best sketch Winnie has ever made—she was only twelve and still honing human proportions, so Darian's head looks a bit vampiric while Andrew's torso is sort of droll-like—but it's obviously them in the drawing, and Winnie obviously sketched it with lots of love.

Because Darian and Andrew—and of course Mum too—are the most important people in Winnie's life. This is why Winnie *knows* she isn't going to fail. There's no room for it. No second chances. No summer programs at Heritage where she will "flourish." In seven hours, she will be going into the forest. In five hours, she will be doing what she has been practicing, and she will make her family whole again.

"Thanks for the hunter stuff," she tells Andrew, stripping off the gear. *Rrrrripppp, rrripppp, rrrippp.* "And for the cake too. I'll eat it tomorrow *after*"—she hits Darian with her most forceful, Wednesday stare—"I pass the trial." Then she stuffs the Kevlar into her backpack.

And Darian sighs. "Come on, then. Let's get you home. Mum's probably wondering where you are."

Dinner with Mum is a quiet affair in the family kitchen. Steam coats the lone window over the crooked farmhouse sink, despite the draft that scourges through said window (because it is very old and the sash doesn't close properly).

"More birthday lasagna?" Mum offers the ceramic dish. She ran out of mozzarella and substituted pepper jack, which has definitely changed the overall flavour. It is less lasagna now and more quesadilla.

"I'm good," Winnie says. It was a struggle to get the first serving down. She's too nervous for food. Mum starts scooping out the lasagna anyway. "No, no—Mum." Winnie grabs her wrist. "I said I don't want any more."

"Oh." Mum's forehead knits and she drops the serving spoon back into the lasagna. "Sorry." She shoots to her feet and hurries to the sink, which is filled with dishes from Mum's rare attempt to cook.

The water turns on; Mum hums the Beach Boys and starts cleaning in a spray of water. She is even more wound up than usual, and as relieved as Winnie is that Mum isn't noticing her own anxiety, she also wishes Mum could just settle down.

But it's always like this on her birthday. Every year, Dad sends a card via mysterious means, and Mum wages an inner war over whether or not to share it—not with Winnie, of course. She *never* shares it with Winnie, and Winnie only even knows the cards exist because two years ago, she found one before Mum did. It had no return address, but she'd recognised Dad's handwriting immediately.

He always wrote in print ("Who has time for cursive?" he'd say) and he always dotted his *i*'s at the end, so the dots were never quite over the proper letter. Plus, it said very obviously, *For my daughter Winnie.*

She did not open the letter, because she didn't and still doesn't care what Dad might have to say to her. Instead she returned the envelope to the postbox before Mum would realise she'd seen it, and then she'd waited to see what Mum would do.

What Mum had done was exactly what Mum is doing now. At first, Winnie had assumed Mum was debating whether or not to deliver it to Winnie . . . but last year, she'd overheard Mum muttering, "The cause above all else. Loyalty through and through," before she'd shoved the letter in her purse and vanished.

Winnie can only assume Mum will make the same decision this year: she will deliver it to the Council. And that is fine by her. Let the Luminaries have the card. Let the Luminaries deal with her dad.

"I'm gonna go do some homework," Winnie says, and since it isn't *technically* a lie—she'll be preparing for the trial, which is work done at home—the words come out only partially stilted. "And then I'll probably go to bed." This is also not a lie, since Winnie *will* get there eventually.

Mum just nods from the sink and tries for a smile. "Your glasses look really good, Winnebago. Did they work okay?"

Winnie nods. "They worked great. Thanks, Mum. And thanks for dinner."

Mum's smile relaxes. She uses a soapy hand to swipe hair from her eyes, and she seems to be taking in Winnie for the first time since getting home. Like really taking her in, gaze roaming and expression softening, as if a forest mist has swept in to blur away the edges she and Winnie share. "I'm really proud of you, you know."

Winnie gulps. Her teeth start clicking.

"I know it hasn't been easy since Dad left, but you've done such a great job—"

Nope. Winnie can't listen to this or she is going to erupt with a confession. Darian might have grudgingly released her for the trials, but she doesn't know what Mum will do. She might approve—she might even support her more than Darian has. Or she might strap her to a chair and stand guard until sunrise.

And honestly, Winnie would actually prefer the latter option. It was bad enough seeing hope lurk in Darian's eyes; she doesn't think she can handle seeing it in Mum's.

"Love you," she blurts. Then she power walks from the room, through the low-ceilinged living room, up the creaking stairs (third from the bottom is a real doozy; watch out), and into her bedroom, tucked at the end of the hall where the ceiling slants down and squirrel feet patter all summer.

She "studies" for an hour, jumping every time she thinks Mum might be coming upstairs, and taking pee breaks every ten minutes because for some reason her bladder has shrunk to the size of a raisin.

Finally, 8:00 P.M. clangs out from the downtown bells, and Winnie jumps into action. She stuffs pillows under her covers, turns on her white-noise machine, gathers up Andrew's gear and her new leather jacket, and on the tippiest of toes, she sneaks out of her room and into Darian's. He hasn't lived at home in almost two years, but like everything he touches or has ever touched, the tiny room is a spreadsheet. Even the colours feel vaguely Excel—green and grey with black lines to separate it all.

Winnie opens the slate-grey curtains, and the first hints of moonlight spear in. Scarcely enough to see by, but enough to get dressed by. This window, with its warped glass that hasn't been updated since the house was built almost a hundred years ago, is going to be Winnie's escape. The roof juts out below it, and it's an easy hop onto the woodpile and then to the ground. Winnie has actually done it many times as part of her makeshift "obstacle course" inside the house.

She pulls on old black jeans that are a little tight and a lot too short thanks to an unexpected growth spurt last autumn, and a black turtleneck she got while second-hand shop scrounging with Darian the month before. The teakettle whistles downstairs. The TV flips on with the local Luminaries news.

"Vampira hordes are on the rise again," says the local news anchor, Johnny Saturday. Winnie can just imagine the way he gels his black hair. Mum used to jokingly sigh about how handsome he was; Dad used to jokingly mutter how he wasn't impressed.

Winnie wonders where this year's birthday card might be hiding.

"There has also been a surge in hotspot activity," Johnny continues, "and boaters are warned to avoid the red buoys in the Little Lake as well as all staked areas outside the usual boundaries. For a complete list of coordinates, check the hunter website." Johnny spells out the website, and Winnie pauses in mid-grab for her leather jacket.

In all the anxiety and frustration of the day, she completely forgot about Mario. He must have emailed her by now. "Shit," she whispers, mentally adding a dollar to the swear jar in the kitchen that is almost entirely filled with dollars shoved in by Mum.

There is no way Winnie can sneak back downstairs to the family computer to check her email. And unlike almost every other teenager in Hemlock Falls, she does not have a phone. Cell service doesn't work here—the forest interferes with signals—and though there is local Wi-Fi for phones, Winnie is denied access until her family's time as outcasts is complete.

She'll have to check tomorrow. Besides, it's not as if the answer will change anything right now. Whether she won the wager with Mario or not, she is going to the first trial. She is going into the forest.

Once the leather jacket is on, Winnie finds the box labeled BAGS in Darian's closet and fishes out a mostly black one. It's old, the straps are worn, but it will hold the copied pages from the Rulebook and Mum's old copy of the abridged Nightmare Compendium. It holds Andrew's gear and the two poison-mist traps as well.

Lastly, she pulls on the locket Darian gave to her. Her heart thumps against her fingers as she tucks it under her shirt. She regrets eating dinner. She feels like she needs to pee again. But it's too late to turn back. She is doing this.

The forest awaits.

CHAPTER
10

I t takes Winnie longer than anticipated to walk to
the Thursday estate. She is afraid Mum will notice if
she takes the family's shared bike, and despite Mum's
repeated insistence they practice driving, Mum has yet to
actually make time for it beyond a handful of lessons over a
month ago. Back in the day when Erica and Winnie had been
friends, Winnie had trekked to the estate regularly. A mile
and a half seems really short in her memory.

Memory, she realises, is a liar. Especially when you *have*
to arrive at nine o'clock on the dot. And even more so when
you really should have skipped dinner, and crap on a cracker,
you really do need to pee.

She ends up jogging most of the way, which leaves her
sweating inside the Kevlar she'd pulled on behind the family
shed. She's desperately thirsty by the time the long driveway
to the estate comes into view.

Cars pass her when she finally slows to a walk; no one
offers a ride. They don't even decelerate as they drive by,
though Winnie does feel eyes staring.

It used to be that coming to the Thursday estate was
exciting, since Erica's mum is head of the clan and Erica lives
on the estate. Winnie always felt so *fancy* going to her room

on the top floor, passing all the cool tile and tall windows. If the Monday estate feels like a campus, then the Thursday estate is a modern-art museum. It's all clean, contemporary lines set in a low pocket surrounded by hill and forest. Retaining ponds thick with lily pads and cattails surround the grey stone.

All the lights are on in the building as Winnie finally reaches the end of the driveway and the full expanse of the estate rises before her. Floodlights beam in front, revealing hedges so perfectly square only a Thursday could have trimmed them.

Culture runs thicker than blood.

On instinct, Winnie glances at the window into Erica's room. It's dark, but light flickers as if someone is watching TV—which surprises Winnie. Erica's mum used to be so opposed to a TV in the bedroom.

Black SUVs are parked in front of the wide stone awning that leads to the front door, and teens dressed in much newer, fancier gear than Winnie's mill about. She counts five, and she recognises all of them from school. Two Sundays, a Tuesday, a Thursday, and Fatima Wednesday.

The rule is that anyone in the Luminaries—except nons who join from outside—can try to become a hunter during the month of their sixteenth birthday. If they fail, though, that's it. No do-overs. No mulligans. The stakes are too high to risk anyone in the forest who isn't a peak performer.

"Winnie!" cries a chipper voice. Then a second, "Oh my gosh, what are you doing here?" Bretta and then Emma dart out from behind a nearby SUV (bringing the applicant total to seven), and Winnie has to fight the urge to curl in on herself. The twins bound toward her, skipping in much newer, full-body armor, and despite Winnie's not-subtle retreat, they envelop her in a hug.

They smell like a floral perfume. Lilacs, maybe. It's actually quite nice.

"You were right," Emma says breathlessly.

"He *was* there," Bretta chimes.

"Who?" Winnie asks as she peels herself free from the embrace.

"Jay." Emma fiddles with her braids. "We didn't know what to say to him, but we did at least get him to promise to talk to us after his performance on Saturday."

"Us, and like four other people," Bretta says with a giggle. "In the spirit of sportsmanship, we had to tell Angélica, Katie, Marisol, and Xavier. But *oh*, thank you for telling us, Winnie. And gosh, the jacket looks amazing on you." She pinches the leather with gloved hands.

Emma, meanwhile, hesitates. Then cocks her head. "But why are you here, Winnie? Are you taking the trial?"

Heat scorches up Winnie's neck. She shoves at her glasses. "Yeah. I'm sixteen today, so I'm allowed." She sounds a lot more defensive than she wants to; the twins have absolutely no accusation in their tones, stances, or expressions.

Bretta grins, and her curls, pulled back into a ponytail, bounce. "You didn't say a word this morning at corpse duty!" She punches Winnie playfully.

Winnie cringes. Fortunately, the twins don't seem upset, and Emma continues: "This is *so* exciting, Winnie. The three of us taking it together! And Fatima too!"

Before Winnie can agree that yes, it *is* very exciting, a voice cuts over the twins' enthusiastic giggles: "What do you think you're doing here?"

Aunt Rachel.

Winnie knew this moment was coming. Every Lead Hunter attends the trials, so Winnie has been imagining this moment for a long time.

"Nightmare alert," Emma whisper-hisses nearby, and Bretta replies, "*Eek.*" Then the twins twist away and scamper off at top speed.

Winnie's teeth start clicking. If she weren't so desperately wishing she could chase after the twins, she might have giggled. Unfortunately, the "nightmare" in question has now reached Winnie, and Winnie's tongue is tying itself in knots. *Click, click, click.*

"I repeat," Aunt Rachel says, "what do you think you're doing here?"

"I'm taking the first trial."

A snort. "Right." Rachel looks away as if the conversation is over. Then she stops. Frowns. And her gaze shoots back to Winnie, taking in the Kevlar vest and thigh plates. "Holy crap. You're serious."

"Yes." *Click, click, click.* Winnie pulls her backpack around and unzips it. Her fingers shake; the zip is not smooth like her jacket's. It gets caught and she has to yank, yank, *rip* the damned thing sideways a few times before it finally opens. All while Rachel watches with increasing horror.

Horror and something that might be rage.

Winnie yanks out the copied pages and shoves them at her. "These-are-the-pages-from-the-Rulebook-and-no-where-in-them-does-it-say-I-can't-take-the-trials." Her memorised words erupt forth like pus from a manticore sting. "I-have-been-training-on-my-own-for-the-past-four-years, so-I'm-ready-to-do-this-and-if-you-look-at-page-seven-you'll-see-that-because-I-have-arrived-on-time-and-it's-the-birth-month-of-my-sixteenth-birthday,you-have-to-let-me-participate."

Rachel doesn't take the pages. Her mouth is hanging open, and the tic at the edge of her left eye is definitely from rage. It is the sort of face that would normally cow Winnie. The face that everyone in the Luminaries gave her after Dad got caught. The face that she herself wants to give her dad if he should ever show up here again.

She wishes Aunt Rachel would look away. She wishes other people weren't gathering nearby, whispering and pointing. She wishes she hadn't just heard Casey Tuesday say, *Witch spawn gonna be bait or something?* And then Astrid Söndag laughing.

At last, Rachel does break eye contact, and Winnie has to fight the instantaneous reaction her body has to wilt on the spot. Instead, she holds her stance with the copied pages offered and the backpack dangling off her shoulder.

Rachel swipes the pages from the air. She doesn't look at them, just rips them in two. "Get out of here," she says. "Before you embarrass me any more."

Winnie does get out of there.

Sort of.

To her surprise, she is just as furious as Rachel is. She is so furious that as she stalks back down the driveway toward the main road—laughter following behind her—she is imagining all the various ways she can break her aunt's nose. Winnie is not a violent person, even by a long stretch, but she suddenly feels like punching something.

It's a delicious feeling. It makes her spine stretch long and her blood pump hot. She's invincible. *Dangerous,* and she imagines this must be what it feels like to drink melusine blood. No wonder the rare substance is classified as addictive; she could get used to this feeling.

She reaches the main road leading north with only an occasional streetlight to mark the way. The Thursday estate is one of three on the east side of the river. It's a long walk from here to the forest. Fortunately, there's a closer alternative: a narrow swath of forest that stretches down to the edge of the Wednesday estate grounds like a finger beckoning you in.

It's far from the heart of the forest, so there will be fewer nightmares there than where the other hunter applicants go. But theoretically, Winnie could complete the trial in there. A nightmare is a nightmare, after all. It doesn't matter where she slays it.

All Winnie has to do is go inside the bounds of the forest, wait for the mist to rise, kill the first monster she sees, and leave again.

Is it riskier? Sure, since there won't be any hunters nearby to rescue her if she needs it. But she has armor to protect her and rage as fuel. She is Gran Winona in that old photograph, and nightmares don't stand a chance.

Aunt Rachel is about to see that. Darian and Andrew are about to see that, and stupid Dante with his stupid birthday song is about to see that. Then stupid Casey with his stupid comment calling her bait and stupid Marcus with his smug smile and squeaky voice—they'll all see it.

Stupid Jay and stupid Erica too. Even stupid Ms. Morgan with her art programs and printed applications. Winnie doesn't need them; she never needed them; and soon all the Luminaries are going to see that she, Winnie Wednesday, is meant to be a Luminary still.

She can run an eight-minute mile and cut it down to six and a half minutes if she adds in sprints. She has practiced falling and jumping and spinning so many times in her empty house that there are hard calluses on her elbows and shins. She knows *every entry* in the Nightmare Compendium, *every entry* in the Addendum, and she can draw an accurate manticore with her eyes closed.

All of that counts for something. It *has* to count for something.

It feels like only minutes before Winnie spots the first stake marking the forest: yellow and with a reflector that glints in the nearest streetlight. It means that if she heads inward, she will find the forest's edge. A natural fog whispers at this hour, but all is silent. No cars have passed, and the nocturnal creatures of the forest—the raccoons and foxes and nightjars and bats that would thrive in other spaces—know better than to live this close to where the spirit's dreams come into being.

Any moment now the thicker, gnarly mist that carries the nightmares each night will rise up from the soil. Winnie has never seen it up close, and for that matter, she has never seen a living nightmare. She isn't frightened, though. Instead, as she veers off the road's shoulder and away from the streetlamp's bright embrace, she feels only excitement.

The world is sharper behind her new glasses. Her muscles sparkle and stretch. And her mind runs through the pages of the Nightmare Compendium as if it were right before her. Page after copied page that she has slowly memorised every night when Mum thought she was sleeping. All the anatomical diagrams she has copied with her own pens, then drawn again from memory, then improved upon once her stint with corpse duty began.

Changelings: These daywalkers can perfectly mimic any human they see. Long claws give them away, and they cannot speak.

Werewolves, were-cats, were-stags: Human by day and monster by night, these rare daywalkers blend in easily and are unrecognizable from other humans in their daytime form.

Melusine: These beautiful, mermaid-like creatures inhabit the rivers and lakes of the forest. They are not aggressive but will attack if humans get near.

Revenants, banshees, drolls, manticores—Winnie's mind buzzes through them all. How to recognise them, how to fight them, what they eat, and how they move. She is absolutely ready for this moment.

Which is why she shoves her glasses up her nose one last time, pats at her new locket for luck, and steps into the trees.

CHAPTER

11

It is dark. Darker than Winnie has ever experienced before. Darker than a windowless room with no lights even though a waning gibbous moon flickers down. It's as if the forest canopy presses around her, squeezes in. An iron maiden of shadows and shapes and noises unlike any Winnie has ever heard before.

It is also cold.

She stands for a time at the edge of the red stakes. A hemlock stretches skyward beside her, twice as wide as she and with grooves in the bark that glow like old scars. Two hops and she will be outside of the forest boundary again. Not safe, but at least safer, since if any nightmares chase her, the sensors will be tripped. The Thursday-night hunters will come this way.

They must be out there now, preparing for the mist that coils up from the soil. Searching for the nightmares that will form tonight or reappear from last night. There is no consistency to it, no pattern. No guessing where specific creatures will arrive or which ones might wreak death. There is only entering the forest and killing any that try to leave.

Underbrush rustles nearby. Winnie goes cold. Not the outer cold that was already numbing her fingers and toes, but an inner cold. Like the north wind has pushed beneath her skin and found all her organs.

Then she spots it: the mist. It is white, thick, and hungry. Moment by moment it slithers over the forest, erasing the trees from sight. In seconds, Winnie sees nothing. Not the nearby oak or balsam fir. Not even her feet, and soon, not even the hemlock.

She clutches a poison trap to her chest and watches the mist tendril upward. Strangely, the mist warms her. She knew, in theory, that this would happen—just as she knew the mist would erase her sight. But learning facts from the Compendium is nothing like experiencing it.

Plus, the mist isn't something Winnie could draw, so she never quite focused on it like she did with all the nightmares.

At first the heat is welcome, melting away the numbness and caressing her muscles like a bath. Then it is hot. Cloying. Claustrophobic. She cannot see a thing. Panic heaves up her throat along with the night's lasagna. *You're fine,* she shouts at herself. *You're fine!* The mist is only temporary, and all she has to do is stand here and remember how to breathe.

If she were still training with the others, she would have practiced breathing, moving, and hunting through this in an obstacle course on the Sunday estate called the "hot room." As if in some massive spa, steam is pumped into the sprawling underground chamber. But Winnie only ever saw the entrance when she trained under the Sundays. She never got to go inside.

Spirit mist, she mouths to herself, *is both the origin of and end of the nightmares each night. It rises once the sun is fully set and dissipates once it rises again.*

She wants to take off the jacket. She wants to rip off the Kevlar and sprint back out of the forest boundary. But she doesn't. She just sucks in clotted heat and continues to recite the Compendium.

Though initially thick and hot, it quickly fades into a more typical post-rain fog. The mist acts like a stage curtain. First it cloaks, then it reveals. Hunters are at their most vulnerable during the mist rise.

Winnie definitely feels vulnerable, and though the mist is already starting to diffuse, she still cannot see her hands or the trap clutched within. She palms the device carefully. There was a button—she'd *seen* the button—but now she can't find it, and the last thing she needs is to have the trap explode in her face.

Since there is no predicting the location of a nightmare's arrival, the hunter must keep moving. Otherwise, one could appear exactly where the hunter stands. In such cases, the hunter does not survive the experience.

Winnie doesn't move. She just continues to search the trap for a button and imagine what it had looked like by the lamp in her bedroom. All while the Compendium pours silently from her mouth.

Some believe the mist is a warning for the natural creatures of the forest to flee, and this is often the first sign a hotspot will soon form outside the forest's primary boundaries: the flight of local fauna—

A wolf howls.

Winnie jumps. The trap falls from her hand. She doesn't hear it hit the soil, and she realises with a fresh surge of cold that the wolf must be near if she can hear it so clearly.

The creature howls again, farther away this time, and the first stripe of hemlock bark wavers before Winnie's eyes. She can see; the mist is fading; no nightmare has formed directly atop her.

She drops to the forest floor and pats around for the trap. Each second that passes reveals more pine needles and soil. More moss and stone. And cold—the usual forest cold is leaking into her bones again.

Her fingers land on the trap, and when she squints down, she sees the button. It is very red, and she doesn't know how she missed it before.

Another wolf howl, still farther, and Winnie finds her lungs are loosening. Her confidence is returning, and long-forgotten instincts are prickling to life beneath her skin. It's as if the mist were paint thinner that just ate away years of grime gobbing up Winnie's insides.

She has carted countless nightmare corpses to the Mondays. She has drawn and redrawn every nightmare that lives beside Hemlock Falls. She can do this. Oh yes, she can do this.

The cause above all else. Loyalty through and through.

Winnie hefts her backpack into place and adjusts her glasses. Her front teeth click silently. If the wolf... or *were*wolf... is the only nightmare that formed nearby, she will need to go deeper into the forest to find her prey. And though she supposes she could just track the werewolf, she isn't *that* confident. After all, she saw what happened to that halfer, and paint thinner can only remove so much paint.

Fortunately, were-creatures hunt more than just humans. They also feast on other nightmares, so if Winnie can follow the wolf from a distance, she can assume it will lead her to different monsters.

As if on cue, the wolf howls again. Northeast, Winnie decides, and she pastes on her vicious hunter smile before setting off after that sound, her thumb beside the trap button and her throwing arm ready.

The wolf howls intermittently, which later Winnie will realise is strange. Normal wolves howl as a way to communicate to their pack, but werewolves are solo creatures. So for whom is this one howling?

Yet as she creeps through the wispy fog, watching for movement and straining to see in the forest dark, she only thinks about which direction the wolf hunts. What creatures he might be after.

Which is why she misses the second sound. It is soft, subtle, and so human it takes her a moment to register what it is: someone is crying. Not a mournful wail or a hiccuping sob, but more like a sniffling. As if someone attempts to stifle tears so no one else will hear.

Winnie stops moving, and instantly the page in the Compendium scrolls across her mind along with the drawing she'd sketched beside it.

Banshees: Known for weeping and wailing, they lure prey to them via the natural human instinct for empathy. From afar, they appear as gnarled, elderly women, but closer examination will reveal their differences: vertical pupils, green skin, and claws that come to needlelike points. Their tears produce a lethal poison that burns to the touch.

The sniffling ping-pongs around Winnie, hiding where the creature might be. She tightens her grip on the trap. Mum always warned about banshees because they're good at disorienting, and one almost took her down eighteen years ago. Before Dad left, before Winnie was even born.

Mum has a long, jagged scar the entire length of her leg from that encounter, and Winnie always thought it was the coolest feature Francesca Wednesday bore. A stretch of puckered skin to wear proudly. But that's because Winnie has never considered how much it might have hurt to receive. She has never considered that her mother *almost died* from it, and that she wouldn't exist today if not for Aunt Rachel right there to help her.

I shouldn't be here.

The thought interrupts the constant flow of the Compendium, and with it comes fresh cold in Winnie's organs. The winter that doesn't like to let go.

Winnie can't believe she was naive enough to walk into the forest alone. Naive enough to think she could follow a werewolf. Naive enough to think she could face the mist— face any nightmare—without backup.

She is not invincible. She is not prepared for this, and Darian and Andrew and Aunt Rachel were all right. Now she is too far from the red stakes to escape. Now, she will die and

BANSHEE

Known for weeping and wailing, they lure prey to them via a natural human instinct toward sympathy. From afar, they appear as gnarled, elderly women, but closer examination will reveal their differences: vertical pupils, greenish skin, and claws with needle-like points.

Their tears produce a poison that burns to the touch. If collected from a banshee corpse, it can be used to induce temporary comas and even a mimicry of death, slowing the recipient's heartbeat to near stillness.

Note: Never run from a banshee.

the Thursday-clan corpse duty will ziplock her body with the same bored detachment Winnie uses.

Banshees, her mind repeats—she can't stop the Compendium from playing like some macabre song stuck on repeat. *Known for weeping and wailing, they lure prey to them via the natural human instinct for empathy.*

Winnie squints around her. She is surrounded by evergreens with twiggy lower branches. The sniffling is louder, she thinks, though that might be her growing panic playing tricks on her. Doesn't matter one way or the other. She needs to think. She needs to act.

From afar, they appear as gnarled, elderly women, but closer examination will reveal their differences: vertical pupils, greenish skin, and claws that come to needlelike points.

Every muscle inside Winnie screams to run. Her bladder wants to release, and she wants to sprint away from here as fast as her legs can move—even as another part of her wants to move toward the tears and ask what's wrong.

Fortunately, tucked beneath those warring instincts is another footnote. Another piece of the Nightmare Compendium Addendum she was smart enough to read.

Never run from a banshee.

She can't remember the exact reason. Something about how they hunt—like maybe they follow exhalations. Or they move too fast to escape. But it doesn't matter. The fact is, *never run from a banshee* is definitely in that appendix and Winnie is going to obey.

Mum ran, and it didn't work out for her.

The sniffling tears are getting louder now, and though Winnie would really like more space in her brain for planning, she can't seem to turn off the Compendium.

Their tears produce a lethal poison that burns to the touch. If collected from a banshee corpse, the venom can be used to induce temporary comas and even a mimicry of death, slowing the recipient's heartbeat to near stillness.

Winnie has no plans to collect tears and no need for a false death. Her only choice right now is to lay this trap and hide.

Except there are no branches she can climb onto, no convenient logs to clamber under. There are only herself and the red button that looks grey in this leached light. *Press it,* she tells herself, and somehow, her thumb obeys. Prongs poke out, although in the darkness, she feels more than sees how metal spines eject like scarab legs.

She sets it down, then slings her backpack around to grab for the second poison-mist trap. The zip gets stuck. The bag won't open.

The crying is now overwhelming in its nearness and its power. Winnie's chest twists in on itself, a sponge wringing out. There's something so familiar in that sound, as if this creature has lost her own father and been cast out from all she ever knew. As if she too knows how big loneliness can feel. How it settles over everything, muddying edges the way tears muddy ink.

Winnie yanks at the zip, again, again. Harder, harder, her fingers numb and pulse booming against her eardrums. The banshee will be here any moment. Winnie needs the second trap. She needs to set it down and move—

The underbrush shivers. The banshee appears.

She is close enough that there is no mistaking her for human. What might look like a green cape from afar is actually her skin, sagging off bones with a velvety sheen. Her hair, spun silver, hangs in long strands that shine as if lit from within. Her humanoid face is strangely smooth, strangely serene, as if this crying frees her. As if it will free Winnie too if Winnie will only give in to the pain.

Winnie drops her backpack and straightens. She knows not to run, but she has to move *some* if she doesn't want her lone, pathetically tiny trap to release while she, Winnie, is still in the way.

It's all she's got. This one trap she almost didn't have at all is her only chance.

The banshee, still crying, wipes her eyes. Her claws glint, and Winnie realises that the creature has no knuckles. That each finger is like a fat syringe waiting to inject. As illogical as it is, she thinks, *I need to update my drawing.*

The banshee takes a single step forward. Winnie takes an achingly cautious step backward. Surely this is safe. She's not running, after all. She takes a second step. A third—

The creature lightnings toward her, a streak of silver hair and a scream to shred hearts, and where Winnie has always believed time must slow in moments like these—isn't that what the movies and stories say?—it doesn't. The banshee is somehow before her. Somehow on top of her while her back crashes against the ground, and the poison-mist trap hasn't fired.

She can't see the creature's face. The banshee is too close and there isn't enough light. She can feel the weight of her nightmare body, though. She can smell a breath that is fetid and ancient like a sarcophagus opened for the first time.

Winnie wants to fight. Deep down, along with the footnote not to run, she *wants* to fight this nightmare and get away. But she can't, because she is so overcome by grief that now she is crying too. And not just the sniffling tears like the banshee had made, but a rough, heaving sob that scratches up her throat and ejects from her mouth.

She misses her dad. She wishes he hadn't chosen the Dianas over his family. She wishes he hadn't chosen the Dianas over *her.*

A teardrop hits Winnie's cheek, but it doesn't burn. It's like the mist when it first enclosed her: warm, soothing. It melts down her cheek to her jaw, where it mingles with her own tears. And somehow, that feels even better.

She doesn't smell death anymore, nor does she feel the banshee's weight. Her sobs are quieting, her chest relaxing, as if the banshee tears are an antidote that have somehow smoothed away scar tissue Dad left behind.

Thank you, she wants to say, but her lips don't move and her body has gone completely limp. She would have thought herself asleep and dreaming if she didn't still see the silver hair cascading around her, erasing the forest, encapsulating her, not like an iron maiden, but like a cocoon. She will awaken from this and be a different person.

The wolf howls. An odd sound that pierces Winnie's awareness and punctures her cocoon. Another howl, nearer this time and almost frantic. Distantly—in a tucked-away spot still functioning—Winnie wonders if it's the werewolf and if it now hunts the banshee. If she is about to have two nightmares to contend with.

The banshee's head turns. Silver hair scrapes Winnie's face, stealing away the warmth of her tears—and stealing away the cocoon and the safety and the certainty that everything will be all right.

Reality crashes into Winnie as hard as the banshee had only moments ago. She is trapped beneath the creature, and three needle claws are stabbed through her Kevlar vest. Pain scrapes the surface of her skin, and rotten, wasted death fills her nose.

She needs to get out of here.

Winnie arches her back upward, slinging up a single knee. She has practiced this move a thousand times, but never with a partner. She's weak and clumsy.

The forest seems to favor her, though, for the banshee is distracted by the wolf howling. With Winnie's kick, the monster slings sideways like a pile of shed clothes, skin sagging and body unresistant. Needle-claws snap—still stuck in the Kevlar—and fragile light slices into Winnie's vision.

She scrabbles away. Then to her feet. She doesn't flee but instead dives for the trap and her backpack. The werewolf is almost to her, and it could be coming from anywhere. Its howling bounces and flings around her, so loud she worries it isn't alone. That others like it might follow.

And underneath that sound, she hears something else. Something whispery. It susurrates like wind through branches and bites like winter grey. It's different from the banshee's crying, and Winnie doesn't recognise it. This isn't something she remembers from the Compendium, isn't something she remembers *ever* hearing about or studying or sketching from an anatomy book.

Winnie slings on her backpack and swoops up the trap, still her only weapon. She will trigger it manually if she has to. Better to risk the poison than get eaten alive by the forest. The banshee is now on her feet and racing into the trees, her silver hair a vanishing moonset.

Not far ahead, a white shape streaks through the trees. It is the wolf, and it is not in fact running toward Winnie. It is zooming away and yipping with alarm.

Behind it, the forest seems to change. At first, Winnie thinks it just a trick of her eyes, the result of filthy glasses. But no, the longer she stares, the more the forest really does *change*. It warps and bends, it shivers and quakes. Trees undulate and shadows stretch long—all in time to that frozen whisper that seems to bleed out from every pore and surface in the forest.

Then the wolf is past. The kaleidoscoping thing behind it disappears. And the forest falls silent as a grave.

Winnie shoves at her glasses and runs.

CHAPTER
12

Winnie doesn't know how she reaches the red stakes. Maybe it's luck, maybe it's the forest's will, but she isn't foolish enough to question it. Somehow, she gets to the boundary, and somehow, she sprints past. She has twisted her ankle three times in unseen holes or hidden roots. She has fallen once and scratched up her palms, muddied her knees, and almost lost the trap. But every time, she has scrabbled back upright and sprinted onward.

She trips a fourth time and flies forward, toward a splintered spruce with low branches. She catches herself. Glances back to make sure she has left nothing behind, that the trap is still clutched in one hand with metal spines retracted.

That's when Winnie spots what she tripped over: the banshee's head.

No body—just the head, silver hair now grey, and green velvety skin now pasty. Its eyes are vacant, and for the first time, Winnie sees those vertical pupils the Compendium describes. The creature has no teeth, only gums, and it has no life, only the memories of it coiling upward like steam off hot coffee.

Whatever killed the halfer is what killed this banshee. The shredded pieces of the neck and spine look exactly like the body from this morning.

Winnie draws in her legs, heart pounding while she gapes at the banshee head. It was *just* alive, and unlike the halfer's feet, it could not have been thrown out of the boundary. She's closer to the road now than the edge of the forest mist.

This head was *carried,* and only a daywalker could have done so without tripping the boundary alarm.

Or maybe the alarm was *tripped,* she thinks. Maybe she's just too far away from the Thursday estate to hear the blaring alarm. Maybe hunters will swarm this area at any moment. *Or maybe they won't and I am the only person who knows this banshee was dropped here.*

"Dropped by what?" Winnie croaks, rising stiffly and flinging a cautious glance around. She sees nothing, hears nothing. Her ankle throbs. "Crap." She grabs for the banshee's hair before she can think too hard or look too closely.

The hair feels like spiderwebs against her fingers, and the head is lighter than she would have guessed. Human heads, she knows from experience, are heavier. She takes a few steps to make sure her ankle is okay (it hurts; she'll manage) and that the head won't fall. Then she picks up her sprint right where she'd left off.

The forest and its nightmares recede behind her.

Winnie doesn't know how long it takes her to reach the road. She is so focused on just propelling herself onward and not dropping the banshee head or her trap that it could be anywhere between midnight and dawn—and once she does reach the street, the sky offers no answers. Clouds have swept in to hide the moon.

Her stomach hurts. Her ankle hurts. Her fingers hurt from holding the silver hair so tightly. The last thing she wants to do right now is walk back to the Thursday estate. But loyalty demands it; the cause demands it.

Not only is this banshee head useful for science and resources—after all, banshee tears and venom have multiple uses—but *someone* needs to know about what killed it. *Someone* needs to know about a nightmare that distorts the forest, can walk outside it, and frightens even a werewolf. They'll be able to, at the very least, ID it and then determine a threat level for Hemlock Falls.

After shoving her glasses with her forearm, Winnie aims south. She skips from streetlight to streetlight like a melusine hopping streams. The night is quiet. No alarms sound from the Thursday estate. No cars vroom past. She hears only her footsteps and the occasional *drip-drip* of banshee blood on pavement or the *click-click-click* of her teeth as she replays what just happened in the forest.

What had the werewolf been running from? What had killed the banshee?

Winnie wishes she'd checked her email from Mario now. She also wishes she'd brought a weapon into the forest or else gone home entirely. This isn't going to end well for her, showing up at the Thursday estate and explaining what she saw and how badly she failed.

She can just imagine Aunt Rachel's face, eyes ablaze and lips pressed into a furious line. Or Dante's laughter and the new songs he'll compose in homeroom tomorrow. Or worst of all, the almost certain pity and secondhand embarrassment in Emma's and Bretta's eyes. *What* had Winnie been thinking? She should be dead right now. She really should be dead.

Her heart feels like it's breaking all over again, her soul awash in banshee tears. This had been her only dream: to become a hunter. Now she has failed the first trial. She will never get another chance. The only path left for her is art school, assuming she can even get in—but then, all she's ever really drawn are nightmares. She probably can't even qualify for that summer program, no matter how many strings Ms. Morgan might try to pull.

This must have been how Darian felt when he saw his Council dreams shatter. No going back. No rewriting history. Just . . . broken glass.

And *god,* Winnie has probably made things a lot worse for Darian now, hasn't she? And for Mum. What the hell was she thinking, going into the forest like that?

Winnie stops her forward march beneath a streetlight. The river glimmers nearby, slow and wide as it curves. Birch trees peel as if sunburned. Waters lap and laze. It should be soothing, but it isn't. Winnie used to swim here with Erica and Jay. She can just imagine their expressions. Cold disgust from Erica. Bored disapproval from Jay.

It is as she stares at the river with unseeing eyes that an engine revs into her hearing. It is moving fast, and she knows with a sickening lurch that there can be no avoiding it. This road is too long, too straight. The fact that she can now see headlights means that they can also see her.

She draws back her shoulders and waits for the inevitable slowdown. The inevitable window-roll and questions.

Her teeth click. The car takes clearer and clearer shape beneath each streetlamp. It's a black SUV like all hunters drive, and soon Winnie spots the Thursdays' silver bell sigil on the front plate. *Please don't have Aunt Rachel inside,* she begs. *Please don't have Aunt Rachel inside.*

Aunt Rachel isn't inside—but Emma and Bretta are. They're with others that Winnie can't see as the SUV grinds to a stop and the back door slings open.

"Oh my *god,* Winnie!" Emma shrieks, clutching her dimpled cheeks as she leaps out.

"You killed a banshee!" cries Bretta. Then they both launch toward Winnie, hands clapping and steps bouncing.

"Winnie killed a banshee!" Bretta screams as she runs, and Emma joins her: "Winnie killed a banshee!"

CHAPTER
13

It all happens so fast Winnie can't seem to stop it. Like the banshee's attack in the forest, there is no slowing of time. No pause for assessment. No life flashing before her eyes. There is simply beat after confusing beat to slam into her while she is trapped by the weight of a banshee with silver hair.

First: The twins assume Winnie killed the banshee and they scream this at everyone in the SUV. Repeatedly.

Second: Everyone in the SUV—two Thursday hunters and Fatima—scrambles out and rushes toward Winnie. Everyone is talking at once, inundating Winnie in words and sound and, to her utter confusion, claps of congratulations or smiles with open respect. There is no space for her to reply. She can barely keep up with what anyone is saying.

Winnie vaguely notices how filthy everyone is, coated in nightmare blood of varying shades as well as dirt and sweat and pine needles and leaves. Winnie realises that the same thing coats her, except there is no blood.

Just the three banshee needle-claws, still poking out of her Kevlar.

Third: She is herded toward the SUV, where one of the hunters (Ernesto, a distant relation of Erica's) takes the banshee head and dumps it in the while the other hunter (Lucia Giovedì, not related) pushes Winnie into the back seat and offers her a swig of celebratory whiskey from a silver flask at her hip. The twins and Fatima cram in with Winnie, all of them asking her some variation of *How did you kill it? Where did you find it?* Or alternately squealing, *Holy crap, you killed a banshee! Wow, wow, wow, you're gonna be a legend!*

They also mention they'd seen a werewolf—Bretta, Fatima, and Ernesto too all saw a werewolf, and oh my gosh, Winnie, a real *werewolf*! Ernesto is the only one who seems worried by this development instead of exhilarated.

Fourth: When at last Winnie does manage to speak, her throat and chest still burning from the whiskey, she croaks out exactly what had happened—with the wolf howling and the banshee arriving and the trap she'd placed on the forest floor. But like some horrifying game of telephone, the twins take over the story before she's done and finish it for her. They assume the trap fired; they assume Winnie then used a standard hunting knife (that no one seems to notice she doesn't have) to saw off the monster's head.

Emma even points to the needle-claws as evidence of Winnie's epic skills and hair-raising escape.

Fifth: Winnie doesn't contradict Emma. She knows she should. She watches the scene in detached alarm, like some omniscient narrator removed from her body that can assess and disapprove in real time. But she can't seem to get back *into* her body to tell Emma and the others they're wrong.

Because as she sits there squashed into the middle seat, basting in the stench of nightmare viscera and hunter sweat, no one in the SUV is laughing at her. No one is calling her names. No one is looking at her like they just wiped her off the bottom of their shoe.

Instead, they're all impressed. Even awestruck, and they are welcoming her into their ranks with not only open arms, but smiles and laughs and whiskey flasks. Emma killed a will-o'-wisp; Bretta slew a manticore hatchling; and Fatima gutted a sylphid. And of course, *they* all did it with hunters nearby in case anything went sideways.

Winnie did it solo. Winnie is a queen.

But when Winnie asks them all about a weird whispery creature that makes the forest look like it was smashed through a meat grinder, no one knows what she's describing. Fatima even regards Winnie with a worried frown and offers a power bar "in case your blood sugar is low."

Winnie doesn't take it, but she does wonder—again—if she might have missed something in the Compendium. For all her memorizing and sketching, no brain is perfect. Surely that creature she saw has a name. *Surely* someone in Hemlock Falls will know it.

Sixth: The SUV pulls up to the Thursday estate. The clock on the dash says 12:42. The Thursday-night hunters will still be at large until dawn, but most hunter applicants seem to have already returned. Casey Tuesday wears his arm in a sling and Astrid dances off her adrenaline to music that only she seems to hear. A third SUV is shifting into park as Winnie and the rest of her crew pour out.

Seventh: The twins and Fatima relay Winnie's story to everyone, complete with hand motions to mimic what she'd done. They make it sound a lot more badass, and the second half of the story remains completely untrue.

Winnie still doesn't contradict them. *Later,* she tells herself. *I'll tell the truth later.* When not everyone is nearby to impale her with stares and frowns and words thickened by hate.

Eighth: The fourth and final SUV arrives right as Ernesto pulls the banshee head from the boot and as everyone starts cheering and patting Winnie on the back. The banshee claws glint on her vest, which Casey keeps gaping at and saying, *That's so cool, that's so cool.*

Ninth: Aunt Rachel disembarks from the SUV and assesses the situation with her usual blank expression, listening while the twins, yet again, relay a story that is only 50 percent true. And while Winnie, yet again, finds her throat closed off and her words far, far away.

Rachel studies the banshee head, then leans in to study the claws on Winnie's vest. Winnie's heart thunders almost as hard as it had in the forest. She prays Rachel doesn't notice that she has no banshee blood on her. That her leather jacket is only streaked in red clay. She *will* tell the truth, just not yet. Not here.

Then it happens. The tenth and final beat of the night: Aunt Rachel's expression transforms. From acute angles to obtuse, her entire face opens up. The lines on her forehead relax, and she even cracks the barest glimmer of a crooked smile. Her dark eyes meet Winnie's—the same hemlock-bark brown as her sister's, as Darian's, and as Winnie's too—and she says, "Well, shit, Winnie. I guess I need to apologise."

She thrusts out a hand, and Winnie is almost too stunned to take it. She is definitely too stunned to speak as Rachel pumps it and says, "Good job, kid. You passed the first trial."

Winnie's night is a continued roller-coaster blur. Everything happens *to* her instead of *by* her, and each new smile or pat on the back or word of congratulations leaves her less and less able to speak up. Until finally, it is almost dawn and Mum is coming to pick her up because Rachel called and told her everything.

"Everything" in quotes because the reality is that no one actually knows what happened. The reality is that Winnie didn't kill this banshee and something else did—something that is now *outside* the red stakes and forest boundary. Maybe it was the werewolf . . . or maybe it was that unidentified thing she saw. The one nobody else noticed or seemed interested in hearing about.

Werewolves, however, are a known quantity, and while the hunter applicants speak excitedly about such a monster, the adults are very clearly on edge. Winnie hears Aunt Rachel say, "I'll notify the Council first thing tomorrow."

Mum is in her robe and pajamas when she arrives in the old Volvo, the Beatles keening rhythmically, audible before the car headlights come into view. Then she is parked and stumbling out with a combination of fury, relief, and pride on her face. Mostly just fury, though she doesn't let any of it loose until Winnie is in the front seat and the Thursday estate is shrinking in the rearview mirror.

Then she lays into Winnie with a rage that Winnie hasn't seen since Mum caught Dad and he fled. It starts off seething and whispered, her grip white-knuckled on the steering wheel, but it has reached "inside voice" by the time they hit the main road. Then "outside voice" by the time they turn onto their street. And finally "concert shrieking voice" by the time they park on the curb in front of their house.

The actual words circle around three main themes: *How could you be so reckless?* Followed by *What if you had died?* And lastly, *Why didn't you tell me?* Once Mum reaches the end of those subjects, she loops back to the start.

As she has done most of the night, Winnie holds her silence. There is an ache in her chest that feels like the banshee is crying again and her heart is going to split in two. She can't stop cleaning her glasses the entire drive home. Like if she pauses for even one second with her furious scrubbing, she will burst into tears and confess everything. And though she knows she needs to eventually tell someone the truth, she can't bring herself to do it now. Not while three sips of whiskey are still hot in her throat and all those Luminary cheers are still fresh in her ears.

Once they're parked, Mum marches around to the passenger side and yanks Winnie out. She's not yelling anymore. Instead, her eyes are wet and she pulls Winnie in for a hug. The Kevlar and leather jacket are in the back seat, and Winnie melts into her mum's arms. She can't remember the last time they hugged like this. Not since Dad left.

Somehow, Winnie doesn't cry. Somehow, her mum's pajamas (blue stripes) and familiar soap scent (verbena) give her more warmth than the whiskey and more calm than even the banshee tears.

At least until Mum whispers into her hair, "I'm really proud of you, Winnebago. I'm so, *so* proud of you." Mum pulls back then. The sun is rising behind her, just a faint kiss of pink to glow around her like a halo. "Furious, but proud." She cups Winnie's face, and her nose scrunches playfully. "My wittle baby is all gwown up. And did Rachel tell you? Thanks to you, we're invited to clan dinner next week. It's just a . . . a trial visit, but it's something."

Winnie's insides go cold. "She invited us already?"

"Yep." Mum grins, and the wrinkles that Winnie thought were permanently creased between her eyebrows slough away. "*And* you're allowed to return to afternoon training at the Sunday estate."

"Oh," Winnie rasps. Something as sharp as banshee claws is spiking in her stomach. Something hot as the mist when it rises. This is all she has ever wanted and all she has dreamed about for the past four years. She should be happy, but instead she wants to vomit.

Worse, Mum wears an expression that takes ten years off her face and makes her shoulders seem higher, broader, stronger. Winnie doesn't want that to go away. She doesn't want this smile around Mum's eyes to disappear or their world to return to forest grey.

"Darian is going to be so excited." Mum slings her arm around Winnie's shoulders.

And it is the final nail in Winnie's coffin. Winnie can't tell Mum the truth now. She can't tell *anyone* the truth now.

"How do pancakes sound for breakfast, Winnebago?" Mum hauls her toward their front porch with its peeling paint and the dangling chains where a bench used to swing. "There's a second trial to prep for, and a hunter needs her carbs. *Lots* of them, with as much syrup as we can squeeze on top."

CHAPTER
14

Winnie doesn't think she can possibly sleep, yet after pancakes and a hot shower, she crashes the instant her head hits the pillow. She doesn't hear Mum get ready for work (a long running argument between them is that Mum makes coffee *way too loudly*), doesn't hear the Volvo's engine rumble to life, and doesn't notice the light change outside.

When she finally wakes up, it's 3:00 P.M. She doesn't know if she was supposed to go to school—it's a Friday, after all—or the Sunday estate after, but considering the time, she decides it can wait until tomorrow. Especially because she has no interest in ever leaving bed again.

Instead, she lies under her old sunflower covers and stares with weak eyesight at the dust motes and a forgotten spiderweb beside the ceiling light. Her tiny desk, with the napkins stuffed under one leg to keep it stable, is littered with sketchbooks and pens that Darian always begs to organise. *At least let me label them,* he says. *And dates—don't you want to know when you drew all these nightmares?*

She doesn't. In fact, she wants to rip down the sketch of a hellion she'd made, all doglike and drooling, taped to her wall beside a shadowy kelpie sketch, its underwater horse form murky and vague.

How naive she'd been to think she could ever capture the forest on a page, that a pen could *ever* transfer the three-dimensional reality of spiderweb hair against her face or green, velvety skin bearing down.

"No," she mutters, shooting up in bed. Her comforter falls off and cold air swirls in. Rain has started to patter against her window, and the sunlight diffusing through the curtain is turning greyer by the second. Eventually, thunder rumbles—unusual for spring in other places. Not unusual for Hemlock Falls.

She flings her gaze to a banner that hangs over the back of her bedroom door: the Wednesday bear. It's faded. A piece of pine-green felt that stretches two feet and is gifted to every Wednesday when they first start training at the Sunday estate at age five.

Darian threw his away after Dad. Winnie just put hers where she could never stop seeing it.

"The cause above all else," she says, swinging her legs from bed. The floor groans beneath her feet; the ancient beige carpet is cold. "Loyalty through and through." Yes, she sucked at hunting. *Really* sucked at hunting. But she isn't going to let that stop her.

So what if last night didn't go according to plan? So what if everyone was right and she hadn't been ready for the forest? She still got what she wanted and what her family *needed*. There's no reason not to keep going. She has been gifted with a second chance. Her dream could still become a reality. All she has to do is stay this course and take the second trial.

To pass the first trial, the Rulebook says, *an applicant must track and slay a nightmare without any interference from an adult. To pass the second trial, the applicant must spend a night in the forest alone; no adult hunters are allowed to interfere except in emergency situations. Lastly, the applicant must pass the family trial. These trials are unique to each clan and subject to change at any time.*

Spending a night in the forest alone. That is what Winnie has to do next, and four years ago when she'd decided to take these steps, it had seemed so easy. After all, Francesca Wednesday was her mum, Winona Wednesday was her grandmother, Maria Mercoledì was her great-grandmother. She'd thought that had to count for something.

It hadn't. It doesn't. Winnie'd choked last night, and the "hunt" she'd always assumed was in her blood . . . Yeah, it hadn't been there.

Have you given any thought to that summer program at Heritage?

Winnie leaps from bed and lurches out of her room, aiming for the tiny bathroom everyone shares. But once she's bent over the old porcelain toilet, the vomit doesn't come. She just stares at a collection of blue-stained cracks in the bowl from the winter three years ago when money had been too tight to keep the heat on during the day, so Mum had dumped antifreeze into the toilet.

It's not that Winnie's family doesn't get by. Mum makes an okay wage at the Revenant's Daughter and some of the nicer Luminaries do pity-tip her a lot. Plus, she works at the grocers once a week and picks up occasional shifts at the bakery—and then Darian chips in whatever he can too. So they have shelter, they have heat 98 percent of the time, and they never go hungry. But back when Mum had been Lead Hunter and Dad had contributed an income too, life had been a lot . . . well, easier.

Breakfast spins a bit faster in Winnie's stomach. She clutches the toilet seat. The ankle she'd twisted on her escape from the forest throbs. She hadn't even wanted the pancakes, since they were overcooked to the point of rubbery, but Mum had been so . . . well, *Mum*ish. "Birthday pancakes," she kept calling them as she flipped more onto Winnie's plate. "Next stop? Lead Hunter!"

Winnie has to pass the second trial. She doesn't want to go to art school, she doesn't want to leave Hemlock Falls. And if that means she has to spend the night in the forest alone on Sunday—if it means she *has* to keep pretending that she killed the banshee—then so be it. That's exactly what she'll do.

It takes a few minutes, but the nausea subsides without any vomit to show for it. Winnie hauls herself out of the bathroom, shoves on her old glasses (the new pair got pretty bent up last night), and slumps downstairs for a ginger ale from the supply kept only for emergencies. The sparkly candy juice slides down Winnie's throat, sharp and brisk and grounding. After a few big gulps, she heads to the family computer in the living area, an ancient PC that they got before Dad left.

It takes a while to boot up, and she gazes around the room, taking it in with lens-sharp eyes. The couch with the spring hanging out of the bottom. The TV with the remote that got smashed (and then trashed) after one of Winnie's more spectacular attempts to dive and roll when no one was home. The framed sketch of the house Winnie had made when she'd briefly flirted with architectural drawings . . . then decided she hated composing anything that wasn't alive.

Beside the house sketch are four faded patches where pictures of the family once hung. Where Mum keeps saying she'll put up new ones; Winnie and Darian know she never will.

There used to be plants in here too that Dad and Darian lovingly talked to. A money tree, a ficus, and an African violet. They all died after he left, and no one has wanted to replace them.

Winnie hasn't thought of those plants in years; she wishes she hadn't remembered them now, but it's like the banshee opened a door she has kept shut. The closet she has shoved all her memories into. The way things *used* to be before Dad became the enemy.

He'd had a mini basketball hoop in the kitchen with a foam ball that always knocked over the salt by the stove. One time the ball even fell into a pot of boiling rice water, and because Dad hadn't wanted to start a fresh pot (brown rice takes forever, you know?), he'd made Winnie help him pick out all the blue plastic flakes that had sloughed off between the grains. *It's just micronutrients,* he said. *They're good for us! Also, don't tell Mum.*

They'd giggled through the whole meal that night, and to this day, Mum still doesn't know why.

Winnie fingers her hair. She inherited the auburn shade from him, along with her nearsightedness.

She used to wonder sometimes if maybe Dad *hadn't* done it. If maybe Mum had been wrong when she'd found him. Except that guilty people don't knock out their partners and run away, leaving their family in ruin.

The computer screen finally winks on, revealing its puppy desktop menu, and Winnie opens her email. As expected, there's a message from Mario.

The Council is in agreement with you, it reads. *Though I'm honestly still not sure a werewolf is what we're dealing with. Nonetheless, I'll let you win this one. Congrats! There's a tab under your name at Joe Squared. Get as much coffee as you want.*

Winnie drums her fingers against the desk. Her teeth start clicking too, and though she would rather *never* think about last night again, she forces her mind back to the forest—to the banshee and how it had fled.

And how the werewolf had been running from something . . . something *whispery* she couldn't quite see. Could that . . . whatever it was, be what Mario is now talking about?

She should go find out. She doesn't have to admit to him that she didn't kill the banshee, but *someone* needs to know what she saw. And maybe he'll recognise something about the description that she doesn't. She might know the Compendium backward and forward, she might have sketched enough manticore hatchlings to make her fingers callused, but that obviously didn't count for much when she was faced with a nightmare.

Her fingers and teeth pause their percussive beat. What she needs is someone to help her. Not Mario, but someone who knows what they're doing in the forest and won't ask too many questions. If experience is what she lacks, then experience is what she should find.

She glances at the clock in the screen corner. It is almost 4:00 P.M., meaning if she gets dressed now and takes the family bicycle, she could probably reach Gunther's before five.

And just like that, the final shreds of nausea crumble away. The living room comes into focus around her; her muscles come alive. Winnie is done dwelling on last night and on Dad and on pancakes with syrup out of date.

She has a new plan, and it's time to put it into action.

CHAPTER
15

Despite being one of only two petrol stations in or near Hemlock Falls, Gunther's Garage looks like it hasn't been updated since the 1960s. Because it hasn't. Neither has Gunther. He is an odd breed of non who seems to know about the Luminaries and the forest but has never shown any desire to join the local society or flee the area for safer grounds. The Luminaries grudgingly allow him to remain, since his booze and petrol are cheap.

That said, the Wednesdays do regularly check his background, and the Thursdays regularly check that he hasn't shared what he knows.

He keeps his pavement station on the lone road leading into Hemlock Falls, about two miles outside of the roundabout that marks the edge of town, and Winnie is both freezing and boiling by the time she gets there on her bicycle. The earlier rain has drooped into a halfhearted drizzle, leaving behind a bone-chilling humidity that has numbed her fingers and toes despite the cardio of a five-mile bike ride. Her hair is practically soaked through too, and she's glad she traded in her leather jacket for an anorak.

Or she *was* glad until she saw how full the petrol station parking lot is. It's literally every possible cool kid. There's

Xavier and Marisol beside the open garage door. There's Peter, Imran, and Angélica on the bench out front while Dante and Casey act out something for them that might be a replay of last night's trial or could just be a bad attempt at breakdancing. Winnie can't be sure.

There are also a ton of other kids actually *inside* Gunther's, combing the two aisles of sweets and crisps as if they might discover secret treasure by lifting every package and inspecting underneath.

This is not what Winnie was expecting, and nowhere in all the chaos does she see the one person she needs. She stops at the edge of the parking lot, beside a pothole that has grown like tree rings for the past decade.

Then Dante spots her and elbows Casey, who in turn knocks on the petrol station window. Next thing Winnie knows, silence descends and everyone turns to face her.

She swallows. Dante's lips part, and *now* is when time finally slows and her life flashes before her eyes. It's one thing to sit in homeroom and be the butt of the jokes. It's another to be faced with every popular Luminary in Hemlock Falls while they rake their collective gazes across her. She should have worn the leather jacket, dammit. And why didn't she put her hair in a sensible bun instead of letting each miserable hank soak up the rain?

Her fingers squeeze around the brakes, pulsing the tires in time to her clicking front teeth. *Never run from a banshee,* her brain provides uselessly, followed by *Vampira hordes are never to be faced alone.*

Then a familiar voice chirps, "Winnie!" and suddenly Emma Wednesday is skipping out of the garage with a grin so bright it could make a rainbow.

And it's like some cork has been popped, releasing all the churned-up carbonation. Suddenly the air changes and everyone is saying Winnie's name. It's like last night after the trial, but a thousand times more overwhelming because it's more people and all the cool ones too and now Dante is chanting *banshee slayer, banshee slayer* in his Italian accent.

Winnie doesn't know what to say, not that anyone actually seems to want her to speak. They might shout, "Tell us how you did it!" but then someone else answers and she's just left gaping at the people closing in around her.

This is almost as bad as the mist.

Until she sees Jay. He is coming out of the garage now, and though his expression is as buttoned-up as his blue flannel, Winnie recognises a caged animal when she sees one. He doesn't like that these people have invaded his spot. He knows that Winnie is to blame for it.

He wipes his hands on a greasy towel as he strides toward her. People move out of his way, not because he tells them to or because they even seem to notice him, but because he just has that effect on people. An unconscious force field that pushes humans aside.

Then he's standing before Winnie, still wiping his hands, and he says, "You're late."

"I'm . . . what?" She squeezes the bike brakes again, and he repeats, "You're late." This time, he beckons for her to follow and turns around.

Where he immediately careens into Bretta along with Katie Tuesday. "You're giving a ride to Winnie?" Bretta asks, offering a half pout, half smile that makes only one dimple form. It's intriguing, and every other person in the vicinity seems to melt at the sight of it.

Not Jay, though. He just goes, "Yep," and strides right past. Then in a louder voice, "Come on, Win. I don't have all day."

Winnie has no idea what he's talking about. However, since he *is* the person she came here to see and walking with him means escaping all these people, she rolls her bike around the pothole and follows him toward the back of the garage.

"We'll see you when you're done?" Katie trills after him, and pity spikes through Winnie's gut. All these adoring fans, and he scarcely recognises their existence. It spikes a second time when Jay grunts noncommittally as he rounds the garage corner and disappears.

She flashes an apologetic face at Bretta and Katie. Then at everyone else, who, thank the forest, seems to have forgotten her.

Her bike clickity-clicks, and in seconds she's behind the garage, where an old Wagoneer awaits.

"Mathilda!" she exclaims. She hasn't seen the navy beast in years. It looked rough back when Jay's aunt drove it. It looks a lot rougher now. "I can't believe she still runs."

"Define 'run,'" Jay says as he opens the boot with a clang. "If you mean she gets me where I need to go while my bike is broken, then yes. She runs." He grabs the greasy rag from his pocket and wipes his hands again. Then he reaches for Winnie's handlebars.

She scoots back. "What are you doing?"

He frowns, the barest pinch across his brow. "I thought it was clear." He nods his head toward the front of the garage. "I'm giving you a ride."

"A ride to where?"

"Literally anywhere that isn't here, Winnie Wednesday." He reaches again.

And Winnie scoots again. "I'm not getting into a car with a strange man."

This startles a laugh from him. Or the closest to a laugh that Jay ever makes: a soft cough while his left eyebrow lifts. "I am not a strange man. You've known me since you were five."

"I've known a lot of people since I was five, and a lot of them turned out strange." Winnie regrets this declaration as soon as it leaves her mouth, because even though Jay doesn't mention her dad, she can practically hear the thought crossing his mind.

It certainly crosses hers.

He sighs. "Look, Win. You obviously came to Gunther's for a reason. And since you don't need petrol and can't buy liquor, I'm going to assume you're here to see me."

She doesn't contradict him, and when he grabs for her handlebars a third time, she doesn't pull away. There's still a streak of grease on the back of his right hand. "I need a favor," she says as he tries to pry her fingers loose. "If you agree to said favor, I will get into Mathilda with you."

"Okay. Deal." He digs harder at her fingers. She grips more tightly.

"You don't want to know what the favor is?"

"You can tell me while you give me the bicycle."

Winnie frowns. This isn't going how she'd imagined. For one, he has agreed much too easily. For two, there are people nearby and she doesn't want to be overheard. She flings a cautious glance behind her, but no one has snuck around the garage. Still, she finds her voice sinking to a whisper as she says, "I need you to tutor me."

"In what?" He's still trying to grab the bike. Winnie is still resisting.

"Hunting."

"I see." Now his hands pause, resting atop hers. They're warm despite the cold around them.

Do *you see?* she wants to ask, suddenly afraid that he does. That somehow he knows she didn't kill the banshee and that everything about last night was a lie.

His fingers start moving again. "Okay," he says. "I'll tutor you in hunting. Now, can you please get into Mathilda?"

Winnie's lips part. Then pinch shut again because this *really* has been too easy, and were he a member of any other clan but Friday, she'd worry he was tricking her. That he was about to drive her a mile away from Gunther's only to dump her on the side of the road and declare all bets off again.

But Jay *is* a Friday, and though they might be the smallest, least powerful family in the Luminaries, they still live by their motto like everyone else. Their culture still runs thicker than their blood. *Integrity in all. Honesty to the end.* If he says he'll tutor her, he means it.

"Jay?" comes an alto croon that sounds like Angélica. "Are you still here?"

His eyes widen like a cornered ghost-deer's, and Winnie almost laughs at that. He is projected to be the next Friday Lead Hunter before he's even eighteen, yet he's terrified of the Luminaries. Namely, female ones. It almost defies believability.

"We start tutoring right now," Winnie says. Her ankle has mostly stopped hurting, and there's no time to waste.

He nods, gaze fixed over her left shoulder. "Yep."

"Excellent." She grins, releasing the bike handles, and with superhuman speed, Jay yanks the bicycle from her and flings it into the boot. "Hey," she barks. "Be gentle with that."

He says nothing. Just slams the boot shut and lurches for the passenger door, where he shoves Winnie inside. He then propels himself to the driver's seat, and before Winnie is even buckled in, he is twisting Mathilda's key.

The Wagoneer quakes to life. A smell like old exhaust hits Winnie's nose, a familiar smell that makes her chest hurt—which in turn reminds her of the banshee. How it could stir up feelings she'd thought she had scrubbed away so many years ago.

While Jay backs them up with almost reckless speed, Winnie shoves at her glasses and pulls on her own seat belt. The twins are waving at her in the side mirror by the time Jay peels away. She waves back. Jay doesn't.

CHAPTER

16

"Y ou could be nicer to them," Winnie says. She has to yell to be heard over Mathilda's nightmarish howl and the squeak of windshield wipers. The rain is picking up again.

"Be nicer to who?" Jay yells back. It's weird to see him driving.

"Literally everyone," she replies, although it's only the twins' feelings she personally cares about.

Jay glances at Winnie, gaze vacant while woods stream by outside. It's *really* weird to see him driving. *Squeak-squeak. Squeak-squeak.*

"All the people at Gunther's just now?" Winnie elaborates. "Emma? Katie? Bretta?"

"Oh, right." His attention locks back on the road. "I didn't realise I was mean to them."

"You just ran like vampira from garlic."

He has the decency to flush. "I'm sure they're all very nice. I just . . ."

"You just?" Winnie presses.

"Don't have time."

"For what?"

"For other people," he replies, and Winnie makes a mental

note to actively steer Bretta and Emma away from him. They deserve better than a slacker/stoner/deadbeat, and they *especially* deserve better than a slacker/stoner/deadbeat who clearly has no interest in them or anyone else.

"Where are we going?"

"Your house."

"What?" She sits taller in the cracked leather seat. "You said we could start training now."

"And we can." A glance in the rearview. A glance in the side mirrors. His posture might have relaxed, but his eyes are still hunted. "We should wait for the rain to end. Plus," a cool side eye, "you need different clothes."

Winnie doesn't argue with this. She is soaked through from the rain on the outside and sweat on the inside. "Fine," she agrees. "I'll just pop into the house, change into something fresh and 'foresty,' then we can head off to train. Okay?"

He grunts an acknowledgment.

Soon they reach the roundabout that leads into Hemlock Falls. The first exit heads for the eastern side of the river, the second for the western side. Jay lugs the steering wheel around the circle, recently repaved and buttery smooth, then veers them onto the first exit. The river appears to their left, rough, choppy with fresh rain. Trees hug the bank here, green sprouting off their limbs in a way that it never will off the limbs of forest trees. Blue crocuses wink like police lights within the underbrush.

The windshield wipers still squeak.

"I heard about your trial last night."

Winnie pushes up her glasses. "And?"

A shrug. A pinching of his lips that might be approval or might just as easily be disapproval.

"Did you hear about the werewolf?" she asks.

"It's all anyone has talked about today. So yes." He sounds neither alarmed nor concerned by it.

"Have you seen it?" Rumor has it Jay picks up a lot of

hunting shifts with other clans, in addition to his required Friday nights.

"No."

"I did."

"Huh," he replies, and Winnie scowls. Talking to him is like talking to a piece of cardboard sometimes, except that cardboard still emotes more than he does.

They reach the stretch of neighbourhoods where Thursdays mostly reside. Mathilda slows to accommodate a reduced speed limit. Her growl softens; the windshield wipers seem louder. *Squeak-squeak. Squeak-squeak.*

Though not required to, most families live near their clan's estate. More often than not, the homes pass from generation to generation. Gran Winona's house passed on to Mum, and one day she will pass it on to Winnie, while Darian and Andrew will likely move into Andrew's ancestral home.

As Mathilda clears the neighbourhoods, the old trees that line the streets give way to rolling green lawns on the right. Then there's the Thursday estate, grey stone gleaming. Mathilda groans past, and they finally reach a new stretch of neighbourhoods, where most Wednesdays live.

"Jay," Winnie says. He grunts. "Have you ever seen a nightmare that's . . ." She pauses. Articulating what she saw keeps proving near impossible. "Well, it's a nightmare that's whispery. Like . . . like a wind that's going backwards. Or a lawn mower from another dimension." She feels absurd as soon as she utters these descriptions, and when Jay gives her a sideways look that says *Huh?* heat rises to her cheeks.

"It's just that I saw something," she quickly explains. "It wasn't like anything I've ever read about in the Compendium. It made the forest look all distorted. And it *sounded* distorted too."

Mathilda hits the intersection at Hawthorne, and Jay turns them right. He isn't saying anything. Winnie's face gets hotter by the second.

"Are you listening to me, Jay?"

"Of course I am, Win." He pulls against the curb where Mum usually parks. Once Mathilda huffs a final automotive sigh, Jay withdraws the key and twists toward Winnie. "Have you asked Mario about it? He'll know more than I do."

Winnie deflates. "Yeah, that's my plan."

"Well, let me know what he says. Also, be careful. Two hunters have died recently, you know, and the forest is dangerous—"

"For a Luminary untrained. Yeah, I *do* know." She grabs on to the door handle. "That's why I'm asking you to help me." She kicks out of the Wagoneer, only to find Jay doing the same. Winnie scrabbles toward him on the lawn. "I thought we had to wait before we trained?"

"We do."

"Are you going to wait *here*?"

"Oh." There's the flush again. He rubs at his hair, and for some reason Winnie feels embarrassed that he's embarrassed. "It just seemed easier to wait together. But sure." He stuffs his hands in his pockets. "I'll call you when the rain eases up."

"Or just come in," Winnie says with a sigh, and she shuffles past him toward the front door.

Before he can inevitably protest, she snags a finger in his button-up and tugs him along. Her skin touches his undershirt. It's warm like his hands were, and he doesn't pull away. In fact, he lets her drag him all the way to the porch steps.

"You sure?" he asks as he follows her up the creaking wood.

"Obviously," she replies. The rain stops misting her as the porch ceiling stretches over them. The cold vanishes too when she steps inside the house.

"I see you still don't lock the front door." Jay slumps in behind Winnie.

"And I see you still have a problem with that." Winnie dumps her anorak on the front-stairs banister and cuts into the kitchen. "Want something to drink? We have water and we have water. Or I guess I can make you tea." There is also ginger ale, but he is not special enough for one of those.

"I'm good." He joins her in the kitchen, and as Winnie sets about making her own pot of Earl Grey, he hovers awkwardly in the tiny space. It is even weirder seeing him in her house than it was to see him drive. Last time he'd stood in that exact spot, he'd been a whole head shorter. Probably a whole head thinner too, since his shoulders have expanded from growing boy into best hunter in Hemlock Falls.

He also stands differently. It used to be that nothing could keep him still. He was always bouncing or tapping or fidgeting or shifting. Like a runner about to start a race, he had this potential energy always ready to go kinetic. Winnie could never sketch him quite right—though she tried hundreds . . . maybe even thousands of times. Her skill just wasn't there.

Or maybe he was just too alive.

Now, though, she thinks she can capture him. He stands, hands in his pockets, shoulders bunched toward his ears, and his grey eyes not vacant . . . but not quite alive either. Like the forest winter refusing to let go.

From her side-eying vantage at the kettle, Winnie can't even see his chest move. He is as still as a vampira waiting for its prey.

The act of making tea saves Winnie from conversation, but once the kettle has whistled its readiness and the Earl Grey is steeping in her unicorn mug, she has no choice but to face him head-on.

Except that he is the first to speak. "Why me?" he asks.

"Huh?" Her glasses slide down her nose.

"Why me? For tutoring you, I mean. There are other people you could have asked." He dips his head in the vague direction of Gunther's. "In fact, it seems to me there are a lot of people who want to help you."

Winnie wets her lips, frowning at her tea bag as she dips it in and out of the mug. She can't tell Jay the full truth. She also can't lie, because he will see through that in an instant. But the argument she'd mapped out earlier while riding her bike to Gunther's (*You don't want me to die, do you?*) now seems unhelpful. He has agreed to help her; he just wants an explanation.

Auburn tea swirls outward, thicker with each of Winnie's strains. Her dad used to joke that his hair was Earl Grey because it was a mixture of black tea shot through with silver. He also used to leave her coded messages on the tea-bag tags. Goofy things like *Steep me!* or *Address me as "my lord,"* and the cipher would hide somewhere in plain sight in the kitchen. Usually a circled barcode on the spaghetti package or a starred phone number on the fridge.

Winnie drops the steeped bag and sighs. "Last night didn't go as well as everyone thinks, Jay, and you're the only person I can trust to help me."

It isn't a lie, and Jay's eyebrows rocket skyward. His posture straightens. For a split second, he looks like the old, animated Jay she used to know. "You trust me."

She pushes at her glasses. "You're the best hunter in your year." Also not a lie. "And you've known me a million years." An exaggeration, but not a lie. "And I trust you not to tell anyone that you're helping me." Very, very true.

"Because I'm a Friday."

"Because you're a Friday. Honesty to the end, right?" She yanks out the tea bag and drops it into the rubbish. Then she fastens her gaze on Jay and waits for him to press her for more answers.

Instead he says, "You're supposed to put that in the compost." His tone is light, and there's something that could almost be called a smile towing at his lips.

But Winnie can't smile back. "We haven't composted in four years." She strides past him toward the stairs. "I'm going to change," she calls. "The remote is broken. You've got to turn on the TV by hand."

By the time Winnie has changed into dry clothes and grabbed her Kevlar gear from the night before—the banshee needles still poking out of it—she finds Jay sitting on her couch. He has fallen asleep, his boots propped up on the old trunk turned coffee table, arms folded over his chest, and chin slouched against his clavicle. His watch winks out from under a flannel sleeve. It's old and requires daily winding, but it used to belong to his dad—a man Jay never actually knew.

Somehow Jay looks as young as he did when he and Winnie used to be friends, the angles of his face eroded away. Gone is the sense that he is hunted; gone is the sense that he is hunting.

He is just Jay Friday, tired and familiar.

Which is probably why Winnie finds herself sneaking up on him like she would have all those lifetimes ago. Then bending over, vertebra by vertebra, and reaching for his nose. "Boop!"

She doesn't actually make contact before he has her pinned to the opposite wall.

It happens so fast, she doesn't feel the movements. Doesn't see him leap to his feet or have time to feel fear or the physical crack of her skull on plaster. She just goes from hovering over Jay to her back slammed beside the TV.

He has one arm under her throat, the other around her wrist, and his right thigh is pressed up against her legs, trapping her in place. Vaguely, Winnie thinks this must be how insects feel when collectors pin them.

"*Ugh,*" she coughs against his arm. "*Jay!*"

He blinks. His pewter eyes have turned to gunmetal. His pupils throb and expand.

"*What the hell!*" she continues, and this time she shoves her left arm against him. But it's like hitting an oak tree. He doesn't move.

His pupils do constrict, though, and a confused frown hatch-marks over his brow. Then colour ignites on his cheeks. At first she thinks it's another flush, but when she shoves against him a second time, his nostrils flare.

He's angry.

"What the hell?" she repeats as he finally drops his arm. "What the hell was that, Jay?"

He shakes his head. The hunted energy from before has returned. His gaze darts around the room. Up, down, sideways—he looks at anything that isn't Winnie. "That was your first lesson," he says eventually, voice raspy. As if he has just slept a lot longer than ten minutes. Like he has been sleeping his whole life and these are the first words he's ever needed to say. "Never surprise a nightmare." He dips toward her until his face is only inches from hers and she can smell bergamot and lime. "*Never*," he repeats, "surprise a nightmare." Then he stalks for the door and leaves.

Winnie shouts at his back—to return, to explain, to actually train her, dammit—but Jay doesn't look her way again. He simply crosses the garden to Mathilda and awakens the car's smoker's cough with a scowl.

Seconds later, he is gone.

CHAPTER
17

Winnie is stranded. She can't believe it. Jay bailed and he took her only form of transportation. Like, he just drove off with her bike in the boot after the most cryptic nonlesson of all time.

No kidding, she shouldn't startle a nightmare.

If she had his cell phone number, she'd call him right now and scream into his ear. Or, because (let's be real) she has total phonephobia, she'd at least text him in all caps ABOUT WHAT A JERK HE IS AND CAN I HAVE MY BIKE BACK? But she doesn't have his number, and for all she knows, he doesn't even have a phone. He's a Friday clan ward, meaning both his parents died and he relies on the clan for necessities, so money is even tighter for him than it is for Winnie.

She debates calling Darian for a ride to the Friday estate so she can fetch her bike, but decides against it. She doesn't know if that's where Jay has gone; she suspects he goes to other people's houses a lot to party when he's not at the old museum, and she has no desire to track him down.

Ultimately, she decides to go upstairs and try on clothes. Luminary training, unlike regular school, happens seven days a week—meaning tomorrow, Saturday, will be her first day back at the Sunday estate in four years.

She needs to look her best.

When she sees her reflection in the mirror beside her desk and taped-up nightmare sketches, she winces. She had dressed so quickly in preparation for training with Jay, she hadn't fully seen the damage the rain had wrought: her hair has quadrupled in size, and curls she doesn't normally have are springing up in strange locations atop her head. She also has a brown fuzzball on her jaw from the turtleneck she'd so hastily dragged on, and now that she's looking, did she put the shirt on inside out?

Winnie yanks off her glasses, suddenly glad Jay left before he could have noticed any of this. Then again, with his hunter instincts, he probably saw.

Not that she cares. Of course she doesn't care. It's just Jay.

After trying on an assortment of clothes that still fit and squeezing into a few that don't, Winnie settles on her favorite corduroys, a loose white peasant top Darian got her for Christmas that she's been too afraid to wear in case she ruins it, and finally the new leather jacket.

She looks whimsical, she decides. Almost as cool as Ms. Morgan, and the new locket from Darian makes her collarbone look nice.

At the thought of Ms. Morgan, Winnie's eyes drop to the desk. To all those unlabeled and lately untouched sketchbooks. Her teeth start clicking. She fiddles with her locket. She should try to draw the banshee—she *knows* she should, while the skin and the claws and that wretched, slippery hair are still fresh in her memory . . .

"Winnie!" Darian's howl pierces the house.

Her heart lurches into her throat. She barrels into the hall right as Darian comes hammering up the steps. "What is it? What's wrong—"

He tackles her in a hug. Then he starts whooping and hauling her around the narrow hall in an awkward square dance. He is speaking a mile a minute, but Winnie manages to tease out "I got promoted, I got promoted, thanks to you, I got promoted!"

He stops abruptly at her bedroom door and thrusts her in front of him, hands on her biceps and face aglow. "Holy crap, Win, I can't believe you're still alive."

"Um, thanks?"

"And you killed a banshee—a *banshee*! Andrew started telling me how they like to eat their prey still alive, and I was just like, 'Stop! I don't want to know!'" He yanks her into another hug. "I was wrong to doubt you. I was really wrong, and you are my hero."

Winnie draws in a slow breath. Darian smells like spearmint toothpaste, as he always does. It would be a comforting smell if she weren't presently freaking out. If anyone can catch her in a lie, it's Darian. *Don't say anything,* she tells herself. *Don't say anything.* She'll just keep her mouth shut, and he'll move on.

Except he doesn't move on. "Tell me what happened. I want the whole story."

"I mean," she squeezes out, "it's pretty much what everyone is saying—"

"But I want to hear it from *you.*" He pushes her toward her bed and then slings himself into the desk chair, where he used to sit almost every night while he and Winnie hashed out, yet again, what had happened with Dad. How had they missed the signs? Where had he fled to? What would they do if the Council decided to cast them out forever?

It's nice seeing Darian there again. Winnie doesn't want to ruin the moment.

She pushes at her glasses. "Okay, I'll tell you, but first." She holds out her arms. "What do you think of my outfit?"

As she'd hoped, his eyes light on the leather jacket. He gasps. "Where did you get that? It's gorgeous."

"Isn't it?" She strokes her forearm like a cat. "It's buttery soft, and look at this." *Zip-zip, zip-zip.* "Emma and Bretta Wednesday gave it to me."

Darian's expression moves from skeptical awe to envious awe. "I knew being a networker paid well, but . . ." He scoots from the chair to the bed. "Maybe I should consider a career change." He sighs. Then his gaze scans over her, taking in the rest of her outfit. When he spots the locket, he smiles. "You like it?"

"Yeah." She pats her sternum where it rests. "I like it."

"These, though." He flicks her old glasses. "Please tell me the new ones got smashed by a banshee."

"Kind of." Winnie forces a laugh. They are returning to dangerously boily waters. She shoots to her feet. "What's this promotion? Are you no longer assistant to the assistant of the illustrious Mr. Dryden Saturday?"

"Nope." A sly smile spreads over his lips. His dark eyes crinkle behind his own, much more stylish glasses. "I am now straight *assistant* and Cindy Thursday got punted over to the filing desk. Oh, man, Winnie, I wish you could have seen her face when Mr. Saturday told us about the 'internal rearranging.' She looked like her head might explode, neck straining, lips so tight they turned white—"

"Are you coming?" a voice hollers from downstairs. Andrew. "Dinner is getting cold!"

"Dinner?" Winnie asks as Darian flashes her an *oops!* face and pushes to his feet.

"Indeed, madam." He offers her his arm. "We have brought you the finest fare from Très Jolie, and Mum will be home soon for our celebratory meal. You can tell us all about the banshee hunt then."

It takes every ounce of wiles Winnie has to navigate dinner. It's worse than being in the forest, all the dodging and ducking and deflecting. Yet somehow, over the dinner of coq au vin, baguette, and a family-sized salad, Winnie manages to successfully steer the conversation away from the banshee.

And if anyone thinks it strange that she keeps removing her glasses to clean them or that she keeps asking everyone else about *their* days, no one says anything.

They also don't say anything when she declares exhaustion and an early bedtime. On her way toward the stairs, though, Winnie's attention snags on the PC and she remembers that she hasn't heard a word from Jay—meaning she also has no ride to the Sunday estate in the morning.

It's a long shot, but maybe Jay still uses the old email address he used to have. Before she can actually write to him, however, she spots a new email from Mario.

I heard what happened, it reads. *Congratulations! You're either completely bananas or an evil genius. I'm guessing the former, but I'm impressed all the same. And now that you've got clan privileges again, come by my office. No need to wait for corpse duty. I want to discuss that wolf theory. See you soon!*

All thoughts of Jay diffuse like forest mist. Winnie's eyes unfocus and her teeth start clicking as she closes the browser. As she puts the old PC to sleep and slides out of the squeaky swivel chair. As her feet shuffle her upstairs and into her bedroom, where the door shuts and softens the sound of wine-happy Darian and Mum.

Winnie is welcome back on the Monday estate. Just like that, she is allowed to come and go as she pleases. And if she wants, she can waltz right into the main building where Mario's office is and visit him at any time. It doesn't even matter that she doesn't know where it is. She's allowed to be on the campus, and people will actually respond to her when she waves.

For some reason, this feels more real than anything else has. Or rather, it's like the final adjustment on the eye-doctor lens that makes the hot-air balloon come into focus. She actually did it. Her family is accepted again in the Luminaries. *She* is accepted again in the Luminaries.

She sits on her bed, teeth no longer clicking. Everything inside her has gone as still as the forest—and as cold as the forest too. She should be happy. It's been so long since she heard Mum and Darian laugh like they are right now downstairs.

But she isn't happy. Not merely because it's all a lie and she'll have to maintain this lie for the rest of her life, or because her odds of survival on Sunday night are feeling terrifyingly low and her plan to get Jay's help has already dissolved like cotton candy in the rain . . . but because of the werewolf.

Her reaction isn't logical. She should feel fear, but instead, she feels only a sluggish, almost angry resistance. What if the Council and the hunters have it all wrong? What if the werewolf hasn't killed anyone at all, and instead, all the recent deaths of hunters and nons were caused by that whispery kaleidoscope thing?

Yes, werewolves are bad. Period. If one is out there, then Hemlock Falls needs to be on high alert. When the werewolf emerged from the forest seventeen years ago, he killed six people before the Tuesdays were able to kill him. The whole city was on lockdown, and the collective memory of that imprinted on everyone. Even on the people who, like Winnie, weren't yet alive.

But there was also that *other* thing, whatever it was. Even if no one else seems to have seen it, she knows she saw the forest crack into fractals. She knows she heard a sound like melting car speakers. And she *knows* she found that banshee outside the forest lines.

She will just have to go tomorrow after training and talk to Mario. It's as simple as that. If anyone in Hemlock Falls can ID the whispery nightmare, it's him. He has always listened to Winnie before; she has absolute faith he'll listen now.

CHAPTER

18

The next morning, Winnie is halfway through crossing her neighbourhood on foot (fortunately, her ankle is doing much better) when a sound like a dragon trapped inside an old tugboat hits her ears.

Mathilda.

She whips around just as Jay pulls over beside her, right blinker flashing. At the sight of his tired face through the eighties glass, Winnie's temper shoots straight into her skull. She propels herself to the passenger door and swings it wide.

"You stole my bike."

He has the decency to flush. "Sorry."

"I was stuck at home because you stole my bike."

"It was an accident."

"I don't care." She slings herself into the front and yanks on the seat belt. Then she crosses her arms and scowls out the windshield. "Drive."

Jay obeys, shifting Mathilda forward. She *blub-blub-blub*s toward downtown. Winnie peeks at Jay from the corner of her glasses. As usual, he looks like utter crap.

"You bailed on me," she says as Mathilda whines to a stop at an intersection. "What happened to tutoring?"

The flush returns, brighter this time. And laced with something else. Something . . . empty. "Sorry," he repeats, and he actually sounds like he means it.

Which surprises Winnie. She expected him to come back with *I'm not going to train you,* or at the very least *I'm the one doing you a favor here.* And for some reason, the fact that he isn't arguing makes her insides scoop out uncomfortably. Or maybe that's just her nerves, twanging higher the nearer they get to the Sundays.

Jay maintains silence the entire drive, through downtown with its local shops and perfectly manicured hedges, then over the dam to the west side of Hemlock Falls. The river wears white chop from yesterday's rain. It plays tricks on Winnie's tired eyes. She thinks she sees fins where there are none. She thinks she sees scales.

It makes her think of the Whisperer—that's what she has started calling the mystery nightmare. It also makes her wish she'd slept more last night, so she'd be prepared to face the Luminaries and professors. But her mind had gotten stuck in a *you are a liar* and *you will fail the next trial* cycle all night.

Normally, when she can't sleep, she draws. Droll hands are especially soothing, since there are so many little bones to get just right. Last night, though, she hadn't even looked in her desk's direction, much less crawled out of bed to grab a pad or pen. She'd just stared into darkness and stewed.

Mathilda hiccups over the dam, bringing Jay and Winnie into the Monday and Tuesday neighbourhoods, then onward to the sprawling grounds of the Sunday clan, where a morning sun gleams halfheartedly over a soccer field, a football field, and a wide running track. Tucked beyond is the stately Sunday mansion with its brick face, wood-shingled roof, and neat, square windows perfectly spaced throughout.

For the past four years, Winnie has avoided staring too closely at the Sunday estate when she passes by (or on the rare occasion she drives herself by without stalling between first and second gear). Why look at what she can't have? Why remind herself of the days when she used to be happy? Even now, her first instinct is to avoid the way those multipaned windows wink at her. To instead gawp with vacant eyes at the grass streaming by in a perfect buzz cut.

Winnie pushes at her glasses, teeth clicking, while Jay parks in the student lot. They are early, which should be a relief, except her thundering heart doesn't seem to have gotten the memo. As on the Monday estate, there are multiple annexes around the main mansion, but here each one is devoted to the training of a Luminary.

There's the library, a vastly truncated version of the two libraries on the Monday estate. There's the massive glass-roofed indoor pool and, beside it, a pond made to mimic the lake above the river's falls where aquatic nightmares thrive. Beyond that is a small building that leads into the underground hot room. Finally, circling around all of it is the obstacle course—which has grown more intense since Winnie was last here. More columns to dive around, more ladders to scramble up, more tires and mud and marshy pools to race through.

Winnie spots Coach Rosa Domingo, the professor in charge of physical training, out checking a particularly daunting stretch of tightropes. She's originally from the Brazilian Luminaries, and her green, almost ocher eyes glow beneath a brief burst of morning sun. She keeps her dark curls and coppery highlights forever in a ponytail, which bounces now against her muscled back.

It has been years since Winnie has spoken to any of the Sunday professors beyond the occasional awkward encounter at the Revenant's Daughter. *This is what you want,* she tells herself, rubbing her clammy palms on her corduroys as Jay cuts the ignition. *This is what you want.* She and Coach Rosa always got along well enough; maybe Rosa will be glad to see her.

After several moments of watching professors leave their vehicles and aim for the double doors at the back of the estate, Winnie realises she hasn't moved since Mathilda's engine quieted. Nor has Jay. Instead, he studies her with that flinty arrowhead gaze of his.

"Do you want me to walk in with you?" he asks eventually.

Winnie feels her face warm. For half a stuttering heartbeat, she wants to blurt out, *Yes*. Instead, she says, "You're not going in?"

"I had the hunt last night. I'm tired."

"Oh." She cringes. She's really out of practice with Luminary life if she forgot he had the hunt. "Did you wake up just to give me a ride?"

"Yep."

"Oh," she repeats, annoyed that that's the only word she can find. And annoyed that Jay is still looking at her. "Well, that was silly," she finds herself saying, even though she actually wants to thank him. "You should have slept in."

"You're welcome." He taps the steering wheel faster. "I'll remember that the next time I steal your bike."

"Yeah, okay." Her cringe deepens. She zips her leather jacket all the way to the top, then snags her backpack and grabs the handle to leave the car.

"Wait." There's an authority in Jay's voice that Winnie isn't used to. It makes her actually pause her fingers on the worn handle. "Do you want to train today?"

"Yes. Please." Winnie runs her finger over the handle. The metal is scratched and chipped. She knows she needs to get out of the car, but she's finding it hard to move, even though today can't possibly be worse than yesterday at Gunther's. It can't possibly be worse than the four years she spent outside looking in.

Jay exits first, finally jolting her back into action. By the time she is out of the Wagoneer, he has pulled her bike from the boot. "How about this afternoon?" he asks, his grip lingering on the handlebars as Winnie tries to pull it away. "Cool?"

"Yeah." She avoids Jay's eyes as she takes the bike. Neither of them says goodbye.

Clickity-clickity-clickity. Winnie has rolled her bike halfway around the estate when footsteps hammer behind her. Then a voice, slightly accented, calls, "Winnie. It has been a long time."

Coach Rosa. Beyond the aforementioned awkward encounters, Winnie hasn't seen her at all in the past four years. Now she falls into step beside Winnie as if nothing has changed and Winnie has always belonged here.

"You're in my third-period training." Coach Rosa rubs her hands together against the wind. Her tracksuit billows. "It's the easier class, but don't worry. I'm sure you'll get bumped to second period in no time. A banshee." She grins sideways. "I don't think anyone has killed a banshee solo in . . . well, not as long as I've lived here. And with only a poison-mist trap too! You will have to tell the class how you managed that."

Winnie thinks she might vomit. "Yep." She rolls a bit faster toward the bike rack ahead. "Looking forward to it."

"Great." Rosa claps her on the back. "See you in a few hours, then." She hops up the steps into the estate entrance, taking two at a time with enviable ease, while Winnie fumbles with her bike chain.

"This is what you want," she tells herself. "This is what you want."

It's not only physical training that has Winnie placed into introductory courses. "You are four years behind," Headmaster Gina Sunday (who is also Councilor Gina Sunday and head of the Sunday clan) explains in her soprano voice. "But you always were an excellent student, and I have no doubt you will advance quickly. Though"—she wags a red-painted finger at Winnie from across her broad desk—"you will have to study a bit more than everyone else to catch up. Now, if you need anything, don't hesitate to ask."

She smiles, her warm, dark brown skin stretching across high cheekbones, and Winnie ventures a smile of her own. Headmaster Gina is another one who has always been kind to Winnie when they meet, and she's kind now, wheeling her chair into the halls so she can guide Winnie to her first class.

The school looks like Winnie remembers: polished wood paneling, heavy oak doors, and dangling candelabras that are much too nice to be appreciated by a bunch of teenagers. Winnie certainly didn't appreciate them four years ago. Now, she just sees how many light bulbs the Sundays must have to change.

All down the main hall hang the banners and sigils of the families. *Culture runs thicker than blood,* she thinks as her eyes skim down each one.

First is a white swan for the Sundays. Their motto is *Patience inside. Calm under pressure.* Next, a white scroll with a black ribbon for the Mondays. *Intellect at the fore. Knowledge is the path.* A red scorpion for the Tuesdays. *Strength of body and heart. We hold the line.* Then comes the Wednesday black bear. *The cause above all else. Loyalty through and through.* A silver bell for the Thursdays. *Always prepared. Never without a plan.* A grey sparrow for the Fridays. *Integrity in all. Honesty to the end.* And lastly, a golden key for the Saturdays. *Leadership in deed and word. Persuasion is power.*

Each person in Hemlock Falls will mold themselves into their clan's needs, all in the name of the Luminaries. All in the name of keeping an oblivious world safe from the fourteen sleeping spirits. Winnie is one of those people—again. Finally.

Pride swells up from her belly. Loyalty through and through.

The first two-hour period of class is—thank god—easy for Winnie. It's nightmare anatomy, and if there is one thing she actually *does* know, it's where a changeling liver is or why vampira don't have livers at all. Before the first hour is up, she has already been bumped ahead three classes. Goodbye Professor Anders, hello Professor Il-Hwa.

Second period proves harder. Winnie has never been interested in Luminary history. Nightmares, sure. But the politics and history of the Luminaries, no. She knows the first spirit formed in what is now northern Italy, and it was the only spirit for almost a thousand years. The second appeared in Norway, a third in Russia. After that, spirits spread much more rapidly, leaping across continents, until the most recent spirit formed here, near Hemlock Falls, in 1901. The various Luminary branches sent members here to deal with it, and eventually the American Luminaries were formed.

Of course, that's the basic stuff, and the students—all of whom are thirteen years old (or in the case of her cousin Marcus, who keeps grinning smugly at her, fourteen)—are learning more nitty-gritty stuff like names and dates . . . and more names and dates.

Because Professor Samuel is a jerk (*that* definitely hasn't changed), he keeps calling on Winnie when he knows she doesn't have the answer. It's mortifying and Marcus's grinning face isn't helping.

She doesn't even have her usual margin doodling to save her. She is too busy taking notes, so she can't pause for sketching or shading or nightmare adornment. Although, she does vaguely think that might be a good thing. Like last night, her fingers feel empty. No spark, no itch, no desire to transfer a banshee's empty eyes into solid lines.

Overall, the morning passes in a big Alice in Wonderland blur. People aren't just nice to Winnie, they're *too* nice. The sort of nice you use when you feel really guilty about something but don't want the other person to know.

Not that Winnie thinks any of the Luminaries actually feel any guilt for how they've treated her over the past four years. After all, she had been labeled an outcast—what did she expect? No, it's more probable they don't know how to be friendly, so they're turning into creepy, unnatural versions of themselves. Like when video game characters smile—it's not *quite* human, but it's close enough to make you uncomfortable.

Every fist bump makes Winnie flinch as if someone is going to smack her. Every call of *banshee slayer* makes her shrink as if it's *witch spawn* they're saying instead. And every brilliantly white smile makes her recoil instead of smile back.

This is just all too, too weird.

And as the day ticks past, as Winnie shambles through classes and the people, the cold inside her spins a little bit wider. By the time third period rolls around, she is exhausted in a way she didn't know a human could be exhausted. Too many eyes have been upon her. Too many false grins she didn't earn.

At the doorway that will lead into the locker rooms— where Winnie can hear all the same thirteen-year-old voices chattering away while they change for third-period physical training, while Coach Rosa chatters away too—Winnie realises she can't breathe.

Like, really can't breathe. She has gotten too close to a kelpie and now it's dragging her underwater, away from air, away from life.

Winnie bolts into the girls' bathroom. Four stalls meet her eyes, ancient but clean, as well as three sinks that look like they came out of an old-timey photograph. She bursts into the first stall, drops onto the toilet seat, and dunks her head between her legs. *Breathe, breathe, breathe.* She can do this, she can do this, she *has* to do this. Coach Rosa won't be the first person who makes her tell the tale of the banshee slaying; she's got to get this figured out.

She can do this. *Breathe, breathe, breathe.*

The bathroom door squeaks outside. Heeled boots click past Winnie's stall. She doesn't look up. Her focus is on the tiny hexagonal tiles that cover the bathroom floor. A

thousand grout lines for dirt and grime to squeeze into—
but where it never does because the Sundays keep this
place spotless.

She can do this. She just has to manage to relay the story
that the twins told two nights ago. Act like it was somebody
else who went into those trees. Act like it was somebody else
who met a banshee and killed it—because it *was* somebody
else in the end. Or some*thing* else, rather—

"I know you're in there." A voice cleaves through Winnie's
thoughts. Familiar, if sharper than it used to be. Carved by
razors into a voice like her mother's.

Erica Thursday.

She is standing directly outside Winnie's stall. Her booted
toe with its gleaming steel cap is tapping a rhythm on the
floor.

"What do you want?" Winnie asks. Shamefully, her voice
quavers.

"I need to ask you something."

"I'm busy."

"No you're not." Erica's right foot kicks up, and with the
perfect poise of a dancer, she lightly kicks the stall door with
her toe. The latch falls. The door swings wide. Then Erica
herself comes into view.

She is perfectly made up, as always, the shading of her
makeup enhancing the natural warmth of her amber skin,
while thick burgundy liner brings out the autumnal red
shades in her brown eyes. She's gorgeous, her raven hair in
long, sleek lines that reach down to her waist. She wears a
leather jacket not so different from Winnie's, but in black and
over a baby blue turtleneck that looks like an angel made it
for her out of clouds. Her impossibly long legs hide beneath
a long grey skirt that would, on anyone else, look dowdy. But
on her, it looks like High Fashion with capital letters and an
exorbitant price tag. The only part of her that isn't perfect is
the plaster wrapped around her thumb.

She looks so much like Jenna, her older half sister who died four years ago, that Winnie can't help but wonder if it's intentional.

Winnie bolts to her feet. The stall—and Erica—spins. Erica is taller than Winnie with her boots on; it's jarring. Winnie was always the taller of the two. It's also jarring to see the mascara on Erica's lashes, the glossy perfection of her lips, the contouring that Winnie wouldn't even know was there if she weren't used to the curves of Erica's natural face.

Four years since she has been this close to her best friend, and it's like staring at an illustration. This is both the girl she knew . . . and somehow not her at all.

"What," Winnie repeats, "do you want?"

Erica lifts her chin, appraising Winnie through half-lowered lashes. First she takes in Winnie's hair (a mess), then Winnie's clothes (suddenly not as cool as Winnie had thought they were), and finally Winnie's collarbone, where the locket from Darian rests.

"Where did you get that necklace?"

Winnie's hand rises to the locket. A thousand things she might have expected Erica to say, and this certainly isn't one of them. "My brother gave it to me."

"When?"

"On Thursday. On my birthday."

"Where did he get it?"

"I don't know." Winnie glares and shoves past Erica, getting a whiff of a musky perfume that literally reeks of money. Being a clan leader's daughter has its perks. "Why the interrogation?" Winnie stalks to the sink and turns on the faucet. Three pumps of the soap dispenser and Erica sidles up beside her, arms now folded over her chest.

"Because I used to have one like it, Winnie Wednesday, and I want to know where it went."

"Are you saying Darian stole it from you?" Winnie means it as a joke.

Erica responds as if it isn't. "Maybe."

"*What?*" Winnie spins toward Erica. Soapy water sprays the mirror. "If you're accusing him of a crime, just say it."

A splash of suds mars Erica's sweater. For several seconds, she holds Winnie's gaze, but there's uncertainty in it. Maybe even a little embarrassment. She doesn't blink, though, and neither does Winnie.

Cold water drips to the floor from Winnie's hands. The faucet still gushes beside her. Until finally, Erica breaks the stare down. "No," she says primly. "I don't think anyone stole it. Just . . . ask Darian where he got it, okay?" She lifts a single eyebrow, gaze briefly flickering back to Winnie. "And let me know what he says."

No, Winnie thinks as she watches Erica stalk away. *No way in hell.* Winnie isn't going out of her way to help Erica with anything. Or to talk to Erica, for that matter, ever again.

Winnie twists back to the sink to finish washing her hands. In the mirror, she spots two flags of colour on her cheeks and a crystalline edge to her eyes that hadn't been there when she'd first walked into the bathroom. It's what she looked like on Thursday night, she bets, when she'd walked right into that forest so certain she could slay a nightmare.

Suddenly, training with Coach Rosa doesn't sound so daunting, because even if nothing went according to plan on Thursday night, even if Winnie found herself horribly outmatched, she *had* survived an encounter with a banshee. Erica, the Luminaries, Marcus with his awful grin—they were nothing compared to that. Winnie can face all of them.

CHAPTER

19

Physical training goes better than Winnie could have hoped for. A million billion times better because Marcus gets a nosebleed, forcing Coach Rosa to leave with him—and forcing Rosa to command the class to run laps on the obstacle course while she's away.

Winnie discovers very quickly that despite her four years on a homemade obstacle course, she is excruciatingly not equipped for this one. Tire jumps? Rope climbs? By the time the seventh and eighth graders are back to the starting line, Winnie is only halfway around the track, panting like a hellion and regretting ever wanting to be back in the Luminaries again.

She can't even enjoy the scenery of the Sunday estate as the track loops through trees and past the hot room with its mausoleum-like entrance, then past the lake where a lonely mallard watches her mournfully. She just wants to be done and for this searing heat in her chest to recede.

By the time she does get back to the starting line, the day is basically over and the final bell is about to toll.

"That wasn't *too* bad," Rosa tells her. "You just need to do it a few more times."

Unlikely, Winnie thinks. Out loud she heaves, "I . . . hurt my ankle . . . in the trial."

Rosa pops a skeptical eyebrow. "Of course," she murmurs politely as the bell rings.

Winnie flees for her bike. She doesn't even care that she's still wearing her training clothes; she needs to escape before everyone swarms her like they did at Gunther's.

Or that's the reason she tells herself. Deep down, though, she knows she just doesn't want to see Erica again. It was hard enough having her raptor eyes ignore Winnie for four years. It's a lot harder having them trained on her directly. There is nothing left of the Erica from before. She has painted that person away with expertly applied eyeliner and blush.

Winnie hops on her bike and aims for a trail that connects the Sunday and Monday estates. The paved and perfect lines of Sunday melt into the natural orderliness of Monday with burgeoning trees and daffodil shoots just thrusting up from the ground.

She passes faces she vaguely knows and waves to. This time, they all wave back or at least nod. And when she asks one older woman with turquoise hair where to find Mario, the woman smiles and offers detailed directions.

His office, it turns out, is on the top floor of the main mansion. Winnie parks her bike out front, beside a tendril of ivy that looks like it might be interested in turning green soon. With legs that have turned to rubber bands, she hauls herself into the building.

No one interferes when Winnie pants upstairs and through the halls. They don't even seem to notice her, and it occurs to her that she probably could have been doing this at any time over the past four years.

But then she remembers that Mario hasn't exactly invited her until now. He might have been her "friend," but he wasn't her *friend*. Like everyone else, he followed the rules on outcasts.

Winnie kind of wishes she hadn't considered this, and her spine droops a bit by the time she reaches Mario's door. Someone is already inside when she arrives—she hears a man speaking in authoritative tones: "I want tests ready to go, Mario. I don't care what supplies you're lacking. I don't care what crackpot theories you're developing. Get this done. We can't have a daywalker on the loose in the city. Do you understand?"

A pause. Then: "Yep. Got it."

"The Masquerade is soon, and I won't have anything interfering. This werewolf *will* be dealt with by then."

"Yeah, Dryden. I get the picture."

"Good." Footsteps clatter. "Don't screw this up."

Winnie scoots away from the door just in time to avoid being caught as an eavesdropper. A moment later, Dryden Saturday—head of the Saturdays, head of the Council, and Darian's boss—emerges. He wears navy slacks and a tawny tweed jacket with a red bow tie over a white button-up (always the white, always the bow tie), and his grey hair encircles his head like a wispy crown. Round pince-nez perch on his nose.

Winnie waits until he has vanished down the hall before slinking to Mario's door. "Hey," she calls, poking her head inside. The room is exactly what she would have expected: books everywhere, paper everywhere, shelves with bones and vertebrae and skulls, all laced with a slightly overpowering scent of bubblegum.

Mario sits at his desk, his focus on a sleek monitor that's thin as paper and curved like a droll rib. His fingers fly over a keyboard. "I was wondering when you'd come," he says absently as Winnie creeps into the room. "Guess you found me okay?"

Winnie doesn't answer. Her eyes have caught on a podium that was hidden by the open door. On it is a book as thick as her forearm is long. It's open, Post-its and papers poking out from a thousand different spots.

"The Compendium," Winnie breathes reverently. She stumbles toward it like a revenant toward blood. "And the newest edition too. Can I look?" She glances at Mario.

He grunts, fingers still rattling away. *Pop-pop-pop!*

She leans over the open page, the text small and sharp. Nothing like the copied pages and sketchbook sheets stuffed in her closet at home. This is the Real Deal, complete with all the latest research from Luminaries around the globe.

She thumbs from one page to the next. A solid half of the creatures aren't in her edition because they only exist in other parts of the world. Since the spirit that sleeps by Hemlock Falls is so young, it hasn't had time to evolve its own unique nightmares yet.

Mum always used to say it was like a Lego starter kit. When a new spirit is born, it comes with a standard set of monsters—vampira, hellions, harpies, melusine, and so on—but over the centuries, it starts to create its own. As its mind expands with age, its dreams in turn grow more vast.

Winnie is so absorbed reading about sylphids that she doesn't notice when Mario has reached her side until suddenly he's there and grinning. He clearly appreciates Winnie's awe.

"All these," he says, ruffling the Post-its that poke out the side, "are notes I hope I can add. The global Mondays will have to agree, of course, but . . ." A shrug, almost shy. "Twenty-six years I've been doing this. I've seen our nightmares evolve in real time. Like this"—he flips toward the back of the book, to *W*—"doesn't apply to the were-creatures here. They don't transfer their were-blood via bite."

Winnie frowns at that, reading Mario's sloping scrawl: *No evidence of nightmare transmission.*

"How do you know that? Was someone bitten seventeen years ago?" She's never heard that before—she only knows of the six deaths: two women, three men, one child.

Mario pauses a beat, and she has the sense that he just shared something he shouldn't have. When he speaks again, it's unnaturally casual. "Yeah. Seventeen years ago."

"I saw the new werewolf on Thursday night." She twists toward Mario, who is hastily closing the Compendium. "You lost our bet pretty badly."

"That I did." He saunters—still too casual—toward his desk, and Winnie trails after. There's nowhere for her to sit, so while he settles back into his swivel chair, she stands on the other side.

"But you still don't think the wolf killed the halfer?"

Mario's chair groans as he leans back. He smacks away at his gum. "Of course I do. Forget my email."

"Liar." Winnie glares at him. She plants her hands on the edge of his desk. "Here's the thing, Mario: I don't think the wolf killed that non either. I think it was something . . . big. Something . . . whispery." She shivers.

And Mario's whole body goes stone-still. Gone is the fake nonchalance, and in its place is sharp-eyed, scientific interest. "Explain."

So Winnie does. She's vague about the banshee, careful to sneak around the lies and hover on a curved tightrope of truth. "The banshee almost had me until this whispering began. The wolf was yipping—like a warning sound—and running away from it. Then I saw the . . . the *thing*. It was . . ." She gropes for words like she had with Jay. "It was like a warped glass got placed over my eyes then smashed with a hammer. The forest seemed to change shapes. To . . . to grow." She opens her hands. "To shrink too, and to bend and to morph." She squiggles her fingers.

At that demonstration, Mario snaps to his computer. A flurry of typing, and then he grips the monitor and spins it Winnie's way. "Did it look like this?"

She gasps. "Yes, exactly like that." An image fills his screen with the black-and-white glow of night vision, but there's no mistaking what she sees. There is the fuzzy edge, there is the rounded warping, there is the shrinking and the stretching and the morphing. "That's exactly it, Mario. Where did you get this?"

Whisperer?

"Lizzy Friday," he says, naming Jay's aunt. Part tinkerer, part scientist, like many Luminaries, she was born to the wrong family. And like Winnie, she should have been born a Monday.

Winnie's heart gives a little pang at that thought. She had loved Lizzy almost as much as her own family. But when Jay had ditched her, she'd lost Lizzy too.

"She has those surveillance cameras set up along the Friday estate boundaries," Mario explains. "She captured this the night the halfer died. I think *this* is what killed him."

"Me too." Winnie swallows. "What is it?"

Mario takes a beat before he answers, blowing a huge bubble. *Pop!* "I have no idea. I have gone over everything I can think of in the Compendium. Nightmares that distort vision, nightmares that bleed mist, nightmares that can become invisible . . . I even found a Pakistani nightmare that purportedly has its own gravitational field. But nothing"—he taps the monitor—"looks like this. Or makes the sound you're describing. Which is new data, by the way." He grabs for a note pad, the frown now replaced by wide, elated eyes. "Describe it to me again, Winnie. Every detail you can remember."

Winnie's teeth start clicking, an unconscious movement because even if Mario isn't afraid of the creature, *she* is. Whatever was in that woods scared a banshee. It scared a werewolf. It scared *her.*

And twice now, she's found its leftovers on the other side of a sensor.

When she doesn't answer right away, Mario glances up, red pen hovering as he takes in her clicking teeth. He knows her well enough to understand what that movement means. "Hey." He sets down the pen. "Don't worry about this thing, okay? Lizzy and I are on it."

"The Council isn't, though, are they?"

Pop-pop! "Did you just hear Dryden scolding me?"

Winnie nods. "Sounded like he cares a lot more about his precious Nightmare Masquerade than a murderous daywalker outside the sensors."

"You're not wrong there." Mario rubs tiredly at his eyes. "And it's not just Dryden acting that way. Dignitaries from all over the world will be showing up soon, evaluating our little corner of the Luminaries. A werewolf is easy . . . easy*ish* to stop. Just test everyone's blood and remove the one that doesn't look right. But a . . . what did you call it? Whisperer? No one has ever heard of that, so there's no easy way to deal with it. As such, unfortunately"—he opens his arms in defeat—"until we have more proof than just a blurry image, no one is going to listen to us."

"Even though I *saw* it?" Winnie waves toward her face. "With my own eyes?"

"Even though you saw it, Win. No one else has, and you wear glasses—I'm not saying that makes you unreliable," he hastily adds. "I'm just sharing what the Council would probably say. But hey, don't worry, okay?"

Winnie makes a face. "Yeah, sure. Don't worry about the nightmare that makes banshees and werewolves run in fear. That sounds like another dimension piped through a carburetor."

"You'll be safe on your next trials," Mario insists. "Hunters will be nearby the entire time. So whatever this Whisperer is, it'll die just like every other nightmare out there."

But will it? Winnie thinks. She doesn't say it aloud, though—there's no point. She's going into the forest tomorrow night for the second trial, whether or not the Whisperer is real. All she can do is pray she doesn't run into it.

And pray someone else starts taking it seriously—before it's too late.

CHAPTER
20

Winnie has only just gotten home and is making tea when Mum pounces on her. Literally pounces, like a harpy with claws bared. "Jay Friday called."

Winnie pauses her steeping of Earl Grey. This is unexpected. She'd thought Jay would just show up, haunting her doorway with his grey, tired eyes and forever mussed hair. That seems more on brand for Jay than calling ahead. "What did he say?" Winnie tries for nonchalance, succeeding about as well as Mario had.

"You haven't heard from that boy in four years." Mum leans onto the counter. She reeks of hash browns and bacon, and Winnie spots two ketchup stains on her T-shirt. "Now he wants to be friends again?"

"It's not like that," Winnie tries, but Mum is having none of it.

"Then what is it like?"

"He's helping me."

"Oh, yeah? And why now?" Mum pushes off the counter to start pacing. "For four years, everyone in this damned town has acted like we were poison because of Bryant."

Winnie flinches at the sound of her dad's name. It's so unexpected—so unlike Mum to say it—that Winnie doesn't even point out she owes a dollar to the swear jar. She just watches with widening eyes as Mum walks faster.

"I thought Jay would be different though. He loved you, you know? Erica too, though she had *Marcia* to contend with. I know you think I'm an overbearing mum, but I'm nothing like *Marcia*." She keeps saying that name like it's a cussword all on its own. "It was less of a surprise that Erica pulled away, but Jay? I really thought he'd be different. Now here we are, four years later, and he's not. He's just like everyone else. Lizzy too!" Mum rounds suddenly on Winnie. "You know, she came to me at the Daughter this morning, asking me all about you. She and every other Luminary are acting like they can get some of your banshee-killing shine if they just talk to me . . ."

Mum's face is red. Her eyes are bulging like two manticore pustules about to explode. All Winnie can do is stand there, holding her Earl Grey while it oversteeps and Mum storms and stomps and racks up a colossal tab for the swear jar.

Her stomach knots as she watches. First just a little tangle, like a kink in a gold chain. Then a full-on snarl that's so chunky, so clotted there can be no saving the chain. Because if Mum is this upset that people are suddenly paying attention to her, then why did Winnie bother doing this? Sure, she wants to be a hunter, but a huge calculation in her risk assessment had been how much it might help her family.

It's too late now for her to admit she didn't kill that banshee. Darian got promoted. Mum gets to go back to Wednesday dinners. And Winnie thought that was what they *wanted*.

"I thought you were happy I did this, Mum." The words whisper out, hollow and meek.

Mum freezes in mid-stride, cheeks ablaze and arms high. And Winnie's knotted horror must have reached her face, because suddenly Mum rushes to her. "Aw, hon." She takes the mug from Winnie's hands and sets it on the table. Then pulls Winnie to her for the third hug in just as many days. It has to be a record. "I'm sorry. I shouldn't have unloaded like that. I *am* happy. I'm just . . . I'm ashamed you had to do this, you know?"

Her voice cracks, and a new sort of knotting coils into Winnie's belly.

"I'm embarrassed it couldn't be me to solve it all." Mum squeezes, talking into Winnie's hair now. They're the same height, but Winnie feels so much smaller. In a good way. "I am so, so, *so* proud of you, Winnie. You did what I couldn't do, and you earned respect that I lost for us."

"You didn't lose it. Dad did."

Mum doesn't say anything to that, but she nods. "It upsets me how quickly the clans can change their tune. After four years of shouting at me for more ketchup, now they want to be friends. But . . . let's be real, Winnebago." She withdraws, grinning slyly. "I don't mind either. Even Marcia Thursday invited me for coffee next week—and yes, *I* did accept."

Winnie attempts a smile of her own, but it's snagged because the gold chain is still snagged. And Mum can tell. "I'm sorry I got upset that Jay called. I just don't want to see him hurt you again."

Winnie drops her gaze to her toes. "It's not like that." Her glasses start sliding. "We aren't friends. He doesn't want to be friends. He's just tutoring me."

Not a lie.

"Because I'm so behind in my training."

Also true.

Mum sighs, a defeated sound, but also an accepting one. "Okay. Then I'll give you a ride. He said to be there at two, and . . ." She glances at the clock. "It's a quarter till. You'll never get there in time on the bike."

"Get where in time?" Winnie hurries after Mum, who is now pouncing for the Volvo keys and then pouncing for her jacket.

"The Friday estate." Mum slips into her navy fleece. "He said to meet him outside."

Nothing has changed since the last time Winnie visited the Fridays, four years ago—except that everything is even more run-down than it used to be. If the Thursday estate is an art museum, then the Friday estate is something out of a horror movie. It is a haunted Gothic mansion brought to life, with its sloped, mossy roof, with its three stories and chipped white paint, with its tall, slender windows (two of which are broken and boarded up) and two gargoyles that loom over the eastern and western wings.

Then there is the crowning horror: the burned-out tower on the west side. It was round and stately once, according to the black-and-white photos that peer out from heavy frames on several halls inside. But now it is a charred skeleton, missing a roof, a top floor, and any dignity it might have once possessed.

The clouds have briefly abandoned their usual post, leaving the sun to sweep down. Unusually cheerful for Hemlock Falls in spring, but almost garish when beamed upon the Friday estate. This is a house meant for gloom.

While the estates exist for clan operations, the Fridays are the tiniest clan on the Luminary tree—meaning the Friday "work" has always been filling whatever spot might be vacant in the Hemlock Falls ecosystem, from cleaning to catering to running the Revenant's Daughter (Archie is a third cousin of Jay's).

Four years ago, Winnie had never thought this collection of odd jobs strange. The Fridays were just that extra family that made some of the best hunters, and that was that. Now, driving toward the house, Winnie realises how very strange it actually is. Every other clan has a function in the global society. Sundays teach new Luminaries; Wednesdays handle basic life needs and logistics; Thursdays ensure no one ever learns of the forests or the spirits or the society. But the Fridays . . .

They're just *there*. The only clan without a clearly defined role. Is it because there aren't many of them? And why hasn't Winnie ever considered this before?

Culture runs thicker than blood. That truth doesn't only apply to the clans and their ideals; it defines the entirety of the Luminaries. Except that while Winnie has been trapped on the fringe, the culture in her blood has . . . Well, it hasn't gone away so much as thinned. Just enough for her to question things she'd never questioned before.

Jay waits on the bottom step of six that lead up to the black front door. He is still as the gargoyles, staring at the ground. Even when the gravel crunches under the Volvo's tires as Mum drives up, he doesn't move.

I could draw him like that, Winnie thinks, mentally taking a snapshot—even though she hasn't drawn Jay in years. Even though she hasn't touched her pens since before the first trial. Something about him right now, so far away despite being right here, feels actually sketchable.

"When should I pick you up?" Mum asks, eying Jay warily behind glasses she only wears when driving.

"Jay can give me a ride," Winnie answers, and though Mum's lips purse—she clearly still doesn't trust Jay's motives—she does at least nod.

Winnie exits the Volvo and Jay finally reacts. It's like a robot coming out of power-save mode: his spine straightens, his gaze solidifies with focus, and he even offers the slightest twinge of a smile. He wears loose black sportswear, not so different from Winnie's clothes from training at the Sunday estate (which yes, she still has on), except that his hoodie and joggers are fresh. Winnie's, meanwhile, are coated in sweat with an extra fragrance of *eau de Revenant's Daughter* thanks to the car ride with Mum.

For some reason, as Jay approaches her and Mum drives away, Winnie is keenly aware of her filthy state. Which is weird, because it's not as if Jay ever looks put together. "Do you have your hunting gear?" he asks.

Winnie lifts the black backpack that used to be Darian's.

"Great. Then follow me." Jay slides his hands into his pockets. The loose trousers cling in places on his body that Winnie wishes she weren't noticing. She doesn't remember Jay having thigh muscles before.

He saunters off, as oblivious to Winnie's scrutiny as he is to the rest of Hemlock Falls' rapture, aiming for the mansion's eastern corner. Grass pokes up from the gravel. A few snapdragons too.

They reach a cluster of trees that has a path lined with massive stepping-stones. Winnie's heart gives a little sigh at the sight of it. She used to love this path; it was so magical. So *un*-nightmarish. Like if she took this path, she'd end up at a castle far away. Unlike the grounds around the Friday estate, which are overgrown and long since evolved from chaotic garden into full-on nature, the path is cleared, the saplings and undergrowth kept gently at bay.

When at last Jay guides Winnie out of the trees, it's to find a familiar training ground. They used to sneak out here with Erica, all those years ago, and play hide-and-seek within the wooden platforms and rope ladders, the ditches and walls. Somehow, it looks even more run-down than the house. The man-shaped targets have plastic flaking off them in vicious curls—as well as a galaxy of holes from various weapons. The platforms, meanwhile, appear rotten, and the rope ladders have mostly just become ropes.

It is a downright perilous series of obstacles, and Winnie suspects any one of them might actually kill her if she doesn't navigate them *just* right.

As Jay leads her toward a table at the far corner of the field, Winnie remembers something Dad once said about people who excel. She'd been complaining that Erica had a nicer bicycle, and couldn't *she* have a nicer bicycle?

Listen, Winnie Benny, some of the world's most elite athletes have trained in the worst conditions. He had on his professor voice, the one that hearkened to his days before joining the Luminaries and that always indicated a lecture was on the way. *The constraints of a partly deflated soccer ball or a twenty-year-old tennis racket can sometimes lead to one-of-a-kind talent because when those athletes do get the best gear—oh, to see them perform then. They become unstoppable.*

For once, thinking of Dad doesn't make Winnie's blood boil. She's too absorbed by the meaning of what he'd told her. By the living, breathing, very well-muscled proof before her. The other clans might have top-notch training gear, but everyone knows that it's actually the Friday hunters who often turn out the best.

Jay has reached the table now, and he's looking back at Winnie. No expression beyond a patient sort of curiosity. Winnie hurries toward him, frowning at her epiphany—wondering if her own constraints might ultimately help her.

Probably not.

On the table is a red compound bow. She reaches for it, but Jay lifts a hand. "Gear first," he tells her. "It's better to train in what you'll actually wear."

This makes sense, and speaking of constraints, the enormity of Andrew's gear certainly is one. She hauls it out of her backpack. *Rrrrippp, rrrrripppp.* Velcro opens. *Krrr, krrrr.* Velcro closes. When she looks at Jay again, she realises he's staring at her chest.

"Hey," she snaps, even though she'd ogled him only a few minutes ago.

"Banshee claws," he replies.

Winnie flushes. Because of course he wasn't ogling *her*. It's just that three claws are still poking out of the Kevlar.

"May I?" He motions to them, and Winnie nods. Now that the vest is on, it *is* easier for him to do it. Even if it's really weird having him stand this near. Even if her chest starts doing this uncomfortable clenching thing as he crooks down to carefully, delicately remove each syringe-like claw.

"They have barbs," he says, wriggling the claw. "But you can spin them counterclockwise to remove them without too much damage to the Kevlar."

"I . . . didn't know that." But she thinks this should really be in the Compendium. She also thinks how Jay's hair is thicker than she remembers. Darker too, no longer the downy blond he'd had as a boy, but a coarse field of wheat.

He smells of his usual lime and bergamot. No smoke or weed or booze. Her glasses slide down her nose as she stares at the top of his head.

Once the first claw is out, he sets it on the table with the bow and glances at Winnie for approval before grasping at the others. Winnie nods, contemplating his face now.

The skin under his eyes is haggard; small capillaries are visible through weary skin. It's like he never sees the sun, except Winnie knows he does. His hands are just as pale too, but callused in a way that they weren't four years ago.

As he wriggles and works at the second claw, Winnie spots a bandage peeking out from under his watchband. Without thinking, she touches it, her fingers sliding onto his wrist.

He goes very still.

"What happened?" she asks.

He takes a beat to answer. "Harpy."

"Oh." She wets her lips. Her glasses perch on the end of her nose, but she doesn't push them up. "Did you kill it?"

"Her," he corrects. His eyes are only inches away from Winnie's, wintery and cold, mournful and lost. She feels like she is staring at the banshee all over again. "Yes," he answers eventually. "I killed her." Then he pulls his wrist from Winnie's grasp.

CHAPTER

21

Winnie keeps the three claws. She wants to look at these barbs under a microscope—and now that she can walk onto the Monday estate whenever she wants, she bets Mario will let her use his lab.

She and Jay don't stay at the training grounds. "It'll get crowded soon," Jay explains, motioning toward the house, where Winnie can hear the sounds of car engines and doors slamming. Friday hunters arriving to train. Jay takes the compound bow, and though Winnie itches to get her hands on it, she forces herself to patiently follow him into the woods.

They pass cedars and aspens, maples and oaks. Birds sing and green shines. But soon, they leave the rough path Jay had followed and cut off into the spirit's realm.

Winnie doesn't need the red stakes to know when they've entered the forest. Sunbeams lose their edge; silence muffles everything, damp and intractable. After another five minutes of tromping, Jay leads Winnie over a small stream— ephemeral, barely a trickle now—and into a clearing. A sugar maple and red pine have fallen recently here, their trunks akimbo on the floor. Already, branches from the surrounding trees have laced together to block the sky. Without sun, there is no secondary growth. Only soft pine needles.

Jay turns to face Winnie beside one of the trunks. He offers her the bow, and her mouth practically waters as she yanks it from him.

"You still remember how to use it?"

"Yes." She tries for a glare, but her body is too pleased to glower. It recalls the shape of the grip in her hand, the way the bow limbs and riser fill her vision while her eyes naturally look past. Yes, there is an awkwardness in holding it—especially since Jay hasn't offered her a trigger release, so it's just her fingers. But the memory is written on her muscles; four years couldn't erase that.

Jay pulls a waterproof quiver from under the nearest trunk, and Winnie realises he must have prepared for their meeting. He offers her a training bolt with a foam tip, and her muscles take over again. *Gimme, gimme, gimme.* She needs two tries to nock the bolt, her fingers stiff with cold, but once she gets it in, she turns a wide grin onto Jay.

He swallows. Clears his throat. Then quickly spins away to hop up the maple trunk in four loping bounds. Winnie is both impressed by and jealous of how easily he moves.

"Ready?" he calls, twirling to face her. He's forty feet away and fifteen feet off the ground.

"For what?" she calls back.

"Target practice."

"What am I shooting at?"

"Me." The word barks out. Winnie's eyes widen behind her glasses. Then Jay is on the move.

She doesn't know how he reaches her so fast. She doesn't know anything at all beyond that word—*Me*—before a blur of wheat hair and black cotton hits her with the same speed Jay had in the living room, the same force. Except this time, there's no wall to land against. Only the forest floor.

She drops the bow. Her back slams against the ground, lungs compressing. Vision darkening. And a Jay-shaped weight bearing down.

"Oh . . . god." The words barely rasp out as she opens her eyes and meets Jay's. If she thought he was close before, this is a thousand times closer—and a thousand times more intimate. Except that she's way too startled and too . . . broken to feel uncomfortable.

Besides, he's already rolling off her and springing to his feet. He offers her a hand. "Good fall."

She winces up at him. "What?"

"You tucked in your chin and threw out your arm." He points to her left arm, which sure enough is thrust out to her side, fingers splayed. It is the first lesson Luminaries learn in physical training: how to fall correctly. Winnie and all the other kids with her, before her, after her learn by falling over and over and over . . . and then over some more, until their bodies instinctively know how to minimise impact.

Winnie has practiced falling a thousand times on her living room floor these past four years (RIP TV remote), but the forest floor feels a lot harder, a lot colder.

"Glad I remembered one thing," she groans, eyes closing. First the failure in the forest. Then the failure on the obstacle course. And now this failure against Jay. As far as she can tell, all her efforts over the last four years have led her basically *nowhere*.

She hears Jay's clothing rustle, then his hand—so warm in this forest cold—wraps around hers. "Up you go, Win." He doesn't give her a choice, just starts hauling, and next thing she knows, she's standing beside him.

He scoops up the bow next, and then the fallen bolt. "Again," he tells her, and he hops once more onto the crooked trunk.

This time, Winnie takes aim. But this time, when he moves, he doesn't come directly at her. He drops to the floor and zooms sideways. She shoots. She misses—horribly misses, because he has already leaped into a forward roll.

He hits her again one second later, and she topples over a mere fraction of a second after that.

"Ow." He is heavier than he looks. All those lean lines are pure muscle. Or maybe lead weights. He certainly feels like lead weights.

"Again." He rises off her and prowls away. She doesn't even have time to fetch her lost bolt—it's landed beside the fallen trunk—before he's charging again.

He hits her. She hits the ground. Then the steps of the dance renew. Every time, she lands on her back with Jay pinning her down, his grey eyes inescapable while the forest breathes around them. With each onslaught, though, Jay seems to change. The skin on his face gains colour, looking less like paper stretched over bone. As if the grey of the forest is releasing him. As if the old Jay is seeping back into his veins with each new surge of endorphins.

Or maybe it's Winnie who's changing, her muscles and brain finally adapting four years of practice to accommodate a partner, a target, a forest. The fallen trees seem to sharpen; the pine needles divide into a thousand amber lines across the floor; she notices small dips and rises in the terrain that she hadn't seen before.

On maybe the tenth, maybe the twelfth try, Winnie finally has the bolt nocked—and she finally has a sense of where Jay is going to go before he moves. She's not fast, but she's faster than she was thirty minutes ago now that her body and instincts have woken up.

He rushes her—and rushes right for the arrow aimed at his head.

He instantly grinds to a stop, hands lifting in supplication. And Winnie whoops with pure elation. It bursts out of her, radiant as the spring sun outside the forest. "I did it! I did it! I did it!" She lowers the bow and skips toward him, shrieking.

Except he isn't smiling back, and for half a moment, she's

scared she shot him. But when she looks down, the bolt is still in her hand.

She looks at him again. This is an expression she's never seen before, his eyes laser-sharp. *Intense,* Winnie thinks. It's the only word to describe him right now. *Intense.*

"Are . . . you okay?" She's panting, and her elation is draining fast. She doesn't like this version of Jay. Or, rather, she doesn't like that she doesn't recognise him. "Did I hurt you?"

He blinks. "No," he gruffs out, abruptly turning away. "I'm fine." He stalks three steps to the fallen trunk, and before Winnie's eyes, he seems to smear away. As if the forest is erasing him, leaving only wind and leaves and misty silence in his stead.

"Good job," he calls eventually, still facing the tree trunk. "A few more weeks, and you might actually hit me on the first try."

Now Winnie is the one to blink. "A few more weeks?" She scurries toward him. "I don't have a few weeks, Jay. I have another trial *tomorrow night.*"

"I know what you're up against." Jay's hands are in his pockets. He is folding in on himself. "I go in the forest at least one night a week, remember?"

Help me, she wants to say, but she stops herself. Jay owes her nothing. She's not even sure why he has done this much for her. Plus, the more she pushes, the more likely he is to push *her* for answers—and if he knows what *really* happened on Thursday night . . .

He won't help her anymore. He'll turn her in for the liar she is because his honor as a Friday will force him to. Because deep down to the very beating core of him, Jay is honesty through and through.

He twists toward her. His cheeks are pale once more, his body back to its unnatural stillness. Mud streaks his joggers. The zip on his hoodie has come halfway undone, revealing a white T-shirt underneath. His hair is mussed and pine-needled. "Surviving the night is the easiest of the trials, Winnie. As long as you know where to go."

"I don't."

"But I do." He reaches for the bow, and she lets him take it. His fingers are icy to the touch, though she swears only a minute ago they were warm. "There's a spot where nightmares don't go. You'll have to reach that spot from the drop-off point, but I'll show you where it is."

"Why don't the nightmares go there?"

"It's surrounded by running water. And while you might get some vampira lurking around the edges, they won't cross."

Winnie's teeth start clicking. There's something off here, something she doesn't quite trust. The problem is, she knows Jay would never lie to her. She squints at him from behind her glasses. "When can you show me?"

"Tomorrow. It'll be best if it's fresh in your mind before the trial. Now, come on." He jerks his chin toward the trees. "It's time to finish our session with a run." He sets off before Winnie can protest, and though the thought of *any more running* today makes her want to die inside, she also knows she asked for this.

She chases him into the forest.

The sun has already begun its descent by the time Jay leads Winnie back to the Friday estate. If she'd thought her legs were made of rubber after Coach Rosa, it is nothing compared to their absolute uselessness after a jog through the forest. She had to hop over roots, duck under branches, leap and sideswipe, and at one point wade through a stream that reached above her knees and made her bones hurt from the cold.

But now she and Jay are back at the estate, and Winnie can't deny that, even if everything hurts and tomorrow it's going to hurt even worse, she has enjoyed herself. She spent so long careening around an empty house or jogging through neighbourhoods trying to shave time off her mile—now she's finally using her body *in the forest*.

It's like a plug clicking into a socket: she feels so completely switched on. She is surging and sparkling with power.

Jay leads her around to the front of the estate, where Mathilda no longer awaits. Instead, it's his motorcycle—or rather, Aunt Lizzy's motorcycle that he gets to use and tinker with. Clearly, it's back from Gunther's.

Jay heads for it. "The spare helmet is under the seat."

Winnie stops dead in her tracks. "I'm sorry, what?"

He repeats, louder, "The helmet is under the seat—"

"I heard you. I meant *what* in an incredulous way. In an 'I'm not getting on that death machine' way."

He laughs, that surprised puff of air he always offers, and looks back at her. "You, a Luminary untrained, who went into the forest with only a trap to protect you, but now my bike is too dangerous for you?" He retraces three steps to stand before Winnie. The memory of bergamot and lime still clings to him, but mostly he smells of sweat and forest and fog.

It's not unpleasant.

"I don't like motorcycles, Jay."

"Your house is five minutes away, Winnie. I promise I'll go the speed limit."

"I *don't* like motorcycles."

Another bark of laughter, but this one is exasperated. "Win, this is it." He waves at the bike. "That's all I've got right now. Lizzy took Mathilda for the afternoon, so if you want to go home, then you've got to ride the death machine."

"When will she be back?"

"Really?" The exasperation spreads through his body, sending his shoulders toward his ears. "*Really?* You trust me so little?" When Winnie doesn't answer—it's a trick question anyway—he says, "She won't be back for a while, and I can't waste any time. I've got a show tonight at Joe Squared."

"Oh." Winnie blinks. It's Saturday. She totally forgot that Jay and the Forgotten always play on Saturday. "What time does it start?"

"We go on at nine, and I need to shower before then." He unzips his hoodie, as if to demonstrate just how filthy he is . . .

But Winnie only finds herself eying the way his T-shirt hangs on his frame. It is disconcerting that he can be so extremely well-proportioned while also being, *ugh,* Jay. Part of her genuinely misses the boy he used to be.

Most of her, though, is just impressed by what he's grown into. Hunter training clearly suits him. Not just physically either, but emotionally. In that clearing, on that tree trunk, he'd been more alert, more alive than she'd seen him in years. This is the Jay she can never quite translate onto the page.

It takes Winnie a moment to realise she is, yet again, ogling him. And that this time, he has asked her a question and is waiting for a reply.

"Huh?" She shoves her glasses up her nose. There's so much dirt around the lenses. "Did you say something?"

He sighs. "I said you can come inside and call your mum—if it's really that big a deal."

"Mum's working," she answers absently.

"Okay, option two. You go with me to Joe Squared. Lizzy will be back right before I need to go. We can shower now, and then—"

"Jay! I'm not showering with you!"

He flushes pure scarlet. All the way to his hairline and practically into the hair itself. "I did not mean together, you perv. I meant separately. Separate showers."

"Oh." Now she flushes too, and even manages a little laugh. *Separate* makes a lot more sense.

"I'm sure Lizzy has something you can borrow." He gestures vaguely at Winnie's dirty sportswear, and she flushes even more.

She must really stink at this point. She's still wearing the Kevlar, and now that all her sweat is drying, she is absolutely *freezing.* In fact, Jay's offer of a shower is actually kind of tempting.

However, as much as she doesn't want to ride on Jay's death machine, she wants to go to Joe Squared even less. It will be all the Luminaries, from the twins to Dante to Erica to Marcus, and Winnie has had more than enough of them today. Plus, if she *is* going to show up where Erica is again—or any of the Luminaries, for that matter—she wants to wear better clothes than borrowed jeans and flannel from Lizzy (there is a very direct line between Jay's sense of style and his aunt's).

She also doesn't want to still be lying. Eventually the novelty of her killing a banshee will wear off. People will stop talking about it, stop asking her about it, stop remembering she ever showed up on the side of the road with that creature's head hanging from her hand.

As much as she hates it, her only real option is the motorcycle. Her eyes shutter. "Fine," she moans. "I'll ride with you on that thing."

When she opens her eyes again, she finds something on Jay's face, just pinching around the edges, that is almost sad, almost disappointed. And she realises with a jolt that maybe he actually wanted her to go to the show.

He turns away before she can confirm and resumes his march for the bike. "I'll drive safely," he promises. "You won't even know we're not in Mathilda."

CHAPTER
22

Winnie definitely knows she's not in Mathilda. It's not just that her legs are straddled over a wide, vibrating seat. Or that there is wind to flay against her and turn her into a frozen sweatcicle. Or a helmet to limit her head's rotation, shrink down her field of view, and remove her hearing entirely.

It's the fact that she has to put her arms around Jay's waist—something one *never* has to do in a car. Oh, he might tell her she doesn't need to. He might *tell* her it's totally safe for her to lean back, but in the absence of seat belts, she is going to hold on to him for dear life.

Of course, now that her arms are around him and he's steering them off the Friday estate and onto an actual paved road, she wonders if maybe holding on is a bad idea. Maybe the danger here isn't actually the motorcycle—it's a lot smoother than she expected, and Jay handles it with ease. More easily than he drives Mathilda, in fact.

No, the danger is *him*. Seeing the shape of him in black sportswear is a lot different than feeling that shape. Even when he'd been pressed atop her in the forest, Winnie had been too adrenaline-fueled and skull-knocked to really feel him. Now, there is no escaping it.

He is as muscled as he looks, and Winnie is utterly freaked out by it. Thank god he zipped up his hoodie, and thank god it's made of thick sweatshirt material, or else she'd be touching just his T-shirt with her fingers, and she isn't sure she wants that.

No, she definitely doesn't want that. Jay Friday isn't supposed to feel like this, and *she* isn't supposed to notice if he does.

Fortunately, the ride to Winnie's house is mere minutes. Unfortunately, she is so sore (she should have stretched, why didn't she stretch?) and so cold, she can't seem to lift her legs to dismount. She literally falls in her attempt, and only Jay's hunter reflexes keep her from face-planting onto the curb.

"Whoa." He helps her rise, helmet still on. Winnie's is still on too, which is making things worse—like, even her neck is sore, and suddenly holding up the weight of the helmet seems unmanageable. Worse, she can't seem to move as she wants and it's sending her heart rate spiking.

It's like she's in the forest all over again. It's like the banshee has her trapped while the world slowly ends—

"Off," she shrieks, ripping at the helmet. "Off, off, get it off!"

Jay obeys immediately, unlatching whatever it is that needs unlatching and then yanking the helmet off of Winnie. Cold air rushes in, sharp and fortifying. Bright and alive. She isn't in the forest. She isn't under the banshee. She is standing in front of Jay, who has now removed his helmet too, and she is okay.

She is okay.

"I'm sorry." Jay looks horrified, and he's reaching for her without quite touching. Like he's afraid she'll fall again, so he needs to be ready to catch her. "I shouldn't have forced you onto the bike." His face is stricken. An unusual expression for him, both in the fact that he has an expression at all and that this one is so fierce. "I'm so sorry, Win—"

"No," she cuts in, straightening. Breathing. She wishes she could tell him about the banshee. She wishes she could *tell* him what happened—how the monster's skin looked, how she saw her dad and couldn't stop crying, how beautiful it was and also how devastating. How, as messed up as it is, she would let a banshee cry on her again because she'd never felt so pure. And how, as deeply wrong and *messed up* as it is, she is sad the banshee died.

Instead, she forces out, "You're fine, Jay. The bike was . . . fine. I'm just really cold."

He nods, though his expression stays grim. She can tell he doesn't believe her lie, but he also isn't going to press her for more. It's not his way and never has been. Patient, patient Jay.

Then, as if he actually knows the truth anyway, he says, "We'll go find that safe spot tomorrow, okay? You'll be at Sunday training?"

"Yeah." She winces. Her muscles probably won't get her up the front porch steps, much less through another round with Coach Rosa.

"Good," he replies. "I'll find you there. And hey." He pulls a crumpled Post-it from his pocket. "Here's my number, in case you need something. I know you don't have a phone, but . . ." He swallows. The faintest blush returns.

Winnie takes the paper, so crumpled it's almost soft now. The ink is faded too, like he wrote this a few days ago and it's been sitting in his pocket ever since.

"Thanks," she tells him. Then again—because she actually means it: "Thanks. For this and for the training."

"Yeah, Win." He turns away. "Anytime."

Winnie is just getting out of the shower when she hears an engine pulling in front of the house. She glances out the tiny bathroom window, wiping away the fog, and spots a navy Honda Civic. It takes her a second to place why she knows the car.

Then its owner steps from the driver's seat: Aunt Rachel.

Winnie is so surprised, she doesn't move. She's too accustomed to being ignored for her brain to register that Rachel might be coming *here*. Then Rachel's dark head circles toward the lawn. The fading sunset transforms her into an impressionist painting.

Winnie watches the fog start to reclaim its territory on the window, wondering if she can pretend no one is home. But right as Rachel reaches the first step to the porch, she pauses. Glances up. Spots Winnie and waves.

"Shit." Winnie bolts for her room, mentally adding a dollar to the swear jar. Then mentally removing it because she is certain Mum never paid up earlier.

Though her body is covered in bruises and small cuts, though her arms are so sore she can hardly lift them to put on a T-shirt (white) and her Save the Whales hoodie, though her thigh muscles literally scream (she can definitely hear them screaming) as she shimmies into trousers that maybe have gotten a little too small, Winnie dresses in record speed. She can hear Rachel opening the front door, and she decides Jay is right: they really should lock that thing.

Winnie leaves her hair unbrushed and sopping, and in mere minutes, she is rushing downstairs. Rachel stands awkwardly in the living room, staring at the spots where the photos of Dad used to be.

And photos of her too, now that Winnie considers it. Rachel came over often. She and Mum were more than just sisters. They were best friends, and the two of them had always paired together on Wednesday nights in the forest.

For the first time in four years, Winnie wonders what Rachel felt when she learned her sister's husband had betrayed them. When she learned her closest friend and partner was getting banned from the Luminaries because she'd unwittingly married a Diana.

Rachel speaks first, clasping her hands in front of her,

shoulders hunching slightly. "Your mum's not here, huh?"

"She's at work." Winnie steps warily into the living room. "She has a shift at the Daughter tonight."

"Ah." Rachel seems to hunch even more. It's very un-Rachel of her. "She, uh . . . well, she . . ."

"Yeah?" Winnie presses. She had rushed down here expecting Hard-Ass Aunt Rachel. Instead, she's faced with . . . this. Whatever *this* is, and she feels weirdly like the adult in the room.

"She might not have to keep that job much longer," Rachel continues. "There are some administrative openings at the estate, assuming the whole outcast thing gets, uh . . ." She releases her hands and moves to the couch. "May I?"

"Sure." Winnie shrugs, because she can hardly refuse.

Rachel perches on the edge of the farthest cushion from Winnie, somehow looking even more uncomfortable than when she'd been standing. There's clearly something she wants to say, and Winnie starts to wonder if maybe Rachel isn't here to see Mum at all, but actually came to see her.

Then Rachel confirms it. "Look, I'm sorry." She deflates slightly and rubs at her eyes. "I've been so hard on you these past four years and, uh . . . Well, you did good on Thursday night. You showed real loyalty. All three of you, actually." She lurches to her feet and starts pacing.

Winnie still waits at the edge of the room.

"You, Fran, Darian—you've stuck by the Luminaries, even though none of them . . . none of *us* have stuck by you. I can't imagine it was easy." She pauses her forward march briefly to flick a questioning glance Winnie's way, as if maybe Winnie will contradict her. As if she'll say, *Nah, it was all good.*

But it wasn't all good. Plus, Winnie is too stunned to speak. She's the ghost-deer now, caught in the sights of a hunter.

Rachel resumes her pacing and her monologue. "I don't think there is a . . . a purer embodiment of the Wednesday motto than the three of you. Than, well . . . than you. I'm really proud of you, Win. Your mum and me once faced a banshee, you know." She stops walking and squares herself to Winnie. "We couldn't do what you did, and you were all alone. It's amazing." There's a soft smile on Rachel's lips and genuine awe in her dark eyes at what she thinks Winnie did.

The nausea bubbles up again. The lie of it all cranking inside Winnie, like a jack-in-the-box ready to burst. If she says anything, it will probably be the truth—or worse, a lie that Rachel will see right through.

So Winnie nods. A brusque movement on a neck made of bruises and strained muscles.

But it seems to be enough, because Rachel nods too. "All right. That's, uh, all I wanted to say." She moves toward Winnie, clearly headed for the front door. Right as she reaches Winnie, though, she pauses, staring at Winnie's neck. Her hand twitches upward, then stills. "Where did you get that?"

"Get what?" Winnie clutches at her neck, and of course, there's the locket. "It was a gift."

"Who gave it to you?"

Winnie hesitates, wondering if she should lie. Wondering if she needs to protect Darian. She really doesn't like the way Rachel is looking at it. Erica had stared at it with anger and contempt; Rachel looks only horrified. Her left eye is twitching.

"Darian gave it to me." Winnie notches her chin up an inch. "It was my birthday present. Why do you ask?"

Rachel's lips compress. She's staring at Winnie's knuckles, as if she can see through them to the necklace. "I thought it looked familiar, but I guess I was wrong." Her gaze flicks upward. Then she gives Winnie an awkward pat on the shoulder. "How about I pick you up after Sunday classes tomorrow? We can get some decent gear for you at the estate."

"Sure," Winnie replies—what else can she say?—and Rachel gives her another pat before walking away. Seconds later, the front door shuts. Winnie is left alone, cold hair still sopping.

"I got accosted *twice* today," Winnie tells her brother. He is on the opposite side of the kitchen island, chopping an onion with goggles on because of course Darian would have goggles just for chopping onions. They were his favorite gift from Andrew last Christmas, and Winnie has to admit that she almost wishes she had a pair of her own right now. It's a really strong onion.

"What the heck is this locket?" Winnie lifts it toward him, and he briefly pauses his chopping to glance her way. Tonight, his skin gleams thanks to kitchen cooking steam and the relaxation of a day *not* working for Dryden Saturday.

"What do you mean? It's a locket."

"Well, Erica Thursday low-key accused you of stealing it from her, and then Aunt Rachel looked at it like it contained a nightmare inside."

Darian recoils slightly, his face scrunching into a frown. "That's really weird because as far as I know, it's just a locket."

"Where did you get it?"

"The attic."

Winnie's fingers clench around the golden circle. "Our attic?"

"Yeah." He rushes his chopping. *Clack-clack-clack.* Tears burn anew in Winnie's eyes. "I asked Mum if I could have it, she said yes, so I got it cleaned up—it was so tarnished when I found it. Then I put the two photos in it . . . and yeah. That's it." He lifts the cutting board and heads for the pan of hot oil on the stove. Saturday is spaghetti night, always, and while Winnie and Darian grew up on jarred or canned everything, Andrew did *not*. He insists they make most meals from scratch. Normally, he is here to help; tonight, he is in the loft at his desk studying.

The onions hit the pan, hissing like a basilisk.

"Whose locket was it?" Winnie asks once Darian is back before her—now to peel garlic. He still wears the goggles.

He also wears an apron that says, COOKING HARD OR HARDLY COOKING?, which he and Andrew think is hilarious, but Winnie doesn't understand the joke. In fact, she's pretty sure there is no joke.

"Mum didn't know whose it was, so she said it was fine if I wanted it."

"So it was probably Dad's." For some reason, as Winnie says this, her stomach flips. Dad is gone; anything he left behind should absolutely be used (or destroyed).

Darian pauses his peeling, and this time he removes the goggles so they hang around his neck. "Does that bother you? I . . . didn't think it would. Listen, I'm sorry. I can get you a new—"

"No." Winnie shoots up her hands, sliding off the stool as she does so. "No, it doesn't bother me. Really." Since she's hurrying toward the pan—where the onions are definitely burning—she hopes Darian doesn't notice her lie.

He totally notices. "I'm sorry, Win. I didn't think . . . I mean, we don't know it's his for sure. Mum really doesn't know who it belongs to."

"Right," Winnie says, grabbing a spatula. She is not a skilled enough cook to lift the pan and do the vegetable flippy thing. "But it's probably Dad's. That's why Aunt Rachel looked like she'd seen a nightmare in the living room." She stirs at the onions. A few are stuck to the cast iron because Andrew refuses to use that *cancer substance called Teflon*.

"But if Mum doesn't know that, then why would Rachel?" Darian reaches for the locket and slides it sideways on the chain, so he can study it while Winnie continues prying onions off the iron. He looks like a wild inventor, with the goggles at his neck and the apron and his attention on the locket.

She turns the burner to low and faces Darian. He releases the locket. "Erica Thursday said she used to have one like it, but it went missing. You don't think it's hers, do you?"

Darian blinks. "I mean . . . I sure hope not. I don't know how it would have ended up in our attic. Did she say when it went missing?"

Winnie shakes her head.

And Darian sighs, a forlorn sound. "I'll just get you a new one, okay? Then we can offer this one to her—"

"*No.*" Winnie smacks a hand to her collarbone, covering the locket. "I am not giving this to her. I like it. Really, I do. And it's . . . it's good luck. I passed the trial, right? Maybe this is the reason." She is surprised how easily the lie rolls off her tongue. Maybe because she *did* have good luck that had to have come from somewhere.

Or maybe she's just getting used to talking about the banshee. Either way, Darian doesn't question her. If anything, he looks relieved—like he'd been worried she would want a new one. And now that she considers it, even with his promotion, there's no way he could afford a locket made from real gold like this one.

"The onions are burning!" Andrew shouts from the loft. "I can smell it from up here!"

"No they aren't!" Winnie squeaks at the same time Darian shouts, "Because I know that's how you like them, sweetie!" Then he flashes Winnie a conspiratorial smile and gets back to peeling garlic.

Winnie resumes her stirring.

CHAPTER

23

Winnie is waiting for Mum behind the Revenant's Daughter. She hadn't seen any reason for Darian, who had kindly picked her up, to drive her back home when Mum will be off her shift any minute now.

Or she is *supposed* to be, but for some reason Archie keeps giving her the "just one more order, just one more order, and you can go" line, so now Winnie has been leaning against the brick wall in the alley outside for fifteen minutes' worth of "one mores" and freezing her butt off despite the leather jacket. The open door to the Revenant's Daughter spews a greasy vapor of fluorescent light, while across the alley, another doorway hangs open to welcome cool air into the overcrowded space—but that light is cozy and dim, carrying with it the smell of fresh coffee and the sounds of grinding beans and clinking cups.

Winnie really wants a cup of coffee. One of the fancy ones that has whipped cream on top and flavoured syrups—and that Mum totally disapproves of. She keeps imagining going into the warmth, ordering a coffee on the tab from Mario, sitting in a corner, and savoring the vanilla or the chai or *both*. But she doesn't dare. Because there's a guitar tuning in there. And a sound like tables being moved. Winnie even thinks she hears Jay's voice a couple of times. She *definitely* hears all the Luminaries. That's Xavier's distinctive chuckle, and there is Marisol's excited squeal. It's a ton of people; one of them is likely Erica; no way is Winnie going inside.

Just as she is huddling more deeply into her hoodie and jacket, a head pokes out of the Joe Squared door. "Winnie?"

Winnie jolts upright. It's one of the twins. "Oh, hey . . . Emma." She can always tell the sisters apart when they're together, but solo—and in shadows—it gets tricky. Fortunately, Emma has been wearing her long braids for a while now. "Fancy meeting you here."

Emma giggles as if Winnie said something funny—and not in a mocking way, but in a genuinely delighted way. "Are you coming inside? The show's gonna start any minute now."

"No." Winnie offers what she hopes is an apologetic smile. "I'm just waiting on my mum to get off work."

"Ah, right." Emma traipses out of the doorway toward Winnie, and Winnie has to fight the urge to cower into her hoodie. She definitely keeps her hands in the leather pockets. Her teeth start clicking, and she berates herself for being a coward. The twins deserve better than her flinches and frowns. They aren't going to hurt her; none of the Luminaries are anymore.

Emma only makes it three steps before a cheer goes up in Joe Squared. It's like watching the mist in the forest clear: Emma transforms before Winnie's eyes, somehow becoming even more beautiful. Her eyes literally sparkle, her dimples pucker cutely, and her smile beams.

Winnie is moved by its infectiousness and she finds herself smiling in return.

"They're starting," Emma says breathily, clapping her hands to her chest. "Oh, I hope they start with 'Backlit.'" She gives Winnie a fluttery wave and then half skips, half runs back into the coffee shop.

Winnie watches after her, a frown sewing across her lips. Though she knows that Jay and Trevor Tuesday and L.A. (Louisa Anne) Saturday are in there now, she can't really imagine what it looks like. She can't really imagine Jay playing bass guitar or performing on a stage.

"We're the Forgotten," L.A. says in a crooning voice. "Thanks for coming out tonight"—rapturous cheers!—"and this is a song about a siren."

More rapturous cheers. Winnie thinks she hears the twins shrieking loudest of all. Not that she's really listening to them. The music has started now, and it's so completely different from what Winnie was imagining.

Once, four and a half years ago—shortly before Dad had gotten caught as a Diana—Winnie and Erica had come to Joe Squared to hear a different Luminary perform: Jenna, Erica's half sister. She'd had a whispery voice that had sounded almost otherworldly atop her acoustic guitar. A lot like the siren L.A. is now singing about. Every tune had been soft, magical. Jenna had been really good, and she'd desperately wanted to leave Hemlock Falls. Go to music school, perform on a real stage like her non dad, whom she'd never really known.

But then she'd died during a hunter trial—a trial she hadn't even wanted to take—and that had been the end of her dreams. The end of her music.

Even now, Winnie sometimes wakes up with a hole in her chest and Jenna's voice whispering around her. The lyrics of her songs might be lost to time, but the ghost of the tunes never seems to fade.

Winnie wonders if Erica thinks of her every time she goes into Joe Squared. She wonders how Erica can stand to ever listen to music again.

The Forgotten sound nothing like Jenna and her lone guitar. They are heavy on beat, electric and pointed, the bass sustaining the bulk of the sound while L.A.'s voice flitters around it, tripping out a melody that's part pop, part dance, part . . . Winnie doesn't even know. It's different. It's alive. It's throbbing in a way that she has only felt once before, when she was alone in the forest after the mist had faded. When it was just her and the vast expanse of nightmares.

They're all hunters, Winnie realises, and without quite knowing what she's doing, she finds herself walking toward Joe Squared.

"Winnie." Mum rushes breathlessly out of the Revenant's Daughter, catching Winnie only a few steps away from the coffee shop door. "Hon, I'm so sorry it's taking me forever. Come wait inside the kitchen, where it's warm. I've still got this one table to wrap up, and then we can go."

"It's fine, Mum." Winnie tugs her arm free. She doesn't want to miss this song to conversation. It calls to her, just as an actual siren would. "I'll . . . I'll wait in there." She pops her chin toward Joe Squared.

And Mum nods absently, already hurrying into the kitchen once more. "Meet you back here in fifteen!" She vanishes into the steam.

Winnie tugs her hood low, pulls as much of her hair around her face as she can, and finally ducks into the coffee shop. The song is just ending, everyone's attention focused on the performers. People don't notice her slinking into a shadow beside the coffee bar.

Strings of light drape over the high-ceilinged space. The tables normally at the front of the shop have been replaced by a makeshift stage on which a single, crude spotlight gleams. People are clustered close to it, and only a few sit at the three remaining tables in the back. The owners, Jo and Joe, bustle about behind the counter. Jo is a former Tuesday hunter who had to have her leg amputated after a droll encounter. She moves easily about on a prosthetic, filling orders. She and Joe both pause to cheer along with everyone else when L.A. announces "Misty Nights," Trevor kicks off the beat with a drum machine at his foot, and Jay starts plucking away at his bass.

Winnie can't see Jay from her spot. There's a column draped in fairy lights that blocks him. She sees Trevor just fine, though, his foot hitting pedals to repeat different guitar parts while his fingers slide over the chords with ease. He's tall, taller even than Jay, with tawny brown skin that reflects to almost gold in this ethereal light and long dreads that bounce as his head bobs to the beat. Meanwhile L.A., whose dad moved here from the South Korean Luminaries, wears a rainbow baby dress and monster platform trainers, and she has even added star stickers to the apples of both her high cheekbones.

Jay, Winnie thinks, is definitely the boring one of the three. Even if she can't see him, she can imagine him in his standard uniform, his skin like old fireplace ash. His music, however, is anything but boring. Every piece of the song seems to centre around his bass line—around that thrum in your veins that only comes inside the forest. That *is* the very forest.

Winnie circles around the counter, sliding between two dancing girls she vaguely recognises from school and who she thinks are a couple. Actually, a lot of people are dancing—which again, is not what Winnie had expected for a band called the Forgotten. Or for a band Jay might be in.

She spots Emma and Bretta, dancing with Imran and Xavier. Then Winnie has cleared the counter's edge, and she can see behind the fairy light column too.

Jay wears a black flannel button-up and looks as he always does . . . yet completely different. His eyes are fastened on the stage floor, as if that's where the inspiration to play comes from, and his head moves to the beat. But where Trevor and L.A. are bouncing, dancing, Jay moves with a bare sway that seems to tremble up from the bass guitar. It is hypnotic to watch him.

Winnie suddenly understands what the twins mean about him being in his own head. She also suddenly understands why it's so appealing, and never has Winnie been more aware of how much Jay has changed in the last four years. The thirteen-year-old boy she used to love is well and truly gone. And the twelve-year-old girl that she used to be—the girl who had put whipped cream on his nose and spiders in his backpack—she's gone too.

Maybe it's the music, rattling inside her like a nightmare. Maybe it's Jay, undeniably gorgeous even as he tucks inside himself, a secret message that she used to know but now can't read at all—and could *never* draw . . . Or maybe it's the noise and the pain in her muscles and the fact that this time tomorrow night, she'll be back in the forest trying to stay alive. No matter the cause, she finds tears welling in her eyes and a banshee-sized grief ballooning behind her rib cage.

She shouldn't have come here. She should have stayed outside in the cold that smelled of french fries and burgers.

She swipes at her eyes, ready to flee for the back door, when Jay spots her. It's the first time he has broken his focus from the floor, and he snaps his eyes to her with a violent tension. Like his hunter senses have caught someone here who doesn't belong.

His grey gaze—shadowy in this light—latches on to her face. His lips part. His shoulders rise. He looks like he might attack at any moment, leaving the stage and coming for her with the full power of his hunter speed.

It should be terrifying, but it isn't. Instead, it's just embarrassing. Winnie doesn't think he can see the tears on her cheeks, but he has caught her sneaking in. Watching him like one of his countless fans.

So she does what any sensible person would do: she ducks away and runs.

CHAPTER
24

W innie doesn't sleep that night, though she tries. Her mind is too full, her muscles too sore, her skin too puffy and bruised. She might know how to fall properly, but her body has lost all the conditioning of actually being hit by another person.

This time, when the thoughts start rampaging, she forces herself to get up and try sketching. *Just a droll hand,* she tells herself. *Just a few bones, a few lines.* It has always calmed her before. She opens a pad, picks up a 0.5-tip black pen, and begins with a soft line for the thumb . . .

Her fingers shake. She loses the smooth curve almost instantly.

Worse, when she closes her eyes to try to imagine all the carpal bones near the thumb, she only sees the banshee instead. Green. Glimmering. *Devastating* in its hideousness and beauty. The air reeks of ancient blood. Winnie's eyes, inexplicably, start to burn.

No. She drops the pen. She can't do this. *No.* In seconds, she has crawled back into bed, burrowed deep beneath her sunflower covers.

Her desk light stays on the entire night.

———

Early the next morning, Winnie drags herself to the Sunday estate. Every pump of her legs on the family bike makes her want to cry a little. Classes are about the same: everything is a slog. She's too tired to even care when Erica stares at her in the hall or Marcus sits by her in Luminary history and brags about their blood relation. Or even when Coach Rosa makes her run the obstacle course, and specifically hop the tires *twice*. There is a pit of dread rumbling in Winnie's belly that she cannot evade. It bleeds wider with every hour that passes. Until the end of Sunday training finally comes, at noon, and she drags herself to the bike rack out front.

Where Jay is waiting.

He smells like weed. It pisses Winnie off immediately.

"Hey." He pushes off her bike, which he'd been leaning against all cool-as-you-please, as if he hadn't just skipped all of Sunday training to get high. "Thought you might want a ride."

"No," she lies, even as her muscles shriek, *Yes, you do!*

He frowns. "Okay. Well, do you not want to go to the forest? I need to show you where that safe spot is."

Winnie pushes him aside to reach her bike chain. He *really* stinks of weed, which, fine. If that's what he wants to do instead of school, fine. It's his choice. Whatever. "I don't have time to go to the forest," she says. "Can't you just tell me where it is?"

His frown deepens. "Sure. Though it won't take long, and I think it would be safest if you saw—"

"We're not allowed in the forest." She slings her chain off. It smacks against her forearm. *Ow.*

"Sure, but we went in yesterday." He dips his head to try to look at her. "Is something wrong?"

Yes, she wants to scream. *Everything is wrong.* But she doesn't. It would only lead to questions and questions and more questions. Instead, she skewers him with a glare. "You took me to a fringe spot yesterday. I assume this special spot of yours is in the heart of it all, right? Where a bazillion sensors might notice us?"

"Sure." He shrugs, the frown melting slightly. "But people go into the forest all the time. Mostly to party, but sometimes just to make out."

Winnie pauses, fingers grabbing for her handlebars, as an absolutely unwelcome image bubbles up in her mind. *Jay making out in the forest. Jay making out with* her *in the forest, that colour in his cheeks and intensity in his movements.*

Heat explodes onto her face. She wrenches her bike off the rack. The front tire hits the pavement with a rattly bounce.

"Well, I guess *you're* the expert on forest make-outs." Winnie can't believe such words have blurted from her mouth. She also can't believe that she is still imagining what it would be like to kiss him, surrounded by forest grey and the remnants of winter.

Jay laughs softly. "I do not go into the forest to make out, Winnie. There are better places for that."

She really thinks she might detonate. "I wouldn't know," she bites out, and then she starts wheeling the bike away from him, her stride long and borderline desperate.

Jay saunters easily alongside her. He looks amused, which only makes her angrier. "So if you don't have time to go to the forest, does that mean you also don't have time to train today?"

"No," she snaps before she can consider this. She squeezes her brakes and stops. They are at the edge of the parking lot, cars rumbling away. There go Emma and Bretta in Katie's Prius, waving frantically at Jay. Or, maybe they're just waving at Winnie, since they both seem to be grinning more at her than at him.

She waves in return. Smiles too, and something about that movement is like water hitting magma. She cools, solidifies. Then reassesses all she has just said.

"The next trial is tonight." She pulls off her glasses and rubs her eyes with the knuckles of her hand. "I have to go to the Wednesday estate before that to get some gear that actually fits."

"A good plan."

Winnie shoves the glasses back on. They are, of course, smudged now. "Tell me honestly, Jay—what's the point in practicing more? I don't know what I thought I could accomplish in three days, but now I realise *nothing* is what I could accomplish in three days. I'm so sore just the act of lifting my arm here"—she attempts to raise it over her head—"sends my body into power-down mode."

It really does. She wants a nap very badly.

"No, more training won't do much," he admits. A new sort of frown pinches his brow. He slides his hands into his jeans pockets, shoulders bunching high. "But I do think seeing where that safe spot is would be good. We can get there from the Friday estate, if you're really worried about the sensors. There are gaps over there."

"No." Winnie wags her head. If this spot is in the heart of the forest, it will take too long to reach from the Friday estate. And she really *is* short on time. "We'll go the main way. Can you pick me up in . . ." She grabs his wrist and lifts his old watch to read. The bandage from yesterday is gone, but a faint red line puckers out from under the ticking face.

He swallows.

"Two hours," Winnie says. That should give her plenty of time to visit the Wednesday estate. "At my house."

"You bet," he replies, and for half a minute, they just stand there, his wrist in her hand. Their eyes meeting in the cold.

She withdraws first, a new sort of heat gathering inside her, and he quickly turns away. His long legs carry him into the parking lot. No goodbye, just a hand scrubbing at his hair and a pace that could only be described as *purposeful*.

"Driving high is dangerous!" Winnie calls at him once he reaches Mathilda.

He glances back while he unlocks the door, a crooked twitch on his lips that almost seems to say, *You adorable little human. Is that why you're so mad?* Then he calls out, "It is indeed, and I would never!"

Soon he's gone, leaving Winnie all alone in the cold, waiting for a different ride she really hopes is coming.

Aunt Rachel does come. She's a few minutes late (clearly this runs in the family), but Winnie is too happy for the blasting heater in the Civic to complain. Plus, even with Rachel's apology from last night, Winnie is still terrified of her.

"I don't know where Marcus went," Winnie says, thrusting her fingers into the heater vents.

"Oh, he's with his dad on the weekends."

That's right; Winnie had forgotten: Rachel and Elijah Thursday got a divorce last year, and in the Luminaries, kids automatically go into the mother's clan—even though Rachel and Elijah technically have shared custody.

"I love Marcus," Rachel says, crossing over parking spaces with no concern for the lanes, "but fourteen." She flings Winnie a look that says, *Teen boys, am I right?*

Winnie obliges with a snort of commiseration even though she really has no idea what fourteen-year-old boys are like. When Darian was fourteen, she'd been only nine and *very* obsessed with convincing everyone that Pokémon had roots in the Luminaries.

She still stands by this theory.

Rachel drives like Winnie imagines she hunts: fast and with lots of rolling stops. She gets carsick at the various roundabouts, and it occurs to her that Rachel is so different from Mum. Mum would never speed; Rachel clearly forgets a speed limit even exists. And pedestrians? What are those?

When at last the Wednesday estate comes into view in the early-afternoon light, Winnie is wondering if she can just *walk* home after this. Hell, she'd take Jay's motorcycle over another trip in the navy Civic.

Rachel parks in a lot set off from the main house. It's mostly empty—and newly paved since the last time Winnie was here; the old potholes that always ate away the Volvo's front tires are now smooth as cake icing. Silver maples and black locust trees hug the lot, their leaves just starting to emerge, while the manicured rows of tulips show green shoots that will soon burst with purple and pink and red.

When Winnie and Aunt Rachel emerge from the lot's walking path and onto the main driveway, Winnie's breath catches as the full expanse of the brick estate appears before her. The tall windows and hedges are so perfectly square, you'd think a Thursday had trimmed them, and over the large double doors hangs the same black bear that waits in Winnie's bedroom.

If the Thursday estate is a modern-art museum, the Monday estate is a university campus, and the Friday estate is a haunted mansion, then the Wednesday estate is Pemberley from *Pride and Prejudice.* It used to be that coming here for clan dinner was the highlight of Winnie's week. Sitting in the massive dining hall with its wood beams arching high while course after course was served on gorgeous china with the Wednesday bear painted around the edges—it made Winnie feel like a character in a novel. The *hero* even, and until now she'd had no idea how much she'd truly missed it.

For the first time since Thursday night, she doesn't regret what happened. She doesn't care that she has been living a lie. She's just so happy to come home.

Even if no tears reach Winnie's eyes, Aunt Rachel seems to sense her emotions. She offers a closemouthed smile, the kind that's casually sympathetic. That says, *I get it, kid.*

Winnie appreciates it. She also appreciates when Rachel asks, "Want to go in through the front?"

It's not the most direct route to the hunters' area where gear would be kept. In fact, it's kind of out of the way, since they could just veer right at the forked path ahead and circle behind the house to the basement entrance. But she *does* want to go in the front. She *does* want to savor this moment after four years stuck outside.

She's glad no one is around. It's just her and Aunt Rachel to go up the white steps leading to the green double doors with the bear banner. It's just her and Aunt Rachel to step inside the yawning foyer with its enormous chandelier, the candles unlit at this time of day. The dark hardwood floors gleam beneath thick patterned rugs that stretch down the long hall before climbing the main stairs at the end. Mirrors mark the paneled walls, hanging over antique tables loaded down with busts of every Lead Hunter from the past fifty years.

Mum's bust is conspicuously no longer there, replaced instead by a marble version of Aunt Rachel.

Between the tables on the left are closed doors leading to the various archives and offices that fill the estate. On the right there are only two doors, both open, leading into the enormous dining room. The Wednesday clan is the largest in Hemlock Falls; they need lots of space.

Winnie can't resist poking her head into the dining room. It's empty now, but assuming all goes well tonight—or well enough—then on Wednesday night she and Mum and Darian will be back in there. Back at one of those long tables that each seats a hundred. Tall glass doors peer out over a closed garden just starting to awaken and welcome spring.

Aunt Rachel waits patiently while Winnie takes it all in, which Winnie again appreciates . . . but also kind of resents now. Because all of this is *weird*. Only three days ago, Rachel was rude, borderline hateful. Now she's a sympathizing, supportive kind of aunt. It's enough to give a gal whiplash.

A door opens into the main hall; Winnie jerks out of the dining room doorway. But the person—a second cousin named Arthur—doesn't look at her suspiciously as he strides down the hall with a stack of papers in one hand. Instead, he calls a greeting to Aunt Rachel and then grins Winnie's way. "Welcome back!" He disappears through a different door.

And that weird feeling rises higher inside of Winnie. She loves this even as it makes no sense. Have they all really just switched off how they felt about her and her family? Technically, they're still outcasts. Does killing a banshee really negate a ten-year sentence so easily? Sure, in all her fantasies, it had been exactly like this . . .

Except not really, her subconscious kindly reminds. *You didn't actually pass the trial, so all of this welcome is built on a lie.*

Winnie's teeth start clicking. She shoves at her glasses and motions for Rachel to continue leading the way.

Soon, they've reached the end of the hall, where the stairs rise and then split, aiming upward into more offices and, on the top floor, Fatima and her family's living quarters. Another set of stairs descends on the left. Voices drift up, along with the sounds of jogging feet, of fists against punching bags, of bow bolts thudding into targets.

Winnie's breath catches. She used to love this sound, and whenever Mum had visited the estate for clan business, Winnie had sat right here, at the top of the stairs, and dreamed of the day she'd get to go down.

She's never actually been allowed into the Armory, as they call it. Sure, she got to see it a few times as a kid, but remaining inside for more than a cursory glance is not allowed for anyone who isn't a hunter. Now, Rachel is beckoning for Winnie to descend like she's welcome. Like she can stay. Like she's a hunter who's already passed all three trials. Winnie hurries down the steps, barely able to keep pace with Rachel's leisurely stroll. She wants to run. She wants to see how much the massive gym-like space has changed.

Then she's there, facing it all: the track that circles the enormous room, looping behind the cinder-block wall lined with targets. There are the punching bags and the sparring ring. There are free weights and benches. There is an open space where three hunters are doing yoga.

It could not be more different from the decrepit Friday estate training grounds. The equipment here is all new, all gleaming and clean. Not a one of the fluorescent lights flickers with impending death, and there are even water coolers along a side wall with sprays of colourful fruit tucked inside.

Winnie thinks again about what her dad had said. But just because she knows that she might become a better hunter if she trains as the Fridays do . . . what normal human is going to say no to strawberry-flavoured water or punching targets that aren't dissolving in the rain?

Rachel leads Winnie to a door tucked into the wall behind the coolers. This leads into the actual Armory, a locker room space where all the hunter gear is stored. Winnie has never been inside before; she's pretty sure she's not supposed to go now, since there's a very clear sign that reads HUNTERS ONLY. But no one argues with the Lead Hunter—certainly not Winnie—and she follows after Rachel. The light dims to amber, revealing what could have been any rich country club locker room . . . were it not for the back wall of crossbows and compound bows, of machetes and sabers. Though hunters don't typically use guns—the noise only draws more nightmares—there are a few handguns and rifles too.

And Winnie's whole body is tingling. Her mum used to come here. Gran Winona used to come here—probably Great-Gran Maria too. Winnie can almost pretend the *incident* never happened, and this is just the natural course of things. She is a hunter; she has been invited here; and now she belongs.

"Let's get you outfitted," Rachel says, offering a sly grin.

"Yeah, okay." Winnie fights the urge to pinch herself. "Where do we start?"

"Well, it's called the Armory, so . . ." Rachel sidles over to a panel beside Winnie's shoulder. "How about armor?" She flips a switch, the wall gives off an electric hum, and before Winnie's eyes, a series of drawers along the bottom roll outward, revealing all sorts of leather and Kevlar and fleece and Lycra, each item in forest black. "A hunter needs good gear to survive a night in the forest. Take your pick."

"Anything?" Winnie's eyes bug out.

"Anything." Rachel's grin widens, and Winnie can't help but grin right back. Weird or not to have her aunt be so nice, this is *beyond* even Winnie's wildest dreams. She floats toward the drawers, soaking in all the options. They're so top-of-the-line, she's never seen anything like them. This isn't the gear Mum wore four years ago. This isn't a Kevlar vest with Velcro. These are the latest Tuesday family designs, each stamped with the Wednesday family bear on the chest.

"Might I suggest this one?" Rachel pulls out a black shirt that is so slinky, it doesn't hold its shape—but also so dark, Winnie can't seem to focus on it.

"Yes," Winnie breathes. *Gimme, gimme, gimme.* "I'll take it."

CHAPTER
25

J ay whistles as Winnie gets into Mathilda at two o'clock.
She knows she is smiling like a fool, but she can't
help it. Rachel let her have the "exo-scales," as they're
called, and they make her feel part Catwoman, part
nightmare. Composed of a thin, almost scalelike material,
they absorb all light and hug her like a second skin. She
usually hates tight clothes of any kind, but these aren't
restrictive or revealing. They are freeing.

"How do I look?" Winnie asks, yanking on the seat belt.

Jay pointedly ignores the question, instead saying, "That's
the newest tech. Most clans don't have access to it." Meaning
his clan doesn't have access. To his credit, he doesn't sound
bitter about that fact. He's just observing. Winnie almost
wishes she hadn't kept the exo-scales on after Rachel dropped
her off at home.

Almost. They also feel so amazing against her skin, she
thinks she might sleep in them.

Jay drives them through downtown, over the dam and
then north, past the Little Lake, past the Mondays and the
Tuesdays, and finally onto the dirt road Winnie takes every
Thursday morning for corpse duty. A sign at the mouth
declares, NO TRESPASSING.

Though spring sun may mark Hemlock Falls, the world here shifts to greyscale. Green slowly desaturates. Birdsong drips away. At a narrow fork in the road, Jay pulls right instead of the left that leads to the hunter meeting point—the spot where Winnie and the others will get dropped off tonight.

Somehow, that moment feels much too soon and also still so far away. This day has felt even more eternal than Thursday before the first trial. It's as if knowing what she's going to be up against has distorted the passage of time.

Mathilda heaves and yaws over terrain better navigated by Tuesday Hummers. "Are we going to the overlook?" Winnie asks, referring to a large wooden platform where you can watch the giant falls that are partly the source of Hemlock Falls' name.

"You'll see" is Jay's only reply until they reach the dirt road's end, where forest clusters close. It feels like the end of day here, though the Wagoneer clock only shows ten after two.

Jay cuts the engine and slings himself out. Like yesterday, he wears his black training clothes. He no longer smells of weed, but instead like his usual soap. He also doesn't look stoned (Winnie never would have gotten in the car with him if he did), and he doesn't move stoned. He is, once more, Jay of the forest, slowly sharpening around the edges as if her pen is filling him in.

Without a word, he sets off into the forest, using the trail that leads to the overlook. He only stays on the path for about twenty steps before ducking around a maple sapling and vanishing into the trees.

"Can we go slower?" she asks, hurrying after him. "I need to memorise this."

He lifts a hand. "Not yet. Just walk for now, Win."

So she does. This close to the Big Lake, the forest reigns with a dense grip of pines and hemlocks and oak. Undergrowth slips away, the canopy rises, and the roar of the falls saturates everything. Jay strides with his usual ease, and Winnie finds her sore muscles melting away with the movement. Training with Coach Rosa had made it all worse—every muscle fiber had screamed at her like that painting with the guy clutching his face in visceral horror.

Her muscles aren't screaming now, though. They're relaxing, softening, smiling at her, as if this new gear modeled on melusine scales also transfers some of the creatures' healing magic. *Or,* she thinks optimistically, *as if my muscles know it's time to hunt and they're ready for it.*

Jay leads her ever deeper into the forest, speaking only occasionally, to point out murderously low branches or roots lying in wait. The sound of the falls expands, until Winnie can hardly hear Jay when he points out a lurking hole in the ground. Fog gathers in the air, biting and wet and pure as only spindrift from running water can be. The ground rumbles beneath her feet.

Then they clear the forest, Jay first, Winnie second, and the waterfall right before them. They stand on a stretch of wet stone at the edge of the Big Lake, where the water escapes its rocky jailer and thunders a hundred feet below.

Winnie scoots to the stone edge of their little cliff and cranes her neck to peer down. Fifty feet below is the wooden overlook. Another fifty below that is the crashing falls' end, shrouded in spray.

"This is your spot?" Winnie has to lift her voice slightly to be heard.

He shakes his head. "No." Water beads on his cheeks, dampens his hair. "It's just a spot I thought you might like to see."

Winnie doesn't know how to answer that, so she pushes at her glasses—now speckled with water—and peers once more over the edge. It's a long way down. She's glad heights don't bother her.

Her teeth start clicking.

"You came," Jay says eventually. "Last night."

Winnie swallows and stares harder at the white-flecked water far below. She had really hoped this conversation wouldn't come up. After all, he hadn't looked particularly happy to see her.

"Just for a minute. I was waiting on Mum to get off work." She forces herself to look at him.

But he's staring over the waterfall too, giving her a close-up of his jaw misted with water and his cheeks daubed in pink.

Strangely, she thinks he has a very nice neck, the muscles long and defined where they stretch up from beneath his collar.

"You're good," she tells his profile. "The band, I mean." *And you too.*

He flushes slightly. His gaze darts to hers. "What songs did you hear?"

"Just the first two." She can't remember their names. But like the music Jenna used to make, she remembers the tunes. She remembers the way Jay's fingers flew across the bass, reverberating inside her.

"Okay," he says, and he seems to wilt ever so slightly, like he's relieved that's all Winnie had heard. Clearly he's glad she left early.

It makes her heart feel prickly.

"Come on." Jay twists away from the falls and heads back into the forest, leaving her to scamper after him. Though they move deeper into the trees again, she senses that they are circling the Big Lake. Every now and then, she glimpses dark water through the trees. Wide, long, still, and treacherous. She once had to lug a kelpie corpse out of the lake, and she'd felt something almost sentient in there. She knows the spirit that dwells in the forest technically resides under *everything,* but only in the lake does she truly feel like it's alive. As if even in daylight, it might start spewing out nightmares.

Fortunately, Jay doesn't lead her there. Instead, he cuts west until they reach a stream. Winnie doesn't hear it at all— the forest is too dense here, its grip too tight—until they are upon it. It's small, clearly fed by mostly rainfall, and Winnie realises with dawning horror, as Jay hops easily over the burbling waters, that *this* is the running water he referred to.

"That isn't going to stop a nightmare." She stares down at the little trickle of clear water that fills a ditch no more than three feet across. "This is walking water, at best."

Jay has the decency to look ashamed. "The stream gets bigger in the summer. But," he adds quickly before Winnie can commence a full freak-out, "it still stops most nightmares. The mist doesn't even rise on this patch of land." He leans across the ditch and offers her a hand.

She doesn't take it. The stream is literally *so small* that even with her sore muscles she easily jumps over. Her boots sink into soft soil and she stalks past Jay. A single hemlock owns this island—and it *is* an island. The stream splits about twenty steps to the left, encasing the earth in a pathetic trickle that looks like it might peter out at any moment. It then reconnects another twenty paces to the right.

"If you can get here before the mist rises," Jay says, "and climb that tree, you should be safe for the rest of the night. No nightmares will form here, and the moving water is enough to keep them from stepping over."

Winnie tears off her glasses, reaching for a sleeve to frantically clean them . . . only to then realise the scales on her armor aren't any good for that. Jay realises too, and in an easy shrug, he slips off his hoodie and offers it to her. She yanks it from him and starts scrubbing away.

She also starts pacing. "How far are we from the drop-off point?"

"Close to a mile?"

"Close to a mile *under*? Or close to a mile *over*?" She glares at him as she strides past. "Every second will count for me."

He winces. "Close to a mile over."

"Crap." She increases her pace, her glasses cleaned but her fingers unable to stop scrubbing. *I'm going to die,* she thinks. *What the hell was I thinking?* "So I have to run over a mile in the dark knowing that the mist will rise at any moment, so I can . . . can . . ." She stomps to the hemlock and squints up. Its lowest branches are well over her head. "So I can stand under a tree for an entire night?" Her voice is getting high-pitched with a mixture of panic and fury.

It's not fury at Jay—although he clearly thinks it is—but rather at herself. Because really: What the *hell* was she thinking? She might have real armor now and a satchel full of knives, but she still has no idea what she's doing when it comes to facing the forest.

I'm going to die.

Her breaths start coming in faster. Weaker. She is squeezing Jay's hoodie around her glasses, and she can feel the frames resisting. *I'm going to die. I'm going to die.* At some point, she bends forward, the needle-strewn floor wavering in close.

Jay drops to a kneel before her. "Hey." He wraps a gentle hand around her glasses-crushing fist. "We're going to practice, okay? We'll run from the drop-off point to here, and then I'll show you how to climb the tree. It's easier than it looks, and there's a branch sturdy enough to hold you all night." He pulls the hoodie and the glasses from her grip. For some reason, his eyes no longer look grey. Instead, they are the colour of the hemlock creaking behind him. Of the stream rollicking by. Of the falls' roaring crash when they hit the hard earth below.

"You're not as bad as you think you are, Win," he continues. "All those morning jogs over the dam made a difference." He tries for a smile, and even though Winnie knows he's pumping her full of hot, useless air, she finds herself surprised he'd ever noticed her out jogging.

"Don't coddle me, Jay." Her lungs are still weak and her body still doubled over. "I know how bad I am at this."

"No." His smile vanishes. His eyes turn back to grey. "I wouldn't lie to you."

She wishes she could believe him. Or rather, she wishes she could *agree* with him. She knows he'd never lie; the problem is that he seems to have a lot more faith in her than she does.

She straightens. The forest wavers beneath a head rush; Jay's face scopes upward to track her. He is slightly blurry without glasses to shape him; and he seems to melt into the forest, the colour of his eyes bleeding outward. "Thanks for helping me," she says softly.

Jay sucks in a breath, his chest expanding beneath his white T-shirt, and vaguely Winnie realises he must be freezing without his hoodie on. Then he rises to his feet like a knight who has just been anointed. The hoodie and her glasses dangle from his right hand. His left hand flexes and fists against his side.

Winnie has the odd sensation that he wants to touch her—but the odd sensation that he also wants to run away.

He does neither. He just stares at her with that grey intensity only he can have, and says, "You either trust the forest or you don't, Winnie. You have to make up your mind."

CHAPTER
26

The Sunday estate is lit up, much like the Thursday estate had been three nights before. This time, though, Winnie has a ride. Mum grips the steering wheel with ice-white knuckles. She has also said the same thing four times in a row: "If you think you're in real danger, call the hunters. I'd rather have a living daughter than *anything* else, okay? Do you promise?"

For the fourth time, Winnie promises. When they reach the front curb, where the same hunter hopefuls from Thursday cluster (minus Katie Tuesday, who apparently failed to catch anything last week), Winnie can see her mum forcibly resist the urge to get out and hug Winnie. Instead, she wishes her daughter good luck, asks her please not to die, and says she'll be here waiting at dawn. Then she drives away.

Other parents have gone inside the Sunday estate to ride out the night like it's a sporting event and their kids aren't potentially going to die. Mum is going to spend it with Darian.

"Oh my god," Emma says, skipping over to Winnie with her dimples on full display in her cheeks. "You've got the new exo-scales." She pinches at Winnie's sleeve. "Hey, Bretta!

Come feel this. We have last year's exo-frame"—she knocks a hand against the hard casing on her chest—"which is great. But yours . . ."

"Ooooh," Bretta croons, grabbing at a separate fistful of Winnie's shirt. "How did you get this?"

While Winnie explains (and hopes she doesn't get Aunt Rachel in trouble in the process), the final two hunter hopefuls arrive and everyone heads for the black SUVs. Winnie doesn't see Aunt Rachel anywhere, so she climbs into the jeep Coach Rosa is driving. The Sunday teacher looks completely transformed in her hunter gear, fitted armor similar to Winnie's, except much cooler-looking on her athletic frame. She punches Winnie on the shoulder as Winnie grabs for the back door handle. "Hope you're ready for this!"

Me too, Winnie thinks, stomach sinking. The twins scramble in with her, forcing her into the middle seat, while Fatima takes the front.

"So," Bretta begins as she slings the door shut. "It's official, Winnie: we're having a party for our birthday."

Right. Winnie cringes internally. She'd forgotten all about that. She *really* needs to get them a present. What a great friend she is.

"You *have* to come." Emma loops her arm into Winnie's as if they're the best of friends . . . and Winnie has to admit she appreciates the touch. Unlike the rest of Hemlock Falls, Emma and Bretta have been nice to her ever since they moved here. And now that she knows what fake nice feels like, she can actually appreciate the real kind.

"And get this, Winnie: we've convinced the Forgotten to play." Bretta utters this with such breathy joy, it feels more like they're at a slumber party and not in the back seat of an SUV while Coach Rosa drives them all toward their potential dooms.

"You really should have heard them play last night," Emma inserts. "They were even better than usual."

Fatima sighs from the front seat and twists around. "Trevor was so good."

"And Jay," the twins chime—followed by their obligatory giggle for speaking in unison.

Coach Rosa glances at Winnie in the rearview and then visibly bites back a smile as her eyes meet Winnie's. *Yes, Winnie wants to say to her. I too find this conversation weird given that we are driving toward death.* Except, as the twins tell Winnie where the party will be (in the Wednesday gardens after clan dinner) and describe that it's a *fancy* party ("But really, you can wear whatever you want, Winnie—as long as it's *not* your Save the Whales hoodie") that will be outside with heaters and a net of lights they put together themselves ("Fatima is just brilliant with design ideas"), the drive to the forest blurs past. Winnie doesn't have time to let the leeches gathering in her stomach engorge. Bretta talks too quickly, Emma and Fatima chirping in every few minutes too, and it's all Winnie can do to just keep up with the collective outpouring of words.

It's actually the perfect distraction.

When at last they reach the sign that declares NO TRESPASSING, the SUV crests the shift from smooth pavement to dirt road much more gently than Mathilda had. The twins are still talking, and it doesn't escape Winnie's notice that Emma's grip on her arm has grown tighter and tighter with each bump in the road.

Rosa cuts the engine at the spot where Winnie parks every Thursday morning on corpse duty. The twins go silent. Fatima audibly swallows. Everyone sits there, stewing in the tautness of the moment. The forest looms, stark and forbidding in the jeep's headlights. The trees look like bars on a jail cell.

Rosa moves first, kicking out of the jeep and jolting everyone else to follow. The night is cold. Winnie's breath plumes. She hugs her arms to her chest and kind of wishes Emma still held on.

The twins are latched to each other now, nary a dimple in sight.

Another jeep that was already parked and waiting opens, spitting out Aunt Rachel along with the Tuesday, Monday, and Thursday Lead Hunters. Rachel gives Winnie a nod, once more wearing the hard angles of her hunter persona. This is the Aunt Rachel Winnie is used to, minus the open hostility.

"Just a reminder of the rules," she says. "No leaving the forest, and no working together. Only knives, traps, and stun grenades allowed. Break any of those rules, and you're immediately disqualified. That said—" Her eyes flicker to Winnie as she withdraws a stack of small pager-like devices from her vest pocket, each looped on a lanyard. "—we'd rather all of you live than die trying. Not everyone becomes a hunter, and there's no shame in that. So if you find yourself up against something you can't fight, just pull the alarm off the lanyard like so." She demonstrates detaching the alarm, and Winnie spots a metal pin that will withdraw from the main box. "Then all the nearby hunters will come for you. And we've got extra hunters out there tonight."

Again, her eyes flash to Winnie, and Winnie feels a shamed sort of heat rise in her. Aunt Rachel thinks she's going to fail. For all that she's been nice to her and given her this fancy new gear, she doesn't think Winnie will last the night.

But Winnie was sure then and she's sure now. She has Jay's secret spot, and she will reach it before the mist rises. She is going to be a hunter. She's going to keep passing these trials until her family are no longer outcasts.

More SUVs open, and after handing Winnie her lanyard alarm and then squeezing her biceps in a way that might have been reassuring, Rachel moves on.

Which leaves Winnie and Fatima and the twins just standing there. Winnie looks at Coach Rosa. "Can we—"

She doesn't have to finish before Rosa flings a hand at the trees. "Go, girls. And fast. The mist will be rising soon."

Do not sprint. It was the first thing Jay had told Winnie seven hours ago. *There is too much risk for injury, sprinting in the woods in the dark. You'll want to sprint, but don't.*

Winnie almost laughs at that advice now. She can no more sprint than she can run backward. Just a slow jog is proving harder than she'd thought it would be. The terrain is impossible to see. No moonlight, no starlight, only clouds. Every step is taking her so much longer than it did with Jay. They'd even practiced once with her going all alone, but she'd had no idea how much *illumination* contributed to speed.

She tries not to freak out. She can only move so fast, and forward is all that matters. She has her new machete sheathed at her hip and a hunting knife strapped to her thigh, and in a small pack on her back are four shrapnel traps and three stun grenades. A fourth grenade hangs on her belt. No clunky poison-mist traps tonight.

You'll leave the parking lot between the oak that's lost its branch and those two maple saplings. Then go for a hundred paces until you see an aspen stand.

Winnie doesn't see the aspen stand. She has been a hundred paces, and she doesn't see it. There is only darkness and shadow and more darkness—and branches that keep clawing at her like banshee hands.

For the first fifty steps, she'd also heard Emma and Bretta charging into the trees. But now that she's a hundred steps . . . past a hundred steps . . . closing in on a hundred twenty-five, she doesn't hear anything but her own plodding footsteps.

Sprinting. *Sprinting.* As if.

Then she glimpses two silver maples that have fused into one. *Crap.* She missed the aspens entirely and now she has already reached step two. This is good because she's deeper into the forest than she'd thought—and also bad because it means she is already completely turned around on her directions.

"Go slowly," she tells herself, reaching a hickory tree. "Think it through." For some reason, though, instead of *going slowly* or *thinking it through,* her brain just spits out the Nightmare Compendium.

Basilisks: Though seemingly small, no wider than a cobra, the basilisk can, in fact, stretch up to forty feet long. Fine, hairlike tendrils alert it to nearby movement of prey, and the head can move with uncanny speed once prey is detected.

Revenants: Corpses left in the forest or buried too close to the forest will reawaken, imbued by spiritual energy and hungry for blood.

The Compendium and all its nightmares are exactly what Winnie doesn't need right now. "Trust the forest," she hisses at herself. "Jay told you to trust the forest." She puts her hand on the fused maples, the bark grooved under her gloved palm. "Look left, and you'll see a clearing in the trees. Cross it."

Winnie does exactly that, left at the maples. Cross the clearing. Two hundred and twelve steps onward, then it's left at the fallen pine and another hundred to the little spring that forms the first hint of her special stream.

Winnie is so relieved to see it in the dark, a glittery, burbling thing that makes a small puddle at the top of an incline, she doesn't notice right away that the noises around her have shifted. She's breathing hard already. Her new boots are giving her a blister.

Do not sprint, do not sprint.

She realises too late that she should have sprinted, for the mist has begun to rise.

It's like it was a few days ago, white and thick and hungry, yet it moves more quickly this time, since she's nearer to the forest's heart. The entire world smears away before Winnie's eyes, the warmth of the mist undulating over her. Erasing her legs, then her arms, then her neck and nose. Any second now, it will turn to scalding.

She can't breathe. She can't see, and she certainly can't move—but she needs to. She knows she needs to. The Compendium tells her she needs to keep moving.

Do not sprint, do not sprint.

The hunter must keep moving. The hunter must keep moving.

Which is it? Which is Jay's voice, which is the Compendium, which is her own? She can't breathe, she can't think. Everything sears. She is boiling from the inside out and the outside in.

Left at the maples. Cross clearing. One hundred paces to an aspen stand. Left at the maples. Two hundred and twelve . . .

No, no. She's getting everything out of order—and the Compendium just won't shut up.

Melusine: These beautiful, mermaid-like creatures inhabit the rivers and lakes of the forest. They are not aggressive but will attack if humans get near.

Winnie tries to stumble forward. She makes it three steps before her hands hit a tree trunk. Even with gloves, it scalds.

Two maple saplings growing leaves. Cross the clearing.

Banshees: Known for weeping and wailing, they lure prey to them via the natural human instinct for empathy.

Winnie tries to inch around the tree, even though each pat against its trunk is like touching a hot burner on the stove. Or it starts out that way, but when she has moved maybe halfway around the trunk—or maybe all the way around it twice, for all she knows—she realises it doesn't burn quite so badly. And soon, she can see her arms. Then her hands. Then the tree bark (it looks like oak).

She is so relieved for half a moment that it doesn't occur to her what the vanishing mist might mean—what it heralds. She is just desperately grateful to breathe again.

It is right when Winnie is going to turn away from the oak, right as her head swivels and her muscles coil inward for movement, that she hears it: a soft, skittering sound like mandibles nearby. It's coming from her left.

No, from her right. No, from behind her . . . from beyond the tree . . . from her left and her right because, oh god, she is completely and utterly surrounded.

The mist has created an entire horde of vampira, and Winnie is smack-dab in the middle of them.

CHAPTER
27

*V*ampira: *Also called the praying mantis of the forest, these tall creatures move on stilt-like feet that rest atop the soil, leaving no tracks. They move in hordes, but when tracking prey, they do not move at all.*

They have what appear to be mandibles, but are in fact side-hinging jaws and fangs. To startle a vampira is to startle the entire horde.

Additional tips: Always aim for their knees. A well-placed blade can destabilise them, preventing pursuit.

Winnie does not move. It's only a matter of seconds before the vampira smell her in their midst, but if the exo-scales are as good as Aunt Rachel said, then she should have a few extra seconds before they sniff her out.

She is very careful to breathe through her nose. And she is very careful not to move. The alarm lanyard hangs temptingly around her neck, but even if she could pull it, it would take too long for the hunters to get here. She is on her own for this, and surprise is the only real weapon she has.

She inhales. The faint dregs of a fading mist warm her nostrils. The vampira are still rattling away with their fangs, and she hears a few moving—audible only because they think they are alone and stealth is not their priority. Trees rustle. Two vampira snarl at each other.

Vampira hordes can range anywhere from ten members to over one hundred. Winnie thinks this horde is on the smaller end. *They move with sophisticated coordination and speed, following the lead of a bellwether. To eliminate the bellwether is to slow the horde.*

There is no way for Winnie to sense which one is the bellwether, and her time is almost up. She needs to move, she needs to *move*.

Winnie moves. She shoves away from the tree, unsheathing her machete. It's not graceful, it's not quick, but she gets the blade out before the vampira can fully process that she is there.

And oh god, it's more than ten. There are least twenty directly between her and the burbling stream. They look like long shadows, like crooked saplings in the darkness.

So she doesn't aim for the stream. Instead, she bolts right, where the clattering of fangs is not so thick. There are still two vampira in her way, though.

She hacks at the first—aiming right for the knee like the Compendium said. And it's as if the forest knows what she's about to do. Like it has decided right then and there that if *this* is to be her course of action, then she should really see what she's up against.

Trust me? it asks. *Do you really dare?*

The clouds part. A burst of moonlight flares down, illuminating the vampira in perfect, horrific detail—and now is one of those moments where time actually seems to slow. The creature is both exactly like the diagram in the Compendium, and exactly like her copied sketch of one . . .

And also nothing like it. There are its pointed, needlelike feet that pierce the soil without leaving a mark. There are its long, stilt-like legs covered in a rough silvery skin that could easily be mistaken for bark in the shadows.

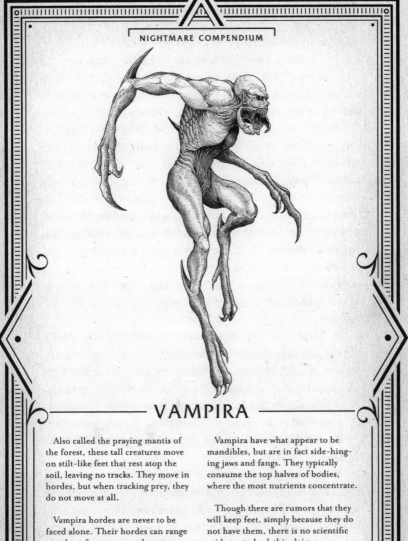

VAMPIRA

Also called the praying mantis of the forest, these tall creatures move on stilt-like feet that rest atop the soil, leaving no tracks. They move in hordes, but when tracking prey, they do not move at all.

Vampira hordes are never to be faced alone. Their hordes can range anywhere from ten members to over a hundred, and they move with sophisticated coordination and speed, following the lead of a bellwether. To eliminate the bellwether is to temporarily slow the horde. However, to startle a vampira is to startle the entire horde.

Vampira have what appear to be mandibles, but are in fact side-hinging jaws and fangs. They typically consume the top halves of bodies, where the most nutrients concentrate.

Though there are rumors that they will keep feet, simply because they do not have them, there is no scientific evidence to back this claim.

Additional tips: always aim for their knees. A well-placed blade can destabilize them, preventing pursuit.

Note: Though not their typical method of hunting, there are records of vampira climbing trees in pursuit of prey.

There is its shrunken torso and its two-jointed arms. There are its bladelike hands with spines along the edges.

And there is its head, hairless and long with a jaw that hinges sideways. Its fangs gleam in the light, three on each side of its mouth, each as long as Winnie's fingers.

There's no time to be afraid of that mouth. No time for anything, because the clock is surging forward again and the vampira's blade arms are rearing back for a slicing attack.

But Winnie has already started her own attack—she can't stop it now even if she wants to. The machete slices into the vampira's knee. It doesn't go through like the Compendium described. She doesn't hit the joint at the right spot or with the proper angle, but the steel still beats against bone. The nightmare still screams.

Winnie yanks back the blade. The vampira falls, and Winnie starts running again. *Sprinting* exactly like Jay told her not to do.

A second vampira lunges. Winnie rolls sideways. Badly, but enough to dodge the monster. And somehow, out of sheer luck, it impales itself on her blade. The machete spikes into its torso, between the bilateral ribs that float like a human's. Then into a heart that Winnie knows beats within. It screams. Winnie releases the blade. It collapses and she keeps running.

No machete now, but not defenceless—because she has an idea.

The forest thrashes behind her as she kicks her knees high. The clouds have graciously remained parted, so she can see the roots to avoid and rocks to leap over. Amazing how she ever thought the forest was dark. There is so much light here it feels like day.

She grabs for the stun grenade on her belt. Assuming every vampira is following her—a safe assumption—she can stun maybe half of them. But she won't have time to see where they are. She's going to have to throw and hope for the best.

Which is exactly what she does. She yanks out the pin, just like Rachel showed her (god, was that only nine hours ago?), and runs left to where the stream is. She prays everything Jay told her is accurate.

Winnie throws the grenade behind her. Three steps become five become—

Crack. The grenade goes off in a burst of light that Winnie was waiting for. She covers her eyes just in time.

The vampira scream. A collective sound that starts with one throat in particular: one that's right behind Winnie. *The bellwether.* She glances back, following the shredding cries of its inhuman throat until she finds it, no different from all the rest except that somehow it's the one in charge.

Winnie reaches the stream and leaps over. The waters are even sadder than she remembers, and already the clouds are returning above. Blanketing the forest in the shadows it so loves.

Winnie sprints onward. Not for long—Jay's advice still rings in her mind, and already she has almost tripped twice— but long enough to put some distance between her and the still-howling vampira.

The vampira don't follow. She doesn't know if it's because of the grenade or the stream, but for now, they don't follow. She slows to a jog. Then a panting walk because she's making too much noise and that grenade will draw new nightmares. But this time as she moves, she withdraws a shrapnel trap from her backpack. She will be ready for whatever comes next.

When she spots the hemlock, a black tower against the sky, Winnie finds herself almost disappointed. While facing the horde, she felt like the bass line in a Forgotten song. She was awake, euphoric, alive. Part of her wants more of that—to take on the nightmares again, hacking through knees and viscera.

Gone is Winnie's guilt over the banshee lie. As she climbs the hemlock, finding the iron spikes Jay put in—spaced in such a way as to be almost invisible—she can't stop thinking how this is where she is meant to be.

She belongs in the forest. She belongs as a Luminary. She belongs as a hunter.

And Jay was right: Winnie isn't as bad as she thinks she is. Hell, she might even be *good*.

She spiders up the trunk, lacking Jay's grace or strength, but the handholds are close enough together that she doesn't have trouble reaching the first branch. Then the second, and finally the third—the one Jay-showed her that could hold her all night.

It's not wide, but she's able to hang her backpack on a separate branch and then wedge herself up against the trunk, one boot on this branch, one boot on a lower one for stability. She shouldn't fall asleep like this, but she also won't topple to her doom if she accidentally nods off.

Of course, the thought of sleep feels impossible right now. She, Winnie Wednesday, just impaled a vampira—after hamstringing another. Then she outran the rest of them. An entire freaking horde. She wishes someone could have been there to see it. Mum or Aunt Rachel or ever doubting Ms. Morgan.

Winnie faced down vampira and she didn't pull the alarm for backup. The rest of the night is going to be absolutely peaceful compared to that.

Still, just in case, she keeps that shrapnel trap on her lap and her right hand on the hunting knife. So far, Jay's rule about the running water seems to be holding true, but there are stronger things out there than vampira.

There are banshees. There is a werewolf.

There is the Whisperer.

Winnie does doze off. A few times, actually. The ankle she'd thought was healed now aches. It's boring in the tree, and she wishes she'd brought night-vision goggles or even binoculars. She hears creatures go by, sometimes with footfalls heavy enough to rattle branches. Sometimes with a softer, slithery sound. And sometimes the faint clacking sound that she thinks is the vampira searching for her.

She sees hunters go by too, and one girl she thinks might be Fatima, since she remembers a spiderweb pattern on her hijab. She hears a wolf howl far, far away. She strangely hopes no hunter finds it tonight, because what if it's *not* a werewolf at all, but just a lost animal caught in an unrelenting forest like she is caught in this tree?

Winnie is about to nod off a third time when a light trickles into her eyes. Instantly, she is wide awake. Instantly, she cranes her neck toward the pallid glow. It comes from across the stream, hazy at first, like the mist rising. She squints . . .

And then gasps.

It is a ghost-deer—a ghost-*doe* actually, with two ghost-fawns beside her.

Ghost-deer, ghost-squirrel, ghost-raccoon, etc.: These ghostly apparitions pose no threat to humans, and will typically flee when hunters or nightmares appear. Much dispute remains around their origins: Are they creations of the dreaming spirits? Or are they phantoms of animals that inhabited the woods prior to the spirits' arrival? In the forests surrounding the Earth's oldest spirits, there are apparitions of primitive creatures long since lost to time.

Though they leave tracks, no known hunter has managed to capture a ghost-creature. Weapons do not pierce them.

Winnie is captivated by the doe and her fawns. They are young, as if born just this season, and tottering on legs that don't quite work. And they look to be grazing on undergrowth just as real deer would do.

Winnie doesn't move as she watches them, even though her left leg is going numb from being elevated too long and her neck is getting a crick from craning. She *dares* not move, for no matter how cautious she is to make no sound, the ghost-deer will hear. The ghost-deer will know, and they will flee.

She doesn't want them to ever leave. If she thought the vampira brought her to life, sharpening the lines of the world and connecting her mind to her muscles in a harmony she'd never known before, then the ghost-deer do the opposite. They smooth down her roughness, stretching her mind outward, weaving her into the world in a way that's wholly new.

Except with the banshee, she thinks, watching the doe nose at the smaller of the two fawns. When Winnie had felt those banshee tears, she'd felt the same sense of beautiful calm she feels now—the same tragic certainty that life can't last forever.

You either trust the forest or you don't, Winnie.

For the first time since her failed trial, since her failed encounter with the forest and its nightmares, Winnie's fingers itch to draw again—even if she knows she can never, *ever* capture these deer. They are more alive than Jay in the forest, and far less tangible. A pen's line would only define something that shouldn't be.

Yet she wants to try all the same. How else can she make this moment last forever?

Eventually, the ghost-deer move on, the fawns frolicking off toward the lake in a way that only fawns can do. Mama trails behind.

Winnie's heart sinks. Her eyelids too.

She falls asleep.

CHAPTER
28

Winnie jolts awake to the sound of clattering mandibles. *Vampira,* her brain provides, heart ramping into overdrive. She readies the trap, fingers moving without her mind to guide them—and later, she will think that she isn't sure where that muscle memory came from. But right now, in the moment, she squints through glasses that have slid down her nose.

The vampira are definitely here. Though cloud cover still blurs the forest shapes into undefined brushstrokes, she senses a weight straight ahead that didn't used to be there. It's where the ghost-deer were; now it's where the vampira wait.

They know I'm in the tree, she thinks at the same time the Compendium unrolls in her mind. *Though it is not their typical method of hunting, there are records of vampira climbing.*

Winnie's teeth want to start clicking, but she shoves her tongue between them. Jay's stream is really going to be tested now. How badly do the vampira want her? What will they do to cross?

Why running water deters land nightmares is something that has been debated for as long as the Luminaries have existed. Back when the Dianas were still a part of the society. Back when there were only three spirits instead of fourteen. Some speculate it has nothing to do with the actual movement of the water (after all, some nightmares live in slow-moving oxbows) but rather the purity of it. Others speculate it's the direction of the flow (east-moving water does seem more effective). And then some say running water does nothing; it's just that the terrestrial nightmares don't like to get wet.

Until tonight, Winnie has always leaned toward the purity theory. Now that she's seen a ghost-deer with her own eyes, though, she's not so sure. Those nightmares were more pure than she knew a creature could be—so much so that even the word "nightmare" seems all wrong for them.

The longer Winnie stares, the more movement her eyes detect. It's like molasses sliding down a mixing bowl—if molasses could click. A hundred little clicks from fangs tapping together. The sounds bounce off trees, making it impossible to tell where exactly the vampira are.

And in that scientist corner of her mind, Winnie thinks, *It's intentional, it's focused.* Yet she has never read of such behavior in the Compendium.

The molasses is nearing the stream's edge. The clicking is slightly closer. One stalk-like shape hovers at the stream's edge. *The bellwether,* Winnie thinks, right as she also thinks, *It's going to cross.* It certainly has the legs for it, and sure enough, Winnie watches as it lifts one spindly limb and stretches it forward like a grotesque dancer.

The clouds briefly thin. Its bald head gleams. Its legs straddle the stream.

Winnie doesn't know what to do. She can't climb down and flee, since she has to assume she's surrounded. She can't toss the trap, because she can't risk wasting it on a single vampira—and she can't see where the rest of the horde is.

The bellwether gives a strangled snarl, as if the water pains it. Winnie thinks she hears a sound like bacon in a pan, but that might also just be the sudden wind now rustling through the trees. Once the bellwether finishes crossing, the others will follow. It is showing them that although slow and painful, it *can* be done.

Winnie's going to have to pull her alarm. It's the only option. And though she's terrified to move, to risk making any noise at all on the off-off-off-*off* chance these vampira don't actually know she's here, she really doesn't have a choice.

If you think you're in real danger, call the hunters. I'd rather have a living daughter than anything *else, okay?*

Winnie finds she is praying to the spirit in the forest. To a god she doesn't believe in. To anything at all that might help her get out of here.

The bellwether finishes crossing, its back leg slipping over the stream. After a stumble, it catches itself with its long, two-elbowed arms. Then it straightens, face aiming toward Winnie. She can see it clearly now, even though the clouds are scudding back across the sky.

Its sideways jaw opens. Its fangs jut outward. It launches for Winnie's tree.

Winnie has no chance to pull the lanyard. She tries, yanking it immediately while her left thumb smashes the shrapnel trap into action. But the alarm gets stuck, and now the bellwether is at the hemlock. She drops the trap, abandons the alarm, and launches herself up the tree. She doesn't know what she'll do when she runs out of branches, but this is her only chance. *Climb, climb, climb.*

The trap fires below. Shrapnel sprays. The bellwether screams, a serrated sound that carves at Winnie's bowels.

She keeps climbing. Her backpack is below her. All she has is her hunting knife—and the lanyard, still hanging. *Climb, climb, climb.* She will try the alarm again when she runs out of branches. She will pray no other vampira start climbing.

The trunk shakes. The sound of clicking fangs rattles over her. At least one more vampira has reached the tree.

She grabs for a branch; it snaps beneath her. *Climb, climb, climb.* She grabs for another; it bows but holds.

It's also the last; there are no more wide enough to clamber onto, and this one is already bending dangerously. Shaking in time to a vampira's spiked hands and feet as it stabs into the tree. Icy wind rushes against her over the forest.

Winnie grabs for the alarm again. She readies her muscles to yank.

And that is when she hears it: the sound like frying bacon, but louder. It's carried on the wind, a growing static that makes every cell inside her glacierise.

The Whisperer.

She snaps her gaze into the forest. A purple light is staking its claim on the eastern horizon. Sunrise will come soon; the mist will come soon.

The tree stops rattling, and a cry goes up from the vampira. A yapping, chirping sound that reminds Winnie of the sonar dolphins use. Then Winnie spots a disturbance in the textured surface of the forest, as if the patches in a quilt are being stretched apart at the seams. The pines and oaks don't move in a physical sense, but rather the *idea* of them shifts, as if they can't quite decide how they want Winnie to see them.

As a kid, she'd had a pair of binoculars, and she'd liked to look through the main lenses to magnify . . . and then switch the binoculars around, shrinking the world down to thumbnails. That is what it feels like she is doing now: flipping the binoculars back and forth while that whispery charge in the air scratches louder.

The vampira are fleeing, though three are stuck over the stream, legs split and throats shrieking. The water has them trapped; they cannot move fast enough to evade what they know is coming.

Pull the alarm, Winnie's heart says. *Badoom, badoom, pull the, badoom, alarm.* She is going to die because the Whisperer will kill her. She will be one more shredded casualty in the forest. *Pull the alarm.*

Yet even as her heart thunders at her, her mind knows that if she calls any hunters, they will die exactly like that halfer without the feet. Like the banshee without the head. Like *she* is about to.

But maybe Mario was right, she thinks. *Maybe this nightmare can die like all the rest of them can.* The hunters have bows and rifles; she doesn't. They have skill and speed; she doesn't.

Winnie pulls the alarm.

Nothing happens on her end. It's anticlimactic, and for all she knows, it didn't work. She just has to pray while she watches the Whisperer approach from below.

It reaches the vampira horde—those not trapped on the stream—and screams tear upward into the brightening sky. It's like the sound of Winnie's blender at home, with its engine half dead and the blades too dull for much blending beyond a chunky smoothie: there is a crunching, ripping sound as vampira are torn to bits—and a high-pitched, machinelike keen as their cries reach a deadly pitch.

The forest swells and quakes.

Winnie closes her eyes. The hunters can't fight that. She has just summoned them to their deaths; Mario was wrong.

The vampira trying to cross the stream are squealing now. They know slaughter is coming, and Winnie doesn't want to watch it, but she knows she has to. It is her own death coming too; she wonders if it will hurt.

The keen of the horde snaps off. The Whisperer moves this way, its rasping voice scuttling over Winnie's skin. She doesn't want to die this way. She doesn't want to die at all.

The branch she is on creaks and bends. It is going to snap, and she has no choice but to turn in to the tree and hold tight. It is much too wide for her to get her arms around. She has no real grip. The Whisperer is almost here.

She twists her head to watch it approach, everything else in the world falling away. She almost thinks she can sense footfalls in the undulation of the forest. A rhythm, a beat, steady and inescapable.

The closest vampira finally gets its second leg over the stream. It tries to flee, but it only manages three skittering steps before a tentacle grabs it.

Winnie can't find another word to describe what she sees: the warping forest snakes out with a tendril made of galaxies, pierces into the vampira's back, and then retracts—carrying the nightmare with it like meat on a spit.

The vampira reaches the bulbous, bilious heart of the Whisperer. It screams. It crunches. Then it's gone, and Winnie can't see it anymore.

The second vampira screeches. It is still trapped on the stream. Yet for some reason, the Whisperer isn't going for it.

Then Winnie spots a flashlight beam piercing the forest. *No,* she wants to scream at the hunters. *Turn back, turn back.* But she can't make words form in her throat. All she can do is cling with aching muscles to a tree that will never withstand the Whisperer. She is no hunter, no Luminary. She is a murderer, luring these hunters to their doom.

Except the Whisperer doesn't seem interested in the hunters. In fact, as Winnie cranes her neck as far as it will go so she can watch its writhing form, she spots the first wisps of a white fog rising.

The mist.

Morning has come to the forest.

The thick fog coils upward from the forest floor, first encasing the vampira—which still screams, still strains to move across the stream. Then it moves over the trees, and over the Whisperer too.

At some point, as Winnie watches the mist saturate and blot out the forest, as it climbs over her, choking and scalding and relentless, tears start to fall.

She will live. The hunters will live.

Except that when the mist finally subsides—the sun a sharp wink on the horizon—she realises there is still a bulbous, bilious shape wandering through the trees. Smaller, yes, but undeterred by the mist.

It prowls despite the day, and soon vanishes from sight.

Aunt Rachel and Coach Rosa find Winnie just climbing down from the hemlock. They all converge on the vampira corpse, shredded by Winnie's trap.

"*Meu Deus*," Rosa says, eyes leaping to Winnie, who approaches on legs that might collapse at any moment. "You destroyed these nightmares." She motions toward the trees. "I don't know how you did it with just a few traps, but . . ."

And Winnie realises with a sickening lurch that they think, yet again, she is responsible for the Whisperer's kill. This time, though, she can't lie about it.

"It . . . wasn't me." Her voice cracks. She thinks she might still be crying. Her chest definitely feels like it. "It was . . . something else. Something that's still out there." She stumbles toward Rachel, who quickly loops an arm behind her. "It's still out there, Aunt Rachel. We need to warn the hunters. And the Tuesdays. The mist didn't erase it—"

"Slow down." Rachel passes a look to Rosa. "Slow down. You're safe now. Whatever it was, it's gone."

"But it's *not*. That's what I'm trying to say."

"Winnie, living nightmares disappear with the mist—"

"Not this one." Why aren't they listening to her? Why are they looking at each other like they're worried she's lost her marbles? "I pulled the alarm because there was a whole horde of vampira here. But then this . . . this Whisperer came—"

"A what?" Rosa asks.

"A Whisperer. I don't know its real name because it's not in the Compendium. But it's all . . . *whispery*. And it just decimated the horde. I killed one vampira, sure, and another, but not the whole horde!"

"Get the emergency blanket," Rachel tells Rosa.

"I don't need an emergency blanket." Winnie tries to pull free. But Rachel is strong, and neither she nor Rosa is listening.

"Also radio in for the four-wheeler. She looks okay"— Rachel gives Winnie a hard once-over—"but I don't think she should be moving too much. Look, kid, you passed the trial, okay? You made it the whole night, and now we're going to get you to civilization."

"Why aren't you listening to me?" Winnie asks. Rosa is now muttering into a small wrist radio, and Rachel is just talking right over her. "I know what I saw, Aunt Rachel. It's like . . . like a supernova made of shotguns, and we need to get the Tuesdays in here right away. And the Council! They need to know."

Rachel tugs Winnie toward the stream; Rosa urges her on from the other side. And for what feels like an eternity of Winnie *begging* them to listen, they just haul her onward until three four-wheelers arrive. Until Winnie is shoved onto one with some Sunday hunter she doesn't recognise, and there's nothing she can do but hold on until they reach the dirt road again.

This is worse than having Mario laugh at her theories and call them *inspired*. This is worse than having the Luminary Council dismiss her like a child with an overactive imagination. Because unlike those times, there is *really a nightmare out there* that she *saw with her own eyes* and now absolutely *no one will believe her*. She tries to tell the Sunday on the four-wheeler; nothing. In the forest parking area she tries to tell Bretta, who is limping, and Fatima, who has a bandaged wrist. Nothing. She tries to tell Rachel again on their ride back to the Sunday estate. *Nothing*.

So she finally shuts up. If they won't believe her, then she's out of options right now.

"I know you pulled the alarm," Rachel is saying as they drive into the Sunday parking lot, where Mum's Volvo puffs exhaust into the morning. "But since we didn't reach you until after the mist, you still qualify as passing. Great job, Winnie. We're really proud of you. *I'm* really proud of you. You killed two vampira and survived the night."

Winnie doesn't answer. She just waits until Rachel has parked, pushes out of the SUV, and rushes straight for Mum—who is practically leaping from the car, excitement brightening her sleepless face like the sunrise behind her.

"How did it go? How did it go?"

Winnie doesn't answer her either. Instead, she strides to the passenger door and climbs inside. She pulls on her seat belt, staring straight ahead, and waits for Mum to finish talking to Aunt Rachel. Waits for her to get back in the car and put it into drive. Only when they are out of the parking lot does Winnie finally move: she curls over and silently cries.

CHAPTER
29

Mum is clearly worried about Winnie but also seems to intuitively understand (in that way only mums can) that Winnie needs space. She offers her a pat on the shoulder when they get to the house and says, "I went through the same thing." Then she lets Winnie climb the stairs and burrow into her room.

Winnie can't sleep once she's there, though. She knows she needs to, but as long as the Whisperer is still out there and no one believes her, she can't relax or lie down or shut her eyes.

She can't even be happy that she passed the second trial and is now that much closer to becoming a full-fledged hunter. That her family might be that much closer to shedding their outcast punishment for good.

The fact is that she'd fallen asleep in the tree. She'd let the ghost-deer lull her into thinking the forest could be beautiful and pure. She'd even *sympathised* with a werewolf. Then vampira had snuck up on her, and a nightmare to kill all nightmares had come.

So much for trusting the forest. It only wants death, and it only knows how to betray.

Winnie sits at her desk, and without thinking—as if she's trapped in a siren's hypnotizing song—she starts to draw.

Just big, sweeping lines with a pencil, even though she *never* uses pencil.

She doesn't know what she's drawing, either, or why. The lines and curves just appear beneath the silver graphite as it scrapes across sixty-pound sketching paper.

Voices rumble in the living room. Hushed tones so as not to disturb her. Mum, who has taken the morning off to be with Winnie, talks to Darian and Aunt Rachel. They're likely speculating about whether or not Winnie's mind has cracked.

Maybe it has, she thinks as she stares at a vampira's grey face, stretched long in horror and mandibles wide with a scream. Its eyes are shaded with panic, fear, a desperation to live that is more real, more true than anything Winnie has ever drawn before.

She rips out the page and crushes it in her fist. It hits the carpet a half second later. Then she tears the hellion off the wall. *Crunch. Drop.* And finally the kelpie too. Three balls of paper she never wants to look at again.

Winnie needs to find someone who will listen to her—not sit here and draw. She needs to find Mario.

Which is why, a mere five minutes later, she climbs as quietly as she can out of Darian's window, onto the roof, onto the woodpile, and finally into the garden. She's wearing old leggings and an even older zip-up hoodie over a long-sleeved T-shirt. Three very different shades of black, and she's freezing. But her leather jacket is in the downstairs closet and her clean laundry is . . . nonexistent.

It takes her twenty minutes to cross Hemlock Falls on the family bike. The grime she'd scrubbed off in a boiling shower two hours ago is now replaced with sweat and rain-damp wind.

A storm is coming.

She doesn't bother chaining up the bike in front of the Monday estate's main building when she gets there. Really, an unlikely bike theft by some asshat Luminary is the least of Winnie's concerns right now. She takes the stairs two at a time, surprised her body has any juice left to give. She knows she's coasting on adrenaline, but she needs to go a little bit farther still.

She bursts through Mario's open office door, only to find he isn't there. She asks people in the hall where he is, but apparently no one has seen him today. When she steps inside to leave a note on his desk, though, she discovers something resting atop the Compendium.

It's a vial of what looks like blood.

She goes toward it, not really thinking so much as drawn by the scientific part of her brain that wants to analyse and study. The blood looks like normal human blood, but there's no label on it. No slip of printed lab paper. It's just a vial of blood atop the open Compendium, which is open to the page on . . .

Werewolves.

There's a general sketch of one at the top that is also in her copied Compendium, and below, a more detailed anatomical breakdown. Normally, that's what Winnie would focus on—trying to memorise it so she can reproduce it later. This time, though, her attention homes in on the orange Post-its stuck all over the page.

Winnie's teeth start clicking. *Unaffected by sunlight,* one note reads. *Bites—nontransmissible,* reads another. *No sentience in wolf form?* reads a third. And last, in large all caps: *SOMETHING ELSE ENTIRELY?*

Winnie has no idea what that last Post-it might mean. The others, though, are pretty self-explanatory. They also make it clear Mario has known of a werewolf in the forest for a long time. But then why did he act like Winnie's theory on Thursday was so far-fetched? She would be angry with him if she weren't so confused—and so worried about the Whisperer.

That thought prompts Winnie to get moving again. She scribbles a quick note on Mario's desk, then heads back into the rain.

Winnie is more wet than she knew was physically possible by the time she reaches the Friday estate. It's raining hellions and banshees as she abandons her bike by the house's side door. She reaches for the doorbell, hoping somewhat desperately that it has been repaired in the last four years.

It has. The dinging echoes inside the empty house beyond. Rain patters down, but she is protected by a slight overhang from the roof. This door leads into a mudroom with old carpet that has gone from red to maroon to almost earthlike brown in the decade that Winnie has been coming here.

She is absolutely freezing when Jay finally appears at the door.

He looks, as per usual, like utter crap. His clothes are rumpled, and his jeans are torn over the left knee. His hair is at all angles, and the bags under his eyes have bags. He looks like he might vomit.

"You're supposed to be at school," Winnie snaps. She shoves inside, checking him with her shoulder. He absolutely stinks of stale cigarettes.

"Ow." He grips at his forehead.

Which prompts Winnie to slam the door behind her. It reverberates across the house.

And Jay really looks like he might puke now. He has to lean against the doorframe, one hand over his face while his fingers dig into the wood. The rain beats against the windows on the mudroom, and out of habit, Winnie pulls off her shoes.

"Is your aunt home?" She flings one sopping sneaker to the floor. Then the second. "I need to see her."

"Yeah," Jay says, "she's here." If he adds anything more, Winnie doesn't hear it. She is already stomping into the house on wet socks.

The kitchen opens up before her, enormous and almost never used except for during Friday clan dinners. Winnie has always thought it sad that only Jay and Lizzy live in this vast old home with its burned-out tower. The clan estates were built for *families,* but with Lizzy being solo and Jay's parents being dead, there's no "family" to fill the halls. There are barely even enough clan members, since the Fridays are so small.

Winnie leaves the kitchen via a narrow hall to the rickety back stairwell that leads to the other floors. There's a main staircase that leads up, but since only Jay and Lizzy live here year-round, they usually use this set of stairs that spirals upward on wood that loves to groan.

Winnie tromps up, the dark panel walls lit only by grey light filtering in through tall windows that span all the way from the bottom floor to the top. Rain flecks against the glass with the steady beat of a typewriter.

Winnie reaches the second floor, amazed by how much something can change, and also how little. She'd felt that at the Wednesday estate; she feels it a hundred times more now. Maybe because the Wednesday estate was *special*—a reward that she only ever got to experience on those lucky nights of clan dinner. The Friday estate, though, was where she and Jay and Erica spent many a weekend, many an afternoon. If Winnie turns left right now, she will find Jay's bedroom at the end of the hall. And if she goes right, she will reach Lizzy's office, Lizzy's laboratory, and after that, Lizzy's bedroom.

It surprises Winnie how much she really wants to turn left.

But she doesn't turn left, and instead she aims right for Lizzy's lab and the familiar sound of tapping metal and a whooshing welding flame. When Winnie finally enters what used to be a sprawling living room, she finds Lizzy's face encased in a protective shield over a lab table.

Lizzy glances up from a metal tripod. Then looks back down. Then snaps up her head again and the flame in her blowtorch winks off.

A few seconds pass, Lizzy clearly taking in Winnie and Winnie taking in the lab.

It looks like it used to but somehow even more cluttered than before, and the glass doors that open onto a balcony over the back garden (or what remains of it) have clearly not seen a bottle of Windex in several months. Possibly years. The mismatched shelves are laden with books, papers, and more beakers and vials than Lizzy can possibly ever need—especially since chemistry isn't her specialty.

She's an engineer, electric, mechanical, even a little software, as evidenced by the line of computers on the left wall that could be a museum display titled "Computers of the Last Three Decades."

Lizzy lifts her face shield. She is a tall woman with broad shoulders and a strong frame, all beneath a devastatingly gorgeous face. Honey eyes and golden hair always tied in a set of braids around her head give her the look of a Scandinavian princess. She wears her usual grey coveralls.

"Wednesday Winona Wednesday," Lizzy says.

And Winnie inwardly cringes at the use of her full name. Her Mum's idea of "loyalty" is truly cruel. Outwardly, she sets her jaw and strides across the room.

"I can't believe you're in my lab." Lizzy sets down her blowtorch. "And good lord, girl, you are soaking wet. You must be freezing. Let me get you something to wear—"

Winnie flings up a hand. "I need to talk." And without waiting for an acknowledgment, she launches into her story. Yes, she *is* freezing, and she is definitely dripping water onto the lab floor, but she can't care about that until someone—literally *anyone*—has listened to her story about the Whisperer.

She tells the tale with more clarity than she used in her

panicked ramblings for Aunt Rachel, though she still finds it impossible to actually describe what she saw. Words are even more limiting than her sketches. "Imagine a broken radio inside a car exhaust. Or . . . or a sledgehammer at the bottom of the sea. And then put a stained-glass window over it. That's what it was like, Lizzy."

As she continues on, describing the vampira horde and eventually the mist, Lizzy's face morphs from happy surprise to a stony shade of pale.

"And Mario wasn't in his lab," Winnie eventually finishes, "so I came here. You have to do something."

"Yeah," Lizzy says, her gaze unfocused—her mind already blazing ahead. She absently unzips the top of her coveralls to peel them down to her waist. As in Jay's usual wardrobe, a white T-shirt waits beneath. They must buy a family value pack or something.

"Mario told me you'd seen it," Lizzy says, beckoning Winnie to follow her across the room to the computers. When she reaches the newest of the desktops, she taps a key to wake it up. The computer hums. "And I have that security footage . . ." She clicks through a few menus before bringing up the video Winnie has already seen. "This is it, right?"

Winnie swallows, watching the footage play again. "Yeah." *Drip, drip, drip.* Water splatters from her trousers. "That's it."

"All right. I'll alert the Tuesdays right away." The video ends; Lizzy hits replay.

And Winnie finds herself looking away. She is shivering, and it's not merely from the cold. She thinks of the vampira sketch she'd just made. She thinks of the real nightmare that had inspired it.

"You say it . . . it shrank?" Lizzy asks. She opens a notes app and starts hammering away at the keys. The beat stutters against the stochastic rainfall outside. "When the dawn mist rose?"

"That's what it looked like."

"Fascinating, fascinating." Lizzy flashes Winnie a wide-eyed grin. "Maybe now they'll actually let me put my cameras in the forest."

"But . . ." Winnie glances at the various half-made inventions across the room. "The mist breaks cameras."

"Not these." Lizzy's grin slips from excited to sly. "My nephew has kindly taken a few items in the forest with him, on Friday nights, and every one of them has survived." She types more quickly, gaze fastened once more on the screen. "Well, they've survived at least one night . . . or *most* of a night."

In the background, the footage of the Whisperer has paused on a moment when the forest looks like a fish eye trapped in a solar flare.

Drip, drip, drip. A pool is accumulating around Winnie's feet, and the longer she stands here, the colder she's getting.

"Speaking of Jay." Lizzy doesn't look away from the screen. Her fingers don't stop flying. "Are you two friends again?"

"No." The word blurts out. Harder than Winnie intends.

And Lizzy's eyebrows bounce, like she's not quite sure what to make of that. "Well, uh, I'm glad you're here." A shrug of one shoulder. "It's nice to see your face."

"You could have seen my face any time over the past four years."

Lizzy's fingers still on the keyboard. She clearly wasn't anticipating a response that harsh—and frankly, neither was Winnie. But she doesn't retract her words. After all, they're true.

"Listen." Lizzy straightens. "It was against the rules to talk to you all."

"So?" Winnie finds that she's glaring. "When have you ever cared about rules?"

"Fair point, but as a councilor, you have to understand—"

"What, Lizzy? What do I have to understand? We were

here all along, you know. My mum, my brother, *me*. We were here in Hemlock Falls where everyone could see us, but no one did because of some bullshit rules on outcasts. You . . . you just ditched us, Lizzy. Without any explanation, you just *ditched* us."

"I—" Lizzy tries, but Winnie doesn't want to hear it. She is glad she came here, but she doesn't want to *hear* it. Not right now, when she hasn't slept in days and she's soaked by icy rain. When a nightmare is on the loose and it took her hours to find anyone who would listen.

And she doesn't want to hear it from Lizzy because Lizzy isn't the one she's actually mad at.

She rounds away from the computer and toward the lab door. Her feet carry her with surprising speed. It isn't like her to be so openly angry—she's not even sure why this is catching fire *now*. But it's as if the adrenaline of last night has stoked flames that have been smoldering inside her for three days.

She knows exactly how Mum felt on Saturday.

She finds Jay in the hall. He holds a flannel shirt in one hand. It's clearly meant for her, but Winnie doesn't want it, just as she doesn't want that look in his eyes either. The intense one that doesn't say he's sorry.

"Let me give you a ride," he offers as she practically runs down the hall. Distantly, she notices he's clean now, his hair damp and his clothes fresh. "It's pouring outside, Win, and you're already soaked."

"Yeah." She pauses at the top of the stairs. Rain slashes against the windows. "I am, but you've never cared before. Tell me honestly, Jay: Why are you helping me? Is it because I passed the first trial?"

"No," he begins.

"Is it because I'm not radioactive anymore and *now* you have permission to be my friend? *Now* that I've got that glossy Luminary stamp of approval?"

"No, Winnie." He reaches for her, but she sidles away. His hand falls. "It's not like that. I've had my own stuff going on, okay?"

"*No*," she snaps. "Not okay, Jay. You were my best friend. You and Erica. And I needed you, but you weren't there."

"I'm here now."

"Yeah, well, you're about four years too late." Winnie snatches the flannel from his grip—blessedly dry—before flying down the stairs to once more face the rain.

Jay doesn't follow.

CHAPTER

30

By the time Winnie gets home, Mum has gone to her shift at the grocers and Winnie feels the beginnings of a cold. Everything aches, her throat is starting to swell, and her ankle is puffy too. Jay's flannel hadn't stayed dry for long on the bike ride home, and she's frozen to her core by the time she strips down and crawls into bed to finally crash.

She sleeps horribly, awakens even worse, and she's so glad she didn't have to go to school today. She doesn't want to talk about last night or the banshee. She doesn't want to deal with Marcus pretending they're friends. She doesn't want to be looked at by anyone except the bear on the back of her door.

She's never noticed before that its eyes sort of follow her wherever she moves.

For four years, she has wanted to be a Luminary again. Welcomed back to the Wednesday estate, back into the clan, back at the Sunday training grounds. And for her *whole* life, she has wanted to be a hunter. But now that she has it all, it's nothing like she'd hoped for.

Part of that has to do with what she said to Lizzy and Jay—and what Mum had vented about too: Why is everyone kissing their butts *now*? Another part of it is that she's still living with this lie about a banshee she didn't kill. But most of it is that nothing feels like she remembers.

She *remembers* giggling with Erica in the back seat of Marcia's van. She *remembers* hiding with Jay in a dusty closet while Erica searched for them in a sad three-player version of sardines. And she *remembers* her dad cooking dinner most nights because his job as an estate gardener ended way before Mum's work as Lead Hunter. Darian still lived at home then too, and it was just all so *different.*

Winnie wasn't naive enough to think she would get all that back if she could regain the family's standing in the Luminaries . . .

But she also was kind of that naive, and as she stares at the bear banner from her spot huddling beneath her covers, she almost wishes she could feel those banshee tears again. It had cleaned out so much poison. It had freed up so much that is now festering inside again.

Winnie flings off her covers and stumbles from bed. Her feet kick crumpled nightmare sketches across the carpet. She grabs a sweatshirt, leaves the room, and aims crookedly down the hall, her ankle tender but manageable, to where the attic hatch awaits. After dragging a folding stool from Darian's room (because of course he has a stool for reaching the top shelf in his closet), she yanks down the creaking panel of wood.

Old dust whips down. Winnie coughs, which then triggers snot-coughing, and she has to hurry into the bathroom to blow her nose. Three times. And grab a cough drop.

Finally, sniffly but soothed by Ricola, she unfolds the ladder on the hatch, and clambers into the attic. She pulls a dangling string and the lone light bulb winks on, revealing the slanted eaves of the roof and old pink insulation.

There isn't much in the attic. Mum has never been a hoarder, and Dad was super organised (Darian comes by his passion for clean lines and containers honestly). So there are only a handful of boxes to explore, one containing holiday decorations, one containing old baby clothes Mum insists she's keeping in case Winnie or Darian ever need them, but they all really know it's just because Mum's a big softie. And finally, the box in which Darian must have found the locket.

It's the biggest of the three, and when Winnie peeks inside, she spies a bubble-wrapped clock that was Gran Winona's, a bubble-wrapped mug that was Grandpa Frank's, and then . . . another box. One Winnie suspects holds stuff that used to be Dad's.

She grabs the box. After all, it's the reason she came up here. She has always suspected her mum hadn't trashed everything from Dad, and the locket is confirmation of this.

It's a big shoebox that probably held snow boots once upon a time. Now, as Winnie folds up the lid, she finds some old sketches she'd given Dad. He'd loved flowers, so she had attempted tulips, carnations, and goldenrods. They're all terrible, since Winnie had still been new to drawing and her interest had never been in plants.

A weird feeling tickles through her. It's warm and heavy at the same time. Like she's sad to see these flowers—sad Dad hadn't taken them with him (which is ridiculous)—but also pleased to know Mum kept them.

She hadn't needed more confirmation of her mum's awesomeness and Dad's crappiness, but she has a boxful of proof anyway.

Below her old sketches, she finds photographs. The real kind, since these came from back when there were more real cameras than phones and real film instead of a cloud and they feature Mum and Dad, not much older than Winnie is now. Like Darian, Mum went away for a year to Heritage University. Her mother, Gran Winona, died facing a pack of hellions that had escaped the forest. Mum had been devastated and abruptly renounced all things hunter or even

Luminary. So the Council had given her permission to leave, along with the usual stipulations: *Never speak of the forest, never speak of the Luminaries.*

While away, though, Mum had realised—just as Darian had—that Hemlock Falls was where she belonged and hunting was in her blood. She *missed* the forest, despite what it had taken from her. But in that year away, she'd also met Bryant, a landscape architecture grad student. He was four years older and almost done with his master's; he begged Fran not to dump him when she went back home; and somehow they'd secretly continued dating until his graduation. Then Mum had brought him to Hemlock Falls, where he had, like all other outsiders, been thoroughly vetted by the Wednesdays before being welcomed in.

In the first photo Winnie studies, Dad has a very unfortunate mustache and sideburns—and he's grinning like the happiest man on earth, his arm slung around a much younger Mum. She is leaning into him, looking safe. Relaxed in a way Winnie has forgotten her mum can ever look. Behind them is a building that must have been somewhere outside Hemlock Falls, since Winnie doesn't recognise it.

She sniffles. Wipes her nose on a tissue in her pocket, and looks at the next photo. It's Dad and Mum in front of this house, Mum's hands on her belly even though there's no belly yet to see. The house looks a lot better than it does now.

And Mum does too. She grins. Dad grins. They are happy and blissfully in love. This is not a man who is secretly the enemy. This is not a man who is plotting to betray his family and steal Luminary secrets for the Dianas. This is a man whom the Wednesdays approved and who is about to become a papa.

Suddenly Winnie doesn't know what the hell she was thinking, coming up here. She drops the photo back onto the stack and grabs the lid to close it again—which is when she notices something under all the pictures. Something that isn't a flower sketch or a photograph, but an envelope. Red, just like the one that came on Winnie's birthday.

She sniffles again. Rubs once at her eyes. Then sweeps the pictures aside. Sure enough, it's the birthday card, and when Winnie digs deeper, she finds eight. Four addressed to her, four addressed to Darian. One for each year that Dad hasn't been here.

One for each year Winnie thought her mum was taking these to the Council.

No, no, she tells herself. *You saw Mum leave.* She must have turned them over to the Council, and for whatever reason, the Council gave them back.

Except as Winnie returns the cards to the shoebox with trembling hands, she knows the obvious truth: all the cards except one are unopened. Mum never turned these in. And if she has kept them a secret every single year . . . not just from the Council but from Winnie and Darian too . . . then what else might she be hiding?

Winnie's teeth click as she slides the card from its envelope. It's just a plain white postcard, and in Dad's print writing with the scattered *i* dots, she reads:

Happy 1-3-Th birthday, Winnie! I wish I was there to see you. It was only last year that things were normal and right, framed like that picture of us in the living room. Stay safe.

Love, Dad

It's a code. Winnie knows that right away. The *1-3-Th* is from the games they used to play—this one a sort of scavenger hunt, where they'd leave messages in books at the Monday history library. He must have left her a message, assuming she'd read this card four years ago, and now that hidden message has been sitting inside a book all this time, where anyone might find it.

Where anyone might have *already* found it.

She feels sick at the thought. Like, her heart is thumping way too hard against her lungs. She should go make sure the message is still there. Then dispose of whatever it is. And she should read the other cards too, to make sure there aren't any other notes tucked inside books a random Luminary might read.

Winnie doesn't read them, though—not yet anyway—because she really thinks her heart might explode if she has to stare at Dad's handwriting a second longer. Her whole body feels tingly; her head feels light. How dare he do this. How *dare* he. Even if she'd read his card four years ago, she couldn't have accessed the history library as an outcast.

Winnie is glad Mum didn't give her the cards. She's also glad Mum didn't give these to the Council—not that Mum or Darian knew the game Winnie and Dad used to play. But they might have figured out the code. They might have decided Winnie, Mum, and Darian had been in cahoots with Dad all along.

For some reason, as Winnie escapes the attic, her eyes ache with tears.

That night, Mum lets Winnie have not one, but *two* ginger ales, as well as a boatload of chicken noodle soup that has that *je ne sais quoi* flavour only found in a can. While she and Winnie are sitting on the couch, sharing a blanket that has seen better days, Johnny Saturday appears on the TV with his too-handsome face that never seems to age. After announcing that the drama troupe will be performing *A Midsummer Night's Dream* next week (tickets are fifty dollars) and that the Revenant's Daughter will be briefly closed while a new stove is installed ("Dammit, Archie, thanks for the heads-up"), he shifts to the usual updates on forest activity.

More vampira. A manticore nest that keeps reappearing on the eastern side of the lake with hatchlings. A melusine recorded near the falls.

Winnie blows her nose three times and takes two sips of tea that isn't quite hot anymore. Every second that she's around Mum makes her lungs swell with a question she's afraid will eventually burst out of her: *Why did you keep the birthday cards? Do you know what they say?* But as long as the TV is on, she's able to quell her need for answers—and the truth is that she isn't quite sure she *wants* to know Mum's answers.

Then comes the moment Winnie has been awaiting from Johnny Saturday: "The Council has also posted an alert for all locals of a daywalker in the forest."

Winnie jolts upright. The couch shakes.

"Until the Tuesdays have captured this nightmare, all nonhunters are advised to avoid the main forest and any hotspots." Johnny pauses, as if he's confused by the teleprompter. Then he visibly blanches on camera. "Wow, so this werewolf rumor is real, then. Good god."

He blinks, briefly breaking eye contact with the camera. A swallow. A twitch of his jaw. Then a return to the teleprompter: "Though no ID has been made, there is strong evidence to suggest a werewolf walks among us in Hemlock Falls. The Council blames it for the recent hunter deaths of Noah Saturday and Claire Tuesday, as well as the increase in non corpses. The Council will host a public forum tomorrow night to address any concerns."

Again, Johnny pauses, and this time he shakes his head too. "Be careful out there, folks. Just . . . be careful." The news cuts away. Mum grabs for the remote. The TV winks off, leaving a black screen with Winnie's and Mum's reflections on it.

Winnie feels as sick as Johnny had just looked. Like she has been punched in the stomach. She knows Mum is staring at her—can even see from her periphery as worry folds over Mum's face.

Mum knows about the Whisperer; Aunt Rachel told her about Winnie's assertions; and Winnie later told Mum about Lizzy having actual footage of it.

"I . . . don't understand," Winnie finds herself saying. "It's not the werewolf that killed those people. It's the Whisperer."

"Well," Mum says with way too much gentleness, "a werewolf *is* something to worry about too, even if you think something else—"

"I don't think." Winnie glares at Mum's reflection. "I know." She had been so sure that with Lizzy and Mario to back her up, the hunters would listen. The Council would listen. Instead, all of Hemlock Falls is fixated on the wrong daywalker because of something that happened seventeen years ago.

Sure, Mum is right: a werewolf is something to worry about. But the Whisperer is incalculably worse. A new nightmare that eats other nightmares like a wood chipper? That walks in and out of the forest at will? And that doesn't disappear when the mist comes?

Nothing could be worse. *Nothing* could be more dangerous for Hemlock Falls and the world beyond.

"I'm going to bed," Winnie says, standing unsteadily.

Mum winces, a knot clearly in her throat at the sight of her daughter's misery. "I believe you, you know," she says as Winnie shambles away. "But the town is focused on the werewolf right now. It's the thing we *know*. The thing we've experienced before. Soon the Council will turn to this . . . this Whisperer. One thing at a time, Winnebago."

More like one death at a time. Winnie's teeth grind, but she makes herself nod before climbing the stairs.

Her throat hurts.

CHAPTER

31

B y Tuesday morning, Winnie feels well enough to drag herself out of bed, shower, and go to school. The fever is gone and her throat has shrunk back down to its normal size. While the new stove goes in at the Revenant's Daughter, Mum doesn't have work, and she gives Winnie a ride—as well as a tight hug and kiss on the cheek, which Winnie isn't particularly pleased by but that she lets Mum have.

Homeroom is a surprisingly calm affair. It would seem missing class on Monday has let the sheen of survival wear off. No one asks her about the trial; most people actually ignore her like they used to.

Darian gives Winnie a ride to the Sunday estate at noon— Mum's orders (along with a reminder to *please* practice driving)—and Winnie is glad to see him, even if another question burns in her: *Do you know about the birthday cards?* After all, he had been rummaging in that box too. He must have noticed them in the pictures.

Winnie doesn't ask, though, and after a hug from him as well (and a fierce "Congrats on the second trial. See you at clan dinner tomorrow"), Winnie makes her way into nightmare anatomy.

The twins are there. So is Erica. Winnie avoids the latter and aims for the former. "Excited for your birthday?" she asks, making Bretta's and Emma's dimples form.

"Extremely," Bretta replies. "See you at the party tomorrow night?"

Winnie shoves at her glasses. She still lacks a birthday gift for the twins, and a "fancy outfit" definitely doesn't exist in her wardrobe (though she would *never* wear her Save the Whales hoodie, haha). But she also doesn't want to disappoint Bretta and Emma. She really likes them, and she wants to give them something nice.

She's wearing her leather jacket right now, and she'll never forget that the twins gave it to her with open smiles and genuine goodwill. It's just . . . a lot of pressure to find something comparably as thoughtful in her price range.

Winnie should have searched more deeply in the attic. Maybe there was a second locket.

As Winnie takes a seat at the back of the room, and as Professor Il-Hwa starts describing local manticore stingers (length of a forearm, width of a finger, survivable as long as no venom is pumped through), she feels eyes on her. And she knows, without turning her head, that it's Erica watching her from her own corner.

Winnie doesn't look her way.

As class progresses (this time about the organic changes to a revenant's skin—something Winnie already knows plenty about), she stares out the window at the parking lot. Spring sun spikes down. She considers who she should approach next about the Whisperer. She's never had much luck with the Council directly, but it might be the only option left.

As if summoned by her thoughts, two black SUVs glide into the estate parking lot like harpies in flight. One has a little flag with a golden key. It's the head of the Council: Dryden Saturday.

A few other students notice his illustrious arrival and sit up at their desks. Professor Il-Hwa lectures on, oblivious. By the time she reaches the end of her current slide, no one is paying attention to her. They're all focused on the parking lot and the entourage following Dryden Saturday toward the building.

One of them is Darian, his skin back to haggard paper and his pace frantic behind Dryden's. Meanwhile Dryden, despite being shorter than Darian, feels orders of magnitude larger. As always, he looks like a slightly scattered professor on his way to a lecture.

A second Council member exits the second SUV, marked by a flag with a scroll. It's Theresa Monday, tall and impeccably dressed in a honey-brown suit that sets off her darker, cooler-toned brown skin. Walking behind her is Mario. He looks harried and grouchy, and he pulls a fresh stick of gum from his lab coat as he follows everyone else toward the front door.

The intercom clicks on. The whole classroom jolts. "Report to the auditorium, please," Headmaster Gina trills. "We have an important announcement."

The Whisperer, Winnie thinks. *Please, let it be about the Whisperer.*

She lags behind the rest of the class so she won't have to sit near Erica, and by the time Winnie sidles into the blessedly empty last row of the auditorium, Dryden Saturday is at the mic on the centre of the stage.

Her teeth are clicking up a storm. Her heart is thundering too.

"Thank you all for coming," Dryden says. The speakers give a kick of static, then a kick of feedback. He glares at the first row, and Winnie has no doubt the recipient of said glare is Darian—as if the technical incompetence of the microphone is somehow his fault. "As many of you know, we've had several recent werewolf incidents. And though we've, thankfully, had no civilian encounters thus far—at least within the Luminaries—our hunters have had several run-ins."

Winnie's whole body deflates. She slumps over in her seat. No, no, no.

"Now, I want to begin by saying you are all *quite* safe, and there's no cause for alarm. There will be a public forum on the issue tonight, but we felt it important to go ahead and speak to students.

"I've invited Councilor Theresa Monday and the lead scientist studying this daywalker, Mario Monday, to update you all on the essential information you'll need to stay safe. Then I'm going to share the steps that we, the Council, are taking to address it."

Winnie leans forward to rest her head on her knees. She doesn't know why she'd hoped they'd be here for the Whisperer. Of *course* this is about the werewolf. Of *course* she's going to have to raise the issue entirely on her own.

She hears Theresa Monday's heels strut across the stage. "Hello, students," she says into the mic. "Like Councilor Saturday just mentioned, we're here to discuss the werewolf. Our lead scientist will explain our preliminary findings, and then we'll answer any question you all might have."

Winnie drags up her head as Mario moves to the mic next. With no preamble, he launches into a dense, borderline unintelligible assessment of the werewolf situation. He has spit out his gum, although he pats at his pockets every few minutes like he wishes he could grab another stick.

Winnie listens, but not closely. Mario knows about the Whisperer. *Surely* he has spoken to Dryden about it—and this time with Lizzy, a councilor, to back him up. So why is no one raising the alarm about it?

"During the werewolf, erm . . . *attack* seventeen years ago," Mario says, "we found no werewolf plasmids typically transmitted via bite. In other words, the local nightmare mutation is *not* contagious. But admittedly, our sample size was small, and we're going off old observational data, which isn't ideal. If you know any werewolves open to a randomised trial, let me know." He gives a gruff laugh and grins at the audience.

Winnie blushes on his behalf while her eyes home in on Dryden Saturday, perched at the stage's edge. Theoretically, she could talk to him. He's right there, and there's nothing to stop her from walking right up and addressing him directly.

Mario clears his throat. "Now, uh, contrary to what you might have read in your abridged Compendiums, this isn't unheard of. All Asian Luminary branches have seen this sort of wolf, and it was recorded in a European were-stag population as well. Which is actually what's most fascinating about this current werewolf: the DNA we managed to get from a fur sample has some overlap with the—"

"Very good." Theresa Monday shoves back in to the microphone, essentially hip-bumping Mario aside. "Thank you so much, Dr. Mario. I'm sure many of the students have questions for us, so if you please, raise your hands and . . ."

As one, almost every student in the room raises a hand. And every single teacher too. Councilor Monday looks mildly ill. Mario looks even more so. He pats again at his pockets.

"Well, then." A huff of unhappy laughter from Theresa. "Let's get started. You there, in the plaid jumper?"

"Who is it?" the girl asks. "The werewolf—is it someone we know?"

As one, almost every other hand drops back down again. Yet before Theresa can answer, Dryden Saturday strides back into the fray. "No, we don't know. Which is actually why we're here. The first step to catching this daywalker is to test everyone in Hemlock Falls. We'll begin with the students as soon as we have enough tests, since you are already in a contained space and easily organised for blood samples."

A few more hands leap up at that.

"Then we'll move to the rest of the city. We're already setting up a mass testing site on the boardwalk near the dam."

Three more hands rise, four drop.

When will you start testing?

What if we don't like needles?

Why hasn't the siren downtown gone off?

What if we think we know who it is? (Cough) Casey. (Cough)

As Dryden, Theresa, and Mario move through each question, Winnie's teeth tap like a machine gun and she keeps removing and replacing her glasses. She is definitely going to talk to Dryden. As soon as this assembly is over, she'll corner him and make him listen. Surely Mario will back her up—and Darian too.

This is her best shot to get someone to take the Whisperer seriously. She has to take it.

Her moment comes when the bell rings, marking the end of class. There are still raised hands, but Dryden promises they'll all be answered at the public forum tonight. Winnie is already on the move, having leaped from her seat the instant the bell began its toll. And by the time she reaches the front row, Darian is out of his seat and heading for the stage.

"Hey." She grabs his sleeve.

He smiles at her tiredly. She only saw him a few hours ago, but he looks like he has endured a week in that time. "Hey, sister mine. What's up?"

Winnie swallows. "I need to talk to Dryden."

His eyebrows rise. "Uh . . ."

"Let me rephrase that. I'm *going* to talk to Dryden."

"Wait," Darian tries, but Winnie isn't listening. She scoots for the stage steps right as Dryden begins his descent. A few feet behind, Mario is shoving a piece of gum into his mouth.

"It's not a werewolf," Winnie says without preamble, moving into Dryden's way so he can't exit. "The thing that's been killing hunters and nons and nightmares. It's not a werewolf."

"I beg your pardon?" Dryden looks at Winnie like she has turned into a harpy fledgling. "Who are you?"

"She's my sister." Darian hurries to Winnie's side. "She just completed the second trial, and she saw something—"

"And I *saw* what has been killing everyone," Winnie interrupts. "It's not a werewolf. It's a Whisperer."

"A what?" This is from Theresa Monday, who clacks down the steps.

"A *Whisperer*," Winnie repeats. Her voice is getting a little frantic now. A few students have paused their exit to watch her. "It's this nightmare that . . . that's all squiggly and makes a sound like a tornado in a deep fryer. And I *saw* it on Sunday night. It killed an entire horde of vampira in seconds."

"No, Miss Wednesday, that was the werewolf." Dryden looks peevishly at Darian—as if it's Darian's fault Winnie has pounced on him. He resumes his walk; Theresa does too. Mario, however, hangs back.

"It *wasn't*, though." Winnie falls into step beside Dryden. "It wasn't a werewolf at all. It was a Whisperer."

"There is no such thing in the Compendium," Dryden declares.

"Because it's new—"

"*Please*," Dryden moans at Darian, "take your sister away."

"No." Winnie fears she might be shouting now. But this is even worse than Monday morning when no one at the trial would believe her. If she can't convince the Council, then she's out of options. All of Hemlock Falls will keep searching for the wrong daywalker. "You have to believe me, Councilor Saturday. I saw it with my own eyes. And Mario!" Winnie flings a hand toward him. "He's seen it too! So has Lizzy Friday. They know what I'm talking about. Right, Mario? Right? Tell them."

She rounds on Mario, but instead of nodding his agreement, he firmly avoids her eyes. A bubble rises from his lips. Then pops.

"Miss Wednesday," Theresa offers, more gently than Dryden had, "multiple hunters have seen the werewolf, and multiple Mondays have confirmed werewolf kills—including Mario here. So we thank you for your concerns, but do leave it to the experts."

No, Winnie wants to shout again. She feels like she's fallen into the Big Lake and now a kelpie is dragging her down. No one is listening to her. Mario is straight up ignoring her, and even Darian looks pained.

Winnie stops walking. Everyone else marches on. Marches away.

"Sorry," Darian whispers as he passes. But that's it. That's the end. The one person she was certain would back her up— who had proof of his own, even if the footage wasn't great . . . Mario has left Winnie here to drown.

His next bubble pops like a gunshot as he leaves the auditorium.

Winnie flinches as if she's been hit.

CHAPTER
32

After Coach Rosa's class and three—*three*—laps around the obstacle course, Winnie is surprised to find her cold mostly gone. Her rage, however, is not. How *dare* Mario. How dare Lizzy. How dare *Darian*!

She's going to confront all of them as soon as she can. She deserves an explanation for what happened after the assembly—especially from Mario. How *dare* he.

Once again, she takes way longer than everyone else to run the track, so she doesn't change back into her regular clothes after class. But when she gets to the front to look for Mum and her Volvo (she's going to insist Mum let her drive this time—really! Second gear won't know what hit it), she finds Jay and Mathilda instead.

He hops out of the Wagoneer at the sight of Winnie and lopes over, hands sliding into his pockets. Although he doesn't look high and he doesn't smell of weed, his eyes are puffy, his hair damp.

Clearly, he skipped school *again* and only just woke up.

"Class is already over," Winnie snaps when he meets her at the curb.

"Oh?" He glances at the sky. "I thought that particular angle of the sun meant morning. Silly me."

Winnie thins her eyes at him. "What do you want, Jay?"

"I thought we could train."

"Are you sober?"

"Yes, Winnie." A soft rasp of laughter. "I'm sober."

Her glare deepens into skeptical. "I thought you had band practice on Tuesday afternoon."

"I'm surprised you know that."

"Is my information wrong?"

"No." He shrugs a single shoulder, hands still deep in his jeans. Today his flannel is a tartan green and blue. "But I figure you need the hunting practice more than I need the bass practice."

Now her glare turns annoyed. "Thanks?"

"Is my information wrong?" His hands finally leave the pockets. "You still have one more trial, and I assumed you'd want to keep practicing."

Of course she does, but she also wants to confront Mario. She wants to rip the gum from his mouth and shriek at him for betraying her in front of Dryden and Theresa. There's something else on the loose, dammit. Something that can eat a werewolf and then eject it piece by piece like some outer-dimensional vending machine.

But, nudges the back of her brain, the part that never forgets the forest—that wants to feel plugged in again, hunting and alive. *You only have one trial left. You're so close to getting what you want.*

She hugs her arms to her chest. Her teeth click. "What was yours?"

"My?" Jay's brow rises. The wind tugs at his flannel. "My what?"

"Your third trial. What did they make you do?"

He grimaces, a mere flash that fades in an instant. "You know I can't tell you that."

Winnie *does* know. Clan trials are secret. "Was it hard?"

"Harder than the others."

Winnie snorts. What a Jay thing to say. "Harder than the others, but not *hard* because you're the Amazing Jay Friday, and you'll be Lead Hunter before you're eighteen. You're adored by all, bass guitarist for the Forgotten, tinkerer of motorcycles, and Bad Boy extraordinaire."

Jay flushes all the way through his eyeballs. It's not an embarrassed flush, though, or even an angry one. Winnie doesn't know what it means, only that she doesn't mind watching him squirm. "Look, I can't train today. My mum is on the way to pick me up . . . What? Why are you looking like that?"

His expression is suddenly pained. "Um, actually, your mum asked me to give you a ride. So either way . . ." He opens his arms, waving toward Mathilda like a maître d' toward a fancy table. "Your chariot awaits."

"What do you mean my mum asked you to give me a ride?"

"I mean, she was here but had to leave . . . so she asked me to do her a favor." He is very still as he adds, "She also told me you said that we aren't friends, but I'm tutoring you."

And Winnie is very still as she responds, "I did say that." For some reason, she feels guilty about it too, which only serves to make her angrier. "But fine, Jay. Let's go train. Just . . . not in the forest today."

"Why?"

The Whisperer, she wants to say. *Obviously the Whisperer.* Instead, she answers, "Because there's a werewolf out there. Haven't you heard?"

Jay takes Winnie to the Friday training grounds. There are three other hunters there, who give Jay waves and Winnie curious glances as they pass by on their circuits around the obstacle course. Winnie wants to die from just watching them do an entire loop with high knees.

Jay, who isn't dressed for intensive training in his jeans and flannel, takes Winnie to the targets instead. They start with compound bow practice. This time, Jay offers Winnie his trigger release. The black strap and metal loop that hooks onto arrows is warm from having been in his pocket; it feels nice against her cold wrist.

Her aim is terrible but better than she expected. Her one session with Jay on Saturday did a lot to reawaken forgotten muscles, but even with a three-point sight on the bow, she's not quite hitting where she aims.

Jay is also shooting, but lazily. Like he needs something to do while Winnie practices. Each of his bolts hits exactly where he aims. Every. Single. Time.

"Do you still hate touching your eye?" he asks as Winnie nocks another practice arrow.

She pauses. "Yes. Why?"

"Because contacts would be a lot easier." He releases the cables on his grey bow, and the bolt looses over the cold earth. It pierces a dummy in the left eyeball. "You keep adjusting your glasses. I noticed it when we were on the move last Saturday."

Winnie swallows. Then finishes nocking. She aims at the skull . . . and she misses. Not by much, at least. The bolt pokes out from a foam throat.

"I like my glasses, Jay."

"I didn't say I don't like—"

"And," she glares his way, shoving the lenses up her nose, "I'm not going to wear contacts."

"Okay." He lifts his hands in surrender. The bow rises toward the sky. "They might make you, though, if you become a hunter. It can be dangerous to have glass near your eyes. But forget I asked."

"I will." She doesn't like touching her eye, and as unstylish as her glasses might be, she can't imagine *not* having them.

She grabs another bolt. Her face is going numb with cold, but the rhythm of reloading is keeping her fingers warm. Again, she nocks the arrow, takes aim, shoots . . . and miraculously hits the target where she'd aimed—well, mostly. She wanted the stomach; she probably hit the bladder.

"I like you in glasses," Jay adds. His hands are down now, and he sets the bow onto the table. "Just so we're clear on that. I, uh . . . really like you in glasses."

Something about the way he says "really" makes Winnie glance his way. But he's not looking at her. Instead, he's watching one of the hunters glide up a rope as easily as if she were attached to a pulley.

The Fridays really are the best.

Winnie wonders what Jay would look like climbing that same rope. For some reason, it makes her blush.

She grabs for another bolt. "Remember when I asked you about . . . the Whisperer?" She's not going to be ashamed.

"Yeah." Jay saunters toward her. "And Lizzy told me why you came over yesterday."

Winnie nods. He is moving dangerously close to her, and they are moving dangerously close to the accusations she'd flung at him from the top of the stairs. She doesn't regret saying any of that stuff. It felt good to get it out after four years. She *does* regret that Jay had nothing better to offer in his defence.

"Have you seen it yet?" she asks. "On the hunt Friday night, maybe?"

A frown. "No. Have you talked to Mario about it?"

She scowls and reorients herself to the target. She pretends it's one of Mario's bubbles. "It's out there, Jay. I *know* the Whisperer is out there. But no one will do anything about it." She nocks the bolt. Aims. Releases. And misses the throat via a shoulder.

Jay is now standing very near to her, and after a murmured "May I?" Winnie nods. But where she expects him to take the weapon from her, he instead moves in to adjust her stance and nock another arrow for her.

Suddenly, she is painfully aware that, yet again, she smells like old sweat while he smells of lime and bergamot and forest. He braces his chest against her back and loops his arm over her shoulders, adjusting her grip and her stance and the angle of her body toward the target. Subtle movements that Winnie is pretty sure she won't be able to replicate without his help.

"Pick your target on the body," Jay says. He is a vague shape in the corner of her vision, hazy like forest trees at dawn. Yet as real and sturdy as them too.

Nonsensical, she thinks. *You're being nonsensical.*

"Heart," she says, and with Jay's finely honed muscles to guide her, she finds the right spot on the target. It is a fraction of a hair higher than she would have aimed.

"Shoot," he tells her. His head is beside Winnie's, the heat of him warm against her.

She fights the urge to click her teeth or swallow.

She shoots. The bolt hits the heart.

Before she can move, though, and release the sudden brilliance in her veins—*I hit the heart! I hit the heart!*—Jay's grip on her hardens.

"Don't move," he tells her. "Hold the position. Just a few beats after you're done. It'll help your muscles learn where they're supposed to go."

"Right," she says. "Hold it." *I hit the heart! I hit the heart!*

"You're a natural, Win." His voice tickles against her ear. "Just remember that: the hunt is in your blood. You belong out there and always have."

Winnie's throat swells up at those words. It might be the nicest thing anyone has ever said to her. She twists her head to peer at him. His eyes are right there, the pupils reflecting her face back to her. "Thank you."

"Yeah" is all he offers in reply. Then very slowly, Jay peels away from her. First his fingers, next his arms. And finally his face and body, too. Cold scrapes in. The heat of him recedes.

"Good job. You can move now, Win." And there's his soft laugh—although Winnie doesn't think it's aimed at her this time so much as cutting inward.

When she does finally release the pose to study him, she finds his hands in his pockets and his pewter eyes skating toward the trees, reaching for the forest.

CHAPTER
33

After target practice, they run the Friday obstacle course (Winnie doesn't even get *close* to climbing the rope, and to her weird disappointment, Jay doesn't try), then finish with basic conditioning. In other words, Winnie gets hit repeatedly all over her body.

Jay does at least promise to look for the Whisperer on the extra shift he's picking up tonight with the Tuesdays, and though it doesn't eliminate the acid roiling in Winnie's gut—or her rage at Mario—it does help. A little.

If just one more person can see it in real life, surely the Council will listen?

It's nearing sunset when Jay drops her off at home. She offers a rushed "Hi, bye!" to Mum, who is folding laundry while she watches the public forum on the werewolf; Winnie feels ill just hearing Dryden Saturday's voice. After a rushed shower that isn't quite hot because Mum must have just showered and the water heater is small, Winnie finds herself sitting on her bed, trying to ignore the TV downstairs.

"When will the blood tests begin?" a woman asks.

"We're hoping to start next week. Right now, our medical teams are working to acquire all the necessary supplies—"

"Shouldn't we *have* them already? After what happened?" Cries of agreement rise. Winnie thinks she hears Mum grunt an agreement of her own.

No. She claps her hands to her ears. Listening to the forum isn't going to help her right now. She needs to focus; she needs to brainstorm. What do you give to the coolest girls on the planet who seem to have everything? Winnie knows Emma and Bretta will love whatever she gives them because their hearts are too big not to . . . which only makes her *more* determined to find the perfect present. She wants it to be something worthy of their year of kindness to her, their always welcoming smiles.

Her eyes scoot around her room in search of inspiration, briefly pausing on her desk. On the howling vampira face still crumpled on the carpet nearby. She could, she supposes, draw them something. Maybe the nightmares they each slew during their first trials . . .

But for some reason, that idea makes Winnie's throat close up. Her chest feels too small too. She doesn't want to think about how moonlight falls on a manticore hatchling's carapace or how a will-o'-wisp might look surrounded by forest trees—because whenever she does imagine it, her brain conjures a carapace that's hacked to bits or a will-o'-wisp corpse shoved through a cheese grater.

Her eyes snap away. *Think, Winnie, think.* There *has* to be something here—something special and unique.

She spots Andrew's Kevlar vest hanging in her closet. Her attention snags. There's something about it . . . Something on it . . .

Just like that, she knows exactly what to do. She bounds off the bed, sore ankle protesting, and hurries for the closet—but not for the vest. Instead, she digs into her dirty clothes, searching for something she definitely left in Saturday's training gear.

When she finds it, Winnie can't help but grin. Because this gift really is *perfect*. It's badass. It's one-of-a-kind, just like Emma. Just like Bretta. And they will, Winnie thinks, absolutely love it.

Wednesday morning arrives with storm clouds and thunder. Winnie crawls from bed extra early. No, it's not corpse-duty early, but definitely early-bird-catches-the-worm early—and she has quite the worm to catch. She cycles across town as fast as the old bike will carry her, and as she'd hoped, Mario is just wheeling in the morning's nightmares (brought to you by the Tuesday teens) when Winnie arrives.

She is boiling in her leather jacket even though her face and fingers have gone numb. The storm hasn't broken yet, but it's only a matter of time.

"How could you?" she demands, coasting to a stop and hopping off her bike. "How could you just stand there, Mario?"

"Winnie." He lifts his hands and glances almost furtively around. "Let's talk inside."

"You know what that nightmare can do, but you just stood there while I pleaded with Dryden. How *could* you, Mario?"

"Winnie, please." His eyes are huge. "Let me deliver these bodies. Then we can talk."

Winnie's scowl doesn't budge. She does, however, nod stormily and lean her bike against the back door. She joins Mario at the corpses. One is another manticore hatchling. The other is part of what *might* be a hellion. But it's in bad shape. Like, Whisperer-level bad shape.

Together, Winnie and Mario roll the table into the lowest level of the hospital and toward the morgue. Winnie has never been allowed in here before, but it looks exactly like she'd imagined: beige walls and floors broken up by the occasional "decorative" blue stripe, fluorescent lights that give everything an unnatural sheen, and thick, windowless doors that say PERSONNEL ONLY. At the end of the hall, they reach metal double doors that open when Mario swipes a plastic keycard over a reader. Cold billows over Winnie. The morgue's lights flicker on.

"We'll just leave these here for now," Mario says, wheeling the cart to the centre of the room, where two empty carts rest.

After a hasty scribble onto the usual clipboard—*pop-pop-pop!*—he beckons for her to follow him again. A brisk walk out of the hospital and across the campus plus a few errant raindrops later, they're at the main building. The ivy really does look like it might wake up soon. They ascend to the third floor and enter Mario's office. He shuts the door behind them. The vial of blood, Winnie notices, is gone from the Compendium.

He motions Winnie to his desk, where he silently offers her a stick of gum (she refuses) and turns on his computer. After a little clicking, he finds what he wants and swivels the monitor for her to see. "Lizzy's cameras," he says. For some reason, he's talking very quietly. Almost inaudibly, even.

Winnie turns a frown onto the screen. Three windows reveal black-and-white footage of the forest. The first window shows a spot along the Big Lake, its waters placid as they move with lazy calm toward the waterfall. A label on the video reads: EASTERN SHORE 7:17 A.M.

The second window reveals a spot in the forest Winnie doesn't recognise but that the label declares to be the NORTHWESTERN EDGE. The final screen shows the border between the Friday estate and the forest, near where Winnie and Jay had trekked only a few days ago.

Mario taps an icon on each window, and a sound like the white-noise app Mum uses fills the room. From camera one: a faint hum like the distant crashing of a cold waterfall. From camera two: wind and rustling leaves. From camera three, where the forest's hold is weaker: a trickle of birdsong.

"Here's the deal, Winnie." He's still almost inaudible. "The Council isn't impressed by our Whisperer idea. They think the footage Lizzy captured is just an anomaly—standard distortion caused by the forest. They think *I* just want to get my name into the Compendium by making up a nightmare. And you . . ."

Winnie huffs wearily. "They think I'm the girl who cried wolf."

"Or in this case, cried 'not wolf.' But yeah." Mario blows a bubble. *Pop!* "The Council thinks this fixation on the Whisperer is distracting from the very urgent threat of a werewolf. I've got Dryden breathing down my neck for a human ID *before* Luminaries start flying in for the Masquerade. I've got Tuesdays breathing down my neck for a kill order, and I've got Mondays pissed at me for studying a nightmare no one has ever heard of and no one but *you* has actually seen."

He pauses and his jaw works with a few forceful gum smacks. Then he offers a pained grimace to Winnie. "I'm really sorry about what happened yesterday. Like *so* sorry. But the only way we can get away with tracking the Whisperer right now is if no one knows we're doing it."

Winnie's teeth click. While she is most definitely less furious with Mario than when she'd first found him, she's still a long way off from forgiving him.

"Jay put out these three cameras last night." Mario waves to the screen. "Despite Lizzy's optimism, I'm not sure they'll last a full hunt. If we're lucky, they'll survive the mist long enough to capture more footage of our unknown nightmare. If we're not lucky, well . . . then we'll just keep putting out cameras until we get it."

"Or until you get caught."

Pop! "Or until we get caught." Mario rubs at his eyes. He looks as stretched out as Winnie feels.

"Or," Winnie begins, pushing at her glasses, "you catch the werewolf. Surely after that's done, then Dryden and the other councilors will listen." *One thing at a time,* like her mum had said. Except that when she glances at Mario for a response, she finds he has stiffened at those words. His jaw has stopped moving, and he stares with unseeing eyes at the cameras. Time trickles past. The forest's soothing sounds rustle through the room.

Until at last Mario says, "I don't know, Winnie. This werewolf has remained hidden for a long time, and I'm afraid . . . That is to say, I think . . . Well . . ." He pulls a fresh stick of gum from his pocket and shoves it into his mouth. Then he finally meets Winnie's gaze, a hollowness weighing at the back of his eyes. "I think we need to prepare ourselves for the very real chance we might never find it. At least not before the creature is ready to be found."

Winnie can't stop stewing over Mario's words while she walks to the history library, rolling her bike beside her. *The werewolf has remained hidden a long time.* How long, she wants to know—and how long has Mario known it was out there? She hadn't been able to ask before they'd heard Dryden's voice in the hall and Winnie had fled.

Not before it's ready to be found.

A werewolf in Hemlock Falls. A Whisperer no one believes in. God, she hopes Lizzy's cameras capture something. She might not have been alive for the werewolf seventeen years ago, but the damage is seared into everyone's DNA. Inherited trauma, inherited fear. Sometimes Winnie has wondered if the reason no one noticed what her dad was—the reason that she and Mum and Darian never noticed—was because they were all so fixated on what might come out of the forest . . . instead of what might try to come *in*.

Yet, for some reason, Winnie has a sickening fear that what's happening now is going to get worse. A *lot* worse.

Soon the Monday library comes into view: two square buildings connected by a covered walkway where morning glories will bloom in the late summer. All is still at this hour;

the library never gets crowded, but especially not before 8:00 A.M.

She hasn't been here but a few clandestine times over the past four years, and she hadn't realised just how much she missed being able to simply walk inside. Four stories rise up, arranged around an open area filled with tables and thick with books dedicated to the history of the Luminaries.

Someone coughs on a higher floor. She thinks she hears a copying machine warming up.

She cuts right toward a row of shelves that stretch alongside tall, multipaned windows. *"1" for first floor. "3" for third row.* This eastern block of shelves is dedicated to the Dianas—and it makes her heart pound when she realises it.

Dad was not being subtle.

A few spiders have taken up residence over the oldest, fattest tomes. *"Th" for author first name.* Winnie finds three of them on the bottom shelf closest to the window, all by the same woman, Theodosia Monday: *The Awakening of the Spirit by Source, Signs of Sources, Soil Composition for Optimal Sources.* Winnie feels ill at those titles.

Don't take my finger bones as a source, sì?

A tiny little piece of her wants to open one of those books and read about sources. Do Dianas actually use finger bones? What might Dad's source have been? A much larger, more insistent piece of her, though, wants to find Dad's message and get the hell out of here.

Winnie shoots a quick glance around. There's no one. The copying machine, on a higher floor, is now thrumming in full force.

Heart pounding, she pulls out each book. Her teeth click double time. But when she shakes the books' pages, nothing comes out. And when she quickly skims through them, nothing rests within. They're just dry texts on how Dianas drain magic from spirits by planting "sources" in the forests. When the sources are full, the Dianas can cast spells with the gathered magic—but the spells come at a price: they leave physical marks on Dianas' hands. Burn marks from the heat of a power that isn't theirs.

Winnie's heart pounds harder. Someone must have found Dad's message, and oh god, what if it had been addressed to her? What if it was turned over to the Council and they know Dad tried to contact her—

"No," she whispers, pushing at her glasses. "*No.*" The more likely situation is that Dad didn't even put the note in a book. He wrote in code; he was obviously being careful; if the message isn't here, she should just keep looking.

Another glance around. Still no one, though the copying machine has silenced. Someone coughs again.

Winnie pats along the shelf. Top, bottom, anywhere a message might be taped. Her fingers feel nothing save a spiderweb that makes her flinch. *Gross.* After confirming no spider scuttles over her, she crooks down to actually peer beneath the shelf where the books had rested.

Her chest is practically on the floor. Her glasses slip down her nose. But there's no paper, no tape, no message. Just a squiggly line and some dots on the back of the shelf, like a five-year-old got hold of a permanent marker.

Except why would a five-year-old be here? And why would they draw back there?

Winnie's teeth click even faster as she yanks more books off the shelf, revealing more squiggles. Six books later, and the whole drawing is on display: a wavy line that snakes right, save for a big gap in the middle with an X floating at the heart. Then, at the top corner, there's a letter *Z* with an arrow pointing left, and beside that are the numbers *1–2–1.*

Winnie has absolutely no idea what it means.

She also has no chance to consider it, because footsteps clatter this way. Heeled shoes on hardwood that move with purposeful speed. Winnie shoves the books back onto the shelf and hauls herself to her feet right as, of all people, Erica Thursday appears.

She draws up short at the sight of Winnie, her cool poise briefly flickering with eye-widening surprise. As usual, she looks like a model on the runway, in designer jeans, her signature steel-toed boots, and a black turtleneck.

"Erica," Winnie says as Erica visibly reassembles her aloof hauteur. "Hey. What are you doing here?"

"Paper." Erica's eyes thin suspiciously. "For Professor Il-Hwa, due Thursday. Tomorrow. What are you doing here?"

Winnie gulps. They might not have been friends for the last four years, but Erica will absolutely see through a lie. "I was looking for something," she says—very much the truth. Then, before Erica can ask *what,* Winnie powers on with: "I asked Darian about the locket. He found it in our attic. So . . . I don't think it was yours."

"Ah." A rusty warmth rises on Erica's face, just visible through her freshly applied makeup. "About that. I . . ." She wets her lips. "I should apologise. I was mistaken about the locket. I . . ." Swallow. "I'm sorry for . . ." Eye twitch. "For accusing you."

"Oh." Winnie blinks. She is stunned. *More* than stunned. She is downright shocked. Like an air sylphid has gotten her with its lightning. "Thank you?"

"It was Jenna's is all." Erica speaks faster now, her attention fastening on the nearest shelf. "I lost it last year, and when I saw yours, I thought . . . you know. That you or Darian or *someone* had taken it. But no. I just lost it because of course I did. I'm very *good* at losing things."

There is so much venom in Erica's voice that Winnie instinctively moves a step closer. It's like the years between them are falling away. Like they're not in the library, but instead are twelve again sitting on Erica's bed while Erica berates herself with one more criticism heaped on by Marcia. "It's not your fault, E. People lose things all the time."

"Hmm." Erica's lips press tight. Her chest stops moving. Her gaze upon the shelf has moved into another time. *Recognizing Dianas,* says the spine she seems to be staring at. A book Winnie could have used four years ago.

She spots diamond studs in Erica's ears that she remembers Erica getting for her tenth birthday. And she spots a patch of shiny red skin on the tip of Erica's thumb, where the plaster had been a few days ago.

Erica also smells like summer rain. The perfume Jenna used to wear.

"I'm sorry you lost Jenna." The words flicker from Winnie's mouth like a candle flame. "I'm sorry you lost her. I . . . I can't imagine how hard it's been for you."

"But of course you can." Erica's gaze moves to Winnie's face. For a split second, it feels like the banshee stare in the forest. "Your dad might as well be dead, Winnie, since it's not like you're ever going to see him again."

Without another word, Erica spins on her heel and clacks away. She doesn't grab whatever book she'd come for, and Winnie doesn't chase after to remind her.

CHAPTER
34

After school and training at the Sunday estate—to which Jay fails to arrive so Winnie can ask him about the Whisperer—Mum picks up Winnie and nervous-talks the entire ride home. Tonight is Mum's first night entering the Wednesday estate in four years, and though she has seen Rachel, she has yet to face the entire clan.

She doesn't say it, but Winnie knows she's thinking, hoping, praying: *Maybe they'll end the punishment early. Maybe we'll stop being outcasts.*

"We leave at six," Mum tells Winnie as she parks the Volvo at the curb. "Be ready, or I will leave without you."

Winnie absolutely believes she will.

For the next hour, they both settle into an unspoken frenzy over what they're going to wear tonight. Winnie digs through what few clean clothes remain in her closet. Then she scours what is dirty (why was Febreze invented if not for this exact moment?), and finally she scours Mum's closet. She has the clan dinner and then the twins' birthday party to look her best for.

Ultimately, with shoulders that gradually slope lower and lower, Winnie is forced to accept there is nothing in their household that would qualify as *fancy* for Emma and Bretta's party. Nor even something that will qualify as a *dress*. Which, now that Winnie considers it, is absurd. She's annoyed with herself and Mum equally for this.

So Winnie returns to her room, scrounges out some black leggings, a longer black sweater that could *almost* be a dress if she tugs a bit, and some black flats that she knows are going to leave her feet freezing. She briefly considers wearing her hoodie, just to make the twins laugh. Then decides against it. What if they or someone else mistakenly thinks she's serious?

"You look nice," Mum says, when Winnie finally comes downstairs and joins Mum in the living room. She wears her usual casual-but-nice outfit for those rare moments she's not in greasy work clothes and has to look presentable: fitted jeans, a silk T-shirt, and a long cashmere cardigan. She has each item in three colours, purchased shortly before Dad left, and since she so rarely dresses up, they still look brand-new.

It is startling to see, actually. Mum with her hair styled, Mum in nice clothes, Mum with small pearl earrings and a dab of blush to make her cheeks glow. For half a moment, between one groaning step and the next (that third stair is *such* a doozy), Winnie feels like she's been shot backward four years in time. Nothing has changed, it's just another Wednesday dinner, and any moment now, Dad is going to come out of the kitchen with his canteen, screwing on the top while water drips down because he is never, *never* without water.

But Dad doesn't come out of the kitchen, and Mum is wringing her hands in a way Mum never used to do—and there's no wedding band on the left one to glint as she does so. Plus, now that Winnie takes the final steps, she can see that Mum's concealer is creasing into lines that didn't used to be there, and she is very conspicuously missing the long crescent-moon necklace she always used to wear. *That* necklace is for Lead Hunter; *that* necklace belongs to Aunt Rachel now.

"You ready?" Mum asks without really waiting to see if Winnie is. She strides to the closet under the stairs. "Darian is meeting us at the estate. No Andrew, since we're not entirely sure what to expect tonight." Mum pulls out an old peacoat that has seen better days—and that permanently smells of hash browns—and offers Winnie her leather jacket.

"Oh," Mum says, as she hands it over. "You're wearing your old glasses."

Winnie winces. "Yeah, just for tonight. The new ones got bent at the first trial."

"Right." Mum winces too, though she quickly schools it away. She doesn't believe Winnie; Winnie feels like the worst daughter who ever lived.

But it's too late now to grab the other pair, and they *are* still bent. So there's nothing to do but follow after Mum, feeling abjectly horrible every step of the way.

Darian looks perfect, of course, because he actually does laundry. And buys new clothes every now and then. And knows how to combine said clothes, because he inherited Dad's sense of style and not Mum's utter lack of it. His heather-grey sweater and dark jeans are set off by tan leather loafers and a wool jacket that Winnie thinks he might have bought just for this occasion.

He chatters away as they walk from the shadowy parking lot—the sun has fallen, the moon has no plans to show—toward the estate. "Dryden had me organizing death certificates today," he tells Mum, "and *Cindy* had to get us all coffees. I made sure to order *exactly* what she always orders: double latte with two and a half—not three!— pumps of vanilla syrup and a sprinkling of cinnamon. It was delicious. Telling her my order, I mean. The actual drink was disgusting." He makes a gagging sound; Mum laughs; Winnie doesn't even try.

She's mad at Darian for what had happened with Dryden. Not *as* mad as she'd been with Mario, but she's definitely hurt that Darian hadn't defended her more. Logically, this is unfair. What could he have said? But the sting remains all the same.

It's also just hard to focus on what he's saying right now, much less respond. For one, she has spent the whole day trying to sort out what Dad's drawing at the library means . . . while also trying to think of *anything* else because she still hates Dad. For two, the Wednesday estate is lit up as it always is after sundown, and the lights from the dining room blaze just as Winnie imagines the pits of hell might. She even smells burning, thanks to the enormous fireplace that is no doubt consuming wood as fast as the Wednesday servers can feed it.

People whisk by the windows, colourful and smiling, moving with the ease of Luminaries who never had to leave. Winnie and Mum and Darian used to move like that; she wonders if the muscle memory is still inside her. She wonders if she'll try and repeatedly miss the target by just a little, and this time, Jay won't be there to help her find the proper footing and tell her to aim higher.

Mum slows as they approach the double front doors, and she squeezes Winnie's biceps. "Thank you," she whispers.

On her other side, Darian quickly grabs her for a side-hug, and he whispers the same. "Thank you, Winnie. *Thank you.*"

Then the doors are opening, leaving no time for Winnie to respond—not that she knows what to say anyway. The banshee lie is churning in her gut again, and humming under that is Dante's voice: *Happy birthday, witch traitor!*, and Ms. Morgan's well-meant but disheartening *Have you given any thought to that summer program at Heritage?*

Winnie doesn't belong here. She doesn't want to go inside. She wants to sprint right back home and hide before anyone can look at her and know she's full of lies—

"Frannie!" Aunt Rachel is hopping down the front steps. She's got a champagne flute in one hand, which surprises

Winnie (it's hunting night, after all), but then she pushes it onto Mum. "Welcome. We're so happy you're here."

Mum seems to melt at those words—Darian too—and Winnie tries to make herself join them in their thawed-out bliss. Because this is exactly what she'd wanted. It could not hew more closely to her daydreams if she had choreographed it herself.

Here is Aunt Rachel hauling them inside the estate, telling them all about the special dinner planned. And here is Aunt Rachel leading them into the dining room, where all the mingling Wednesdays turn as one and start clapping.

Clapping. Actual applause, over which Marcus—who is now weaving his way toward them—throws in an obnoxious *whoop-whoop.* Then Marcus is to them, and he's punching at Winnie's shoulders like they're the best of friends and looking around to make sure people saw him doing it.

Winnie has never hated him more.

Now Leila Wednesday, Fatima's mum and clan leader, is striding across the room, having abandoned her usual spot beside the fireplace, and the rest of the clan is clearing aside to let her through. Winnie hasn't seen Leila in four years, not even from afar, and she's shocked at how much the woman hasn't aged. She looks stunning in a lilac hijab that complements her navy sweater and matching wide-leg slacks. Fatima skips behind her, more casual in all grey and a rose-patterned hijab.

"Fran," Leila says, opening her arms to Mum. Her smile is rich and deep, her brown eyes crinkling. Bangles clink on her wrists. "I am so glad you're here. We all are."

The nearest Wednesdays all murmur agreements, and Winnie realises they're each holding champagne (though Leila's is presumably nonalcoholic). Leila's gaze skates to Winnie next, and her smile widens to reveal perfect teeth. "And the belle of our ball tonight! Other than our birthday girls, of course."

A smattering of laughs, and Winnie hears the twins' telltale giggle somewhere in the vicinity of the fireplace.

"Never was there such a display of loyalty," Leila declares, and she moves to Winnie's side. A scent like gardenias and power settles over Winnie; Leila slides an arm around her shoulders.

And Fatima gives Winnie a reassuring wink.

"A toast to Winnie Wednesday. May we all be as brave and loyal as she!" Leila lifts her glass, and the rest of the room follows suit.

"Hear, hear!" they say. Or, "To Winnie!" Or, if they're Marcus, "Whoop-whoop!" Glasses rise, throats gulp, and like a rain cloud letting loose, conversation bursts forth, louder, happier, sparkling with champagne.

"Sit at the table with me," Leila says, giving Winnie a little pat before she pulls away. Then to Mum and Darian: "You two, as well. We have so much to catch up on."

———

Winnie can see, as dinner progresses through each course, the room vibrating with conversation and firelight, that Mum and Darian are struggling. It's the juxtaposition of it all—exactly what Mum had ranted about on Saturday, exactly what Winnie had ranted about too. Everyone acts as if Winnie and Darian and Mum have just gone away for a while—travelled abroad, explored the world, and now are finally returning home as weary, cosmopolitan networkers. There is no mention of Fran serving extra ketchup at the Revenant's Daughter. No mention of all the years Darian has collected coffee and dusted off Dryden Saturday's desk. No mention of Winnie gathering corpses while the Wednesday hunters pretend every Thursday that she doesn't exist.

Unlike Winnie, though, Mum and Darian have the benefit of champagne to smooth away their discomfort and erase the hypocrisy of small talk and clinking silverware. Winnie, meanwhile, just gnaws on steak she knows is really fancy but can't bring herself to eat.

Oh, she smiles when anyone talks to her. And she laughs (genuinely) at Fatima's funny stories about training mishaps the week before. And she even manages to glide right over how she killed the banshee by spinning the tale over to Fatima, who is practically bouncing in her seat to share.

The night feels interminable, though, and when at *last* the various clocks around the house clang eight o'clock—and all the hunters peel off to get ready for the forest—Winnie is just happy she can take a moment to breathe.

Yes, she has to attend the twins' party soon—which she can see being set up through the back windows (the fairy lights look very pretty)—but she also has an excuse to step away: Mum and Darian are tipsy at this point and need a ride home.

It's a bit of a slog to get them out of the house. They're giggly, and Mum in particular wants to talk to *everyone*. Winnie would be embarrassed by the maternal loquaciousness if not for the fact that everyone seems to genuinely want to talk to her too. And to Darian *and* to Winnie. It just makes Winnie want to shout at them like she'd shouted at Lizzy: *We were here all along! You could have talked to us all along!*

By the time Winnie has Mum and Darian seat-belted into the Volvo, she has already wasted almost twenty minutes of her pre-party hour. Fortunately, Hemlock Falls is small, so even puttering along at fifteen miles an hour in first gear, Winnie *should* be back in time.

Three cars pass her as she aims downtown to drop off Darian. The third car honks.

"Ah, screw you, buddy!" Mum flips them the bird, although she gets her fingers mixed up. So it's really just a stern ring finger. "If we wanna go slow, we'll go slow. Although Winnie." Mum turns a serious face on her. "We are going very slow."

"*Very* slow," Darian intones from the back seat.

"I'm aware." Winnie grips the steering wheel so hard her knuckles ache. "But you haven't taught me how to shift gears yet."

"I taught you." Mum makes a fuzzy face. "Two weeks ago. Three. *Sometime* I taught you. It's just like going into first gear. You just need to be gentle with the clutch."

"Except it's not like that, Mum, because now I'm in motion and can stall. So, if either of you want to get home tonight, we're staying in first gear all the way."

Mum giggles. "That's funny."

"It really is." Darian giggles too.

And Winnie sighs. No more champagne for them. Ever again. Not unless it's the nonalcoholic variety.

After Winnie drops off Darian (let Andrew deal with his silliness), the Volvo becomes much quieter. In fact, Mum goes totally silent—even when *another* car passes and honks. Winnie waves apologetically.

She is just puttering them out of downtown when Mum says something wholly unexpected. "Your dad and I used to eat lunch at that picnic table."

Winnie's gaze snaps to Mum, who slouches against the window and gazes out at a patio surrounded by hydrangeas yet to bloom. "He always talked about how hydrangeas change colour based on the soil's pH. And I always told him it was fascinating."

Winnie remembers Dad telling her the same thing once, but she doesn't dare say that to Mum. This is the first time in four years Mum has mentioned Dad without fury in her voice. She doesn't seem sad either. More . . . fond. Like this is a happy memory and it's making her smile.

"Did you know he once challenged Rachel to a drinking contest at Wednesday dinner, and hellions and banshees did he *lose*. He got through two beers by the time she'd finished almost four. We"—Mum lurches a pointed finger toward

Winnie—"know how to drink in our family. You can thank Great-Gran Maria for that."

Winnie isn't going to thank Great-Gran Maria for anything because Mum definitely *cannot* drink, and Winnie really hopes she never has to be Designated Driver again.

When Winnie reaches their street, she very, *very* slowly turns onto it. And very, *very* casually she asks, "Mum, do you ever wonder how we didn't see it? What Dad really was, I mean?"

Mum's eyebrows bounce to the top of her face, while Winnie's heart thumps into the high gears she can't reach with the car. She's still too scared to ask about the birthday cards, but this . . . it seems innocent enough. She hopes.

"I used to." Mum leans back in her seat. "Hell, I even believed at first that he *hadn't* done it. That he *wasn't* a Diana. How could I not, Winnie? Denial's a pretty strong reflux . . . reflec . . . tion?"

"Reflex."

"That." Mum rubs at her eyes. "We'd been together for almost twenty years, and I'd truly never seen any hints that he might be . . ." She draws in a ragged breath. "The bad guy. No crystal ball sources, no scars on his fingertips. But our minds are pretty good at hiding what we don't want to see, Winnebago. And the truth is that he was a Diana. He *is* a Diana, and wishing otherwise or wondering what we hadn't seen is never going to change it."

CHAPTER

35

W hen Winnie finally gets back to the Wednesday estate, forty-five minutes have passed. The party will start soon. She both dreads going to it and also desperately wants to. *Anything* that will get her mind off Dad and that drawing at the library. Off the Whisperer no one will believe in.

Yet she finds herself just sitting in the Volvo's driver's seat, unmoving, while she stares with unfocused eyes at the twins' gift in unicorn wrapping paper upon her lap.

Someone knocks at her window. Winnie whirls about, fists rising and heart lurching. But it's only Jay, bent over and peering through the glass. He lifts his hands, supplicating.

Winnie swallows. Then opens the door.

"Never startle a Luminary," he says, offering a weak smile. "Sorry."

"You're fine," Winnie lies. She hadn't seen him shuffling about in the shadows. Jay steps closer, emerging from the full darkness into clouded moonlight—and Winnie's eyes almost jump from their sockets. "Are you wearing a tux?"

"Unfortunately. L.A. insisted."

"Did you rent it?" Winnie inspects the black bow tie that suits him surprisingly well.

"No, I own it."

"Really?"

He smiles. "Of course not. I rented it from Falls' Finest." He flicks a cuff link, which Winnie notices is shaped like the Luminary moon. "The shoes, though, are all mine."

No surprise, Winnie thinks, peeking down at the motorcycle boots tucked under fitted tux trousers.

On anyone else, this ensemble would look ridiculous. On Jay . . . Well, Winnie suspects his adoring fans will be *very* happy, and against her will, she finds herself yet again scrutinizing his thigh muscles.

"Did you see the Whisperer?" she asks, finally exiting the car. "Mario told me about Lizzy's cameras."

Jay shakes his head. "No, Win. I didn't see it. Or hear it." He looks deeply apologetic as he says this, and Winnie starts to wonder if maybe he doesn't think it's real either, because people who believe you don't stare at you like that. Like they're both embarrassed for you and sorry for you at the same time.

She finds herself scowling.

"Want to help me carry in my equipment?" Jay motions toward Mathilda.

"Not really." She hugs her arms to her chest. It's cold out. "But I will. Just because it's you."

"I'll take that as a compliment." He smiles, a faint thing that hovers momentarily before will-o'-wisping away. Then he unbuttons his tux jacket and slips it off. The white of his button-up glows, leaching his skin of colour. Before Winnie's eyes, he becomes a ghost.

A ghost with very nice shoulders.

"Here." He offers her the coat. "You're freezing."

She doesn't disagree, and she doesn't argue. The captured heat from his body radiates off the coat, and in seconds, she is snuggled deep inside. It smells like him. Like bergamot and lime and a forest shrouded in spring.

She puts the unicorn-wrapped gift in his interior pocket.

At Mathilda's trunk, Jay offers Winnie the bass while he handles his amp. The tux jacket sleeves hang over her hands, so she has to roll up one to grip the case handle. The button on the cuff winks up at her.

They walk slowly toward the front of the estate, Jay unhurried—as if he too isn't entirely sure he wants to go through with a party. And once Winnie can see the front door, see party arrivals mingling near the steps and in the front hall . . .

"Let's go the back way," Winnie says, cutting them right toward the garden path that circles behind the house.

It is like the trail on the Friday estate, with wide stepping-stones and trees kept in check by human hands. They swish and murmur on the night's icy breeze. Winnie's flats patter softly; Jay's boots squeak; and for a few blissful minutes, it feels like they are the only people in the world. Like they are back in the forest, just the two of them, going to train. Just the two of them, like they used to be.

Maybe one day, he'll tell her why he pulled away.

And maybe one day, she'll forgive him for it.

They reach the garden too soon. It is a huge space, the brick walls thick with burgeoning ivy and morning glories that will bloom in August. Winnie leads Jay to an iron gate, through which hundreds of lights sparkle like a canopy of stars. They even flicker, one here, one there, in a slow twinkle that undulates across the brick patio where a stage has been set up. The main fountain—of a bear and her cubs—has been turned off, and potted plants that usually hug it have been cleared away for a refreshments table.

Winnie wonders if this is what the Nightmare Masquerade will look like, the grand gala that Dryden is so fixated on. It's a huge celebration—more like a festival, really—that marks the true beginning of spring and the full release of the forest's winter. Luminaries from all over the world will come.

Winnie wishes the Council would just cancel it, and she wishes even more that someone would just trust her about the Whisperer.

Beyond the patio, a gravel garden is split and divided by rows of early-season flowers. Daffodils and hyacinths, snapdragons and irises. As spring progresses, new flowers will grow while these ones wither away. Then summer will bring others, and even autumn too. This garden bursts with colour almost the entirety of the year.

Dad always hated it. Not the constant influx of new life— that he could and did appreciate—but its primness, each plant in its place with no interesting elements, no wayward strays. All the rows and diamonds, crosses and circles. *Just like a good Wednesday,* Dad would say. *Growing exactly where it's told to grow. Loyal to a gardener it will never know. Except plants, like people, aren't meant to stay in perfect rows.*

"You okay?" Jay asks, startling Winnie. She hadn't realised she'd stopped moving, or that her lips had parted while she gazed at the tidy expanse of botanical symmetry.

No, she thinks. "Yes," she says aloud. They resume their forward progress toward the stage, though they don't proceed far before Fatima springs into their path.

"Oh my gosh, Winnie! *Jay.*"

"Fatima," Winnie says at the same time Jay says nothing at all.

Fatima instantly snags Winnie's arm, then Jay's, and tows them both toward the stage. "You're the first here, Jay, but L.A. just texted and she'll be here any moment. Do you know when Trevor will arrive?" Fatima flashes Jay what can only be described as heart-eyes.

"Soon," he murmurs, shifting the amp from his left arm to his right—which in turn pulls it free from Fatima's grasp. Not that she seems to notice; they're at the stage now, and in a rapid-fire eruption of words and gestures, she indicates where to plug things in, where to put the cables "so you don't trip on them," and where to stand—although that part seems pretty obvious.

"There aren't any of the heaters over here"—Fatima points to one of the many outdoor heaters spaced across the patio—"but I figured you guys would be moving, so you wouldn't need one. Although . . . Are you wearing his coat, Winnie?"

"Oh." Winnie blinks. Then blushes and hastily shrugs out of the aforementioned coat. She pushes it toward Jay. "Thanks."

He offers her a nod and a crooked smile that doesn't reach his eyes. It's only after he has slipped on the jacket again and Winnie has twisted away that she remembers the twins' gift is still in his pocket. "Oh wait." She scoots back to him and slides her hand inside the jacket. "I forgot something . . ." She trails off, realizing too late that this is an extremely intimate position to have put herself in.

"Sorry," she hears herself saying, a distant sound as she stares at his silvery eyes.

"It's fine," he replies, though he makes no move to help her find the present, nor any move to jerk away as her fingers move across the planes of his chest. His eyes simply stay fused to hers, unreadable. She can feel his heartbeat.

When at last Winnie finds the gift beneath her fingertips, she eases it out—very slowly, because her muscles have become detached from her mind.

She wonders if Jay's eyes have always been this dark or if it's just that his pupils have swallowed up everything. She thinks they might be trembling. Or maybe that's his chest, still pressed against her fingers.

Then her hand and the gift are free. "Sorry," she repeats, voice strangely weak.

"It's fine." His voice is not weak. His eyes are still on hers.

Until Fatima pokes her head between them. "Oh *my,*" she says with the satisfied gaze of a harpy who has just eaten delicious feet. "That was interesting to watch." She loops her arm in Winnie's and hauls Winnie away.

Thank god, Winnie thinks even as her body is weirdly shouting, *Go back! Stop moving!* She's pretty sure Jay is watching her leave. She can feel his pulsing pupils bore two holes into her back.

She and Fatima reach the glass doors into the dining room. Once inside, Fatima gives a delighted squeal. "Oh my gosh, are you two *dating*?"

"No!" Winnie blurts. Two caterers on their way outside the house glance her way.

"The twins are going to be so jealous!" Fatima grins wickedly. "But also *so* excited because they can live vicariously through you."

"We're *not* dating," Winnie says as forcefully as she can. "We're just, um . . . We're just . . ."

"Friends?" Fatima provides.

"Um," Winnie offers again. She and Jay aren't friends, but they also aren't enemies. And they're more than just acquaintances. Truth is, she's not even sure a word exists for their relationship. So instead, she pointedly changes subjects. "Where are we going?"

"To my room." Fatima nudges Winnie with a shoulder. "So we can get dressed for the party. The twins are already up there . . . Wait, where's your dress?"

"Oh." Heat gutters onto Winnie's face. "I don't have one. This is all I've got." She waves awkwardly at her sweater and leggings.

But Fatima isn't fazed. "No problem." She offers another conspiratorial grin. "I have tons of stuff you can choose from."

Winnie isn't sure what to say to that. She suspects that even if she argues against borrowing something, Fatima—and the twins—will just forcibly stuff her into a gown anyway, like a droll stuffs treasure into its hoard. Besides, she's not exactly opposed to the idea. Her black sweater is really depressing.

So she lets Fatima lead her through the now-emptied dining room, past the fire burned to smoldering remnants, past the tables now clean and bare and ready for next week's dinner, and finally into the hall. Each of Winnie's footsteps on the red rug is buttery soft. When she'd come here on Sunday with Aunt Rachel, she'd been wearing trainers. Now, with only a thin strip of leather between her and the rug, there is no missing how it soaks up each of her steps. And somehow, on the staircase up . . . and then up again, to the living quarters on the third floor, it's even softer. Like ascending a ramp of sea foam.

Red, bloodied sea foam.

The flat on the top floor is huge—that's the first thing Winnie thinks when she follows Fatima inside. Before her is a wide living area with high ceilings and windows to overlook the front of the estate. The modern decor is almost at odds with the classical style of the home, except it's so elegant, so sleek, that it ends up blending beautifully. Sharp-lined furniture, modern art on the walls, sculptures that look vaguely nightmarish, and beautiful bookcases laden with a rainbow of tomes—literally, the book spines are all organised by colour to make a rainbow across the walls.

Fatima skips right, aiming toward a hall that leads to the bedrooms, and at the first door, giggles sprinkle through. Fatima skips in dramatically. "We're here!"

Emma squeals and bounds off a sleigh bed with lavender-coloured sheets, and Bretta scrabbles off just behind. A chandelier glitters light across the girls. Both wear neon-yellow lipstick; Emma holds a bottle of champagne.

"Winnie! Have some!" She shoves it at Winnie, but Winnie just shoves it onto Fatima . . . who in turn shoves it onto Bretta, who swigs gleefully.

"They took it from the dining room," Fatima explains, beckoning for Winnie to follow. "It is, fortunately, half empty."

"Half full!" Bretta and Emma exclaim in unison before dissolving into giggles. Winnie feels like she should be annoyed after dealing with two bubbled-up family members, but it's impossible to be annoyed with the twins. Unlike Darian and Mum, they're actually fun.

As everyone piles into Fatima's closet—where the twins' outfits are hanging in protective plastic—and helps find something Winnie can fit into (Fatima is bustier and shorter), she is again struck by the fact that out of everyone in Hemlock Falls, the twins have always been nice to her. Even Fatima has never been mean or two-faced like Marcus. She has stood up for Winnie now and then, like she did last Thursday in homeroom.

All this time, Winnie has been missing her old friends when she could have so easily had new ones. It makes her heart scoop out just imagining.

Fatima eventually settles on a green dress for Winnie that she, with her design eye, *insists* will make Winnie's auburn hair "pop." It's definitely meant for summer, and it's *definitely* not the sort of thing Winnie would ever buy— not merely because this is from Falls' Finest, but because without the silk white shirt Fatima wears under it, the dress shows more skin than Winnie's typically . . . well, *Puritan* wardrobe of crew necks and long sleeves. The straps are fine as melusine hair, the silk as soft as a ghost-deer's glow, and the colour really *does* look good against Winnie's olive skin. It's like the forest in summer, when even winter grey is forced to let go.

Because Fatima is shorter than Winnie by a few inches, the dress does cut a bit short, floating just below her mid-calf instead of her ankles. And unfortunately, Fatima's feet are a totally different size, so Winnie is stuck wearing her flats.

"No one will look down there, anyway," Bretta assures, waving to Winnie's chest, where the fabric droops low and her golden locket glimmers. Fatima has a *lot* more chest than

Winnie, so the droopage is very real. "You've got all this, uh . . . skin to catch the eye right here."

"Skin," Winnie says, "meaning no boobs."

Which makes Bretta giggle. "You're the one who said it, not me!"

"*But,*" Emma chimes in with a meaningful eyebrow bounce. "I mean . . ."

Winnie can't help but laugh. It's been so long since anyone teased her good-naturedly. She's forgotten what that felt like—forgotten it can make your heart surge instead of fall.

Fatima and the twins get dressed—Fatima in a royal purple dress with a high lace collar that is much, *much* better suited to the temperature outside, Bretta in a sleek, neon-green pantsuit that makes her look like a rock star crossed with a girl boss, and finally Emma in a magenta miniskirt that makes her legs look a million miles long and a frilly top that flounces like phoenix feathers.

Winnie helps them all, and she grudgingly agrees to put on lipstick and eyeshadow too, using Q-tips and Fatima's supply. She hasn't worn makeup, like . . . ever, and it takes her a few tries (and Emma's help because Winnie is just *not* applying enough) before she looks glammed up enough for the twins' and Fatima's satisfaction.

And though she wasn't expecting it tonight, Winnie actually has fun. Like . . . a *lot* of fun, even if once or twice she does think of Erica.

It is a quarter to ten by the time they're all done. Emma and Bretta have polished off the last swigs of the champagne. "Let's go, let's go!" Emma claps like the cheerleader she would be if Hemlock Falls had competitive sports teams. Her tiny skirt caroms around her thighs.

"Wait," Winnie says before everyone can skip to the door. "I have a present for you."

This earns a collective *Weeeee!* and Emma and Bretta topple back onto the bed in a flurry of lace and frill. Winnie is almost glad they're tipsy, because now, if her present turns out terrible, they will be too silly to care.

She offers them her gift, the unicorn wrapping paper slightly crumpled from its time in Jay's jacket. "I hope you like it," she mutters at the same moment Fatima croons, "Ooooh, what is it?"

Bretta snags the gift first and rips into it with such gusto that Darian would have cried (he likes to slowly peel off the tape, carefully unfold each line, and generally infuriate everyone waiting for him to just open his presents already). A white box soon appears in Bretta's grasp, and she hands it off to Emma, who plucks off the top.

Within are two glass vials, their corks looped onto simple leather cords. "What's . . . in it?" Emma scoops out one necklace and holds the vial to the light.

Bretta is the one to figure it out. "Oh my god, it's a banshee claw! Oh my *god*!" She snatches up her own necklace and then stumbles off the bed. "You gave us banshee claws! This is *so* cool! Aaaah!" She dives at Winnie for a hug, and though Winnie really, really is not a hugger, she lets the twin have it. And when Emma leaps in for the hug too, she just silently endures—and even ends up smiling.

The twins are thrilled. They really are. Her gift, assembled from some random craft supplies in her closet, has actually been a hit.

"Wow," Fatima breathes after the twins pull apart and Emma lets her study the claw. "This is really special. Put it on, put it on!" She loops it around Emma's neck while Bretta struggles with champagne-fuzzy fingers to put on her own.

Winnie helps her out, and moments later, the twins pose before Winnie and Fatima, beaming in that full-wattage way only they can. The vials glint at their collarbones, maybe not the most *high-fashion* thing ever, but definitely unique.

"How do we look?" Bretta strikes a runway stance.

Emma strikes one beside her. "Like hunters?"

"Definitely." Winnie laughs while Fatima claps and giggles—and yet again, Winnie wishes she'd let the twins and Fatima into her world sooner. Because if anyone is worth lowering her defences for, it's definitely them.

CHAPTER
36

When Winnie, the twins, and Fatima finally head down to the night's main event, Leila and Fatima's dad wave at them from the couch, where they're each reading. "There will be chaperones!" Leila calls after them.

Which only earns more giggles and a "Love you!" from Fatima.

As they descend the stairs, the twins arm in arm, Bretta says, "Guess what I heard."

"What?" everyone dutifully replies.

"*I* heard the third trial doesn't even happen in the forest."

"Oh, I heard that too." Fatima's voice dips to a whisper. She glances back at the top floor, already disappearing from sight.

Winnie shoves her glasses up her nose.

"I heard it happens here," Bretta continues. "Like in the Armory or something."

"Pssshhhh." Fatima swats the air. Her purple long sleeves billow. "If it was happening here, I would totally notice."

"How?" Emma demands at the same time Winnie asks, "Are you allowed in the Armory, though?"

This makes Fatima frown. "Well, no—"

"Then it *could* be here!" Bretta squeals, disrupting the heretofore stealth voices they'd been using. Winnie and Fatima both fling nervous glances around. But there's no one near. They're passing the second floor, and all the office doors are shut and dark at this hour.

"What if it happens tonight?" Bretta asks reverently. "On our *birthday.*"

"Oh, I hope not." Emma hip-bumps her sister. "I'm tipsy."

"Me too."

Fatima looks at Winnie, a tiny frown slicing over her brow. "Have you heard anything?" She seems to realise as soon as she asks it that of *course* Winnie hasn't heard anything. She gulps. Hastily adjusts her hijab (in rich purple to match her gown). Then offers loud enough for the twins to hear: "The hunters are on duty tonight. So they *can't* test us."

But even as Fatima says it, Winnie can tell she's not so sure. And Winnie isn't so sure either—only that she's glad she didn't drink any of that champagne. Alcohol, she has decided, makes her family into fools.

When at last they reach the dining room, darkened save for the final phantom of a fire, the party is aglow outside. Speakers pump out dance music Winnie doesn't recognise. The patio she'd navigated easily before is now *packed,* and the winking fairy lights seem to pulse in time to the music.

It's magical. Otherworldly, with everyone glossy and smiling and alive. It reminds her of something Grandpa Frank once said—which is weird, because Winnie barely knew Grandpa Frank and doesn't think of him often.

That's why we're called the Luminaries, Winnie: we are lanterns the forest can never snuff out.

Yes. Winnie can see that's true; she can *feel* that's true. She watches the twins skip across the dining room toward the open glass doors, Fatima with them, and all three oblivious that Winnie has slowed.

Winnie waits a long time before she leaves the safety of the dining room's darkness. She simply stands there, still as Jay in the forest, watching the party unfold behind clear glass. Glittering and vibrant and beating with life. Lanterns the forest can never snuff out.

Outside, the song has shifted to something gentler. Less beat, more ether. It floats into the dining room and settles over Winnie, giving her other senses space to awaken.

The room has grown cold; the fire has coughed its final breath; the heaters outside flare invitingly. The patio is everything she has ever wanted, but in here, she is safe.

Eventually, L.A. gets onstage—to much cheering—and announces that the Forgotten is about to start, *So get rid of your heels and take off those jackets, 'cos we're gonna be dancing tonight.*

"Winnie!" Fatima cries, materializing at the garden door. "Come *on!*" She waves frantically before flinging herself back into the crowd.

Winnie obeys, her feet carrying her toward the door even if her mind isn't quite ready for the onslaught. But then again, will it ever be?

It's like stepping into the mist. Suddenly there is heat, cloying and wild. It swallows her, briefly crushing her in teeth made of Luminaries. But just as the mist always clears, the intensity of the onslaught fades. People smile at her. There is Carmen Lunes and Lindsey Saturday. Imran and Xavier, Dante and Marisol. Hugh Friday with Galina Vtornika, who just moved here from the Russian Luminaries.

Even Erica glances Winnie's way across the crowd, her hair piled on her head in a way that makes her look like a queen. It's not a smile she offers, but an acknowledgment. An acceptance that this is the way things are now, and so she will be polite.

Winnie drifts through the crowd, letting the tide carry her where it will. First she floats toward the stage. Then toward the fountain. Then toward the symmetrical gardens, where cold night air breathes over flowers in perfect rows.

Even if the Council hasn't officially removed her family's outcast status, for tonight, Winnie is a Luminary again. She is a Wednesday. She is a lantern.

She breaks free from the throngs right where the patio ends and the last of the fairy-light lattice extends. Trevor has just gotten onstage, devastatingly handsome in his tux. Winnie thinks she hears Fatima shrieking.

Next L.A. returns to the stage, drawing plenty of adoring shrieks of her own. She's wearing a tuxedo too, but with glittery trainers that flash like meteors.

Last comes Jay, and it's weird because Winnie saw him only an hour ago, yet for some reason, seeing him on the stage, serious and clearly uncomfortable with how *very much* people are screaming at him, he doesn't look like the Jay she knows. Nor even like the Jay she used to know.

He is lonely and lost, and Winnie hates that she knows the feeling.

His grey eyes—glowing pure silver in the twinkling lights—scan quickly over the crowd. She's not sure what he's looking for, but whatever it is, he doesn't seem to find it. A tiny frown cinches his brow. Then L.A. starts singing happy birthday, and he and Trevor join in with their instruments.

The whole party sings, even Winnie, though she's more mouthing the words than really singing along. *Happy birthday, witch traitor, happy birthday to you!* She has come a long way in six days.

The song ends, and without a pause, the Forgotten kick into a song Winnie hadn't heard on Saturday. It starts with L.A. snapping her fingers into the mic, and the twins lose it. Them and everyone else, really, and when Jay moves in with the bass line, Winnie gets why. Then as soon as Trevor starts playing too, popping in with a vocal harmony, Winnie finds she's dancing.

Not the wild dancing up near the stage, but a rocking that thrums through her. Wind caresses her from the garden, icy and fanged. She scarcely notices. The Forgotten are good. Really good, and she almost wishes she'd stayed on Saturday to hear them play longer.

But you're here now, her brain reminds. *You can enjoy them now.* She is about to push into the thick of it all and find the twins, find Fatima, when Jay looks up. It's exactly like it was at Joe Squared, like he has sensed her movement and his eyes instinctively know where to land.

It takes him a beat to realise it's her, though. She can see the confusion in his glinting eyes as he absorbs her makeup, her dress, her shoulders and neck so completely bared.

Then recognition sets in.

His lips part. He stops swaying to the music. Only his fingers still move, sliding up and down the frets as if attached to someone else entirely. She thinks, weirdly, he might approve of her current look. And she thinks, weirdly, that she's pleased by it.

Then he smiles, and she knows he likes what he sees. It's a tiny smile that only lifts one corner of his lips, but sets all his admirers into shrieking raptures. And it sets Winnie's insides curling. Her toes too. And her fingers into the soft silk of Fatima's dress.

For the first time in four years, Winnie forces herself to look squarely in the face of a truth she has stoutly ignored, denied, buried away since Jay ditched her: once upon a time, she liked him. A lot. More than a friend, more than a best friend. Which was why his sudden departure from her life, his cold rejection of her, had been so, *so* hard to bear.

He'd been her first crush. Her *only* crush and he hadn't even wanted her as a friend anymore.

Now he looks at her like maybe he does want her—at least during this particular fraction of a song while his fingers play and his eyes linger—but rather than be flattered, Winnie only finds anger boiling up inside her.

He's four years too late. Why is he *always* four years too late?

It doesn't help that Winnie's traitorous mind imagines, for the second time in a week, what kissing him might be like, with lips crashing and tree bark against her back, with heat and teeth and hunger . . .

No. She doesn't like Jay now; she doesn't even want to *think* of him in that way; and she really wishes he would look at someone else now. That he would end this silly moment that ultimately means nothing for either of them.

She is the first to take the initiative. She turns toward the garden and gulps in the cold air sweeping off it. As she stares into the shadows and her rage shrinks back to something manageable—the same old pain she has lived with for four years past—she spots movement at the edge of the garden.

A person, dressed in magenta with a skirt that flounces on the breeze, is almost to the gate that leads off the estate. *Emma.* She pauses and glances behind her. It's a furtive look, as if she wants to make sure no one sees . . . except that her eyes land on Winnie—just the barest flicker—and Winnie thinks she glimpses a flash of teeth.

Winnie is suddenly frozen down to her very bones. Gone is the normal spring bite. It's like the forest cold has suddenly laid claim to the entire party.

She abandons the patio quickly, an urgency rising in her that says, *Wrong, this is wrong.* And with that feeling comes the Compendium.

Changelings: These daywalkers can perfectly mimic any human they see. Long claws give them away, and they cannot speak.

She doesn't think that was a changeling. In fact, she's almost certain it was Emma, the real Emma because how would a changeling have come into the party—and why would it disappear again when there is so much here to feast upon?

But something is off, something with Emma isn't right.

Possession: Though rare, there are reports of forest spirits briefly possessing humans and using them to accomplish tasks that nightmares cannot complete, such as destroying sensory equipment or killing hunters. The hosts rarely survive the encounter.

Winnie's feet grind over gravel paths. She is covered in gooseflesh from the cold; her toes are already going numb, her ankle aching anew. But those are cursory problems in someone else's body. Right now, everything inside her has homed in on Emma.

Winnie reaches the garden gate. The latch is dangling, the iron not all the way shut. *She wants me to follow,* Winnie thinks, so she does, stepping through the brick wall and leaving the sound of music and revelry, the light of fairies and warmth behind. There are small torches to illuminate a stepping-stone path here. Right will connect it to the other path and then the parking lot. Left will loop around the estate. Straight will take her through trees, and eventually to the forest.

Winnie goes straight. Not merely because she thinks she spots a wink of magenta, but because she can feel, wrapped around her skeleton, a certainty that Emma is headed for danger.

How much did she drink? Winnie wonders as, still, the Compendium scrolls endlessly through the back of her mind.

Revenants: Corpses left in the forest or buried too close to the forest will reawaken, imbued by spiritual energy and hungry for blood.

Later, when all of this is done and the forest has finished what it set out to do, Winnie will think she should have gone back to the party for help. After all, she is weaponless, alone, and no one knows where she is. She doesn't even have a jacket. It's just her, a flimsy dress that droops over her chest, and leather flats that feel every pebble, every stick that lines the wooded floor.

In this moment, though, all Winnie thinks is that she needs to *hurry,* needs to *catch up.* Then she can grab Emma—who really must be drunk—and guide her right back to her birthday party.

She hears the strains of a Forgotten tune, hungry and haunted. Then it is just the bass line she hears. Then it is nothing at all.

But magenta still flashes ahead, so Winnie shoves at her glasses and moves faster. Her ears ache, the veins in her skull warming and expanding too fast against the spring's cold. Her breaths are already shallow, her toes totally numb.

"Emma!" she shouts at the next flicker of magenta. "*Emma!*"

The other girl seems to momentarily slow ... then somehow fly even faster. Like she knows she's being chased; like that is the whole point of it.

Changelings. Possession. Revenants. Yes, something is wrong, and now Winnie is practically sprinting to try to catch the other girl. Her glasses keep sliding down her nose. Annoyingly, Jay's voice murmurs in her mind, *Contacts would be a lot easier,* a maddening bass line to the endless tune of the Compendium.

Changelings. Possession. Revenants.

Emma reaches the forest, the brightness of her skirt suddenly flouncing into muted shadow. Winnie loses sight of it; horror bursts into her chest. The mist has already risen tonight, and Emma—and Winnie—are both completely unarmed, unarmored, unprepared.

Winnie dares not shout again for the other girl.

At the line that marks the forest's edge, where colour bleeds away and the air shifts from crisp to charged, Winnie finds a red stake. She pauses her pursuit of Emma just long enough to yank it from the ground, a primitive weapon against creatures that exist only to kill. Then she finds one of the perimeter sensors and kicks it over. "Find us," she hisses to whatever hunters might respond to a damaged sensor. "Please, find us."

CHAPTER

37

Winnie has lost all feeling in her hands and feet. She wiggles her fingers constantly around the red stake, but the cold is too determined in the forest. One girl cannot stop this wintry grey that refuses to let go.

At least tonight there is moonlight, even if only a half-moon. It illuminates the forest in an eerie glow, and remnants of mist linger in low pockets of earth. Winnie strides through them, brief bursts of searing hot that cut into her frozen limbs.

Emma always stays ahead—too far for Winnie to catch up to, no matter how much she sprints. But never so far that Winnie can't see her, can't quickly find her again when she loses sight.

So far, they have encountered no nightmares—a blessing Winnie isn't going to argue with. But it's only a matter of time. Winnie prays they meet hunters first instead. She's seen signs of them. Boot prints. An errant bolt stuck in an oak. But never the hunters themselves.

And never Emma either—only the shape of her, the muted colours sapped of life.

Possession. Winnie is leaning more and more toward that. *Though rare, there are reports of forest spirits briefly possessing humans and using them to accomplish tasks that nightmares cannot complete.* It's the only thing that might make sense, even if the how of it isn't clear.

Winnie should have gone for help. Why didn't she go for help?

She doesn't know how long she jogs, frozen yet sweating, through a forest that doesn't trust her while the moon wavers down. She only knows that nothing looks familiar. She might know the forest well after three years of corpse duty, but daylight renders it a different world. Now she is a foreigner, an intruder, an invader the forest does not want here.

Something slithers through the trees ahead. It rustles against multiple trees at once, as if enormously long, and Winnie can just detect a faint scent like rotten fruit.

The forest is dangerous for a Luminary untrained. The lesson prickles over Winnie, and she stops dead in her tracks. Despite the thundering of her heart and aching in her eardrums, she finds her senses rocketing to life. Hunter senses she has tried to develop but that only the forest can truly awaken.

Basilisks: Though seemingly small, no wider than a cobra, the basilisk can, in fact, stretch up to forty feet long. Fine, hairlike tendrils alert it to nearby movement of prey, and the head can move with uncanny speed once prey is detected.

The crown-shaped stripes across its brow are venomous to the touch, as are its fangs and its breath, if inhaled. The greatest danger, however, is its eyes. To make eye contact with a basilisk is to have your own eyes turn to stone. Though animals can survive the encounter (but are permanently blinded), the basilisk usually strikes before they can evade.

Winnie slowly shrinks down to the forest floor. She is never going to spot a black serpent in this moon-leached light. The creature has killed several nons lately and keeps evading hunters. But maybe if Winnie can just listen and stay still, she can wait out the creature's passage. It sounds like it's moving away from her.

It's probably following Emma, her mind kindly suggests, and Winnie swears inwardly. She can't shout; she can't run ahead. She's just going to have to hope that Emma is as aware of her surroundings as Winnie is.

Winnie waits, her lips clamped shut. The slithering continues, travelling through the underbrush in the same direction Emma went.

Basilisks possess hollow fangs that inject venom much like natural snakes. Their venom kills within seconds, disabling a victim's nerves in what is believed to be a painless, sudden death.

The basilisk is still sliding away when Winnie finally discerns part of it. Just a segment sliding near a log. It's picking up speed, clearly on the hunt, and the sensory tendrils—almost hairlike, almost feathery—are briefly visible as they catch the moonlight. No wider than Winnie's forearm, this portion of the monster is far enough away that Winnie can't touch it . . . but near enough that she's pretty sure any movement she makes will reach those tendrils.

She has stopped breathing altogether. Eventually the basilisk will leave the area. She will see the tail slide past, and she'll know she can start running again.

But there are two problems with her plan. First, when she does burst into motion, the basilisk will sense her presence and likely double back.

Second, what if it's currently hunting Emma? Weaponless, maybe-possessed Emma.

The tail arrives. It flicks past from a different spot ten paces away, slipping and sliding and slithering while feathery hairs float on the night breeze. They are far more angelic, almost like a peacock's plumage, than she had realised. She thinks, quite uselessly, that her sketch in the Compendium needs updating.

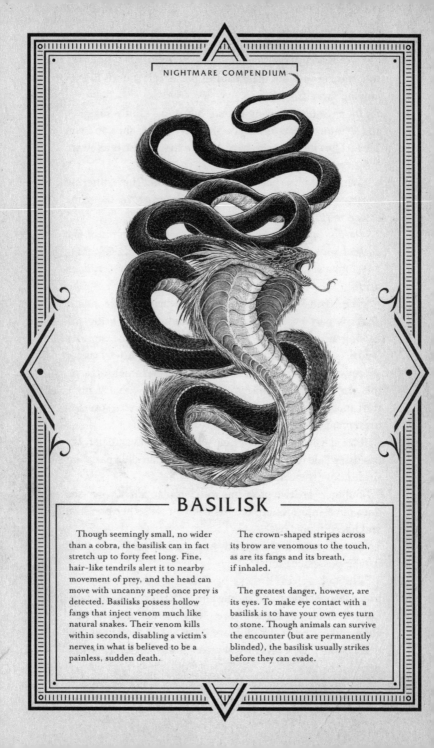

BASILISK

Though seemingly small, no wider than a cobra, the basilisk can in fact stretch up to forty feet long. Fine, hair-like tendrils alert it to nearby movement of prey, and the head can move with uncanny speed once prey is detected. Basilisks possess hollow fangs that inject venom much like natural snakes. Their venom kills within seconds, disabling a victim's nerves in what is believed to be a painless, sudden death.

The crown-shaped stripes across its brow are venomous to the touch, as are its fangs and its breath, if inhaled.

The greatest danger, however, are its eyes. To make eye contact with a basilisk is to have your own eyes turn to stone. Though animals can survive the encounter (but are permanently blinded), the basilisk usually strikes before they can evade.

A scream splits the forest. Winnie's body goes cold. That was Emma screaming, and that is Emma now lifting her voice to shriek, "*Help!*"

Winnie lunges for the basilisk's tail. Up go her arms, stake gripped in both hands. She stabs downward, through the scales and spine and muscle and earth.

But oh god, she wasn't prepared for how fast the basilisk can move. Sketches don't move. Compendium descriptions *don't move.* Somehow, before she can even leap properly away, she sees the head—a crowned queen—flying toward her. It is head-height, moving on an erect body like a cobra. A nightmarish, impossibly tall cobra.

Winnie leaps back, arms windmilling, but she's clumsy on her unhappy ankle. She loses her balance and slings straight down.

Fortunately, the training lives inside her, recently refreshed after hours with Jay on hard ground. She tucks her chin, splays out her arm, and catches herself before transferring into a sideways roll.

The basilisk's fangs slam against the forest floor, exactly where Winnie had just been. She tries to scrabble up, her hands groping for purchase, but all she finds is the stake.

She stumbles against it. Knocks the stake out of the earth and therefore out of the basilisk. Blood spews forth, hissing and grey. It splatters Winnie's hand, and she vaguely thinks that it *really freaking hurts.* But she can't do anything about it, because the basilisk is rising again to strike.

Winnie grabs the stake, bits of it eating away beneath acid blood, and twists her body to face the nightmare.

It lunges, fangs bared.

And Winnie looks right into its eyes.

Not on purpose, because she *knows* what will happen if she meets this creature's gaze, but by accident, because for all her years of solo training, for all her knowledge of the Compendium, her body still lacks experience. The basilisk's eyes are silver with vertical pupils, and in the split second before it hits her, Winnie feels . . .

Sad. Only sad.

Then her glasses turn to stone, and her arms shove the stake forward—a reaction of total panic and no grace.

Scales. Ribs. Heart. The stake pierces the monster.

And, hidden behind lenses of pure stone, the basilisk dies.

Winnie has to ditch her glasses. They are unsalvageable. She also has more basilisk blood on her, and now that the nightmare is dead, adrenaline is receding in the face of pain.

One time, in chemistry class (which Winnie had to take along with six other students who didn't go to the Sunday estate), Winnie spilled a droplet of hydrochloric acid on her wrist. This feels like that times one thousand. She has to forcibly bite her lip to keep from groaning.

It takes her a moment, as she lies there with her skin boiling and her vision a nearsighted blur, to remember why she is here—why she'd stabbed that basilisk in the first place.

Emma.

Winnie pulls the stake from the basilisk's heart. More blood sprays, but she's able to avoid it and she wipes the wooden tip on the ground. Her movements are sharp, perfunctory, and already the horror of the basilisk is fading. Only the pain in her hands remains, but she can ignore that. She *has* to ignore it, along with the cold that has permanently woven through her like that basilisk through the trees.

With the stake clutched tightly, Winnie sets off toward where she thinks she heard Emma scream. And as she moves, over uneven, shadowy terrain thick with pine needles, she wonders where the hell the Wednesday hunters are. Surely Emma's scream would have summoned someone. Instead, Winnie hears no one. Sees no one—and it's not just because her vision is blurred. It's because there's nothing here to see.

She reaches a wide clearing, almost a field really, where boulders thrust up from the soil. Stone Hollow, it's called, and it's a favorite hunting ground for harpies. Wan moonlight slides over the granite megaliths. Winnie squints, trying to force her eyes to see better, to spot where danger or Emma might be.

She glimpses a streak on one stone she thinks might be blood.

After a quick glance at the sky for harpies, Winnie hurries to the weather-carved megalith. There *is* blood on it: three lines, very distinctly spaced like fingers. And on the ground nearby is a shoe.

It's one of Emma's heels, and as Winnie quickly scoops it up in search of something that might indicate what had attacked her—guano from a cockatrice, webbing from a manticore—she realises the glossy leather is completely clean. No clues, no mud, no nothing.

She drops it and scans the soil instead. Maybe the grass is a bit flattened. And *maybe* that stone twenty steps away has more blood on it.

Winnie resumes her forward progress, and with each step, the voice in her head gets louder. *Where are the hunters?* It is louder than the Compendium forever chattering. It is louder than Jay's voice forever playing as the bass line. *Where are the hunters? Where is Aunt Rachel?*

When Winnie reaches the next megalith, she does find more blood and a trail through the grass that leads into the trees.

She is about to set off that way when she hears it: a hissing like a broken time machine. A whispering like a deflating hot-air balloon.

She whips her head backward, toward where she thinks the sound might be coming from. She squints and squints, but there's nothing there. No warping, no bending, no nightmares of any kind. Only moonlight over stone.

Then a herd of ghost-deer break from the trees. They gallop into the clearing, moving with the speed of prey whose death is imminent. Winnie thinks she sees the doe and two fawns, vaguely glowing shapes that melt into one without her glasses.

One of the fawns stops moving. It makes a sound Winnie didn't know a deer could make, much less a ghost-deer.

It disappears. The sound of a broken blender rips out. And Winnie realises the Whisperer is *right there*. Without her glasses on, she simply cannot see it.

Winnie leaps for the trees. Her arms pump, her knees kick, and like the ghost-deer, she moves as fast as prey being hunted. It is almost helpful to lack glasses; there is no awareness of her surroundings to slow her.

Glowing white streaks pass her, blurring at the edges of her vision. *No,* Winnie wants to scream. *Go another way.* They are leading the Whisperer right to her.

Except that when they reach a small brook, the deer spear left to avoid running water, aiming their stampede north. And Winnie just tramples right through, ice-cold water cutting into her ankles and soaking her flimsy flats.

She sprints onward. The other-dimensional whispers fade. She is safe for now, and the forest is empty—nightmares scared away by the Whisperer. And still, somehow, no hunters have come.

Winnie can't stop now, though. If she does, the cold and the venom and the terror of what she's doing, where she is, what she's running from will lock into place. She won't be able to escape it; she'll die here, petrified like her glasses.

She has to figure out where Emma went. She has to figure out what the hell is going on.

CHAPTER
38

Winnie is on the verge of giving up—of finding a tree and trying to survive the night without freezing to death—when she hears a hollow howl. *No.* Her stomach bottoms out. She can't face the werewolf with only this stake. She *has* to find a tree and find it now. Except that as she approaches a pitifully small maple— the only tree her hazy vision can find with low enough branches—Emma screams.

It's visceral and pained and near.

The wolf has her. Winnie knows this right away, despite all the gaps in her knowledge: Why is Emma here? Where are the hunters?

Emma screams again, a sound of terror. A screech of suffering. And Winnie charges straight that way. She holds the stake high, running over tree roots she can't see and stones that want nothing more than to trip her. *This is our forest,* they say. *Go back. You don't belong here.*

Another scream, and with it comes a splash of magenta through the trees. Winnie wants to shout at Emma, *Wait, I'm coming!* But she only runs faster instead.

There is blood on the forest floor. Spatters of it over pine needles.

She gets closer to the magenta and finds the vague outline of a body. Emma is limping like a revenant fresh from the grave, and she is whimpering. Staggering from tree to tree.

Then the wolf is there. It careens into Emma, toppling her to the ground. Pinning her easily, teeth bared. It's larger than any natural wolf, with shoulders shaggy beneath thick white fur. Emma screams again.

Winnie throws her stake like a javelin.

She doesn't know what else to do. The wolf is going to rip out Emma's jugular if she doesn't act, and her arm moves of its own volition. Some long-dormant muscle memory waking up just for this. The stake, red as Emma's blood, whistles through the air and embeds in the wolf's back.

The beast yelps, a piercing cry that strikes a minor chord atop Emma's screams. Then it jumps off Emma and heads straight for Winnie. The red stake pokes from its back, reminding Winnie of a picture she'd once seen of a bull charging a matador. She is weaponless, defenceless, frozen in place.

The wolf barrels for her. One bounding step, two. It leaps. Its front paws hit Winnie with all the force of a freight train. And like Emma only moments before, she goes down.

Her back hits the ground, punching the air from her lungs, and for a confusing half second, she thinks she's back in the clearing with Jay. That it's just him dumping her to the ground as she, yet again, fails to aim true.

But this isn't Jay, and now its teeth are zooming for her face. Foam drips off fangs. Its eyes glow silver as the moon, eerily sentient. And, like the basilisk's, empty and sad.

Winnie struggles. She kicks, she writhes, she claws at fur soft as the shredded silk of her gown. But the beast has survived a stake directly in the back; what good will her human muscles do? She can't believe she ever thought this might be just a natural wolf; she can't believe she ever felt *sympathy* for it.

Were-creatures, when in their animal form, are almost unkillable. However, like the non legends, they are hurt by silver—and, in some rare cases, by gold.

Winnie grabs her locket, snaps it off her neck, and shoves it in the wolf's face. She misses. Her fist and the locket hit a neck thick with fur.

It works. Somehow, the forest has decided *this* wolf responds to gold, and the locket works. The monster yips again with new, nightmare pain and rears away from Winnie's face.

She pushes the locket harder against it, and now it's howling. A sound that will draw more nightmares—or worse, the Whisperer—but Winnie can't stop. This is all she has.

The wolf finally breaks free and bolts. A smear of white, it abandons Winnie and disappears into the forest, taking her locket with it.

Winnie wants to catch her breath. She wants to spend a moment making sure nothing is broken, that no bite wounds mar her skin, but Emma needs her. So she drags herself on wobbling arms and legs—a half crawl, half walk—until she reaches the other girl.

And it's bad. So much worse than Winnie had feared when she'd been tracking Emma's blood across the clearing. Emma's entire left leg is sodden with red, and a bone pokes through thigh.

"You won't turn," Winnie says, panicked words that don't matter, but even now, she can't switch off the Compendium. "The local variety of werewolf can't turn you from a bite."

Emma doesn't say anything. Her breaths are ragged. Her eyes are shut.

Winnie grabs her cheeks; they're freezing. "Wake up, Emma. Wake up. God, wake up."

Emma's eyes flutter open and briefly latch on to Winnie's. "You . . . found me." A smile whispers over her lips. "Rachel will be . . . happy."

"What?" Winnie asks. She doesn't actually care about the answer. She just wants Emma to keep talking—though she's not sure what good that will do either. She can't tend this injury, and she's got no way to contact the hunters.

And *where the hell* are they?

"Loyalty," Emma says. She is smiling a bit more now, and there's a glassiness to her eyes that Winnie doesn't think can be good. "My trial . . . to lure you. Yours . . . to follow. Although." She gives a weak giggle, and blood burbles from her thigh. "I'm not sure I'll . . . pass with a wound like this. Harpy . . . got me good."

"You mean wolf," Winnie counters, even as she assesses what Emma just said.

Emma lured her out here to prove her loyalty to the clan.

And Winnie unknowingly followed to prove hers.

"No," Emma says, "harpy . . . By the stones. Came out of nowhere."

Winnie vaguely hears this and vaguely nods, but the bulk of her focus is now on the heat building in her blood. It's not a heat she recognises. It is incandescent. It is violent. It makes the world look clear even as her vision is still a greyscale blur. And it finally, finally shuts up the never-ending chyron of the Compendium.

She is on her third trial—and Emma is too. This is why there are no hunters near. This is why Emma "lost" her shoe—and why it was so clean. She's wearing combat boots, Winnie now sees. She has a knife sheath at her waist too, though the knife itself is on the leaf-littered earth nearby.

"I really . . . thought I'd do better." Emma offers another laugh. "But you took longer . . . than I thought . . . to find me."

Yes, Winnie thinks, *because this is not where I belong.* She lied about the banshee, and like a cave filled with dynamite, she has set off a gunpowder line to bring the whole thing down. Instead of coming clean and admitting she was out of her depth, she spent the night in a tree—and even then, she still almost died. Now here she is, with Emma's leg gouged apart and red blood seeping into forest grey. A grotesque paint-by-numbers adding colour to all the wrong places.

Winnie isn't just a liar like her dad—she's worse than that. Emma will die and it will be entirely Winnie's fault.

She forces herself to look at Emma's sweat-shining face. At the blood trailing down Emma's jaw like she's a vampira just finishing its kill. Aunt Rachel and the rest of the clan thought Winnie could handle this. They trusted her. Emma trusted her. Now Emma is going to die, and there's nothing Winnie can do to fix it.

"It was a good party, don't you think?" Emma lifts one hand from her leg. It shines with wet blood, and she laughs. "I didn't even drink the champagne. Just pretended. Because..." Her eyes, now sagging, flit to Winnie's. "Because... I knew... of course."

She coughs. Blood spews. A fleck hits Winnie's face.

And there it is. The violence, the silence, the blazing light inside Winnie.

This isn't over yet. Emma isn't dead. And even if Wednesdays won't come to help her, Winnie knows someone who will.

"Emma," she says, pushing to her feet. "I'm going to take this back... just for a minute." She grabs for the vial around Emma's neck. Emma doesn't resist. She just watches with an odd, almost languid smile, as if this is a semi-amusing TV show. Winnie uncorks the glass and shakes the barbed banshee claw onto her palm.

It glistens, and Winnie prays she's doing the right thing. "Can you count to three?" she asks, leaning toward Emma's neck. "Do it with me. One."

"Two," Emma says.

"Three." Winnie pokes the claw into Emma's neck. In her mind, she counts again: *One. Two. Three.* She pulls the claw back out. Emma doesn't react. She still wears a smile. Her chest still moves . . .

Then slowly her eyelids lower. Her breathing slows. When her head lolls sideways against the tree, Winnie feels for her pulse, and though Emma's skin is dangerously, *dangerously* cold, and though her pulse moves sluggish as winter in the forest, the girl still lives.

If collected from a banshee corpse, the venom can be used to induce temporary comas and even a mimicry of death, slowing the recipient's heartbeat to near stillness.

Winnie pushes once at glasses that are no longer on her nose. Then she rises into the night and runs.

Winnie can't be sure where she is, but she can be sure that if she runs southwest, she will reach the Big Lake. And if she can reach the Big Lake, she will find one of Lizzy's cameras.

That is the extent of her plan. The full breadth and width of it: Reach the Big Lake. Do not die. Pray Mario and Lizzy are watching the cameras and will hear her scream for help.

Emma's hunting knife is tight in her grasp, a mirror to flash her face every time she pumps her arms. It offers a reflection she doesn't like. Makeup smeared. Dirt and blood, no glasses. As if the entirety of her being has been distilled down to these elements. As if this is all she is and all she ever can be.

She is no Wednesday. There is no cause inside her, through and through. There is only a shredded dress and a lie hanging by a banshee's severed spine.

Winnie doesn't know what time it is—it's got to be nearing midnight by now, if she's properly gauging the moon that peeks and sneaks between the arrow-tipped trees of the forest. All she has are her feet to keep her moving and this flashing knife to keep showing her a truth she doesn't want to see.

Happy birthday, witch traitor.

The ground starts to slope down. A gentle roll that

heralds the lake. The moon is bright right now. So white it almost hurts the eyes. The trees are thinning out as sandy substrate takes over. Winnie can't avoid the moon's purifying glare.

She is cold. She is hot. She can't feel her feet, and her breaths are loud enough to summon every nightmare in the forest.

Which is exactly what they do, and it's only as she comes upon a rise in the ground that she remembers—too late— what Johnny Saturday had said. *Manticore hatchlings keep reappearing on the eastern shore.*

She has stepped on the mound that marks their nest. She has alerted the hatchlings inside.

They spew forth from a dark hole, hundreds of them, white to the point of transparent—and one after the next, each the size of a small pit bull. They look just like all the corpses she has delivered to Mario, and just like all her sketches too.

Except these hatchlings are on the move.

Manticore: A catchall term for any nightmares with scorpion characteristics, though most often seen with a humanoid head on a six-legged body with a traditional scorpion thorax and stinger.

In the American forest, the manticores lack the human head and are more akin to enormous whip scorpions. While they do possess stingers that lead to painful pustules—and sometimes death—it is their whiplike anterior appendages that do the most damage.

Winnie slings down her knife, ducking to reach the first manticore as it strikes.

Also like their natural cousin the scorpion, a juvenile manticore's venom is more likely to be deadly. Avoid the stinger.

Her knife cuts through chitinous carapace. A stinger flies sideways before her knife pendulums back to cut through anything she can hit. She lurches on unsteady feet, hacking and hacking and *hacking*. But this isn't a knife for brute force, and there are too many manticores to stop. They're still scrabbling out, long mandibles clacking while their whips slash and reach.

Winnie cuts them away, whip after whip, stinger after stinger, but she's not actually killing any of them, and they're still coming. Worse, she can feel a rumble in the earth below that can mean only one thing: Mum is on the way.

Her back hits a pine's rough bark. She hacks twice more— severing a stinger, a whip, a clicking claw—before sidling around the trunk and sprinting again. She can't face those babies; she definitely can't face the mum.

She also can't outrun them. They are six-legged and scuttle easily over this forest terrain spun in moonlight. The only advantage Winnie has is that she is taller, her legs are longer. She gains ground.

But that ground is still shaking. The mother knows she is here.

Winnie angles toward the lake. It's a long shot. It's the longest of long shots, and it relies on even more what-ifs than before. Trees and stone rattle around her. A slash-slash-slash rips through the forest in time to thrashing whips. The mother is moving fast, slowed only by her size.

Winnie looks back once. A sea of writhing white arachnids have engulfed the forest like a tidal wave. Without her glasses, she sees only a frothing, churning mass. And at the back of it all is the wave's crest, her whips swinging left and right like some Weedwacker gone wrong.

Winnie doesn't look back again. She is almost to the shore. Twenty thunderous steps. Ten.

Kelpies: Shaggy water creatures, kelpies are horselike in shape, but close examination reveals algal hair and a bulbous body best suited to high-pressure depths. They hunt at midnight, briefly abandoning their deepwater home for the shoreline. Though legends declare they become human, forest

*kelpies in fact transition to a towering bipedal shape that is
less human and more skeletal. In place of arms, they possess
boneless tentacles.*

*Kelpies are extremely territorial when hunting, and though
they do not actively hunt other nightmares, they are known to
kill other nightmares that infringe upon their shore.*

But there are no kelpies here. Winnie sees *nothing* on the
shore save for silt and rock and still, sentient waters.

She aims south, and doesn't slow. The shore is flatter,
but softer. Each pounding step demands more spring, more
energy from feet encased only in flimsy leather. Ahead is the
camera—a lone tripod staked into the earth, set back ten
paces from the silent shore. She has to squint to make it out,
but it is *there*.

She hears the manticores clear the forest behind her.
She feels the ground vibrate with their legs, and without
trees to muffle it, she hears the chitinous clacking of their
wide mandibles.

She will reach the camera, though. She will reach it and
she will scream into it, and maybe someone will come for
Emma. Maybe at least *she,* the generous, kind one, will make
it out of this forest Winnie was never meant to go into.

Winnie is almost to it. A red light blinks as it transmits
footage. And for the first time since entering the night,
Winnie screams.

"*Help!*" she shrieks at the camera. "*Help us! Emma is in
the forest—*"

A kelpie erupts from the water to Winnie's right. It is
taller than she is, almost vampiric in its bipedal, skeletally
skinny form. But there are the tentacles: two of them as long
as its body now rushing for Winnie like it wants a supremely
messed-up hug.

Winnie slices off both tentacles. It's even more graceless
than her hacking at the manticores, but it does what she
needs it to do. Arm up, knife out. Tentacle one, tentacle two.

The kelpie roars, a strange sound meant for watery depths, and in the fraction of a second before Winnie sprints onward for the camera, she spots gills on its neck. Behind it, more kelpies erupt from the water, bellowing watery roars. Then comes a smashing and cracking like manticore exoskeletons giving way.

Winnie reaches the camera. She snaps it off the tripod and instantly starts running again.

Her plan has worked, but only partially. The kelpies are fighting the manticore hatchlings, but the mum is still coming this way. Winnie sprints, trying to shout and pant into the camera with each step. "Emma! Near . . . Stone Hollow! Badly hurt—find her! Find her!" She says this again and again until she can't hold on to the camera anymore because she needs at least one hand available to face the mama manticore. Though what good will a single knife do against a creature the size of a car?

And now the lake is ending, the trees reclaiming their territory ahead, while the waters move and twine, building toward the falls.

Wind slaps against Winnie in time to the manticore's whips. They will slice right through her, cleave her body in two like too many nons Winnie has never considered much before.

They died like this, she thinks. Whip-whip-whip. *They died like me.* All this time, she has thought vicious death was a fact of life for all Luminaries, and that by inoculating herself against it, she wouldn't fear her own.

She does fear it, though, and she doesn't want to die.

Winnie is so focused on moving, on getting ahead of this manticore—on maybe reaching the trees ahead and trying to find a *really* tall one—that she doesn't notice the white charging toward her. Not until it slams into her and knocks her to the hard shore.

Werewolf, she thinks at the same time the manticore's whips fly over her. Right where her body had been.

Winnie stabs at the wolf, only to realise she has lost her knife—and only to realise the wolf is leaping off her and charging toward the manticore. It is a blur that even with glasses Winnie wouldn't be able to follow. It moves too fast, and she doesn't try to watch it. If this is what the forest is going to give her, then she will take it. And she will run.

She doesn't see her knife anywhere in the second it takes her to rise, so she leaves it. Her arms pump, her knees—bloodied and scraped and attached to a different body with a smarter mind—kick high.

She is almost to the trees and the cover they will provide when the wind scrapes against her. It is unnatural, and she knows by the way everything inside her drops that it's not a natural wind.

Her temperature drops. Her organs drop. The hair on her arms and on her head *drops* like it's all been attached to tiny, icy weights.

Then come the whispers.

She doesn't see it. It's just suddenly there. Directly before her, gusting wind at her along with a coughing, scratching sound like Mathilda when she won't start. It is huge—that much she can sense, even if she can't see it—and it is hungry.

Winnie dives right, toward the lake. It is her only course, because the Whisperer is careening toward her in a way that cuts her off from the trees, like a dog herding sheep. She has no choice but to run right for the water.

If she gets in that water, she will die. If she stops here, she will die. The wind is flaying against her, charged and smelling of melted plastic. It sets everything inside her on a high-pitched edge, like she has just clamped her jaw on an open wire.

Somehow, she is still running, but she's going to have to choose. Lake or Whisperer.

She chooses lake. Her legs splash, cold punching into her—distant, though, and drowned out by adrenaline and electric whispers. She is calf deep, but it is too shallow to dive and the water pulls at her as it sweeps toward tumbling falls she cannot hear.

She splashes onward. The Whisperer follows. She needs to move faster, but the water isn't getting deeper—*why* isn't it getting deeper? And why is the substrate hard?

She's on a rock, she realises. Like the one Jay had walked her onto only four days ago. Like that overhang he'd shown her, this rock leads to the waterfall. And the Whisperer is herding Winnie toward it. Somehow, the running water isn't deterring it at all. It is still coming at her with a voice made of black holes and broken glass.

The water is pulling fast now, shards of granite slick and rough at the same time. Her foot gets caught in an invisible hole. She trips. Hits the water in a splash of cold. It carries her a full second before she gets back up again, soaking and frozen and missing a shoe.

She looks back, wondering if she can cross the whole lake this way. Maybe she can reach that outcropping on the other side if she just moves fast enough.

But no. The Whisperer is right there. She sees it now, a wavering of the world that hurts her eyes. That distorts the shape of manticores and kelpies warring on the beach. Worse, she is out of space. There is nowhere left to run, because the Whisperer isn't just behind her—it's all around, encroaching on her from all sides.

This is the end for Winnie. There is only the lake dumping into frothy, misty darkness. There is no escape. She survived the banshee and the vampira, the basilisk and the manticores and the kelpies and the werewolf. But the Whisperer will get her in the end. The creature no one else believes in.

She looks over the waterfall. There is nothing to see except moonlit death clutched by shadows. But at least that death will leave a mark—an intact body for the kids on corpse duty to find tomorrow.

You either trust the forest or you don't, Winnie.

She jumps.

CHAPTER
39

Winnie falls faster than the water. She plummets through wet air toward what she hopes will not be pain. She hopes it will be a fast death. She hopes she might not die at all.

It is eternal. She passes the overlook. She passes trees. She passes rocks where water catches like meat upon a claw. Then she sees the white, white churn that she is going to fall into.

You either trust the forest or you don't, Winnie. In that moment, right before her feet—one with a shoe, one without—hit the river, she decides she trusts it. Fully and completely. After all, it has gotten her this far, still alive.

She folds her arms to her chest, points her toes, and closes her eyes.

The impact is brutal. Like a sledgehammer to her legs, it beats up through her. Then over her, carrying with it a blanket of cold. She pierces deep into a basin she hadn't known was there while the river grabs and pulls and rips at her like a harpy eating scavenged carrion. She loses all breath, because in cold this complete there is no space for it. It saps every molecule away and then saps everything inside her that keeps her warm.

She is still alive, though—she *knows* she is still alive, because when she starts kicking and grappling, her body moves. The water is a spider and she is in its net; the more she fights, the deeper she seems to sink. She can't see anything. She hears only the constant roar of a waterfall. And each movement grows weaker than the last.

She is so cold. She is sluggish with it, freezing cell by cell into a sculpture that cannot move. *Hypothermia,* she thinks, a frantic almost laugh bubbling from her mouth. Because she survived even the Whisperer, but now *hypothermia* is going to claim her.

And there's nothing she can do about it. Every second she is under water is one more second for her organs to frost over and her blood to Popsicle in her veins. She thinks her lungs might hurt and that she also might need air, but it's the cold that grasps her the strongest.

Until it finally lets go. A beautiful feeling replaced by warmth, warmth, like the mist when it first rises. Her lips part. She lets water into her lungs, too lost to notice because the cold is gone and she is happy.

The world disappears.

Winnie doesn't die. Later she will marvel at it, but in the moment, she is unconscious and has no idea she still lives. All she knows are the three times she briefly resurfaces into awareness.

First, it is to find teeth on her arm and white billowing around her. She glimpses red mixed within silken fur before she fades away again.

Second, she awakens to a song. It is under the water with her, haunting and pure and familiar. *Jenna,* Winnie thinks. *This is Jenna's song.* She is elated to realise this, her heart surging through her—because Jenna is still alive and she is singing. Erica will be so happy.

Winnie wishes there were a way to hold on to this feeling, to sketch out the way Jenna's face must look right now.

The ghost song fades; consciousness does too.

And finally, Winnie stumbles back into awareness to find she is on cold silty ground, breathing air, while an old, damp blanket rests over her.

It smells faintly of bergamot and lime.

CHAPTER
40

Winnie does not come to again for what she will later learn is several hours, and when she finally does, she is in the Monday hospital. The walls are beige with a blue stripe, just like the morgue. Blackout blinds cover a single window to her left. Something beeps—several somethings—and before she can even orient herself in this space, Mum is right there.

She is crying, but it's happy tears, and when Winnie tries to understand what Mum is saying, she finds she can't focus on a single word. Then a warmth spreads through—false warmth, she knows, that is not like the warmth of death's embrace—and she loses all grasp on reality.

For a full day, she drifts in and out like that. Until at last, they let the drugs fully leave her system and clarity sparkle in.

The first thing Winnie says to Darian, who stands beside her, is, "Emma?" Her voice is rusted. Unrecognizable even, and almost inaudible.

But Darian hears. "She's alive." He smiles, and Winnie realises from the red around his eyes and on his nose that he has been crying too. "Thanks to you, she's alive and healing fast."

No, Winnie wants to say. *Not thanks to me. I almost killed her.* "Can I see her?"

"Yes." This is from Mum. She hurries in through the doorway, Andrew behind her. She's wearing her pj's, and Winnie wonders how long she's been here. Andrew looks fresher in scrubs. "You can visit her once the doctor approves." Mum comes to Winnie's other side. "Emma just woke up too, and she was asking for you."

"Banshee claw," Andrew says, and there's something like admiration on his face. "Brilliant of you, Winnie. That saved her life."

Darian grips Winnie's arm, gentle and carefully avoiding several bandages. "Aunt Rachel says you passed the trial. You're a hunter now."

"No." The word slices out, hard on Winnie's tongue. She closes her eyes. "I don't deserve to be. I *can't*. The Whisperer—"

She doesn't get to speak. Doesn't get to confess before a doctor strides into the room. Winnie doesn't know the woman, though she recognises the name Dara Monday as one of Andrew's second cousins. Her appearance renders all of Winnie's protests or confessions moot. Mum, Darian, and Andrew instantly turn to her, an anxiety in each of their spines as if they're waiting for something—some news of some test that Winnie didn't know about.

And then it comes, straight from Dr. Dara's mouth: "Winnie won't turn." She smiles at Winnie while Darian, Mum, and Andrew all collectively whoop. "The old rule still seems to apply. There is no nightmare corruption in your DNA, so you will not become a werewolf."

I got bitten? Winnie thinks at the same time she looks again at the arm Darian had so gingerly touched.

"That said . . ." Dr. Dara gives Mum a pointed look, then Winnie. "Keep up with your tetanus vaccines, okay? Because you're lucky you didn't get *that*."

Mum flushes. Winnie just shakes her head. *I got bitten?* She doesn't feel any pain.

"When can she go home?" Mum asks at the same time

Andrew asks if Winnie wants any food (he's going to the café on the first floor) and Darian says he wasn't *really* worried (lie, lie, lie), and Winnie feels like she is back in the waters of the Big Lake, being swept away on a current out of her control.

She can go home later today. There's just a little paperwork. She can visit Emma on her way out; the other girl is doing well, though her leg is in a cast and she will have some physical therapy ahead.

Then finally, "Congrats on passing all three trials, Winnie." Dr. Dara smiles. "The rumor is you're on track to be next Lead Hunter for the Wednesdays. I'm sure your family must be so proud."

Winnie is released at three o'clock that same day. The outpatient paperwork describes her injuries (werewolf bite, basilisk venom on hands, hypothermia) and their treatments (a lot of fluids and blankets). *Try to relax and allow your body to heal. In one week, slowly reintroduce movement.*

Winnie doesn't feel that fragile. In fact, now that the drugs have fled her system, she feels like nothing happened at all. Only the bandage on her right arm reminds her just how close she came to death.

That and her ever-present shame.

On top of it all, no one saw the Whisperer. Lizzy's camera stopped working right after Winnie screamed into it. All anyone saw was the werewolf attacking Winnie. *That* footage has apparently been all over the Hemlock Falls news.

It is a horrible dream Winnie can't crack out of. Wolf is bad. Whisperer is not real. You are going to be a hunter. Your family must be proud. And deep down, a little tiny part of her keeps saying, *What if they're right? What if the Whisperer isn't real and you are losing your mind?*

On her way out of the hospital, Winnie visits Emma. Somehow, even with her eyes half closed and a ton of tubes hooked up to her, Emma manages to smile and reveal both her dimples. "Thank you, Winnie. Thank you."

Winnie wants to cry. She wants to confess. Instead, she just says, "I'm so glad you're okay. I'm so *glad* you're okay."

"Better than okay." Emma gives a raspy giggle. "First banshee venom and now . . . a melusine blood treatment. I'm basically . . . half nightmare at this point." She laughs again. Winnie's shame just spins wider.

Once she's home, Mum insists Winnie rest. And Winnie does, but only because she is afraid if she speaks to anyone, she might explode. The bear on the back of her door watches her, and she watches it right back with blurry, uncorrected eyes.

It's nearing nine o'clock when a visitor arrives. Aunt Rachel knocks before poking her head in. "You awake?" she whispers to the dark.

"Yeah." Winnie has let the night fall and her room descend into shadow.

Rachel steps in, pats the wall for the switch, and a split second later, light pierces out. Winnie squints as the room materialises into crude focus, Aunt Rachel in simple black athletic gear at the centre of it.

"Hey, kid." She walks hesitantly toward Winnie's bed. "How you feeling?"

Winnie ignores the question, and for the first time in a few hours, she pushes into a seated position. The room spins. "I lied about the banshee."

Rachel stops her forward crawl.

"I didn't kill the banshee. I just found it outside the forest. I was walking to the Thursday estate to warn someone about the Whisperer when the twins and Fatima found me."

Rachel sucks in a long breath, chest expanding. Her expression is immobile and inscrutable—or at least it is to Winnie without her glasses.

Winnie slides her legs out from the covers. Gooseflesh prickles down her pajama-clad body. "The twins assumed I'd killed the banshee, and I just let everyone believe it." She drops her feet to the worn rug.

Rachel still isn't moving.

"And on the night of the second trial, I found a spot surrounded by running water and spent the night there. Emma got hurt because of me. Because everyone . . . because *you* thought I was something I'm not." She braces as if to stand.

But Rachel finally moves, lifting a hand. "Stay." It's a Lead Hunter command, except instead of fury unleashing, Rachel only offers a cool "I know all this already."

Winnie blinks.

"Or, I guessed it." Rachel folds her arms over her chest. "That banshee's head hadn't been cut by a hunting knife, and I saw the running water when we found you on Monday morning."

Winnie blinks again. This isn't making any sense. "But then . . . if you knew, why did you let me keep going?" She shakes her head. Pushes at glasses that aren't there, and ends up scratching the bridge of her nose. "Why didn't you kick me out of the trials right away?"

"Because." Rachel taps a finger against her biceps. "That wasn't really the point, Winnie. I don't care if you can kill a banshee yet—or spend the night in the forest. Those are all things you can learn. But loyalty? Commitment to the cause? That can't be hammered into you."

Of course it can. Culture runs thicker than blood.

Winnie's teeth start clicking, her head starts shaking. "But . . ." *Click, click, click.* "If you knew, then why did you let the third trial happen? I almost died. *Emma* almost died."

"No, actually. Look." She strides to the bed and plops down beside Winnie. Springs squeak. "I know you're blaming yourself right now for what happened to Emma, but it's not your fault. You were *born* to be a hunter. Your mum, me—we have that spark in our blood. Hell, for someone who hasn't been properly trained in four years, you still managed to take down more nightmares in one night than most hunters, and all you had was a green dress and a red stake.

"Emma knew what she was agreeing to, okay? And when she's all healed up, she'll be a hunter too."

"Too?" Winnie asks numbly, still staring at the bear.

"Yeah." Rachel rests a hand on Winnie's shoulder. "I'd be honored to have you on the hunt with me. If you want, of course."

Winnie isn't sure what she wants. Not anymore. Everything is a jumble in her head. Emma trusting Winnie's skills. Aunt Rachel knowing she was liar. No one caring that Emma almost died—that Winnie almost died too. No one caring about the Whisperer.

Death is a part of life in Hemlock Falls, she thinks as the bear seems to laugh at her from the door, just as she'd laughed at Marcus a week ago. *The sooner "the children" learn what the forest can do to them, the safer and happier they'll be.*

She thought she'd understood what being a Luminary meant. What being a *Wednesday* meant. Truth is, she'd had absolutely no idea. And truth is, Aunt Rachel is right: she was born to do this. It is written on her DNA, and even now, after everything, her body aches to go back into those grey-hazed trees.

She kind of hates herself for that. Her head throbs.

Culture runs thicker than blood.

"I . . . need more training." She finally breaks away from the bear's stare and pushes again at invisible glasses.

Aunt Rachel smiles with relief. "I'll set you up with tutors."

"I have one."

"Ah. In that case." She opens her hands, noticeably not asking who the tutor might be—as if she already knows and doesn't disapprove. "You just let me know when you're ready to join us, and we'll be waiting. Oh, and here." She rises to her feet with the fluid ease of a hunter and fishes something from her pocket. "We found this. I thought you might want it back."

Gold glints. A crescent moon dangles, and Winnie finds herself staring at the locket. It should have been lost in the woods, used to burn a werewolf. Before she can ask where Rachel found it, though, Rachel says, "It was your grandmother's."

Winnie frowns. "Winona's?"

"No, on your dad's side. I only ever saw it once, when I helped your parents move in. I thought, when I saw it on you . . ." Rachel bites her lip.

And Winnie finishes, "You thought he had given it to me and maybe I was still seeing him."

"Yeah." Rachel looks pained as she drops the locket into Winnie's cupped hands. "But now I know you'd never do that. And neither would Fran or Darian. You're a bear, Winnie. You're a Wednesday through and through, and I'm proud to be your aunt." She offers what's probably meant to be an encouraging smile, but it ends up looking slightly pained.

Winnie's head throbs even more. "Why did Dad's mum have a Luminary locket?"

"Because it's not a Luminary locket. The moon is backward, and there are three stars instead of two."

Winnie squints down at the gold, only to find Rachel is right. How had she not noticed before? And *ah*, now that she's looking at it properly, ideas are stirring to life in the back of her brain, like silt on the bottom of a pond. Spin, stir, twirl . . .

Click.

Just like that, she knows what her dad's drawing means.

"Stop feeling guilty, okay?" Rachel pats Winnie's shoulder, scattering her thoughts and misinterpreting her frown. "And know that we'll be waiting for you on the hunt, whenever you're ready."

Winnie nods absently as Rachel leaves. The locket glistens on her palm. The bear watches on.

Winnie waits until she hears the front door shut before springing into action and aiming for her desk. Her sketchbook has gathered a little dust since Monday morning, and when she peels back the cover, the lines of a half-drawn werewolf stare up at her.

She doesn't remember sketching this; she could have done it months ago or maybe she did it last year. Darian is right that she should date and label things. What stands out to her most of all, though, is just how wrong she got it all—too vicious, too flat, too small. This isn't what a werewolf looks like.

This isn't what *the* werewolf looks like.

She rips the page aside to find a blank one. Then she snatches up a 0.5 pen, lays her newly returned locket on the left side of her desk, and with quick strokes, draws out what she'd found on the bookshelf at the library—every squiggle, every curve, and even the numbers 1–2–1 and the letter *Z* with an arrow.

Once it's drawn, she rotates the page counterclockwise and draws in the locket's moon and stars.

Now she is staring at a map of the forest. The *Z* is an *N* pointing north. The locket's moon is the stream beside Stone Hollow—the stars representing the megaliths, at the heart of which rests a big X. Dad wants her to go there, that much is obvious. Yet there's still one part of the map she doesn't quite understand.

1–2–1.

Then it hits. *Address me as "my lord."* It's a cipher that's meant for the birthday card in the attic.

In seconds, Winnie has scribbled down the card's message. "First word," she whispers, "in the first phrase." She underlines it. "Second word, second phrase." Another line. "First word, third phrase." A final line—and the final message. Stark, unignorable, and very, very upsetting.

I.

Was.

Framed.

CHAPTER

41

Winnie spends the next two days in bed, not by choice but because Mum is constantly there. She has no chance to make a run for it. So for two days, she does as the hospital discharge notes told her: she rests, recovers, drinks a lot of ginger ale, and stews over Dad's map and message.

And over the Whisperer too. *Is* it real? Maybe her brain imagined the grating sound of a chain saw on starlight. Maybe she never really saw the world assembled like a broken jigsaw.

By Sunday afternoon, when Mum finally ventures out to work at the Daughter, Winnie sees her chance to break free. She has two errands to run on the family bike. The first will take her south. The second will take her north.

At first, lactic acid invades her muscles with a searing pain—though that's more due to underuse than any lingering effects from her fall or hypothermia. She thinks of the song she heard beneath the water as she pedals. She thinks of Jenna and ghosts and the sad look in a basilisk's eyes.

When she reaches the Thursday estate, she cuts onto the driveway. It's got just enough incline for her to coast all the way to the mansion. It's a grey day, perfumed by rain in the night before. Fog rises from the black driveway. Winnie's hair, by the time she reaches the front door and strides inside like she belongs there, is a frizzy mess.

She takes a lift. The mirror within confirms her wet-dog status. She doesn't even bother trying to fix it, and when the bell dings at the top floor, she continues her purposeful march into the tile entryway lit by floor-to-ceiling windows. At the grey door ahead, she pushes a doorbell. It buzzes.

Then she waits. She feels strangely calm, but also very alert.

Heels tap inside the flat before the doorknob turns and the door swings wide. Erica stands on the other side, dressed in a black sweater over black leggings—and her usual steel-capped boots.

She blinks at the sight of Winnie. Even recoils slightly.

"Is that the pizza?" a voice shouts from inside. It sounds like it might be Astrid or Marisol.

Erica doesn't answer. Instead, she recomposes herself, chin rising, and steps outside. The door shuts behind her.

"Hi," Winnie says once Erica is close enough for her to spot the fresh lip gloss sparkling on her lips.

"Hi." It's a wary response, but not a mean one.

"I was wondering if we could talk."

Erica stares at her with no reaction. Laughter peals out from within the flat. Two whole breaths pass before she says, "I'm busy right now."

"It won't take long." Winnie tries for a smile. It's weak, but certainly not the worst she's ever conjured. "I just . . . Look, we don't have to be friends again, but can we at least not be enemies?"

"We aren't enemies." Erica's words are as stiff as her back. She starts spinning a gold ring around her middle finger. Her thumb has a plaster again. "We've never been enemies, Winnie."

"Oh." Now Winnie is the one to stiffen. "I . . . well . . . that's good to know, then. I guess." She had definitely expected a different answer—and a lot more resistance. "I'll see you at school, then?"

Another two breaths. Then: "Yep. I'll see you at school."

And now Winnie's smile is real. "Great." She bobs her head. "Thanks for talking to me."

Erica makes a "hmmm" sound in her throat before slipping back into the flat and closing the front door. Winnie passes the pizza guy on her way out.

Winnie goes next to the Friday estate. The clouds briefly part as she pedals through Hemlock Falls, and she considers how different everything looks now compared to a week ago. The estates are no longer off-limits. The Luminaries are no longer people to avoid. There is sunshine and a wind that could *almost* be described as warm. It carries colour and birdsong.

Any day now, her mum thinks, their outcast status will be fully removed.

Once at the estate, Winnie aims for the garage. The door is open, revealing a huge space packed with tools and cabinets and years of Lizzy clutter that is all too easy to get lost in. Clanking fills the afternoon air. Winnie feels almost guilty that Jay has been forced out of Gunther's and must tinker here instead.

But only almost.

She finds Jay on his back, tucked under Mathilda with booted feet poking out. "Hey." She toes him with her sneaker.

He doesn't react. "I know, I know, Lizzy. You need to get to the Council building. I'm almost done."

Winnie drops to a crouch. "Not Lizzy," she informs him, and Jay's eyes, shaded by the Wagoneer's underbelly, meet hers.

He jolts. Then slides out so fast, he almost knocks over a box of tools. "You're out of hospital." He springs to his feet.

"Yeah."

"I came to see you on Thursday morning, but you were asleep." Jay's eyes, grey as fog, skate over Winnie. Grease is smeared across his white shirt and buffalo flannel. There's a line of dirt across his forehead.

"Oh." No one told Winnie he visited.

"And," he adds, wiping his hands on a cloth, "before you scold me, I visited Emma too. She was only half awake, but she smiled." He tries for a smile of his own.

And Winnie tries to crack one back. Hers falls flat. "I wanted to talk to you about training. We, um, don't have to keep going."

Jay's hands pause mid-wipe. His eyebrows rise, and for half a moment Winnie feels guilty. Like she's rejecting him in some way. She wants to push at her glasses—the new pair, still not fixed and therefore crooked upon her nose. She wants to retract her words and say, *Never mind, I still suck and need your help, haha.* But she does neither, and instead sets her jaw and holds his stare.

"Any particular reason you want to stop?" he asks eventually. He flings the dirty cloth onto the toolbox.

"Since I passed my trials," she replies, "it feels wrong to keep taking advantage of you."

"Taking advantage of me?" He laughs softly. "Is that what you think is happening here?"

Winnie feels her face warming, though it's more from annoyance than shame. "Is it not? I mean, I'm not exactly paying you back in any way."

Now he's the one to flush. "No. Right." He scratches the back of his head. "Not unless you count gracing me with your glorious presence as payback—"

"*Ugh,* Jay." She scowls at him. "Don't be mean. I'm trying to be considerate here. You don't have to help me anymore. End of story." She pushes at her glasses and rounds away to march back to her bike. "I'll see you at school tomorrow."

"What if I'm not joking?" he calls after her. "What if *I* want to keep training?"

"And why would you want to do that?" she snaps over her shoulder.

"Because you're going to get yourself killed?"

Winnie's feet grind to a halt. She has reached the entrance to the garage. Wind sweeps against her.

"You're still four years behind," Jay continues, sauntering toward her. "And believe it or not, I'd like to see you survive more than just your trials." He reaches her side. There's a small smear of grease under his left eye.

"Would we train . . . in the forest?" she asks.

"If you want."

Winnie swallows. She *does* want. Like a hellion tasting flesh for the first time, it's all she has wanted since she woke up in hospital.

It makes no sense to her, this hunger. She should fear the forest after what happened Wednesday night, after all the damage she caused and her near-death leap off of a waterfall. Instead, her body is ravenous to return. To be back within those grey trees.

You were born *to be a hunter. Your mum, me—we have that spark in our blood.* Winnie can't fathom how Mum survived four years without ever going back inside.

"There are Tuesdays prowling around for the werewolf," Jay says, "and new sensors everywhere, but I can get us past those."

Winnie studies his profile. He is the first person who hasn't told her she needs to rest or stay in bed, and as grateful as she is for that, she also finds it weird. Until his face turns and his eyes meet hers.

It's just a brief, crackling connection, his pupils so deep Winnie could fall into them, but in that moment, she glimpses the same hunger, the same aching need to be always among the trees. And just like that, she understands why Jay had transformed within the misty woods a week ago—and why she had transformed too.

It's not just culture that runs thicker than blood here. It's the forest too.

You either trust the forest or you don't, Winnie.

"Let's go now," she tells him.

And with a brief flicker of a smile, he obeys, guiding her into the forest by the same route they'd taken a week ago— and snagging a compound bow along the way. It occurs to Winnie that her mum will probably get home from work and wonder where Winnie has gone, but Winnie will deal with that later. For now, there are just the aspens and the beeches, the maples and the hemlocks, and eventually, a fallen maple and red pine thatched in moss.

New green shrouds this clearing, pockets that wink out from the forever grey because spring really does come to the forest by Hemlock Falls, right after winter like it's supposed to.

Winnie's spine straightens. Her lungs expand. This is where she wants to be. Tomorrow, a new life will begin in the Luminaries. And tomorrow, she will have to deal with her dad's secret map and what his coded bombshell of a message might mean.

For now, though, Winnie is here and she is whole.

"Ready?" Jay asks once he has ascended the maple and Winnie has the bow in hand.

"Ready," she replies.

He charges. Winnie moves. And the forest looks on with knowing eyes.

ACKNOWLEDGEMENTS

This book would not exist if not for the LumiNerds, the incredible online community who first discovered Winnie Wednesday on Twitter in June of 2019. I was struggling with grief from a miscarriage and facing the looming shots of another round of IVF, so while sitting at LaGuardia waiting for a delayed flight after BookCon, I had a thought: *I'll make a story on Twitter using polls.* As a gamer, dungeon master, and occasional interactive-fiction designer, I love interactive story. Plus, I'd had this old idea that had never sold. *I'll let readers vote on what happens in that story,* I decided. *It'll probably go nowhere, but at least it will give me a fun distraction while it lasts.*

Lol. The story did *not* go nowhere, and soon thousands of people were voting each day on what the heroine Winnie would do next. The story lasted for just over six months, with a poll every single day, and during that time, we both hewed to the original vision I'd crafted that never sold... *and* we deviated a lot too. Turns out that letting people decide what to do (aka Hive Mind Winnie) leads to some very unexpected twists—and a lot of fifty-fifty votes when people don't agree!

It wasn't until I was done with the fifth Witchlands book, *Witchshadow,* that I sat down and attempted to write *The Luminaries* as a proper book. I realized quite quickly that I could never replicate the fun of community that came from our crowdsourced tale, so I didn't even try. Instead, I took the characters, the world, and a few homage moments for LumiNerds, then set off into something completely new.

So, dear LumiNerds, *thank you.* This book is for you and because of you. During our months of crafting that "Sooz Your Own Adventure," IVF finally worked, and my little Cricket was born exactly one year to the day after our online adventure began. If that's not fate, I don't know what is!

There were, of course, many other people along the way who also helped me create this book—written and edited during baby nap times: my editor, Lindsey Hall, and everyone else at Tor Teen, who have always supported me, even through the rough IVF years and new-baby months. Then there's my agent, Joanna Volpe, as well as the tireless crew at New Leaf Literary, who are always there when I need them.

And to my brand new team at Daphne Press, I must offer an enormous thank you. Daphne Tonge, Caitlin Lomas, Katie Gray, Jamie-Lee Nardone, Kat McKenna, Micaela Alcaino, and Kerby Rosanes: here's to great things in this new, exciting endeavor!

I also want to thank all my early readers: Cait Listro, Samantha Tan, Sanya Macadam, Praghya Awasthi, Rachel Hansen, Meghan Vanderlee, Jenniea Carter, Jess Holleran, Benjamin Garcia, and Donald Quist. This book got better with every new round of notes, and I am so grateful you all put in your time to help me.

And to all my friends who cheered me on as I navigated my life as a full-time mom and full-time writer *during a freaking pandemic,* I am so lucky to have you. Same to my family—especially my mom, who drove twenty-four hours *twice* to help me care for my baby while I was under deadline.

Lastly, to my MVP, the Frenchman: you're amazing. Thank you for using all of your 2021 vacation days so I could have time to work with- out interruption. *"Maman a fait ... ? Des bêtises!"*

ABOUT THE AUTHOR

Susan Dennard is the award-winning, *New York Times* bestselling author of the Witchlands series (now in development for TV from the Jim Henson Company), and the Something Strange and Deadly series, in addition to various other fiction published online.

She also runs the popular newsletter for writers, the Misfits and Daydreamers. When not writing or teaching writing, she can be found rolling the dice as a Dungeon Master or mashing buttons on one of her way too many consoles. Susan tweets @stdennard.